WINDKEEP

Also by Michael Simms

Poetry Collections

Strange Meadowlark
Nightjar
American Ash
Black Stone
The Happiness of Animals
The Fire-eater
Migration
Notes on Continuing Light

Novels

Bicycles of the Gods: A Divine Comedy
The Green Mage

Nonfiction

Longman Dictionary of Poetic Terms (Jack Myers)
Longman Dictionary and Handbook of Poetry, (with Jack Myers)

Anthologies Edited

The Autumn House Anthology of Contemporary American Poetry
O. Henry's Texas Stories

WINDKEEP

The Second Chronicle
of Tessia Dragonqueen

Michael Simms

MADVILLE
PUBLISHING

Lake Dallas, Texas

FIRST EDITION

Windkeep: The Second Chronicle of Tessia Dragonqueen is a work of fiction. Names, characters, places, and incidents are entirely products of the author's imagination. Any resemblance to actual events, locales, businesses, companies, or persons, living or dead, is entirely coincidental.

Requests for permission to reprint material from this work should be sent to:

Permissions
Madville Publishing
P.O. Box 358
Lake Dallas, TX 75065

Author Photograph: Eva-Maria Simms
Cover Design: Andrew Dunn
Cover Art: Andrew Dunn
Maps: Jacqueline Davis

ISBN: 978-1-956440-71-3 paperback, 978-1-956440-72-0 ebook
Library of Congress Control Number: 2023947055

For Eva

A Commentary
on the Saga of Milon Redshield

by Tatatungia the witch, known as The Wanderer,
visiting the court of Queen Oleanna Vth

-parchment, entered into the Chronicles in the Royal Library of Windkeep

The old songs and stories are wrong in so many ways. Milon Redshield was no hero, but a murderer who violated the will of the Goddess Nilene. It is true, as is sung, that he and his soldiers built a snare of heavy rope and suspended it across the River Iskar and waited in secret until Morf the dragon flew up the river listening for salmon dreaming under the water's surface, and thus distracted, did not see the ropes hanging loosely across the river. At Milon's signal, his men yanked the ropes taut, catching Morf by his talon, tangling him so he fell into the water. The soldiers pulled the dragon to shore half-drowned, wired his jaw shut so he could not breathe fire and tied his legs together, so he could not rip with his talons.

The men lifted Morf into a wide quarry wagon and carried him to Windkeep, the stone tower where Milon Redshield ruled the three valleys. And here is where the sagas depart from true history, for the dragon did not become Milon's willing servant, but rather Milon kept the dragon chained beside his throne as a warning and augury to any who would oppose him. He saddled the dragon like a pony and rode the sentient beast through the kingdom, falsely exhibiting courage to his subjects.

Edwige the Princess was envious of her brother and wished for a dragon of her own. So Milon gifted her Tenwen, the gentle sister of Morf. And Edwige kept Tenwen beside her to impress suitors, but soon the Princess grew bored with her pet and had the unfortunate dragon removed to the dungeon. And there Tenwen, who was known by her kind as The Sweet One, died of hunger and despair.

Following Milon's example, his vassals captured dragons, roasting their hearts and decorating walls with their heads. Wings were clipped to keep the beasts earth-bound, and young dragons were trained to fight each other with their talons while men wagered on the contests. Dragon eggs were sliced open and eaten. In the fashion of the day, women wore bracelets of baby dragon teeth. Thus, all manner of cruelties were done to the dragons who were once protectors of the earth.

At last, the race of dragons who had resided in these valleys since the Age of Ice, and who'd always lived in peace and harmony with other creatures, rose up against men. And Milon rode Morf into battle against the dragons, but Morf turned on his master, so Milon stabbed him through his right heart with a spear.

In his last moments, Morf turned his majestic head to the sky and asked Nilene, Mother Of Us All, to curse the kings and queens of Windkeep until the end of time.

And thus, it was done.

Part One:
Windkeep

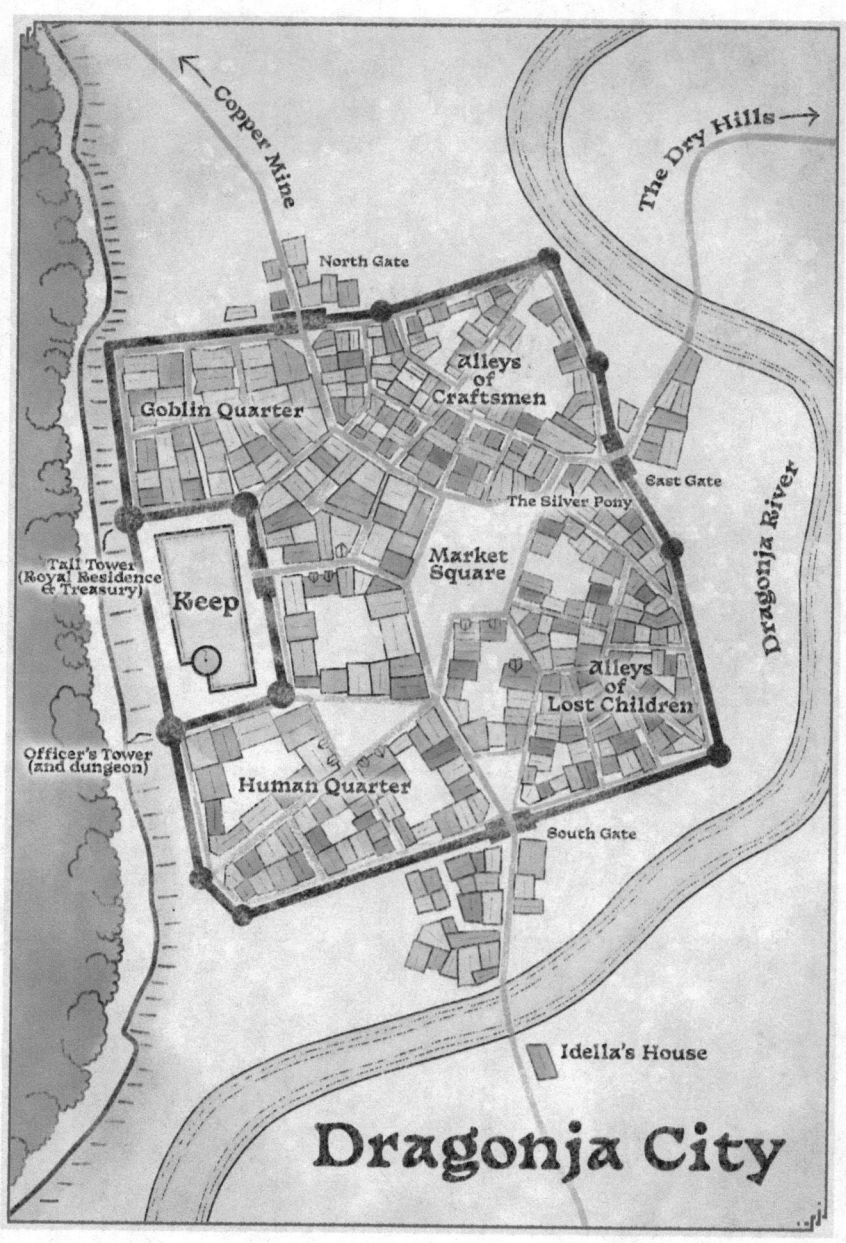

Dragonja City

Chapter One

I was tuning my lyre in the Silver Pony Inn, thinking about a new song I'd been working on, when the Captain of Queen Tessia's guards came through the front door and seeing me, hurried to my side and whispered in my ear, "She's in one of her moods again, Sir Mage. You are the only one who can calm her down when she gets like this."

I nodded, rested my lyre gently in its wooden case, and placed it behind the bar out of sight. Then I hurried with the guard to the high tower.

The Queen's wild black hair was loose, her thin gold crown barely containing it, and her singing sword was drawn. A purple light glinted off the blade, and it was humming like a wasp, so I knew it had just struck something. Or someone. First Minister Caz, the lords and ladies of her retinue, and the palace guards were backing away from her, terrified. I was relieved to see a royal banner lying in tatters at her feet. I thought *At least she's taken out her rage on a flag and not attacked anyone yet.*

I walked quickly up to the queen, gave a curt nod, and turned my back on her, a violation of protocol only I could get away with. Facing her retainers. I caught the eye of Caz and signaled him to leave the hall. After everyone had left, I turned to Tessia and bowed my head, "How may I be of service, Your Majesty?"

Actually, as Tessia's old friend, I knew exactly what the problem was. After two years of wearing the crown, the queen despised her job.

Tessia hadn't always hated being the sovereign ruler of the kingdom. When she first assumed the throne after the death of her mentor Wise Queen Varvara, Tessia had enjoyed the pomp and ceremony that came with the title. Having grown up a coppersmith's daughter in a small village, the luxury of living in a castle, having gold to spend, having as many servants as she could possibly want, and being the most powerful person in the land seemed like a girl's dream.

After the coronation, the first thing she did was to renovate the old pile. Rugs that had been moldering on the floor for centuries were taken out and burned. Priceless tapestries were scrubbed until their colors shone. Furniture was repaired. The kitchen was stripped down to its bones and rebuilt. The Queen's chambers were opened up to let light in during the warm months, and new shutters were installed to keep the wind out during the cold. Spending dragon gold, she recruited the best artisans in the world to create a splendid palace. Every spoon, sconce, bowl, and pennant was crafted to perfection. Her table, heaped with delicious foods brought from the four corners of the kingdom, was applauded by the ambassadors and generals who dined there. Soldiers, craftsmen, and chambermaids worked furiously side by side to bring color and radiance to the castle which came to be known as *Windkeep*. She invited the best painters, sculptors, architects, poets, musicians, and dancers from around the world. (My recommendations may have played a small part here.) Windkeep became a glorious cultural citadel where imagination was celebrated, and visionaries were prized.

Ah, what parties we had! The whole city was turned into a

place of music and dancing. The finest wines and sweetmeats, fire breathers and acrobats. No one was turned away from the sumptuous tables.

I remember how happy Tessia was in those days, dancing with her wife Taja in the streets. Everyone loved the beautiful new Queen who'd been a hero in the war with the evil wizard Ludek. She was Tessia the Dragonqueen, and every schoolboy wanted to serve her, and every schoolgirl wanted to be her. People were now calling our era the *Pax Regina* because Queen Tessia, following Queen Varvara's example, had ushered in a time of peace and prosperity.

I remember inviting legendary mages who brought their various magics. There were Green Mages, like me, who healed the sick and injured, encouraged the fields, orchards, and fisheries to produce abundantly, and blessed honest merchants to thrive. There were Red Mages who encouraged love, blessing us with happy marriages and deep friendships. And there were Purple Mages who inspired our leaders to serve the people's interests rather than their own. Farmers, craftsmen, fishermen, healers, shopkeepers, husbands, wives, children, judges, generals, and the Queen herself thrived in our happy kingdom.

I was glad that Tessia had followed my advice and not encouraged wizards who practice White or Black magic to come to our land. We'd fought a war against the Wizard Ludek, my brother, a master of the dark. I'd advised Tessia against allowing White Wizards to come to our kingdom as well. People tend to think that White Wizards are good and Black Wizards are evil, but the truth is that the two types of wizards have exactly the same powers. They just use them for different purposes. White Wizards encourage harmony and Black Wizards cause disruption, but harmony can be as oppressive as disruption. One of the oldest curses in the Bekla Valley is "May your wish come true!" meaning that unintended and unwanted consequences are inevitable when we change the course of a life. It's best to let

3

the larger natural forces find their own balance without human interference.

In the first months after becoming queen, Tessia tried to adapt to the responsibilities of leadership. Under the tasteful influence of her wife Princess Taja, Tessia changed her outward appearance from a warrior to a queen. She put aside her leather breeches, linen blouse and high boots and began wearing silk dresses and strings of pearls, but as time passed, I noticed the more elegantly she dressed, the less happy she was. She and Taja often quarreled, and recently Tessia confided to me that she worried they were no longer in love.

Two years after the coronation, Tessia's discontent was growing by the day. I told myself that everything would eventually work out. Tessia just needed time to settle into her new role, but as the days wore on, I hoped her acceptance of her responsibilities would happen soon because the kingdom was facing huge challenges, and we needed a queen who could lead our people.

"I don't want to do this anymore," Queen Tessia said, her green eyes flashing in anger.

"You don't want to do what anymore, your Majesty?" I said.

"Stop calling me that, Norbert," she said, gesturing around the empty chamber. "It's just you and me here."

"Sorry, Tessia. What seems to be the problem?"

"The problem is that I'm bored. Heavy bored. If I have to listen to one more farmer complain about his neighbor's cow eating his grain, I'm going to cut off his head."

"Tessia, dealing with the problems of the people is the true work of leaders. Being the queen is not just about leading the troops in battle. You led us to victory, and we are at peace now. This is what we fought for."

"We fought for the right to argue about cows?" She rolled her eyes in disgust.

4

"We fought for the right to have a peaceful life. The people trust you to make wise decisions. They know they'll be treated fairly by you and your ministers. Remember how it was when Ludek ruled the kingdom?"

We were silent for a moment, remembering how Ludek enslaved and tortured people, including Tessia's father and her best friends, and how he'd kidnapped my wife and threatened my son. I'd killed Ludek, my own brother, to protect my wife and son, and years later, the memory of having to make that choice still kept me awake at night.

"Why can't Caz mediate these disputes?" she asked. "Why do I have to listen to them?" Caz was the First Minister, and he handled the day-to-day administration of the kingdom. Caz was very efficient as a manager, but he also could be rather self-aggrandizing at times.

"Tessia, you know that Caz and his magistrates mediate most of the disputes, but there has to be a right to appeal, and those are the cases you hear."

"Well, I don't want to do it anymore," she repeated, sounding like a small girl bored with doing chores, rather than a great general and the ruler of a once prosperous kingdom. In the past weeks, she'd reserved these childlike displays for her wife and me. I accepted my role as her confidante and kept my opinions about her behavior to myself, but Taja was less forgiving, often storming out of the room. In the past, Tessia had maintained her composure in front of her subjects, but now, she was acting in ways that were disruptive to the administration of the kingdom. I felt exasperated by her behavior. For the Goddess's sake, a monarch should not have tantrums in front of her subjects!

For the first time, I wondered whether Tessia was the best person to be queen. Perhaps we were expecting too much from her? Should we spread her responsibilities among her ministers? Perhaps investing so much power in one person is a flawed method of governing? But these conjectures could be seen as treasonous, so I kept them to myself.

"Very well, I'll talk with Caz about referring fewer cases to you, but you're still going to have to hear some of them. This is your job now, Tessia. You can't just refuse to do it, especially now." I glanced out the window at the dry riverbed in front of the castle to signal my meaning. Our people were suffering a terrible drought. She knew as well as I did, we needed her subjects to cooperate with one another if we were going to get through this difficult time.

"Tessia," I said, softening my tone. "We've been friends for quite a while, and we've been through a lot together. You've always displayed uncommon courage. Why are you acting like this?"

She thought for a moment, then said, "Norbert, the challenges we faced in the past I could always solve with gold or a sword. But not now. What can *I* do about a drought?" She asked, turning to face me, her brow furrowed.

I had to admit she was right to be afraid for the kingdom. The farmers and herders were desperate. The spring rains hadn't come. The crops were dying. People had eaten their winter stores, and soon they'd be starving.

"I should be able to help them," she said, shaking her head. "But *I* can't make it rain."

She pulled a pitiful, childlike face. "Can't *you* make it rain, Norbert? Use your magic."

"I've told you many times, Tessia. Bringing rain is beyond my powers." I tried to keep the frustration out of my voice.

"Can other mages bring rain?"

I took a deep breath before responding. We'd had this conversation a number of times in recent weeks, but I told her again of the ancient witches who were said to have been able to influence the weather, and I reminded her that the lore was long lost. "Besides," I said, "controlling a force as large as the weather would be too dangerous. There isn't any telling what might go wrong."

"You don't really believe in some invisible Goddess looking after us, do you?" She asked, almost taunting me. This too was an old debate between us. Tessia was always more interested in the practical application of magic than in the theological issue of the wisdom of disrupting the natural balance.

"I do believe in a merciful Goddess who holds everything in balance, Tessia, and so should you. Disrupting the balance is dangerous. Why must we go over this again now?"

We had discussed the dangers of enlisting the aid of the supernatural when we banned White and Black Magic in the kingdom seven years earlier, during Wise Queen Varvara's reign. The decision had made sense following the war with Ludek, but now, in the face of an emergency, I understood Tessia's view that it would be convenient to have someone just wave a wand to summon rain.

Queen Tessia looked out her tower window at the kingdom stretching to the horizon, and what she saw distressed her. Fields which should have been green with new crops were brown with thirst, and orchards which should have been in flower were dry and brittle. The river which should have been gently flowing past the city was a mud-cracked ditch with pools of water where cattle shoved each other aside to drink.

She turned back from the window and said, "You know what, Norbert? I miss being free. Before we started our quest, I lived in the hills with Anja and Hamlin. Remember? We hunted deer, fished for salmon, ate the wild herbs and berries. When we wanted something, like a new knife or a length of rope, we brought meat or furs into the village and traded for it."

"I remember, Tessia," I said, and I saw her then in my memory, a wild girl roaming the hills of the Bekla Valley where she was born. And I recalled her befriending the dragon, a miracle that ultimately freed not only her father, but the whole kingdom. "I remember the girl and the dragon who saved us from the Wizard Ludek," I said aloud.

"Norbert Oldfoot," she said, addressing me by my birth-name which few people now living knew. "You were the one who defeated Ludek."

She didn't have to remind me of that time when I entered the dark cave of my brother's mind. The pain and horror were etched into my soul.

"Idella told me you captured him and held him long enough for the white bear Tayra to kill him," Tessia said.

"Your Majesty, with all due respect, you exaggerate my accomplishments." I said, bowing floridly like a simpering courtier. "I am but a poor village mage who made his living selling pots and pans, and who followed a talented girl in her quest, helping where he could, and eventually she was kind enough to appoint him Advisor, Bard, and Healer to the Kingdom of Bekla and Dragonja. Yours is a great story that will be sung for a thousand years while I deserve nothing more than a mention here and there in the great epic of Tessia the Dragonqueen."

She laughed at my fatuous flattery, knowing I saw her for what she actually was, a young woman with a talent for fighting and a gift for leading men in battle, but she had not the wisdom of her mentor and predecessor the wise Queen Varvara. But who did?

Our laughter faded quickly, and we sat in silence for a few moments, sadness growing between us, remembering that her childhood friend Hamlin had been kept in a dungeon and tortured by Ludek, trying to turn him to the dark side. He held out for weeks but paid a heavy price for his resistance. Even now six years after the war had ended, Hamlin had not fully recovered. The happy young man we'd known had become a hulking presence in the castle. And as for Hamlin's lover Anja…

"I hate to think about Anja," Tessia said, reading my thoughts, as she often did.

"I do too. But your uncle felt he had no choice but to execute her."

"She died well."

8

"Yes, she was very brave, I'll give her that." I thought back to our friend Anja, whom Tessia had grown up with. A skilled bladeswoman, she'd saved both of us more than once. But Ludek turned her to the dark side without much effort. Anja had always leaned in the direction of darkness. A few threats and a little extortion, and she was ready to betray us.

Tessia turned away from me toward the window which looked out to Dragonja City and beyond to the river and the Dry Hills stretching far into the distance. She chose this room as her private chamber, just as her predecessor, the wise Queen Varvara had. It was at the top of the highest tower in Windkeep. From here, you could see a large slice of the kingdom.

"I'm going for a ride," Tessia said, walking toward the stairs.

One of the improvements Tessia had made to the castle was to install a dragon's lair in the tower below her chambers. A window had been enlarged to allow Tyrmiss's great bulk to fly into the lair. The room had no furnishings other than a large flat stone where Tyrmiss did her cooking. She would bring back a large pike or salmon she had scooped out of the river, lay it on the cook-stone, roast it with a few fiery breaths and then swallow it in two or three large gulps. As a result, the place always smelled of sulfurous smoke and charred fish.

"Tessia!" Tyrmiss said, as we came into her lair. "The Queen herself blesses me with her presence. How exciting! What brings you here?" As an afterthought, she said in a flat voice, "Oh, hello, Norbert."

She'd never liked me because she was jealous of my friendship with Tessia. Still, I always treated her with the respect she deserved. She was, after all, a ten-thousand-year-old creature who'd saved my life, as well as the kingdom, from an evil wizard. Also, she could read people's thoughts, or at least she could hear our dreams, and I was worried that if I harbored resentments against her, she would know it. I really didn't want a fire-breathing flying reptile with talons the size of my forearms mad at me.

"Tyrmiss, would you like to go for a ride?" Tessia asked her friend.

"I would be delighted to do so. You know, for thousands of years I could fly only at night because I didn't want to be seen by people. But now, it's so nice to be, shall we say, out of the closet?"

"Out of what closet?" I asked, confused.

"Never mind, Norbert," Tyrmiss said, condescendingly. "The phrase is after your time."

Tyrmiss had an annoying habit of referring to things in the distant past or future, and then implying I'm stupid for not knowing what she's talking about.

"Are you coming with us, Norbert?" Tessia called over her shoulder. I knew she was just being polite, perhaps to make up for Tyrmiss's rudeness to me. Although I have at times sat behind Tessia on Tyrmiss's back, it wasn't something I would do for fun. It is terrifying and exhilarating, which is why Tessia loved it, but I preferred to take my pleasure in safer ways.

Tessia swung up on Tyrmiss's back, settling comfortably into the spot between her shoulders and grasping the last spine on the dragon's neck. Tessia rode like an expert equestrian, that is, if her steed were the length of six horses, had a wingspan of a dozen eagles and breathed fire like a god from the underworld.

"Where would you like to go, love?" Tyrmiss asked, turning her head to look at Tessia.

"How about we visit your old cave?"

"Good idea, the aspens are pretty in the mountains this time of year with the wind blowing through the leaves flashing green and gray. How about we pick up a salmon from the river and have a cookout? I know a lovely spot up on the mountain. From there we can look down on the Iskar Valley."

"Tyrmiss, the salmon are mostly dead in the river, and the ones that are left are trapped in pools in the riverbed and choking on mud."

"Oh, I forgot about the drought. Well, perhaps we can find a fat doe up in the mountains instead? Any meat that's left over we can bring back to the castle to feed the staff?"

"That sounds lovely," Tessia said, and turning to me, added, "I'd like to talk with you and Caz when I get back, Norbert. Could you join us in the royal chamber?"

"Of course, your Majesty," I said, bowing my head.

With Tessia securely on her back, Tyrmiss leaped out the window, gained speed as she arced down, spread her wings and flew over the city. She made a wide bank, crossed the Dragonja River and let the updrafts carry her into the mountains.

In the afternoon, First Minister Caz and I joined the Queen in the royal chamber, a room in the tower close to her personal suite. Since it was the place where she received foreign dignitaries, the chamber was sumptuous with beautiful tapestries, and she often had a quartet of musicians playing softly in one corner. But today, she had serious matters on her mind, and wished to discuss the emergency caused by the drought, so the musicians were not present.

Caz had several proposals for mitigating the effects of the drought, but each seemed less helpful than the last. We could ask Tyrmiss to fly into the mountains, gather snow and fly it back to the city. But even assuming that the dragon would agree to this strategy, she would never be able to bring more than a fraction of the amount of water the city needed in a day, not to mention the needs of the farmers. Caz's second proposal was to have workmen dig new wells, but this would take months and, again, would supply only a small fraction of the water that was needed. His third proposal was that I examine the ancient texts in the Windkeep library and find the method by which the Blue Witches brought rain in ancient times.

At that last suggestion, I said, "I completely disagree, your

Majesty." I spoke quickly and shook my head. "As I mentioned to you earlier, it is very dangerous to upset the balance of nature. The Goddess…"

"Norbert," Caz interrupted. "This is not a theological problem. There are children who are sick with thirst. We need to do something immediately."

Tessia turned to me, "I hear your concern, Norbert. But I agree with Caz. We are in the midst of an emergency. Extreme steps are called for. Please find an incantation or ritual or spell—whatever is needed—to bring rain. We have to take the risk, even if we upset the natural balance."

I bowed my head in reluctant acquiescence. For Tessia to agree with Caz over my objection, she must feel very strongly that he was right, because she tended to favor me; whereas she tolerated Caz only because he was useful in managing the kingdom's finances.

When Tessia turned away, Caz smirked at me, a childish response. I tried to be friendly with Caz, but he seemed to think of me as a rival for the Queen's favor. Also, I didn't like the way he often went behind Tessia's back and got support from Tessia's wife Princess Taja. Although, like Tessia, I'd never particularly liked Caz, I had to admit that the people of the Kingdom of Dragonja and Bekla had become quite prosperous under Queen Tessia's rule, due in large part to the wise management of the First Minister. I felt confident that once the drought was over, he would help restore the kingdom to prosperity.

I loathed palace intrigue, so I tried to let go of my resentment against Caz and instead to think about what the Queen had instructed me to do. When the Queen dismissed us, I went immediately down the circular stone steps to the library. There were no windows in this room because sunlight is known to destroy books, so I brought a lantern with me.

The library contained most of the written records of the kingdom, but since each book took years to construct and write, there were only a few hundred. The financial records were kept in Caz's chamber while the library contained all the chronicles recording the history of the region. Here were the stories of the kings and queens of the last three thousand years, ever since the first humans settled this region, taking the land from the dragons that had inhabited it since the Age of Ice. There were also commentaries in the chronicles by the Great Witch Tatatungia, old books and scrolls written by wizards and scribes of previous ages and—my favorite—a collection of Beklan folktales collected by the scholar Mihai of Crota.

Since Tessia's assumption of the throne, I had spent many hours in this room studying the spells and incantations that the Old Ones had recorded, and much of what I discovered in these texts was disturbing—dark magic used to terrorize the population, helping the kings to dominate their subjects, and even worse, powerful spells used as weapons against neighboring kingdoms. I knew that my brother Ludek, the wizard who had dominated the kingdom for so many years, was familiar with these methods. A few times, out of curiosity, I had gone into the Dry Hills far from the city and tried some of the spells, but they truly frightened me. Fire and the illusion of fire, lightning, invisibility, disguises, loathsome tricks and permanent lies were the stock-in-trade of these wizards specializing in black magic. I swore to myself I would never use anything contained in these books. It went against everything I had devoted my life to as a Green Mage.

It was easy to determine at a glance the approximate historical order of the chronicles because every few hundred years the method of bookmaking evolved. In the last two hundred years, we've made books of paper, binding the pages with silken thread and covering the sewn volume with a leather cover displaying gold lettering. In the previous era, scrolls were used, and before the scrolls, unbound vellum sheets in an oaken box. And before vellum, there were cattle hides, and so on, back to the oldest records which were little more than scratches on flat rocks. These rune-stones were in the dustiest corner. As I brushed aside the spider webs and mouse droppings to get to them. I suspected I might be the first person to look at these stones in a thousand years.

The spells I was looking for would be scratched into the stones in an ancient language—the forebear of the language we spoke today. I was able to interpret a few of the runes, and eventually came across one stone, the size of my palm, which had a few runes I recognized from what my father had taught me when I was learning the Mage's Way.

A zigzag line was pronounced *Raipah* which meant thunder. Vertical lines connected at the top meant four times. A series of wavy lines was pronounced *Yekhi* which meant rain.

The only other item I could find that might be useful someday was an ancient vellum manuscript titled *A Treatise of Dragon Anatomy* composed by a royal scribe named Zakkik who served in the court of Milon Redshield. Most of the document was badly decomposed, but I thought the information about dragons might be valuable in helping Tyrmiss if she were injured, so I noted the location and returned the manuscript to its oaken box.

I couldn't find anything else which looked even remotely helpful, so I put the stone in my pocket and left the castle. I walked across the central square and exited the East Gate, but instead of turning right on the path which led to my house, I went left and climbed a hill. I looked around. Other than a few thin cows who paid no attention to me, I was alone.

I took my willow wand from my belt, pointed it at the sky, and concentrated. I envisioned large dark clouds coming over the horizon, passing over the kingdom and letting loose their rain. I chanted *Raipah Yekhi* four times. Keeping my eyes closed, I waited.

Nothing. No clouds. The sky remained a bright resolute blue.

I tried a few variations in the spell, reversing the two words, saying them louder, then softer, trying different pronunciations, holding the stone up to the sky, laying it on the ground.

Still nothing.

I walked home, feeling as useless as a single wing on a bird.

Chapter Two

A few days later, my wife Idella, my stepson Alaric and I were invited to dine at the Queen's table. It was an intimate affair, a special occasion because a man named Bastian had returned to Dragonja City after living in a foreign land for many years. Queen Tessia sat at the head of the table with Bastian on her right and Caz on her left. Beside Caz was Kerttu the Coppersmith, the Queen's father and my old friend. I sat next to Kerttu, Idella next to Bastian, and Alaric next to his mother. At the opposite end of the table sat Princess Taja, the Queen's Consort, a woman as tall and beautiful as Tessia, but with blonde hair and light skin, whereas Tessia had dark hair and olive skin. Taja was softer than her powerful wife, both in body and in spirit.

Taja, who had planned the meal with the help of the chef, pointed out that the salmon roe in sheep curd was a delicacy in the Bekla Valley. Idella and I looked at each other, thinking that our neighbors in the countryside were living on weeds and berries from the hills while the Queen's table featured exotic delicacies, but we were guests, so we said nothing about the ostentatious display. Tessia, as usual, ate without discrimination. She didn't care about food. I'd seen her eat raw meat in the wilds when lighting a fire would have given away her position. Her wife, on the other hand, had developed a taste for luxury.

"I understand you've lived many years in Skarsland, Meister Bastian," Taja, always a graceful hostess, said. "I know so little about that land. What is it like?"

"Well," Bastian began, shifting his bulk in the upholstered chair until it creaked. "Skarsland, as you know, your Grace, shares a border to the north with our glorious land of Dragonja and Bekla which the Queen so wisely rules." He nodded his head with its streak of white hair to his monarch at the end of the table, and Tessia looked blankly at him. She was often baffled, or even offended, by flattery.

I thought, *This man is a professional diplomat. As my mother used to say, "Bekla butter would not melt in his mouth."*

"One cannot reach Skarsland by foot," Bastian continued. "The Nordtoppen mountains are too steep and the trails too confusing. Perhaps the goatherds who live in those mountains would know the way, but no traveler such as myself would attempt the journey. I went by sea, boarding a trading vessel in our southern port of Crota and following the east coast northward until I came to Osterbo, the capital of Skarsland."

"You were on a trade mission for King Ottolo?" Caz asked.

"Yes, the Good King," Bastian said, diplomatically referring to the man known in the chronicle as King Ottolo the Befuddled, "King Ottolo sent me to Skarsland in an attempt to establish trade relations. They have valuable minerals, such as purple earth, as well as furs and timber which would be of benefit to our kingdom."

"Was your trade mission successful?" My wife Idella asked. Her voice beside me made me jump—I'd been studying the stranger's manner and I'd practically forgotten she was sitting there, but of course, as a successful baker and merchant, she was always interested in talking about commerce.

"Actually, My Lady, the negotiations were going very well because I am, putting all modesty aside, a brilliant diplomat."

Idella shot me a look that spoke volumes about what she

thought of this man, and I looked down at the food on my plate, so as not to give away my opinion of the pompous ass. He was clearly a braggart and a bootlicker, but he had a tale to tell, and for the good of the kingdom, as well as our own entertainment, it was important to encourage him to talk.

"But I am afraid that while we were discussing the details of the trade deal, I received news that Ludek had become the regent for King Ottolo. Since I knew Ludek quite well, his having been captain of the guard while I was trade minister for the king, I thought it was better if I stayed in Skarsland until the situation at home settled down."

"How long did you live in Skarsland?" Tessia asked, suddenly interested in what this professional guest had to say. Tessia had acted distant through the meal, which had made me wonder if she and Taja had had an argument before dinner.

"I've been away twenty-six years, your Majesty."

"Have you been to the hills where purple earth is mined?" Kerttu asked. Kerttu had invented the secret process of combining copper with purple earth to create the Voprian alloy and he'd become wealthy manufacturing swords for the Queen's guards and soldiers. Caz had called the cozy arrangement *nepotism* and said the secret should be shared with other smiths, but Kerttu kept the formula to himself. Tessia had sided with her father, one of a number of complaints her subjects had with her rule.

"Yes, I have," Bastian answered. "The mines go very deep to find the rare earth."

Leaning forward, eager, on his elbows, Caz asked, "Did you live in the Osterbo palace the whole time?"

"Oh, my goodness no," Bastian said. "With the change in leadership in this country, the king of Skarsland was no longer friendly toward a representative from Dragonja. He thought of me as a representative of the Wizard Ludek although I was not. It seemed that the king had a strong prejudice against wizards." Bastian nodded to me. "No offense intended."

"None taken," I answered. And I meant it. My brother Ludek had been a powerful, evil wizard while I was merely a mage. There was a big difference.

"I barely escaped being arrested and had to flee the city and go into the icy barrens. One of my servants, a woman named Auli, led me to her home village deep in the mountains. It turns out that she was the daughter of the chief of the village and had been kidnapped as a child. When I fled, she no longer had a master in the city and saw the opportunity to escape to her homeland. She allowed me to come with her, partly I suppose out of pity—I had no place else to go—and partly out of her need to travel with a man. Women are very vulnerable there and need the constant protection of men."

I saw Tessia's jaw tighten, and the three women at the table—Taja, Idella, and Tessia—exchanged a look of mild disgust. For a professional diplomat, Bastian had a surprising ability to offend people. I wondered whether the change in leadership in Dragonja decades ago was the only reason Bastian had fled Osterbo.

"Auli's people are called the Renetu. Their homeland is made up of steep ravines and mountainsides in the Nordtoppen. It is a beautiful country but very harsh. Long bitter winters and short, glorious summers. They survive as goatherders, primarily, but they have been known to be raiders as well, coming down from the mountains to attack the lowlanders and steal their stock, even carrying off their children." The man made this pronouncement as if it were nothing, continuing, "But nowadays, the king's soldiers have put a stop to the raids although the Renetu still have beautiful songs and heroic tales about their brave ancestors."

At this, my interest was piqued. "I would like to hear one of those songs if you might share it with us, Meister Bastian."

"Norbert is the Queen's Bard, among his other titles," Taja said, generously.

19

"Oh, sorry. I did not know that you were a poet," Bastian nodded to me. I waved my hand dismissively, signaling him to continue.

"Let us see… It's been months since I listened to one of the Renetu shamans sing, but I think I can give you the feel of a song. It would be best, of course, to hear the song sung by a shaman-healer in front of a fire in the deep winter with the wind howling outside. I'm afraid that listening to it here in an opulent palace does not carry the full weight of the words."

Bastian touched his fingertips together, forming a globe, and said, lost in thought, "The strange thing is that although the bear is a god, in ancient times the male bear was ritually hunted; his body was then reverently buried, and his skull was hung upon a sacred pine tree, symbolizing his ascent back to his heavenly home. But anyway, here's the opening of a song called *Karhu*, which refers to one of the great bears that live in the mountains and which the Renetu hold to be sacred:

> *Where was the bear born?*
> *Where was the beast made?*
> *By the moon,*
> *with the day,*
> *on the shoulders of the Plough*
> *lowered on golden cords.*

Bastian had a surprisingly pleasant voice, deep and soothing, a chant with just a hint of melody. I wished I had my lyre. We could have played well together.

"These are very old songs," Bastian continued. "They may go back to the time when men hunted the great bears, but now, they try to stay away from the bears although the great beasts will sometimes feast on a goat. It has been a very long time since bears and men were enemies."

"So, what did you do in the mountains?" Tessia asked.

"I met Auli's father, and we became friends. After a few months, I married Auli and became the chief's advisor. Following the example set in the old songs and stories, we started raiding the flatlanders, stealing their livestock and taking prisoners for ransom. When the chief was killed in an avalanche, a very common way to die for a people who live on the sides of mountains, I became chief. Auli and I had several children, and with the fourth child, she died in childbirth. Her sisters were raising the children competently without my help. There were younger men who wanted to challenge my role as chief, so I could see that my position in the tribe was untenable. There was really nothing to keep me there. I had heard that the crown here in Dragonja had passed to Queen Tessia, and the city had become beautiful and prosperous, so I decided to return."

"Did you know a merchant named Janne Salo?" Caz asked. "I sold spices to him years ago, and he paid in gemstones."

"Oh yes," Bastian replied. "He was the brother of Eliel. I am sorry to say that Janne died of the coughing disease some time ago before I left the city. But his brother is still running the family business, as far as I know, although by now he may have passed it to his son."

Caz, who had spent his early years traveling the world as a trader and adventurer, reminisced with Bastian about mutual acquaintances in the far north. I could see Tessia's eyes glaze over, bored with the conversation. I knew her well enough to surmise that she was planning some kind of adventure. Before she'd become a warrior, she'd spent most of her time hunting. She'd told me that she, Anja, and Hamlin had once killed a bear, Hamlin saving Tessia with a well-timed spear thrust. I wondered whether Bastian's account had inspired her to think about a bear hunt in the Nordtoppen mountains.

As Idella and I were saying our goodbyes to Tessia and Taja, I asked Tessia, "Are you planning to go to Skarsland, your Majesty?"

I could see Tessia's eyes shining. I decided to have a private conversation with Bastian at some point to find out more about the Nordtoppen Mountains that separated our country from Skarsland.

The next morning, I was scheduled to preside over a trial. Normally, Caz and his assistants heard lawsuits, and the more difficult ones they referred to the Queen, but in this case, the litigant was a farmer who was suing a woman who claimed to be a witch. He alleged that she had cheated him. Caz thought that since I was the Court Mage, the case fell into my bailiwick.

The farmer's name was Horak, and I'd known him for many years. When I was a shireman trekking through the kingdom with my donkey loaded with kitchen wares to sell, I often visited his farm in the Valley. The alluvial soil was rich, so he had an abundance of grain and fruit, and he raised pigs and cattle as well. Horak was a stout, square-headed man with tall, pointed ears, typical of the river-folk in my home region. He was also typically Beklian in his stubborn honesty and his belief that everyone should be as hard-working as he was.

"What is your name?" I asked the defendant.

"My name is Zamarrra, known as Windblown," she answered. I didn't recognize her, and she was so strangely beautiful I felt certain I would have remembered meeting her. She was thin and small with quick darting eyes, and her ears were round, a characteristic that Beklians found exotic or even threatening. Her hair was thick and gray, almost silver. And most amazing of all, her skin was so translucent that she appeared at times to be blue.

"Where are you from?" I asked.

"My family was originally from the Dry Hills in the middle of the kingdom," she answered. "As you may know, it is a sparse land unsuitable for farming, and people must live by their wits." She gave a sly look which I interpreted to mean she was still living a sly life. "My clan now lives in the mountains beyond the Iskar River."

"She took my money and said she would bring rain," Horak was saying, pointing at Zamarrra.

"It would have come if only he had waited," she said firmly. I recognized her dialect as that of the Dry Hills, but it seemed strange, perhaps some archaic variant.

"How much did you pay her, Farmer Horak?" I asked.

"I paid her three silver coins, Meister Norbert."

"Did you receive these coins as payment for services?" I asked, turning to Zamarrra.

"Yes, I did." Her light gray eyes held my gaze steadily as she spoke. Her beauty was distracting, and I wondered whether Horak hadn't been thinking clearly when he contracted her services.

"And did rain come?"

"No." They answered simultaneously.

"Are you actually able to bring rain?" I asked the woman.

"Yes, I am."

"Then what went wrong this time? Why didn't the rain come?"

"It was coming, Mage. But this clod interrupted the ritual."

"I'm not familiar with rain conjuring. Tell me about the ritual," I said evenly although I was beginning to feel a glimmer of hope for our sad kingdom.

"I cannot, Mage."

"And why not?"

"Because it is a secret among the Blue Witches, Mage. We take an oath to hold our spells closely."

"The Blue Witches? I have heard of your kind. You are a guild of some sort, aren't you?"

"We are an ancient society, Mage. We live in the land to the west."

I turned to the farmer. "Did you know she calls herself a Blue Witch?"

23

"Yes, she told me." He looked at her with disgust. "But now I know everything she said was nothing more than cow droppings."

She looked at him angrily, but before she could reply, I held up my hand.

"Would you be willing to let her have another try at bringing rain?"

"No, your honor. It is too late now. If rain does not come soon to the Bekla Valley, I and all the farmers will lose our crops."

Yes, I thought. *This drought will be the death of us all.* I turned to the woman and asked, "How long does it take to bring rain?"

"Four days, Mage."

"Would you be willing to bring rain to the entire kingdom?"

"Yes, I would, but..." She shifted her eyes back and forth as she calculated her advantage. "It would cost a lot of silver."

"No, Witch Zamarrra, it will not cost a lot of silver," I said, believing that there was a good chance that she was little more than a charlatan, cheating desperate people. "The Queen will pay you five silver coins if we see rain on the entire kingdom within five days. If we do not see rain, then you will see the inside of a prison cell for having defrauded this farmer. Do I make myself clear?"

"Go back to your farm, Horak," I said. "It will either rain or not. Your part in this suit is over. Go to the purser and collect your refund of three silver coins." I turned to Zamarrra and said, "We will deduct the three silver coins from your fee, Witch."

After Horak left, I asked Zamarrra, "Can you actually bring rain?" She nodded and said matter-of-factly, "Yes, I can, but I will need to be in a high place where I can see the whole sky, and I will need to have uninterrupted time to work the rituals."

"We can put you in a high tower, and someone will bring food and water every day and place it outside your door. And," I said to her, raising my eyebrows in order to emphasize my control over her. "There will be a guard outside your door who will not allow you to leave." I gave instructions to the Drekavac serving as bailiff, and he led her off.

My stepson Alaric was planning to leave with his business partner Hamlin the next day on their trading journey down the Dragonja River to where it joins the Bekla, and then down the river road to the southern villages where Tessia and I grew up. The two young men were shiremen, as I was when I was their age, and they had taken over my old trading route which had been passed down through our family for generations. I knew from my own experience that shiremen were much appreciated by farmers and villagers because we brought not only trade-goods, but also news from other parts of the kingdom.

Idella had prepared a lovely farewell dinner for the two young men. And our five-year-old daughter, Ena, joined us as well. Idella had made a special pastry that when you cut open the bread shell, a rich stew of rabbit, olives, fruit and turnips spilled out. It was delicious and plentiful. We still had ale left from the winter, so the conversation was lively.

After dinner, as we sat in front of the fire, I told them about the day's court proceedings.

"Can this Blue Witch actually bring rain?" Idella sounded skeptical.

"I hope she can," Alaric said. "The land is parched, and if we don't get rain soon, there will be no crops to harvest this year. The people in the Dry Hills are said to be eating their children."

"I'm not sure about that," Idella said, skeptically.

"Actually, I'm not either," Alaric admitted with his fetching smile that showed his dimples. "But the rumors give an indication of how desperate people are becoming."

I looked at my tall stepson, with his black pebble eyes and curly hair which he wore long. A gold ring hung from his right ear. During his adolescence, Alaric had been forced to live by his wits in the alleys with orphaned children who had to steal to survive. Although I would never have wished this hardscrabble life on any child, it had given Alaric a shrewd sense of survival. I'd heard he was good with a knife, but I hoped I'd never find out whether it was true.

Hamlin listened to the conversation and nodded, but stayed silent as he usually did. Ever since he was rescued from the dungeon after the war he'd seemed distracted, as if he weren't completely here. But he was trustworthy and a good companion for Alaric.

They make a good team, I thought, looking at the two young men: Hamlin big and blonde, strong as a Bekla ox; and Alaric tall, thin, and dark like his mother. Alaric was good with customers, friendly yet shrewd. He always left the customers feeling that they had gotten a good deal. Hamlin was better with animals than people; he cared for Ottolo, the donkey named for a foolish king, which carried their trade goods, and fished for salmon and hunted rabbit when they camped between farms. I missed the open road and envied the two young men the freedom they enjoyed, but I was also happy in my little farmstead with my beautiful wife and daughter.

Alaric looked at me, quizzically. "What is a Blue Witch, Norbert? You've always said that there are only five kinds of magic. Green for healers, Red for lovers, and Purple for leaders, as well as White and Black which are combinations of the three. So, what is Blue magic?"

"I'm not sure," I said, honestly. "I've heard of it before, but I always suspected it was just a way to take money from desperate farmers. We'll see whether Zamarrra can bring rain, and if she can, then perhaps I can learn more about the Blue."

"When I grow up, I want to be a Blue Witch," Ena announced confidently. "And I will bring rain and make everything grow."

"Then you better eat your vegetables, little one," her mother said.

We all laughed, but when I turned my head and looked at our

orchard of walnut and apricot trees, I was saddened. It was early spring, and the branches should have been greening with buds.

The next morning, I saw Alaric and Hamlin off as they trudged down the road with Ottolo laden with trade goods. Idella had already left with her helpers carrying breads and cakes to the city. They would deliver the baked goods to the inns and return in late morning. Idella had told me that this was her last delivery of bread to the city because our flour barrel was almost empty and there was no grain of any kind to be had in the market. She was planning to keep what was left for our own larder though it wouldn't last long.

It was a spring morning, but it felt like high summer. The sun blazed down, and each footstep brought up a small cloud of dust, and each breath felt heavy.

I walked toward the city gate, saddened by what I saw. This time of year, the farmers' tables should have been overflowing with strawberries and spring greens. Instead, the morning sun shone down on bare tables. The sparse produce the farmers had brought had been snatched up, and the farmers were already packing their carts to return home.

Overnight, it seemed, the city had run out of food. I realized that many farmers were doing the same thing that Idella and I were doing—saving the last of their stores for themselves. It would be only a matter of days before the city was starving.

In the city, I stopped by the Silver Pony Inn to see my friends Femke and Heikum. Femke, a large powerful woman, was in the kitchen cutting carrots for soup. Normally, she would have had a variety of meats and vegetables to put in the pot, but all I saw that morning were carrots, probably from the root cellar where they'd sat all winter. She smiled at me and

27

asked about Idella and Alaric, and I asked her about Heikum and the inn.

"Oh, farmers don't have the money to spend on ale, so all we get are the Drekavac soldiers. They're a glum lot, they are, but at least they behave themselves." She looked at me with a twinkle in her eye. "Not like the old days, eh, Bard?"

We both laughed remembering the rough days when the Wizard Ludek ruled the kingdom, and ruffians did as they liked. In those days, I made my living singing songs in the inn, and Tessia earned her keep as a serving wench. Once, Tessia, armed only with a tankard, and Femke, armed only with a broom, fought every man in the house until the place was empty. It was a matter of honor: Tessia's bottom had been pinched once too often.

"Ah," Femke sighed. "Heikum is worried about silver. If we don't take in more from the sale of drink, then we will have nothing to pay for repairs to the roof and whatever other expenses that crop up. By the goddess, if it doesn't rain soon, we'll see riots in the street."

I nodded. The situation was dire. I didn't tell her about my arrangement with the Blue Witch to bring rain this week. No sense in raising people's hopes for something so unlikely.

Four mornings after Zamarrra was locked in her room at the top of the tower, I woke to the sound of people shouting. I looked out the window of my bedroom. Idella, her helpers and a couple of neighbors were standing behind our house and pointing to the east. I couldn't believe what I saw. A bank of dark heavy clouds hung in front of the morning sun, and the storm was moving toward us.

For breakfast, I ate the last of the bread Idella had made the day before, along with some dried apples from the previous year's harvest, thinking—no, hoping—that it would be only a little while before we would have fresh fruit and vegetables on our table.

As I walked toward the city gate, I could feel the excitement of the people I passed. A palpable wave of emotion radiated from them. Everyone nodded a greeting before returning their gaze to the eastern sky. We all felt it: there was hope at last.

In the castle, the Drekavac guards were uncharacteristically cheerful. Although I've always found their sharpened teeth disconcerting, this morning their smiles looked almost pleasant.

Queen Tessia was in her private chamber in the tallest tower, looking out the window at the approaching storm. She turned to me and said, "You've done it, Norbert. You've brought rain! Thank you! Thank you! Thank you!" She hugged me.

Caz shook my hand, tears in his eyes. "I didn't think you could do it, old man. Congratulations!"

"I need to tell you, your Majesty, that I didn't..." But neither Tessia nor Caz wanted to hear my half-hearted protests, so I stayed silent.

All morning people looked at the sky, their excitement building. And shortly after noon, small drops started to fall, and the citizens of Dragonja City went outside to dance and cavort in the first rain they'd seen in months. Children and dogs splashed in the puddles. Men held their faces up to the sky, catching drops in their open mouths. Women placed buckets in front of their front doors to catch the water they would use to wash with, not having to worry about rationing anymore. Tyrmiss the dragon stuck her head out the wide opening of her lair in the tower, letting the drops cool her black forked tongue. Even battle-hardened veterans headed out into the street to dance in the rain like happy children.

I climbed the stairs of the second tower where Zamarrra had been imprisoned for four days. The Drekavac guard smiled and nodded to me, and I dismissed him from his duties for the day and told him to go home to celebrate the rain with his family. He thanked me and scurried happily down the stairs.

The walls of the room the witch occupied were covered in

chalk runes and diagrams. Triangles within circles. Maps of constellations. There were also drawings of wolves and bears and a blue painting of two witches stirring a caldron. In the middle of the room sat a large copper bowl full of water with a clay pitcher sitting at its center. Beside the bowl was a long-handled spoon. I recognized these items as the traditional tools of a storm-born witch, a wind-whistler. I thought that the lore had been lost generations before, but here was the evidence that Zamarrra was an experienced practitioner. A sense of foreboding came over me. I had vastly underestimated this woman's powers.

Zamarrra sat in a chair in front of the open window, smiling. A broom was propped against the wall next to her. The cool moist air blew her thick silver hair, and the delicate blue skin of her cheeks shone beneath a fine mist. For the first time, I wondered how old she was.

"Congratulations," I said. You've brought rain to the kingdom. The Queen will reward you handsomely."

"Oh, I require no payment, Mage," she responded, still looking at the storm blowing in from the east. "It is enough to know that I brought happiness to your people."

Remembering our last conversation when she was demanding silver, I was puzzled. "Why then, did you drive such a hard bargain?"

She turned away from the window and looked at me with a slyness I didn't like, "Mage, if I'd agreed to bring rain for no payment, you would have been suspicious. You doubted not only my magic, but my honesty. You needed to feel you had me under your control, didn't you?" She narrowed her eyes. "You would have been afraid of me if you had known how powerful my magic is."

And she was right. She had made me think that she was a charlatan, out to cheat the farmer and me, so I had given her a chance to fail. She'd caused me to underestimate her. But why?

"Who are you really?" I asked.

30

"I am a Blue Witch," she said. "And I have accomplished what I set out to do."

She grabbed her broom, straddled it, her dress riding up her thighs, and leapt out the window, *whooshing* low over the castle walls before disappearing into the sky beyond.

I found Tyrmiss in her chamber, sitting comfortably watching the rain come down on the hills and the valley below.

"Hello, Norbert," she said, stretching her legs like a cat waking from a nap. "Congratulations on the rain. Did you have something to do with it?"

"Well, sort of..." I told her what had happened with Zamarrra. As I told the tale, Tyrmiss seemed more and more alarmed.

"You brought a Blue Witch into the castle?"

"Why, yes, she was in the top room of the second tower. Didn't you know?"

"No, I didn't. How would I? No one tells me anything, and..." The dragon's voice trailed off. "Lately, I haven't been able to hear anyone's dreams, not even Tessia's."

"How long has it been since you've heard a dream, Tyrmiss?"

"Almost a week," she said. "I think someone has put a blocking spell on me, but before the blocking spell took hold, I heard someone, perhaps it was the Blue Witch, dreaming about creating a drought in the kingdom."

"Why would Zamarrra cause a drought only later to bring rain?" I asked, puzzled.

I don't know..." Tyrmiss said slowly, looking out the window. The rain was coming down hard now. "Norbert, it may be that you've made a serious mistake."

Chapter Three

"Norbert," Tyrmiss said, "Sit down. The story of the Blue Witches, who they are and where they come from, is a tale that takes a while, so make yourself comfortable.

"As you know, I was born ten thousand years ago at the end of the Age of Ice. At that time, dragons ruled the world. The Goddess gave us wings to fly over the mountains, talons to catch the salmon, and fiery breath to carve great caverns into the glaciers where we built beautiful cities of ice and light. I still remember flying into the city at night, my brothers and sisters, wingtip to wingtip beside me, the walls and towers reflecting the moon and the stars. It was truly magnificent when the extended wings of thousands of dragons darkened the sky at the same time.

"After the ice retreated, the valley warmed and became verdant. Grasses spread over the plains, and forests grew where there had been only rock and sand. Deer and elk migrated from the south. When men began to arrive, we paid them little heed. We thought they were reckless and sacrilegious in the ways they treated the Goddess's bounty, but they were few in number, and they seemed vulnerable and perhaps a little pathetic, so we let them be. But our cities of light and ice were melting, and we moved into dark caves where the air was rank.

"As the numbers of men grew, their hatred of every living thing became apparent. They cut the skin of the Goddess with their ploughs. They fouled her waters. They dug up great stones and piled them high, making castles modeled on our cities. Everything men saw, they thought was theirs to waste and destroy. They killed every living thing they could find, including dragons. Since we were large and numerous with long talons and dangerous breath, men thought it was great sport to hunt us. They killed us and collected our feet and jaws as trophies. They hung our body parts on the walls of their feasting places. They drank our blood in empty rituals to prove their courage. They even stole our eggs to use in their ceremonies. And worst of all, they captured dragons and kept them as pets. My own brother Morf and my sister Tenwen were kept in chains by the rulers of men. Tenwen died in a dungeon when the Princess grew bored with her, and Morf was killed for refusing to help the king hunt other dragons. Men were a scourge on the land.

"Disgusted with the ways of men, the dragons held a council in the mountain meadow where our city once stood in the Age of Ice. We decided to do what men would do in such a situation. We would go to war. The concept of war, one tribe attacking another tribe, had been unknown to dragons until the men showed us how it was done. The very idea of it was abhorrent to us. Of course, we hunted other species, such as deer, elk and salmon, but the concept of an organized attack against another nation was strange to us. In our philosophy, every living thing was part of the whole fabric. Individuals die, but the tribe, the nation, the species survive. By living as part of the whole fabric of life, we serve the Goddess. But it had become clear that not only dragons were at risk from men, but all of life itself. We felt called by the Goddess to defend Her creation.

"So, we organized squadrons of dragons who would fly together, and these squadrons would be coordinated by a general, a great she-dragon named Ynu, which means *Eternal Fire*. Ynu was magnificent, with a wingspan the width of ten horses and a fiery breath so fierce she could melt the armor off a man.

"In order to please the Goddess, Ynu built a great fire of birch wood, and she sat in front of the fire for five days, eating nothing but snow. Ynu stared into the fire without moving, her eyes taking in the future of our race. In the evening of the fifth day, she rose and ate a few bites of salmon and lay among the rocks and wept. She said she had seen the dragon Morf, my brother, my littermate, in a dream. He was a captive of King Milon who wanted to ride the dragon into war. When Morf refused, Milon ran a spear into Morf's right heart, and then Milon reached into the chest of the dragon and pulled out the heart and ate it while he stood beside the still body of the dragon. Milon gathered my brother's blood in a chalice and offered a sip to each of his chosen warriors. In this way, Milon and his men prepared for war. On hearing this, it became clear to all of us what Ynu had seen in the fire and why she wept. The time of the dragons was over, and our race would die in the coming war.

"The next day, we looked over the valley and saw a great army of men marching toward us. They were so numerous they looked like grains of sand beside the sea. We could hear their war-drums and their horns calling for war, and we knew that our ten thousand dragons were no match for so many men. Nevertheless, we organized our squadrons and lifted off the ground as one.

"We flew down to the army of men, raking our talons over their numbers and killing many. We breathed fire, scorching them and making them scream in terror. But their archers were many, and a cloud of arrows met us wherever we flew. Their ballistas, huge crossbows that sent giant bolts into the air, killed many of us. Finally, rising high above the battlefield, I looked around and realized that I was the last dragon left. Exhausted, terrified, with one torn wing and a hide full of arrows, I abandoned the field and flew into the mountains. There, I lay down beside a stream and waited to die.

"I woke to find a young dragon, only half-grown, ministering my wounds, carrying water to my parched mouth by the only container she had, her own mouth. Her name was Rilla, which means Little Stream, and it seemed that she and I were the last dragons left in the world. When we were called to war, her mother had hidden her in a cave. Rilla had watched the battle from a nearby peak, and she saw me fly wounded to the stream. She helped me hobble to her cave, brought me water and venison, and kept me safe until I was healed. Rilla became my companion, and when she came of age in her two thousandth year, we had a small ceremony to become mates. She was the light of my life for eight thousand years, until…"

Tyrmiss's voice trailed off, and her eyes filled with tears. A teardrop rolled down the side of her face and she licked it off with her forked black tongue.

"Until soldiers killed Rilla beside the very stream where she saved you," I said, completing her thought. I had heard the story before. "And so, you resumed the war against men, killing soldiers at night as they patrolled the Dry Hills. And you continued the war until you and Tessia took the castle during the revolution that ended the reign of the evil wizard Ludek…"

"I am too sad to continue the story any longer today, Norbert," Tyrmiss said wearily.

"Please, Tyrmiss," I said, somewhat desperately. "I need to know who the Blue Witches are and what kind of threat they pose to Tessia and the kingdom."

"I know, I know, Norbert. We'll continue the story tomorrow. By that time, the nature of the threat will be clearer."

I looked out the large opening in the wall at the rain pouring down on the kingdom. Lightning was flashing in the eastern sky, and thunder was rolling over the land, shaking the very bones of the castle.

35

It was early evening as I left the high tower and walked across the empty market square. Evidently, people had grown bored with dancing in the rain and gone inside to dry off. I was soaked by the time I entered the Silver Pony. The place was crowded, but Heikum, was standing behind the bar with his arms crossed, scowling.

"What's wrong, Heikum?" I asked. "You should be happy with so many patrons in the inn."

"Yes, well, they are here, aren't they? But do you see any of them drinking?"

I scanned the room. He was right. Most people were sitting quietly at the tables or standing near the walls, but few of them had a tankard in front of them.

"People came here to get out of the rain." Heikum grumbled. "No one has any more money to spend than they had yesterday. A few even asked me to hire them."

I went into the kitchen where Femke was scowling into a cauldron of her famous soup. She was usually pretty cheerful, so I asked her what was bothering her.

"Heikum says that if people don't start buying ale, then I am going to have to start charging them for a bowl of soup. He says, 'We can't be feeding the whole city for free,'" she said, lowering her voice to a grumble in imitation of her husband.

I laughed, then caught myself. Their predicament was serious. If their customers didn't have any coin, then how could the inn keep its doors open? I realized that this problem was being repeated thousands of times in shops, taverns, and farms across the kingdom.

"At least we have rain now," I said, trying to lighten the mood.

"Yes, too much rain," she said, nodding toward the puddle forming just outside her back door. "We already have leaks in the roof. Maybe tomorrow it will stop raining and Heikum can climb on the roof to fix the thatch."

She handed me a bowl of soup which I ate greedily, not having had anything since the stale bread at breakfast.

On the way out of the Silver Pony, I handed Heikum a few coppers, telling him they were for a bowl of soup. He nodded thanks as he pocketed the coins.

When I got home, Idella was already asleep, and I crawled into bed beside her. All night the storm kept me awake. The rain poured down. Lightning struck close. Thunder rolled through the valley, and I regretted inviting the Blue Witch to work her magic.

The next morning, there was nothing to eat in the house. We had finished all the winter stores, and Idella had not been able to use her ovens behind our house because they were half under water. The rain continued to beat down. The trees swayed dangerously in the wind. The valley was dark under the black clouds, lit sporadically by lightning.

Idella wouldn't look me in the eye, no doubt because she didn't want to seem to accuse me. I went outside and waded through our flooded orchard and climbed a small hill where I knew wild herbs grew. I picked some greens, seeds and berries and brought them back to the house. As Idella and I ate, the tension between us eased.

"What's going to happen to us, Norbert?" she asked.

"We will survive, Idella. I promise we will survive."

"And what about the kingdom? Food was already in short supply, and now it will be impossible for farmers to plow."

"I know." I looked out the window at the flooding fields, the trees whipped by the wind, the lightning hitting the mountain peaks. I hoped the Queen had moved out of the high tower. I wondered how Tyrmiss was faring.

"Has the Blue Witch cursed us?" Idella asked.

"It appears so." I looked at my beautiful wife and felt a terrible guilt that I had brought this suffering on her and on so many others in the kingdom.

"Where are you going, Norbert?" she asked, seeing me packing my kit and putting my sheathed wand on my belt.

"I'm going to the castle to talk with Tyrmiss. I need to find out more about the Blue Witch. I can't fight what I can't see."

I found Tyrmiss in one of the horse stables on the castle grounds. I wondered whether her lair in the tower had become too wet. Here, Tyrmiss occupied the entire passage between the rows of stalls. The horses stamped and snorted, their eyes wide with fear as they looked at the dragon in front of them. Tyrmiss ignored them.

"Well, little Norbert, I'm glad to see you came back to hear more of the tale."

"Tyrmiss, tell me about the Blue Witch. Who is she? Where did she come from? What are her powers? And most of all, how do we end this blasted rain?"

"Norbert, calm down. There's nothing we can do about the rain right now. Princess Taja—what a jewel that woman is—sent over dry clothes for you. She somehow knew this stable would be your first stop." Tyrmiss nodded her head to a linen bag hanging on a hook.

As I changed into dry clothes—*how did Taja know my size?*—Tyrmiss said, "My ability to read dreams has returned."

"Zamarrra made a gift to you by restoring your psychic powers?"

"I don't think so. More likely, the block had to be renewed every day, and once she left, she was unable to continue the spell."

"So, what did you discover last night as you listened to the dreams of the people in the castle?"

Tyrmiss shook her head sadly, "Nothing good. Taja…" Her voice trailed off.

"What about Princess Taja?" I asked.

"Nothing. I just don't want Tessia to get hurt…"

Before I could ask what she meant, Tyrmiss picked up the

story of the Blue Witches where she left off the day before, and for the time being, I forgot about Princess Taja.

"Norbert, I have heard you explain many times that there are only five types of magic, and I have never contradicted you because what you said was true for this kingdom, and I didn't think anyone here, even you, needed to know that in other kingdoms there are different kinds of magic. But you seem to have forgotten that you learned from Idella that there is brown magic, which empowers a witch to speak to animals. And you might want to know there are also orange magic, which encourages inanimate things to speak; and yellow, which enables people to hear the music of the spheres, and even a few that have variegated colors because they combine different kinds of magic. By the way, Norbert, did you know that there are colors no human has ever seen? The Goddess does not allow you to see them because doing so would risk blindness."

Tyrmiss thought for a moment, then resumed. "And that brings us to Blue Magic. What do you associate with the color blue, Norbert?"

"The sky. The sea. Certain flowers. Certain stones."

"Exactly. Blue Magic encourages rain to fall, wind to blow, clouds to form. Thunder, lightning, floods. Also, the gentle rain of summer, the harsh wintry blast. These are the domain of the Blue Witches, also called the Weather Witches."

"How long will this rain last?"

"Not much longer."

"How do you know?"

"Norbert, you are an accomplished mage. You know that a mage, or in this case a witch, can *encourage* things to happen, but she cannot *create* them. For example, as a Green Mage you can encourage crops to grow, but can you make them grow in poor soil?"

"No."

"It is the same with the weather witches. They can encourage

39

rain to fall, but they cannot create rain where there is no moisture. Eventually, all the moisture will be squeezed out of the air, and it will stop raining."

"And then, things will go back to normal?"

"Probably not. Instead, the weather witches will cause another kind of mischief. They may make a cold wind blow down from the mountains, for example, and freeze the rivers."

"Zamarrra is definitely a weather witch?"

"Indeed. She is one of the most powerful witches of that tribe of women who live in Sheonad."

"Do you think she was working alone?"

"Probably not. The witches of Sheonad almost always work together, amplifying each other's powers. It is one of the reasons they are so powerful."

"Have you ever been to Sheonad?"

"Not in a very long time."

"Why did Zamarrra need to be in the tower to cast the spell?"

"A weather witch needs to be up high where she can see the whole landscape. She could have done her magic from the side of one of the mountains, but it would have been uncomfortable sitting up there for days. You gave her a pleasant room, had food brought to her, and placed a guard at the door, so she would not be interrupted." Tyrmiss looked at me with disgust. "Norbert, you were the perfect dupe for her. She played you like a cheap lyre."

I felt angry at myself for having been taken in so easily.

"Don't feel bad, Norbert. Most men would have been fooled by her. You were expecting to see a stupid woman who lacked your sophistication, a charlatan who was profiting from the ignorance and superstition of farmers, so that's what she gave you. If you had been more open to the idea that a witch could be more powerful than a mage, then you would not have been tricked so easily."

"You are saying that we should fight this tribe of witches?"

"You must go to Sheonad, the place where they live, and talk to them, and if necessary, kill them. Otherwise, they will find new ways to destroy this kingdom."

"Where does this tribe live—this Sheonad?"

"Over the pass between The Two Thumbs of the Giant. Then down the cliffs to the Iskar River. Then follow the river upstream for a few weeks. Then climb another mountain and through another pass to the top of a mountain. The land of the weather witches is not far from here as the dragon flies, but it is a difficult journey on foot."

"They live on top of a mountain?"

"Yes, but remember they can influence the weather, so what might otherwise have been an inhospitable wasteland of ice, has been turned into a place of continual summer. It's quite a beautiful place, actually."

"You have been there?"

"As I said, I have been there, but not in a very long time. The weather witches are not fond of dragons."

"Can you take me there?"

Tyrmiss shook her head wearily, "Norbert, you must be very careful. The weather witches would cut out your heart and roast it on a spit. They are not fond of dragons, but they really hate men."

"Why do they hate men?"

"Oh, that is a long story, so I am going to save it for another time. Right now, I believe the Queen requires your presence," Tyrmiss said, tipping her large head toward the doorway where two Drekavac guards, dripping wet, stood at attention.

Queen Tessia had taken up residence on the second floor of the keep, the oldest building in the castle. The name Windkeep had been given to this place a thousand years ago, and Tessia had brought back the name to refer to the entire castle. The Queen was sitting in a large oaken chair with a high back, a throne to signify her authority. Her wife Princess Taja and her First Minister Caz sat in smaller chairs nearby, and Bastian, the diplomat who had spent many years with the mountain tribes, stood nearby. Taja smiled at me, and Caz and Bastian nodded in my direction.

"Norbert," the Queen said, "Thank you for joining us. Tyrmiss told me that you have a plan for dealing with the Blue Witch and this interminable rain."

"How did Tyrmiss—" but I caught myself. Of course, now that the dragon's psychic abilities had been restored, she knew what I was thinking as I thought it. Not only could the dragon read our dreams, but she could also surmise our plans as we made them. I wondered what kind of blocking spell could have kept her unaware of the presence of the Blue Witch in the castle. I was beginning to realize just how much I had underestimated Zamarrra.

"Yes, I suppose I do have a plan. You know about the tribe of Blue Witches and their mountain fast?"

The Queen nodded her head.

"We must organize a diplomatic expedition to go there and parley with them," I said.

"And if they refuse to parley?" she asked me, narrowing her eyes.

"Then we must destroy them."

The rain had stopped, but during the day and night it had fallen in such abundance, everything was flooded. The Dragonja spilled over its banks, covering the fields and orchards. Thatched roofs had grown so sodden that many of them had collapsed into the rooms below. The roads had become impassable quagmires. Riverboats had broken loose from their moorings and drifted far downstream. People and animals had drowned or been buried under mudslides. Parts of the city wall had collapsed, undermined by running water. Lightning had hit the tallest towers of the castle, including the Queen's own chambers. I realized that the dragon lair, directly below the Queen's chambers, must have been damaged as well, which explained why Tyrmiss had taken refuge in the horse stables. Needless to say, the poets, goldsmiths and tapestry artists that Tessia had invited from other lands had all left in recent months to pursue opportunities elsewhere. Even our own people were emigrating to other lands.

The most serious problem continued to be the shortage of food. Queen Tessia, on the advice of Caz, had sent out heralds to recruit skilled hunters to go into the mountains and bring back meat, boat captains to sail to the coastal cities to purchase fish and to make arrangements to buy food from foreign lands, and farmers to make seining nets to pull fish from the swelling rivers. The Queen also had midwives teach the women how to gather herbs and mushrooms from the fields. However, even after a few days, it was becoming clear that these trading missions were not helping most citizens because the people who obtained food tended to distribute it only to their own families, or they profiteered by selling the food outside the city walls.

"What we're lacking," Caz pointed out to the Queen. "Is a sense of shared obligation. Your subjects have no loyalty to the kingdom as a whole."

Tessia looked puzzled, not having any idea how to inspire devotion in the people of Dragonja.

When I got back to my house after a hard slog through knee-deep mud, Alaric and Hamlin were there to greet me. Idella, who'd been worried about them, was glad to have them home safely.

"Back already?" I hugged the two young men. I too had been worried about them.

Alaric grinned. Clearly, he was glad to be home. Then his expression changed. "We lost Ottolo," he said, looking at the floor sheepishly.

"You mean he ran away? Was he frightened by the lightning?"

"No, he was stolen."

Oh no, I thought. *Poor Ottolo has probably been butchered already, and some starving family is eating him right now.*

"I'm sorry," Alaric said. "We stopped to camp in a stand of trees on high ground. And in the middle of the night when we were asleep, we were attacked by a group of men. I don't know how many, maybe four or five?" He looked at Hamlin for confirmation, and Hamlin nodded and then looked down. I realized that Hamlin must be heart-broken over the loss of Ottolo. He had loved the old donkey.

And I'd loved Ottolo as well. He'd been my faithful companion for years when I was traveling the roads as a shireman. My eyes filled with tears. "Remember the time that the white wolves attacked us in the Dry Hills?" I asked Hamlin, putting my hand on his shoulder.

"Yes," he nodded, crying. "Anja rode Ottolo into the midst of the wolves, scaring them off. You said he fought like the 'Donkey from Hell.'"

"That was the only time I ever saw him be mean in all the years he and I were together."

The four of us, with my little daughter Ena playing under the table, sat in silence for a while, mourning the brave and faithful Ottolo.

Chapter Four

We were sitting at the kitchen table sharing a rabbit that somehow had survived the flooding only to be caught in Hamlin's snare, when we heard a loud knock. Idella opened the door to a Drekavac guard who snapped to attention and said, "The Queen requests that your husband Norbert, your son Alaric, and your friend Hamlin join her in the dragon lair at the castle. I shall accompany them."

I looked at Alaric who shrugged. "I have no idea what this is about," he said. I looked at Hamlin whose face was also blank. Idella looked at me with fear in her eyes.

"I don't want Alaric to go," she said.

"Mother, I have no choice," he said. "A Queen's request is not to be ignored."

As we walked toward the castle, I saw people struggling with the deep mud that was everywhere. The heavy rain had lasted only a day and a night, but it had made ordinary life impossible. If this much damage could be accomplished by the spells of just one weather witch, then what could a whole tribe of them do to us?

We climbed the spiral staircase in the tallest tower to the floor occupied by Tyrmiss. It looked like one wall had been blasted away by lightning and we now had a view of the Two

Thumbs of the Giant. Tyrmiss lay comfortably in the middle of the floor, her wings tucked at her side. Beside her sat the Queen, her wife the Princess Taja, First Minister Caz, the diplomat Bastian, and someone I had not seen in a while—Sergeant Zrul.

I bowed to the Queen, then turned to Zrul. "Hello, Sergeant, it's nice to see you again."

The old Drekavac, veteran of many battles, gave a snarl and put a scowl on his scarred face. I recognized this particular scowl as his version of a smile. He nodded at me. He'd been Tessia's drill sergeant when she first joined the rebel force led by her uncle Zygmunt. Other than Tessia herself, Zrul was undoubtedly the best warrior in the kingdom.

"I have called you here to ask for your help in saving the kingdom," Queen Tessia said in a formal voice. "The Weather Witches have committed an act of war against the kingdom. They created a drought and then followed it with a deluge. As a result, our people are starving. We cannot wait for them to commit another act against us. We underestimated the Blue Witch Zamarrra to our detriment. We cannot make that mistake again. I plan to go over the mountains to Sheonad, the land of the Weather Witches. There I will address their leaders and parley for peace. If they refuse peace, they will face doom. I ask that you join me in this quest."

She looked around the room. "Each of you brings essential skills to the expedition. First, let us consider provisions. It will be a long journey, and I will not take food away from our people, so we must live off the land during our journey. Hamlin, my old friend, we grew up together, and I know what a resourceful hunter and fisherman you are. We will need your skills. Also, you know how to cook and tend camp. Alaric, in your youth, you lived as an orphan in the alleys of Dragonja when the city was in chaos. We will need your scavenging skills and your shrewd ability to survive. You will assist Hamlin in providing for us.

Hamlin and Alaric bowed their heads in acknowledgement of the honor the Queen was giving them.

"Sergeant Zrul, my old commander who taught me how to be a soldier, will you accompany me in one more mission?"

Zrul saluted, ready to obey his Queen.

"Thank you, Sergeant. I need you as second in command. You are an expert fighter, skilled with many weapons, and you are able to improvise in the middle of battle. If I should fall, you will finish the mission and bring the survivors safely home.

"Bastian," Tessia said, turning to the diplomat. "You lived in the mountains near Sheonad. You know the land. You have family in the Renetu tribe that lives near Sheonad. We need your diplomatic skills."

Bastian nodded. "I am honored, my Queen."

"And Norbert," Tessia said to me, her voice turning gentle. "You are the Green Mage, my advisor and companion through the long journey that brought us here. We need your skills to understand and to fight the Weather Witches. Also, if any of us is hurt in battle, we will need your healing powers. Will you join us?"

I bowed my head to my Queen. I had learned long ago that I could refuse Tessia nothing.

Tessia walked over to Tyrmiss and put her arms around the great scaly head. The dragon gave a deep purr. Tessia said something in the large, pointed ear I didn't catch, then turned to us. "My dear friend Tyrmiss has agreed to help us, as she has so many times before at great risk to herself. She will be our scout, our eyes and ears on the trail. And if the Goddess wills us to fight the tribe of witches, Tyrmiss will be their nightmare."

Finally, the Queen turned to her two advisors, Princess Taja and First Minister Caz.

"I am appointing the two of you as regents to rule the Kingdom while I am gone. Princess Taja, my love, listen to Caz. He has a brilliant mind and will administer the rule of law with exact precision. And Caz, listen to the Princess. Her wisdom is of a different kind than yours. She thinks with her heart and can see the wider good. Her decisions are soft, yours are hard. You need to balance each other."

Caz bowed his head in obedience. Taja stood tall and erect, her eyes filling with tears as she looked with great sadness at her wife, the Queen. Taja wiped away her tears, then exchanged a quick look with Caz that seemed oddly conspiratorial. It was only a small moment among many that day, but I know now that I should have paid more attention to my instincts.

"Now," Tessia said, wiping away a tear. "I have asked Tyrmiss to tell us what she knows of these Weather Witches."

"Two thousand years ago," Tyrmiss began. "After the dragons had been conquered, the center of this kingdom, the region we now call The Dry Hills, was an ancient cedar forest. The trees were tall and wise and stood guard over the animals and plants who paid them homage. Over time, humans, who'd always been destroyers of the Goddess's gifts, eventually learned to live in the forest at one with the other animals. When a human killed an animal—and every living thing depends on death to survive—the human thanked the soul of that which had given its life so the human could live. In this way, life was a circle. The soil, the plants, the animals all lived in harmony, each one having its turn to live and then giving itself to the next living thing.

"Among the humans, there were those who had special powers. At first, these powers were small: an ability to smell rain the way animals do, a skill at starting a fire with wet wood, a talent for singing a child to sleep or for telling a story that enchanted a family gathered beside a fire. But over time, these talents grew. Women, in particular, learned to use their talents in ways never seen before. One woman discovered how

48

to whistle up a wind. Another developed the ability to start a fire by pointing a willow wand at dry tinder. And still another invented chants that could put a person to sleep or make them think thoughts not their own. Over time, these practices grew into what we now know as *magic*. And it was a woman's art. Men were not allowed to learn it."

Tyrmiss looked at me out of the corner of her great yellow eye. I said nothing but understood that this story was meant for me.

"Over the next thousand years, the practice of magic became more sophisticated. As new spells and charms were invented, the knowledge became too great for any one woman, or even one group of women, to hold. So, the witches, as they came to be known, divided themselves into guilds, each one taking on a color to signify the kind of power it specialized in. There were the green witches who practiced healing and nurturing, the red ones who focused on love, the purple who loved leadership and politics, the orange who directed fire, the brown who could converse with animals, and the blue who learned how to influence the weather.

"As time passed, the witches became more powerful. They sent out emissaries to other lands, eventually establishing convents and schools, encouraging reforms and even revolutions that changed the world. Many of the things the witches did were good, teaching people to have respect for nature, for example. The Goddess cult which people practice in the kingdom to this day is an artifact of their teachings. But some of what they did was not good. Some witches were interested only in enriching themselves at the expense of the people they supposedly served. They installed kings who ruled with cruel oppression. They established sham religions that kept people in ignorance. A few even set themselves up as goddesses who insisted on being worshipped and obeyed.

"Eventually, the men and women who didn't have magical

powers rose up against the witches. A great war ensued in which the witches killed many, but the unmagical people, who were far more numerous than the witches, slaughtered them and burned the great cedar forest which was their home.

"One small band of witches escaped through the pass between the Two Thumbs of the Giant and went into the Iskar Valley."

Tyrmiss nodded toward the gaping hole in the wall where we could see the two peaks.

"On the other side of the pass, the witches followed the river further and further into the wilderness of ice and came to a place in the mountains so dismal and unfriendly to human existence that they knew no one would follow. There, they used their powers to influence the weather to make a home for themselves. And this is the land of Sheonad.

"Meanwhile here in this Kingdom of Dragonja and Bekla, the land between two rivers, magic has slowly been re-discovered in recent generations. It is now becoming powerful again. But this time, magic is not a woman's art, but primarily a man's art."

Tyrmiss paused, looking at me. "Norbert, you are a threat to the witches."

"Me?" I was caught completely by surprise. "Why me?" I noticed everyone in the room was looking at me. They seemed as baffled as I was.

"The witches of Sheonad have not forgotten their previous glory," Tyrmiss said. "Nor have they forgotten what was done to them by men."

"So, you think they want to kill Norbert?" Tessia asked.

"No, killing him would not accomplish their goal. He has students and apprentices who are growing in power. There are green mages living in the river valleys, helping crops grow and businesses prosper. Red mages practice midwifery in the villages. There's even a budding purple mage who helps rule the kingdom." Tyrmiss looked at Caz who put his hand that bore the purple stone ring in the pocket of his robe. I remembered that Caz had been spending a lot of time in the library studying the old scrolls.

"Then what is it they want?" Tessia asked.

"They want to destroy the kingdom, so they can return to their ancestral homeland," Tyrmiss said.

Later, when I told Idella about the witches and how Tessia had recruited Alaric and me to go with her on the quest, she responded, "I understand why the Queen needs for you to go, Norbert, but why does Alaric have to go? He is not a mage like you or a warrior like Zrul, he's just a shireman."

"Tessia is a very perceptive leader, my love. She must see something in him that we need on the journey. And I will be with him, so I will make sure no harm will come."

"How can you promise such a thing, Norbert? You don't—"

"Mother, I really don't like it when you talk about me as if I weren't here," Alaric said, rolling his eyes.

"I'm sorry, Alaric, but the last six years have been so wonderful. When you were young, and Norbert was off in the mountains fighting in the rebel army, and I was kidnapped, and you were all alone, having to survive in the alleys..." Idella started to cry.

Alaric, his eyes also filling with tears, went to her and the two of them held each other.

"You know I love you and your sister so much," Idella said, her voice muffled as she leaned her face on her son's shoulder."

Alaric held his mother tightly in his strong wiry arms, and I was very aware that he was a man now. *They look so much alike,* I thought for the thousandth time. Both of them tall with dark skin and curly black hair. To me, Idella, Alaric, and Ena were the most beautiful beings in the world.

B ased on reports from Tyrmiss, Tessia had decided that the country we would be covering would be too rough for mules, so each of us would carry our own weapons and tools. I packed my medical kit, including herbs and knives, my wand and warm clothes. After thinking about it for a moment, I decided to bring my lyre. It has often proved useful for casting spells and for making friends. Also, I slipped the emerald ring on, which Idella had given me as a symbol of my commitment to the goddess. I'm not much good as a fighter, so I didn't take any weapons.

I checked on Alaric's preparations. He was packing warm clothes, a small shovel for digging up plants to eat and a few copper knives for cooking. Then he slid a sword from under his bed, and I could see it was made of Voprian, the alloy discovered by Tessia's father, Kerttu. The purple blade shimmered in the morning light. All of the Queen's soldiers carried Voprian blades, but the swords were illegal for civilians to own.

"Where did you get the sword, Alaric?"

"I took it off a bandit I killed in the Dry Hills last summer," he said, meeting my eye.

This was the first I knew of Alaric having killed anyone although I knew he had a reputation for ferocity that he'd earned when he was living by his wits in the alleys of Dragonja City. I wanted to ask him whether he'd killed other people as well, but I decided that this wasn't information I wanted or needed to know.

"Let's say goodbye to your mother, and then we need to meet the others in the castle."

W e met in the lair with Tyrmiss lying quietly behind the Queen, who spoke first. "Thank you all for joining me in this quest. Again, our mission is to go to Sheonad and try to negotiate a peace treaty with them. However, we need to be prepared for them to be hostile toward us. I have asked Bastian to make a map to show us the basic path. I've also asked him to decide on rendezvous points in case we get separated. After each day's march, we'll take a look at the path for the next day and note these rendezvous points." She nodded to Bastian who unrolled a map he had created on vellum. Zrul, Alaric, Hamlin and I moved closer to see it better.

"You see this zigzag line going up to the pass between the Two Thumbs of the Giant?" Bastian began. "That's the trail up the mountain that starts downriver from the city. It will take us about two days to get over the pass, then the trail becomes easier because we'll be going downhill to the Iskar River." He moved his finger over the map. "Then we follow the river up into the mountains for about twenty days." He took a deep breath. "And when we come to the Cliffs of Tortora, we have to climb using ropes. This will be difficult and dangerous."

"Couldn't the dragon take us two at a time up the cliff?" Zrul asked, glancing at Tyrmiss who scowled at him.

"No, we need Tyrmiss to be flying patrol over the cliff to make sure we are not ambushed. Also, I don't want to tire her out by ferrying us. If we get in a fight, she'll be invaluable and I want her fresh," Tessia responded.

Zrul nodded at Tessia's tactical foresight.

Bastian continued, "Once we are at the top of the cliffs, we will use a narrow steep trail up the mountain and across the frozen plain for another ten days to get to the pass into Sheonad. The pass is probably heavily defended, so we'll have to either surrender ourselves to the guards or use guile to find a way around them."

"Can't we just kill them and force our way through the pass?" said Zrul.

Bastian looked at Zrul impatiently. Obviously, he did not like being interrupted. "If we kill them, Zrul, then there is no chance that we can negotiate with their Queen. We need to start peacefully and then use violence only if we have to."

Tessia interjected, "This is very important. We must go to Sheonad with the intention of making peace. We do not want to do anything that will provoke them into attacking us." She looked at Zrul, then moved her eyes to Alaric and Hamlin. "Am I clear?"

All three men nodded assent.

"How long will the journey to Sheonad take?" I asked.

Bastian looked at the map and creased his brow, "With good weather, on foot it will take at least thirty days."

"Did everyone hear that?" Tessia looked around at us. "We need good weather for our journey, so we need stealth. The Weather Witches cannot know we are coming, or who knows what weather they will send us."

Because it was almost a certainty that the Witches had spies in the city, Tessia ordered us to leave the castle one at a time and meet downriver where the mountain trail begins. First Zrul left, followed a few minutes later by Alaric, then Hamlin, then me, then Bastian. Tessia and Tyrmiss would fly out of the lair in the afternoon as they normally did but would take the opportunity to scout the trail up to the pass to make sure it was safe for us. They would meet us at the cave in the mountains where Tyrmiss used to live and where Tessia and I had first encountered her.

When it was my turn, I left the castle carrying my pack, walked across the market square past the Silver Pony. I would have liked to say goodbye to Heikum and Femke but refrained out of respect for Tessia's warning about keeping this quest a secret.

The Witch's Tower

~the first two pages of a bound manuscript composed by the philosopher Linnaeus of Iskar in the reign of Ottolo the Befuddled; the rest of the manuscript illegible having been damaged by water

*T*atatungia, the greatest witch of her age, practiced neither white nor black magic, for she'd moved beyond such distinctions and had a vision that revealed the essence. She'd come to understand that all things are one thing, that most of what we think of as the world is actually empty space with tiny particles she called wu vibrating at a speed beyond our comprehension, colliding, entangling and breaking loose, and we apprehend this never-ending activity of wu as objects and as motion. But nothing we see is as it appears to be. The tree, the bird in the tree, the breeze moving the branches, the light by which we see the tree, and even our minds by which we perceive these objects do not exist. Nothing is real in the way we believe it to be. Everything we know or think we know is created by a Great Mind that is and is not a mind that holds everything in a dream.

When Tatatungia told her students of this vision, they grew excited and went home to tell their families that their wise and esteemed teacher claimed there was no certainty in the world; therefore, they no longer had to obey their strict fathers. The rebellion of the daughters enraged the fathers, and they called a council to denounce the teachings of Tatatungia. If there was no good or bad, right or wrong, they asked, then what will stop the evil impulses that reside in a man's soul? What will stop a man from killing his neighbor? Or a woman from sleeping with her son? Or a daughter from wandering off? Tatatungia claimed that life itself is a dream, so did it not follow that nothing matters? Could it be true that even a mother's love for her infant is nothing but a trick of light? Tatatungia had let go of certainty itself, and the beliefs and traditions that made life possible no longer carried authority. The council of elders, of which Tatatungia had never been a member because she was a woman, cautioned the witch that by convincing the young women that nothing could be known, she may have unlocked the gates of Chaos itself.

When Tatatungia disagreed with the council, claiming she brought light, not darkness to the people, it was said she was unrepentant, and she was banished from the village where she was born. And thus, Tatatungia began wandering. Leaving the high dry plains of her people, she walked through the mountains, foraging roots, leaves, seeds and berries like a wild animal. When she crossed paths with fellow travelers, she ate what she was offered and fasted when she was not. After years of wandering, Tatatungia came to a broad, fast-running river full of fish. She called the river Iskar, which means in the first language, she-who-is-water, and beside the river she made her home.

During her time in the mountains, the witch had watched how the wind moved through trees, how the sun rose and set, and how animals lived on the earth. In this way, she made a study of aging and of death itself, and she knew she could live as long as she wished in this narrow valley protected from the wind. As for the dragon Tyrmiss she knew lived in the mountains, she doubted the creature would even notice her as long as she kept her dreams to herself.

Tatatungia built a small stone tower, a keep, and there she amused herself by considering the animals of the valley. She wanted to know what made one animal different than another. What gives the fish gills and the bird wings? Why do rams eat grass and wolves eat lambs? As the centuries passed, she eventually came to understand that the difference between one animal and another is very slight, a minor variation in wu which could be controlled through the judicious application of herbs in combination with music.

She began to experiment in the transformation of animals. She gave a fly the wings of a moth and a flea the strength of an ant. Then she learned to transform larger animals, creating whole new species, flying cats and walking fish. Deer that could burrow in the ground and wolves that ate only apples. Eventually, the meadow, the forest and the river were teeming with her inventions, her favorite being Narrra the gentle ewe who spoke many languages.

After centuries of living alone with her work and her extraordinary animals, Tatatungia had her first visitor. A tall confident woman showed up at the door of the tower. She introduced herself as Faba, known as Windstorm, and said she'd been carrying out experiments with the weather, and having wandered far from home, she was hungry. Tatatungia invited her into the tower, had her sit at the table, and placed bowls of seeds and berries in front of her, but refrained from offering her meat since the enchanted animals of this valley were the witch's friends. She watched Faba's slim fingers pick up seeds and berries one at a time, as a blue jay would with its beak. Faba was the most beautiful creature Tatatungia had ever seen, with hair as full of lightning as a stormcloud and skin so translucent she was blue. Watching her eat, the witch realized how lonely she'd been these many years.

Part Two: The Trail

Chapter Five

"Have you been up this way before?" Bastian asked me, as we moved up the switchback trail above Dragonja City.

"Oh, yes," I answered. "Many times. My father, who was a shireman, took me with him up the trail to carry trade goods to the copper mining camp. It was my job to care for the donkey."

"In those days," Bastian said, shifting his backpack to a higher, more comfortable position. "Wasn't the mine worked by slaves? Boys that the king's Drekavac soldiers kidnapped from villages in the Bekla Valley and forced down into the mines?"

"That's true," I answered, recalling how shocked I was the first time I saw the lash marks on the boys' backs. When my father passed away, I had taken over his trade route, but didn't go to the mining camp any longer because it was too disturbing to have supper with the guards and make small talk with them when on the other side of the camp boys were sleeping in chains and girls were being molested by the soldiers.

"When was the last time you were here?"

"About seven years ago after I joined the rebels' cause, I visited the mining camp to reconnoiter the defenses. After I reported back on the weakness of the guards' defenses, General Zygmunt led an attack that freed the slaves, some of whom joined the rebel army."

"Who works the mine now?"

"Well-paid men and women who live in comfortable huts close by." I was puzzled by Bastian's interest in the mine. But after all, he was a former ambassador from Dragonja, and he had an interest in the commerce of the kingdom.

"Tessia and her mentor, the Wise Queen Varvara, instituted reforms that made people much happier and more productive," I explained. "Caz, with imminent practicality, persuaded them that having well-paid citizens is far more profitable than having slaves. Not only are healthy well-treated workers more productive than sick, surly slaves, but well-treated workers are much less likely to slit their bosses' throats."

Bastian nodded, conceding the wisdom of Dragonja's rulers.

At the end of the first day, Zrul, Alaric, Hamlin, Bastian and I stumbled into the mining camp. It had been a long trek up the mountain, and we were exhausted. The last time I had made the climb seven years before, I had been in much better shape. However, my current companions were carrying more weight than I. Each of them had a Voprian-tipped spear in one hand and a Voprian sword at his belt. Moreover, Hamlin and Alaric were also carrying rope and cooking pots, and from the look of Zrul's pack, he was carrying additional weapons.

Looking at Bastian hiking up the trail, I wondered how old he was. At Taja's dinner party, he'd seemed a handsome dandy, but he said he'd left Dragonja before Ludek had become the ruler, so I guessed he was in his late fifties, about twenty years older than me, and yet his shoulders were broad and muscular, and he didn't seem to be as exhausted as I was. His hands were square and his fingers thick. The top of one of his pointed ears was missing. Despite being a diplomat, he was someone who had seen his share of hard work and close-in fighting. I looked around at my other companions and suddenly realized that I was the only one in the group who was not a warrior, unless you count the damage I could do, reluctantly, with my wand.

The soldiers, the miners, and their families shared a common mess where they sat at long tables in an open-sided building next to the community kitchen. We were joined by two traders from the Iskar Valley who were bringing dried food—meat, beans, and fruit—across the pass to sell in Dragonja City. One of their donkeys was loaded with bags of barley grain. They had heard about the drought and flood and surmised they could charge high prices for their goods. They were right, of course. The citizens of the capital were starving, and I hoped that there would be a hundred traders like these two bringing food to the city though I worried about the inevitable price gouging that would go on.

Meanwhile, dinner at the mining camp was a welcome feast. Up here, they hadn't experienced the drought and floods of the valley below. Their kitchen gardens supplied them with strawberries and fresh greens. Their hutches gave up rabbits, and one of the men had killed a wild boar, so there was meat on the table. My companions and I had climbed the mountain on empty stomachs, eating only the sparse weeds we found beside the trail, so we devoured the food they generously offered us. I was embarrassed by how much I ate but felt somewhat better when I noticed that Hamlin ate twice as much as I did.

The traders from the Iskar Valley were glad to share what they knew about the region upriver. I noticed one of them eyeing the weapons we'd stacked in the corner, but he knew better than to ask what our business was. As the Queen's Mage and Advisor, I was known to be her emissary, and the Queen was very popular here, so they knew they could trust this group of warriors who'd shown up unexpectedly. Besides, the people in our region don't ordinarily ask a person's business. Curiosity about strangers was a dangerous luxury most of us had given up during the years of Wizard Ludek's rule.

"The area up the Iskar River has few people," a trader named Gaspar said, wiping pig grease off the whiskers of his chin with the back of his hand. "People generally settle downriver where the water is wider and slower, and the land more fertile."

"Are there hostiles in that area?" Zrul asked, his mouth full of rabbit meat.

"There may be a few bandits, but I've never encountered them," the trader answered.

"What about farms and villages?" Bastian asked.

"Not that I know of."

"What kind of game is there?" Hamlin asked.

Gaspar glanced uncomfortably at his companion who looked at his plate, avoiding our eyes.

"What is it, Meister Gaspar?" I asked. "Is there something about the animals in that region that we need to know?"

"There are stories that the woods in that part of the valley are bewitched," he muttered.

"What do you mean 'bewitched?'"

"The animals are strange. They are not like animals anywhere else."

"What do you mean?" Hamlin asked, leaning forward, his food forgotten in mid-chew. Hamlin had always been more interested in animals than people.

"Some of the animals are evil crosses between one kind of animal and another," Gaspar said. "I myself have seen a rabbit spaniel. It had the body of a rabbit and the head of a dog. Also, it is said that some animals in that region behave like humans."

Gaspar's friend piped up, "Sometimes shepherds take their sheep into the hills above the river and when they return, the new lambs learn to speak like people. They call them mimic lambs."

"You mean like a parrot?" Bastian asked.

"No, not like a parrot. The lambs actually have conversations with people."

"So, you can talk about the weather and the price of hay with these sheep?" Zrul asked facetiously. He obviously thought that these two men were putting us on, and Zrul had decided to go along with the joke.

"I've never actually encountered one, but travelers to that area say the sheep can talk to humans. I'm not sure whether they can actually understand our language, or whether they just imitate us," Gaspar said cautiously, seeing that he and his friend were losing credibility with each claim.

Hamlin, who seemed to believe Gaspar's descriptions of these fantastical animals, asked, "Which animals are good to eat?"

"The honeydew lobsters and lemon pike in the river are delicious," Gaspar answered.

And what about animal pelts?" Hamlin asked.

"The ermine horses are said to provide beautiful fur, and the hide is large enough for a bed."

Gaspar's friend plunged on, undeterred by the skeptical looks on the faces of Zrul, Bastian and Alaric. "There's also a tan Bonobo which is a kind of ape, a donkey hamster which looks like a fist-sized donkey, and the legions of army hawks which attack large bears. But the most dangerous of all is the flaming cockroach, which can crawl into your blankets at night and light you on fire."

Zrul started laughing and after a few seconds was joined in loud guffaws by Alaric and Bastian. "You had us going for a while, you two scoundrels. Rabbit spaniels and flaming cockroaches!" He was laughing so hard, he nearly choked on his food.

The two traders looked puzzled, then embarrassed. Gaspar signaled his friend to let the subject drop, and they went on to ask about the price of food in Dragonja City and who they should talk to first about selling their products.

"First, take the bags of barley to my wife Idella at our farm just south of the city gate. She's a baker and will turn the grain into bread. Then, take the dried meat and fruit to the Silver Pony Inn on the market square. Enter by the back door and ask for Femke. The two women will pay you a premium price for the food and share with others, but do not gouge them on the price, or the Queen will be sending Sergeant Zrul to pay a visit to you."

The traders looked at Zrul who was scowling at them.

"Do you understand?" I asked sternly, and they both nodded.

That night before going to sleep, I checked my blankets carefully for flaming cockroaches, something I planned to do every night until I was safe at home in my own bed.

The next day we said goodbye to our hosts at the mining camp and bid the two traders a good trip down the mountain to the city, glad to see food going where it was needed.

Then our band headed up the mountain to the pass between the Two Thumbs of the Giant. In late afternoon we arrived at the cave where Tyrmiss and Rilla had lived for thousands of years. With the increase of travelers through the pass in recent years, I had put an invisibility charm on the entrance to discourage the curious. The opening was quite large because it had to allow the bulk of a dragon into it, but as we approached it, all we could see was a pile of brush and behind it a rock wall covered with vines. The others were surprised when I walked straight through the brush pile and disappeared behind the vines. Alaric followed me without hesitation, but the others held back.

"Norbert! Alaric!" Tessia shouted as we entered the cave, and she gave an enthusiastic hug to each of us. "Where are the others?" she asked, worried. She'd flown up the mountain on Tyrmiss's back, so she looked fresh as a spring rose.

"Oh, they're outside," Alaric answered, laughing. "They're afraid to walk through the illusion Norbert created."

"Well, please go get them. We have food here. And we have lots to talk about," Tessia said urgently.

As my stepson left, I looked around the cave. The evening light came through the mouth of the cave, unblocked by the illusion of brush, rock and vines. Tyrmiss lolled at the back of the cavern, half of her body in the neighboring chamber where she and Rilla had once made their bed. Tyrmiss looked at me and yawned.

In the middle of the room was a large flat stone with two huge pike-fish lying on it. Tyrmiss lifted her great head, opened her mouth to show rows of knife-like teeth, and breathed fire on the fish, roasting them. The cave filled with the aroma. Beside the cooking stone was a large bowl of fresh greens which Tessia must have gathered from the nearby field. Also, there was an amphora of spring water and six silver goblets.

Bastian, Hamlin and Zrul came into the cave, looking disconcerted at having passed through what seemed to be solid rock. But once they saw the feast and smelled the roasting fish, their expressions changed to excitement. We hadn't had anything to eat since the gruel we'd had at the mining camp that morning.

There was an unspoken agreement not to discuss the quest while we ate. Instead, we laughed and joked and complimented Tyrmiss on her cooking. Then we ate some more. I pulled out my lyre and sang them a song about heroes and the maidens who love them. It's a corny song, I know, but very popular with men who risk their lives fighting for what they believe in. I thought, *Let's let them feel like heroes for an evening. What's the harm?*

After the last notes of my lyre faded, Tessia stood up and addressed us. She called us the Heroes of the Dragonja Valley, a nice turn of speech she borrowed from my song and praised us for leaving our homes to defend our people. She asked for a report from Zrul; as second-in-command he deserved to speak first. Zrul was not much for talking, so his report was sketchy. Then Tessia turned to me, and I filled in the gaps about our uneventful trip up the mountain. I started to tell her about the strange animals of the upper Iskar Valley, but Zrul interrupted me with a guffaw.

"Don't you know that they were putting us on? You believed that tall tale?" He jeered, shaking his head in disbelief.

"I don't think they were putting us on, Sergeant," I replied quietly.

Zrul guffawed again and looked around at the other men, but they were not laughing. Clearly, they thought that the animals may be real, not just a joke that was being played on gullible strangers.

"Sergeant," Tessia said, looking at him levelly. "I'd like to hear what the Mage says." She turned to me, "Please continue, Norbert."

I told her what Gaspar and his friend had said about the strange animals in that region: the mimic lamb, the tan bonobos, the army hawks, the flaming cockroaches.

"Don't forget about the honeydew lobsters and the lemon pikes, Norbert," Hamlin interjected. "They sound like good eating."

This was too much for Zrul who shook his head disgusted.

"Do you believe these traders, Norbert?" Tessia asked neutrally.

"I believe they were reporting things they'd heard from other travelers. Whether the animals actually exist is a different issue altogether. Clearly, there are strange things happening in that land."

"Do you believe that the place is bewitched?"

"I would guess so, but I cannot fathom for what purpose."

"Could the Blue Witches have created strange animals to protect the path to their kingdom?"

"I don't think so. If they were capable of creating new breeds of animals to protect themselves, then they would have created threatening species, not lambs that speak and lobsters that taste like melons."

"So, someone else has created these animals for their own purposes?"

"It would appear so, your Majesty. Perhaps they were created as some kind of experiment."

We sat in silence for a while, each of us contemplating the journey ahead.

"Well, enough talk of fantastical beasts," Tessia said. "Tyrmiss and I have been scouting the path ahead and we have something to report."

She unrolled the sheet of vellum on which Bastian had drawn the map leading to Sheonad. Tessia had added more detail to the map, so we could see what lay along the way. She pointed at a place in the Iskar Valley marked with a circle.

"In this place, there is a castle, just one fortified building, a single tower. It is surrounded by green fields of crops, an orchard, and pastureland. Whether there are talking sheep there, I don't know," she said, winking at Zrul who emerged from his sullenness and gave a little chuckle.

"This tower is strategically placed at the foot of the trail that leads up the steep sides of the valley, known as the Cliffs of Tortora. If the stronghold is controlled by our enemies, then it will be a problem for us. If we climb out of the valley with the stronghold behind us, then we would be open to attack from our rear. And if we engage in battle and are unsuccessful and have to retreat, then we could be attacked from front and rear. And if we have to escape Sheonad quickly, we may be carrying our wounded with us, making us vulnerable to attack. So, we cannot let this castle stand behind us if it is held by hostile forces."

Not for the first time, I was impressed by Tessia's tactical genius. In battle, she and Tyrmiss were an unbeatable force.

"So, your Majesty," Zrul said. "We must take the tower before we leave the Iskar Valley?"

"Shouldn't we talk to them first?" Bastian asked. "They may

be valuable allies. Let's don't assume they are allied with the witches."

"Exactly, Bastian," Tessia said. "Let's talk with them and determine their relationship with the Blue Witches. We will fight with them if we have to, but it would be better to be friends with them... Whoever they are."

Tessia looked around the cave, assessing the remaining strength of each man. "There's more to be said about the road that lies ahead of us, but I can see that the long trek and the feast has made you sleepy, so let's save the rest of the briefing for another time."

Zrul was the first to go outside with his bedroll. It was clear that he planned to sleep in the open, despite the coolness of the Spring night. After thanking the dragon for her hospitality, Bastian and Hamlin followed Zrul.

Tessia signaled that I should follow her outside as well. Once we were away from the men laying out their blankets, Tessia said to me in a whisper, "The men are not comfortable sleeping in a dragon's lair. I don't want them to think that I've chosen Tyrmiss over them, so I will sleep out here under the stars with them. Will you and Alaric sleep in the cave, so Tyrmiss won't feel abandoned?"

I wasn't fond of the idea of sleeping in the cave either, given the dragon's ability to listen to dreams, but I understood that Tessia was trying to maintain good relations with her men. Zrul was obviously feeling embarrassed by Tessia believing my interpretation of the tales of fantastical animals rather than his, and Tessia wanted to show that she still felt he was a valuable leader. I didn't envy Tessia's task of smoothing each man's pride, but if she didn't, then the group could easily descend into petty rivalries. Tessia understood men, especially warriors, and this group had to be able to work together, or we'd have little chance of success.

I went back into the cave. Alaric had unrolled his blankets

on the cave floor close to the flat cooking stone, and I made my bed beside his. The warmth of the stove gave us a comfortable sleep, despite the sound of the dragon snoring in the next room.

The next morning, Alaric and I rolled up our blankets and packed our kits. I could hear Tessia and Zrul outside discussing the day-long journey down the mountain into the Iskar Valley. Tessia would take point followed by Bastian, Hamlin, Alaric, and me. Zrul would be in the rear. I was not trained in military matters, but the order made sense to me. Tessia was the best fighter and could command the rest of us from the front. Bastian who knew the route, having climbed the mountain on his way to Dragonja City a few months before, was right behind her to provide guidance if she needed it. Hamlin and Alaric, in third and fourth positions respectively, could move to the front or rear if needed. Fifth in line, I was in the least vulnerable place which was appropriate since I was civilian and not much good in a fight. And Zrul defended our rear from attack.

As we left, Tyrmiss said, "I'll just be tidying up here. I'll meet you in the valley."

"She'll be scouting the route ahead of us and reporting back to us as needed," Tessia said, turning to go.

We followed the trail which led past the old rebel camp where Tessia, Hamlin and I had spent a winter seven years before. Other than the cookhouse, which was built of stone, nothing remained of the camp.

"That's where my tent was, over there," Zrul said, nodding his head toward a spot in the clearing.

Alaric turned his head toward me walking behind him. "Norbert, you've never told me what you did in the war."

"Oh, not much," I said. "General Zygmunt assigned me the rank of Captain. I was unsuited for serving in the military, but I was able to help keep the rebel force healthy and patch up a few battle wounds before we finally took the city. Others sacrificed a lot more than I did."

I glanced at Hamlin, who was walking in front of Alaric. Hamlin had been captured by the wizard Ludek's Drekavac soldiers, held in a dungeon and tortured for a month. He returned to us a ruined man, and it had been only recently after seven years that he seemed to be well enough to take on duties. Hamlin had a special place in Tessia's heart. They'd grown up in the same village and hunted in the hills together. The Queen loved to tell the story about how Hamlin had saved her life when they were both fifteen years old by killing a bear that was charging her. I watched him up ahead. He was carrying his spear with the Voprian point leaning slightly forward. A large blonde man with huge shoulders and a lumbering gait, he looked as if he had taken on the spirit of the bear he'd killed when he was a boy.

Alaric walked a few feet behind Hamlin. He was tall and dark like his mother with a handsome face, full lips, and long dark lashes. Women fell in love with him instantly. But ruffians who thought this pretty boy was a pushover were surprised by his ferocity. When he was a boy during the war and the chaotic years following, he'd lived in the Dragonja alleys for months at a time, stealing, fighting, and scavenging to survive. He was tough as an alley cat. I had seen him throw a copper knife at a running rabbit, killing it instantly. I was sure he would be quick and deft with the Voprian sword hanging from his belt. Moreover, he knew the wild herbs almost as well as I did, which ones were edible and which medicinal. Like Hamlin and me, Alaric could find plenty of food in places where others would starve. As his stepfather, I was worried for him to be on this dangerous mission, and terrified of his mother's wrath at me if he were to be injured or killed, but as someone who was depending on the others in this band to defend and provide for us, I was glad Alaric was along.

Every now and then, Alaric or I would reach down and

pluck a plant out of the ground, or we would leave the line of men to gather a few berries or nuts. Tessia and the men tolerated this idiosyncrasy because they knew we were gathering the evening meal. At one point, Tessia raised her hand and we stopped. She nodded in the direction of the woods next to the trail, and Alaric slowly pulled a sling from his belt, leaned down to pick up a stone, whipped the sling over his head and let the stone fly. He walked a short way into the forest and lifted a rabbit for us to see.

As we moved down the slope, scrambling down the limestone formation Bastian called the Stairway of the Giant, we looked down the mountain into a green valley. The rich soil was perfect for nourishing a forest or for growing crops. To our right, there were farms and small villages, most of them established by settlers in the last few years under the *Pax Regina*, as our era had been dubbed. We could see smoke rising from hearth fires all along the river. To our left, on the other hand, there was uninterrupted forest as far as the eye could see. There must be some reason why all the settlers turned north at the bottom of the slope, rather than south.

In late afternoon, Tessia raised her hand and nodded at a small meadow next to a stream. "We'll camp here," she said. And without being instructed, we each settled into our chores. Alaric pulled out the brace of rabbits he'd killed along the way and started gutting and skinning them. Hamlin gathered dry moss and started a fire. I took the greens and berries I'd foraged to the stream and washed them. Tessia, Zrul, and Bastian unrolled the vellum map and talked about the route ahead.

I noticed Bastian had developed a slight limp, so when they finished talking, I said to him, "Let me take a look at that ankle."

Bastian nodded gratefully and sat on a log. I put my medical kit on the ground beside him, carefully took off his boot and looked at his swollen ankle. "How did you get injured?" I asked him.

He laughed ruefully, "I was looking at the valley below instead of looking where I was walking. A stone rolled away when I stepped on it, and I almost fell."

I washed Bastian's foot, held it on my lap and reached into my medicine bag. I applied a balm made of arnica and red picaron in a base of guringa oil to the injured area. As his skin absorbed the balm, the tension in his face eased and he relaxed his leg. I wrapped the ankle in a piece of cloth and tied it with a string. For good measure, I took out my wand, waved it over his foot and said a few words of gibberish. As any healer knows, a patient needs to believe that magic is happening, or he will not heal, and as Tyrmiss pointed out to me recently, a mage cannot create magic, but only encourage it.

I told Bastian to stay off his foot until morning, and I added he should rest with his foot raised above the rest of his body. I made a mental note to observe his gait the next day to make sure he was healing. I glanced around at the others, doing a quick check of their fitness, and noticed Tessia and Zrul looking at me, nodding with silent approval. Veteran warriors like these are aware of the importance of having a competent and attentive healer in the company.

Everyone else seemed to be tired, but healthy and strong, so I sat down with them and ate a dinner of rabbit, berries, and greens. I was already missing my wife's fresh pastries and warm bed.

The next morning, we rose at dawn, packed our kits and bedrolls, and set off along the trail leading south beside the river. I stayed alert, noting Bastian's gait, which seemed strong and even, as well as the bodies of each of the others. As a healer, I preferred to catch problems early, rather than wait until the patient complained. These men, as well as Tessia, were used to hardship, and by the time they started complaining, they were likely to be experiencing extreme pain. Bastian, for example, would not have asked for my help the previous day if I hadn't insisted. When I was the Healer-in-Chief for the rebel army, I often saw men and women with stab wounds or broken bones refusing medical attention because they thought others were more seriously wounded and should be treated first. We riverfolk and the Drekavacs who live beside us are of hardy stock. For example, it is not unusual for a Drekavac woman to go into a field and give birth without telling anyone until after the baby is born. Zrul, who was the toughest Drekavac I'd ever seen, worried me more than the others. The old sergeant would undoubtedly continue marching and fighting until his last breath, not giving me a chance to bind his wounds or set his broken bones.

The route through the valley that Tessia and Bastian had planned was an easy one, and we settled into a daily routine. We woke at dawn, packed our kits and bedrolls, and marched down the trail single file with Tessia in the lead. At midday, we stopped and rested, drank water, and nibbled on whatever Alaric and I had found along the way. Close to sundown, we made camp, Hamlin started a small fire, we ate a dinner of whatever fish, bird, or rabbit Alaric could supply. After dinner we sat around the fire, and I played my lyre, sang a song, or told a story. The next morning, we woke at dawn and started down the trail again, Tessia in the lead.

Sometimes, though, I grew tired of paying close attention to the gait of my comrades and searching for edible plants growing along the trail, and I let my mind wander. We'd been on the trail for about a fortnight when something remarkable happened that none of us had ever seen before.

Hiking down the path for hours every day was monotonous, so one of the games I played to entertain myself was to imagine each of my companions as an animal. Hamlin, with his great strength and deliberate lumbering walk, was definitely a bear. Bastian's short legs, squat body and his ability to move from home to home, clan to clan, I could identify as a badger. Zrul would be some kind of canine, perhaps one of those fierce dogs who live on the midden, fighting over bones with the other dogs. Although I'd started the game by thinking of Alaric as an alley cat, I later began to see him as a raptor, perhaps a hawk who dives into the middle of a flock of sparrows, grabs one and flies off with his prey to feed his family. And I? What was I? A mouse always hiding? But I would like to think of myself as a wise being, perhaps an elf. River folk like me are often said to resemble elves, with our pointed ears and broad feet, but never having seen one, I doubted that elves were real, but rather the stuff of story. On the other hand, I'd thought the same of dragons until I met Tyrmiss... As for Tessia, I'd often thought of her as a lioness—powerful, deadly, regal—but I doubt that a lioness would have become such close friends with a dragon. Tessia and Tyrmiss were best friends, almost like sisters, devoted to one another, to the point of thinking the same thoughts. So, perhaps Tessia was a dragon, at least in part?

My mind snapped back to reality when Tessia lifted her hand and stopped. The six of us stood, rock-still. I noticed Tessia and the others had their hands on their weapons, ready to draw and fight. I slowly moved my hand to my wand, sheathed at my belt. Tessia had heard or seen something. The trail we were following looked like it was used only by game. Hamlin, who was an expert tracker, had said that since we turned south at the river, leaving the settlements behind, he'd seen no human sign. *People must be frightened of something in this area*, I thought. *Why else would they settle the area north of here, but leave this area alone, not even hunting here?*

The six of us held our breath, waiting and listening until we heard a noise in the underbrush to our left. At a signal from Tessia, the men slowly changed their formation with Zrul moving closer to the sound and the others forming a wedge behind him, their weapons ready. Tessia and I held back, alert, ready for anything.

Suddenly an animal leapt out of the underbrush and ran quickly past Zrul. Alaric hit it with the butt of his spear and sent it rolling. Then Zrul grabbed the animal by its back legs and held it up so we could see.

It appeared to be a small deer, but with the head of a dog. The little animal was yapping and twisting, trying to free itself. Zrul swung the animal against a tree, killing it. Zrul held up the lifeless body and said, "Looks like dinner to me, boys!"

The other men smiled and laughed, but Tessia and I looked at each other, aghast. "Was that a magical beast, Norbert?" she asked softly.

"I think it may have been," I answered.

"Oh, by the Goddess, what have we done?" she said, under her breath.

Chapter Six

That evening, Hamlin flayed the animal and roasted it on a stick. Alaric and I shared the greens, nuts and wild pears we'd gathered during the day's march, and our troop sat and ate around the fire. We'd covered difficult terrain through ankle-deep mud, so we were even hungrier than usual. Nevertheless, as Hamlin cut off pieces of the animal and distributed them, I felt I had to warn the men.

"I don't think it's a good idea to eat the meat."

Zrul laughed and tore off a piece with his teeth. Drekavacs have long narrow teeth which they regularly file to sharp points. Tearing meat came easily to them.

The other men paused at my words, but seeing the sergeant eating gustily, they began eating the meat as well. Alaric bit off a small piece, chewed it slowly, then looked at me. When I shook my head in warning, he swallowed the piece in his mouth and gave the rest back to Hamlin. Even Tessia nibbled at the meat, glancing at me guiltily, before setting it aside. Hunger is a harsh mistress.

"Give me the boy's portion," Zrul said to Hamlin who glanced at Alaric and then at me. Not hearing any objection, he handed the sergeant the small haunch Alaric had been nibbling. Later, I noticed that the piece of meat that the Queen had nibbled was missing, and I thought that Zrul had probably eaten it as well.

When Hamlin had butchered the animal, he'd left the offal lying at the edge of camp, with the head, like that of a small dog, facing the cookfire. The shining eyes seemed to be following Zrul as he prepared for sleep.

Zrul was the first to be affected. The morning after the men had eaten the dog-deer, he was in his usual rear-guard position when I heard him panting loudly. I turned to see him with his mouth open and his tongue, which seemed abnormally large, hanging past his chin. I asked him whether he was alright, but he merely growled at me. Later, when we stopped to rest at midday, I noticed that his ears seemed to have grown. Drekavacs are naturally hairless, but his arms were now covered with short white fur.

I looked at the others, but none of them seemed to have noticed the changes that Zrul was going through. Instead, they seemed to be going through their own metamorphoses. Bastian's hands had widened, and his nails had thickened into powerful claws. Hamlin's face had elongated, and his nose had blackened. And strangest of all, Alaric 's sleeves had split open, revealing that his arms were now covered in feathers.

Only Tessia and I remained unchanged. She looked at me with wide eyes, and for the first time since I'd met her many years before, she was obviously frightened.

"What is happening, Norbert? Are they changing into animals?"

"Yes, the animal they ate last night must have been enchanted. When the men ate the animal, they absorbed the spell."

"But I ate some of the meat as well, and I don't feel any different." She checked the skin of her arms and touched her nose and ears. "Why am I not changing?"

"You didn't eat very much of the meat, Tessia. Perhaps you will not be affected."

"We should set up camp here," I said. "Let's see what happens with the men, how far these changes go, and then make a decision on what we should do."

Tessia and I helped everyone off with their packs and stacked their weapons against a tree. The men lay on the ground, gradually taking on more animal-like characteristics. As the afternoon wore on, Alaric's arms turned to wings, and his head became cat-like. Bastian grew beautiful black and white fur and wandered off into the woods to dig holes and, presumably, to find grubs to eat. Zrul turned into a great white mastiff with long legs and powerful jaws.

Trying to feel useful, I gathered edible plants, washed them in the river and brought them back to Tessia who was looking with horror as her old friend Hamlin turned into a blonde bear. She and I sat on a log, and I encouraged her to eat what I'd found.

"Is this permanent, Norbert? Will they stay in this form?"

"I don't know, Tessia. Let's let them go through their metamorphoses, and then we'll decide what we should do."

She nodded, chewing a few leaves of sapphire parsley I'd given her. It couldn't do her any harm, and I was hoping that it might counter-act the tainted meat she'd consumed the previous evening.

Zrul was becoming a dog, Bastian a badger, and Hamlin a bear. I wondered whether I'd unwittingly played a role in the spell they'd succumbed to. I remembered that shortly before they'd eaten the enchanted dog-deer, I'd been playing a game of imagining each of them as an animal. And I remembered not being able to decide whether Alaric was an alley cat or a bird of prey, and now I could see he was developing the body and wings of a bird and the head of a cat. I silently prayed to the Goddess asking forgiveness for my mistake in mocking the forms she's given us.

"I'm afraid that this change will happen to me, as well," Tessia said, scratching her arm where a small scaly spot had appeared.

In panic, I remembered that as part of my game I'd imagined that Tessia was part lioness and part dragon.

By dawn the next day, everyone's transformation was complete. Sleeping on the ground in front of me were a dog, a badger, and a bear. Sitting on a branch above the camp, there was a large hawk with the head of a cat. At the edge of camp, a dragon with the head of a lioness sprawled.

I checked my own body carefully. Nothing was amiss that I could tell.

"Norbert," I heard Tessia's voice say. "My body has changed, but I still have my own thoughts and memories. I wonder whether the others have retained their essence as well."

I heard Alaric's voice coming from the cat-hawk above, "I feel the same, my Queen. I am still a man in my thoughts, but I can fly."

As each of our other friends woke, I spoke to him, asking if he knew his name and why we were here. Each of them seemed to recognize me, and Hamlin and Bastian could answer simple questions with a nod or a shake of their heads, but they couldn't speak. Only Zrul, who had eaten a triple portion of meat, seemed to have completely transformed into a dog. Tessia and Alaric, who had only nibbled at the meat, still had their human essence.

I sent Hamlin lumbering off to the river to catch fish for breakfast, but not to eat anything until I'd had a chance to inspect it. I asked Alaric to reconnoiter the trail ahead, checking for any dangers. I assigned Zrul and Bastian to gather firewood, telling the latter, who was more human, to keep an eye on the dog and make sure he didn't eat any carrion. No sense in making our situation more dire.

Tessia walked toward me and sat beside the fire, her wings folded beside her body and her claws in front of her. I noticed that her torso and wings were those of a dragon, but her head, paws and tail were those of a lioness, and also that she was small for a dragon, much smaller than Tyrmiss. Whereas Tyrmiss was the length of four horses, Tessia was about half that length. She seemed downcast, so in order to give her something to occupy herself, I asked her to help me understand her new body.

I piled up a few dry sticks on the ashes of yesterday's fire. "Can you breathe fire, Tessia?" I asked pointing at the sticks.

She opened her leonine mouth and breathed. Nothing came out but air.

"Remember that Tyrmiss once told us that she had a special pair of teeth at the back of her mouth that when they clicked together made a spark? Can you feel those teeth with your tongue?"

I saw her moving her large lioness-tongue around the back of her mouth, her eyes rolling as she felt the area. She shook her head.

"No, Norbert. I seem to have the body of a dragon, but the head of a lion."

"And who are you?"

"I am Tessia, Queen of Dragonja and Bekla, daughter of Kerttu the Smith." She turned her head to look at the wings at her side. "They call me the Dragonqueen, so now the name seems apt." She shook her head ruefully.

I looked up at the sky. Alaric was gliding in circles very high in the air, his wings barely moving.

"Can you fly?" I asked Tessia.

She looked surprised. She hadn't thought about the possible advantages of her new form.

Tessia walked, uncertainly at first, then with more confidence, to the sandy shore of the river. She carefully unfolded her wings, then looked at them, studying each one carefully for a few moments.

Then she took a few quick steps, flapped her wide wings, and rose slowly into the air. I caught a glimpse of her regal face bright and excited before she disappeared beyond the trees down river.

Chapter Seven

We stayed in place for a few days while my comrades got used to their new bodies and I tried surreptitiously to undo the stubborn spells that had changed them. After a number of tries, I gave up and considered our options. Trying to fulfill our diplomatic mission seemed too difficult. Would the Blue Witches take a lion-dragon who claimed to be a queen seriously? But declaring the mission a failure and turning back home seemed pointless as well. So far, we had accomplished nothing in terms of helping our kingdom. *Perhaps*, I thought, *we should push downriver and see what we might learn about this enchanted valley and perhaps discover what caused the transformations of my friends.*

One night I woke beside the fire with the familiar feeling that someone was listening to my dreams. *Tyrmiss!* I sat up and looked into the dark forest. I couldn't see or hear anything, but I felt her nearby, and her presence gave me a strange sense of comfort. This ancient wise being would know what to do. Surely, she knew what spell we'd fallen into. I went back to sleep, feeling that we would be able to make a decision in the morning.

After a breakfast of sparrows that Alaric had hunted, as well as roots that Bastian had dug up, I asked my friends to gather around for a meeting. Bastian and Zrul lay down beside the fire. Hamlin sat on his haunches at the edge of the clearing. Alaric perched on a large oak bough above us. And Tessia folded her wings and settled with her head in front of the fire and her body stretched out into the woods behind her.

"We need to make a decision about what we are going to do," I began. When no one immediately responded, I outlined the three alternatives: return home; complete our mission in Sheonad; or explore the valley in search of a way to reverse the spell on us.

"Where is Tyrmiss?" Alaric asked, sounding bewildered. "We haven't seen her since we entered the Iskar Valley. That was weeks ago."

The others nodded, even Zrul who, unable to understand what we were saying, was reacting to our body language like the good dog he was. Bastian reached over with his large paw and scratched Zrul behind the ears, and the mastiff pumped his back leg in ecstasy. Zrul, I have to say, was a much better dog than he was a Drekavac. He was perfectly content to sit panting with his tongue hanging out, happy in our company and the only one of us unconcerned with the future.

"I have a feeling Tyrmiss is nearby," I said, watching as the others suddenly sat up straighter. "I've felt her listening to my dreams."

"Then why doesn't she show herself?" Tessia asked.

"I'm sure she has her reasons," I said.

We sat for a while, each of us considering the choice we had to make.

Finally, Tessia spoke up, "Before we continue, I need to know whether each of you still recognizes me as Queen. I will forgive you if you can no longer be loyal to me but let me assure you that I am still Tessia, warrior and hunter from the Bekla Valley. I still have my mind, my desire, and my love for each of my subjects as I always have. I can no longer throw a spear, but I have claws. I no longer can run, but I can fly. In other words, I am what I have always been, but now I am more. Do I have your loyalty?"

I bowed my head to her, "Your Majesty, my allegiance to you is unchanged."

"As is mine, your Majesty," Alaric said.

Bastian and Hamlin bowed their heads and made soft noises showing their respect for their Queen. Zrul seeing the rest of us show our loyalty to her, made graceful obeisance to the dragon-lion Queen.

Taking charge of the conversation, Tessia said, "I would like to explore this valley and discover what has caused this transformation in us." Turning to me, she asked, "Would there be a wizard or witch behind this spell?"

"I need to tell you something, your Majesty," I took a large gulp and said in a small voice, "I may be responsible for your transformation."

Tessia stared at me, as did the others, except of course for Zrul who had taken a strong interest in a butterfly fluttering over his head.

"WHAT?" Tessia shouted, glaring at me. "You are responsible for this... this unnatural assault on your Queen? Down on your knees, Mage. I am tempted to bite off your head and lap up your blood."

I fell to my knees in front of her. "It was not...well, it actually was my fault.... But I had only a part..." I stammered.

"SILENCE!" the Queen shouted. I had seen her angry in the past, but nothing like this. I thought that she may very likely rip me to pieces with her deadly new claws.

As I kneeled in front of her with my head bowed, I felt her anger slowly subsiding. Of course, she knew that her best chance of resuming her normal form lay with my skills as a mage.

"How did this happen?" she asked between gritted lion-fangs.

I explained how shortly before the dog-deer had been killed and eaten, I had been playing a mental game, imagining each of my companions as an animal.

"So, this was merely a game you were playing?"

"Yes, your Majesty, merely a game. Normally such a thing would have been harmless, but I seem to have somehow triggered a latent spell."

"And so, you imagined me as a combination of a lioness and a dragon?" She seemed, for a moment, pleased that I saw her in such heroic imagery. "And Bastian as a badger, Hamlin as a bear, and Alaric as a combination of a cat and a hawk?"

I nodded.

"And what about Zrul?" she asked nodding to the dog sleeping beside the fire. "Why is he more affected than the rest of us?"

"The strength of the spell seems to have been determined by how much meat was consumed. Zrul ate more meat, so he became more fully a dog. Bastian and Hamlin consumed less meat, so some part of their humanity remained. Alaric had only one bite of the venison, and so only his outward form was changed. And you, your Majesty..." My voice trailed off.

"I merely nibbled on the meat, so, like Alaric, only my outward form has changed. And my human speech and reasoning capabilities have remained intact?"

"Yes, your Majesty."

"Have you tried to undo the spell?"

"Yes, your Majesty, but undoing a spell is like trying to un-ring a bell. The best we can do is to replace the existing spell with a different spell, and the mage must be very careful."

"You mean by trying to change me back to my human form, you may change me into something else like, say, a flaming cockroach?"

I almost laughed but caught myself. If she thought I was amused by her condition, I may yet lose my head.

"Very well then, Mage, you may rise. It seems that I need you more now than ever, my friend."

I started to apologize, but she held up her claw to stop me, and then seeing what her right hand had become, shook her leonine head ruefully.

"What do you suggest we do from here, Mage?"

"When you and Tyrmiss reconnoitered this valley, you saw a tower upriver from here, with cultivated fields and pasturelands. I suggest we make our way there. I would guess that the occupants of the tower are familiar with the magic that holds sway here."

"You think a witch or wizard lives there? Perhaps this transforming spell is his or her doing?"

"There is certainly someone or something that created these spells, your Majesty. Dog-deer are wholly unnatural, not one of the Goddess's creations. A human or Drekavac made this creature using powerful magic."

Tessia flew off, scouted the river valley and reported to us that there was a round stone tower a few days march ahead. It seemed safe to eat fish from the river and nuts and berries from the woods, and Bastian seemed content every evening to dig for roots, grubs and beetles, so we were well provided in this verdant valley. On the third day after our meeting in which I'd confessed my mistake to Tessia, we headed off, following the river trail. Hamlin the bear was in the lead, attached to Zrul on a leash to prevent the dog from wandering into the woods on his own. I walked behind the bear and the dog, and ambling along in the rear was Bastian the badger. Alaric flew in wide circles high above our heads, and Tessia covered long distances up and down the river, meeting up with us before sunset. I knew she was keeping an eye out for Tyrmiss who had been separated from us for so long.

Eventually, we came to a place where the forest ended. We looked out on a large sunlit field covered with a crop I didn't recognize. In the distance was a round tower that looked very old. The battlements had fallen from the top and lay in a ring of stone blocks around the walls.

Bastian tapped me on the hip from behind. Not for the first time, I thanked the Goddess that he'd learned to be careful with his sharp claws. When I looked back at him, he gestured toward the ground.

The green field before my feet had small plants with tiny leaves. I squatted on the ground and looked closely. Each plant was a small oak tree, not a sapling mind you, but a fully-grown tree the size of my hand.

We crossed the field, walking between the lines of tiny trees, trying not to step on them. We came to a wide pasture which surrounded the tower. Sheep stopped their grazing and looked up at us. In a soft *baa*, one of the sheep said to her companion next to her, "Look, we have visitors. It's been ever so long since we've had guests."

Having experienced much more threatening kinds of magic than talking sheep, we paid them little heed and went directly to the front door. I pounded on the door with my fist and waited, but there was no answer. I tried pounding again, but still no answer.

I considered entering, but I was afraid that if a powerful being lived there, then he or she might not take kindly to uninvited guests and may have laid traps in the tower.

I walked back into the pasture and introduced myself and my companions to the ewe who'd spoken before.

"Yes," she said. "We've heard there were creatures coming up the river valley trail." She looked at each of us for a moment, then said, "My name is Narrra and we are known as the mimic sheep, but I don't really like that name for us because we are just ourselves. We mimic no one. What kind of beings are you?"

I explained that I was a mage, and my friends were men who'd been transformed into animals.

"How did this happen?" Narrra asked.

"My friends ate a creature in the woods, a small deer with the head of a dog, and they were transformed into the creatures you see before you."

"They ate a woodland creature?" she said in horror.

The other sheep who'd been grazing peacefully looked up wide-eyed and started talking among themselves in panic.

"Why would they eat a creature?" The sheep next to her asked. Narrra shook her head incredulously, looking at my companions.

"Where we come from, men eat animals," I said flatly. Best to get this out of the way, I thought.

"With so many delicious plants, why would anyone eat an animal?" Narrra mused, obviously not expecting an answer from such primitive beasts.

"Does anyone live in the tower?" I asked.

"Oh no, there used to be a witch named Tatatungia who lived there, but she died a long time ago," she looked at Zrul standing beside me. "There were also packs of animals like your friend there, but Tatatungia turned them into deer in order to protect us."

That would explain the dog-deer we encountered in the woods. Evidently there was residual magic clinging to the creature which my imaginings awoke, I thought, as I returned to the tower entrance, put my hand on the heavy door and pushed it open.

Judging by the thick dust which lay on the floor, the tower had obviously not been occupied for many years except by birds and rodents. Upstairs, there were two rooms. One looked like a mage's workshop, and the other held a wide bed covered with rotten linen and human bones picked clean by animals. By the shape, assortment, and position of the bones, it appeared that a man and a woman had died in each other's arms.

In the workshop, clay jars lined the shelves, each one displaying a symbol of some heavenly body. I knew that magic spells were often associated with particular stars and constellations, and I guessed the jars contained mixtures of herbs and rare earths whose purpose was to aid in casting such spells, but these symbols represented a kind of magic far beyond my skills.

I'd read in the Windkeep library of Tatatungia the Wanderer, who is said to have been the most powerful practitioner of magic who ever lived. She was the only practitioner known to have gone beyond White and Black to understand the true essence, the reality that lies beneath all we know in this life. Although I respected her brilliant accomplishments, in truth, I found it offensive to experiment with nature's forms. I never enjoyed shape-shifting or the magic of metamorphosis because it seemed blasphemous to change what the Goddess has created. To me, all life was and is sacred, and to meddle with creation as if it were a child's toy was the darkest magic imaginable. For the magic to remain in this valley for years after the death of the one who cast the spells affirmed that half the bones in the other room were not those of a mere mage like myself, but of a powerful being who changed the world.

I searched, but found no books or scrolls that would tell me how the metamorphosis of animals had been achieved, or how the spells could be undone. Like most witches, it appeared Tatatungia had kept her discoveries to herself, not wanting others to duplicate her magic, fearing such power could be used for evil purposes.

Alaric flew in the window and glanced at the dusty jars on the shelves. "Can you undo the spell?" he asked, a desperate look on his feline face.

I shrugged and gave a small sad shake of my head.

"I'm sorry, son," I said. "There's nothing here that tells me anything about the spell you are under or how to reverse it."

When I went outside, Tessia was there, and the sheep were gone. Evidently, tolerating Zrul was one thing, but they wanted nothing to do with a dragon who had the head of a lion.

I told her what I'd found in the tower.

"I'd hoped you would be able to reverse this spell, Norbert," she said, sadly.

"I did too, Tessia, but for now it looks like we're going to have to accept the forms you and the others have been given."

Tessia looked around the pasture. It was a beautiful summer afternoon. "Let's make camp here," she declared.

After a dinner of trout caught by Hamlin, roasted tubers that Bastian had dug up, and milk the ewes kindly shared, we looked toward Tessia. We were willing to trust her as our leader to come up with a plan to deal with our current predicament.

"It would appear," Tessia began. "That there is no spell to undo what has happened to us."

Tessia pointedly didn't look at me, but the others did. I felt a flush of shame coming over me. *They rightly blame me,* I thought. *I did this to my friends and to my son, and now I cannot undo it.*

"Be that as it may," Tessia continued. "We still have a mission to accomplish. Our kingdom still needs to reach an understanding with the Blue Witches of Sheonad. However, the Cliffs of Tortora are too difficult for most of you to climb in your current forms, so I'm sending Bastian, Hamlin, and Zrul back the way we came. But I think you know you cannot return to Dragonja City. The citizens would not recognize you, and you would not be able to explain what happened. So, I want you to take shelter for the fall and winter in Tyrmiss' cave. In the forest, you will be able to hunt game as well as find nuts and berries. Hamlin, you know that area well. Can you find Tyrmiss' cave even though the entrance has been hidden by magic?"

The bear nodded his large head.

"Bastian, do you agree to this plan?"

The badger nodded as well. Zrul wagged his tail agreeably.

Tessia turned to Alaric and me. "The three of us are going to fly to Sheonad to parley with the witches. We need to find out what they want and then reach an agreement for them to stop attacking Dragonja."

The next morning, we said goodbye and watched as the bear, the badger and the dog traipsed through the forest of tiny oak trees toward the dark forest of tall trees from which we'd come. I agreed with Tessia; they would be much safer in Tyrmiss's cave than in Dragonja City.

"Alaric," Tessia said, and the cat-hawk raised his head attentively. "Do you see the cliff on the other side of the river? I want you to fly there and scout the area for hostiles. Also, look for a safe place for us to camp on the cliff if possible."

"Yes, your Majesty," Alaric said. "But first I want to say goodbye to our friends."

Alaric flew over to our three friends. He nuzzled his head, the way cats do, on the necks of Bastian, Hamlin and Zrul. It was touching to watch, and not for the first time I wondered why we men cannot show our feelings the way animals do.

"Do you want to say goodbye to your sheep-friends, Mage?"

"Thank you, your Majesty. They have shown us hospitality and tolerated our strangeness, so I think a few words are called for."

"I don't want to frighten them any more than I already have, so I will remain here," Tessia said.

"I think that would be wise, your Majesty."

"See whether they know anything about this spell we are under, and also whether they know anything about Sheonad."

As I started to leave, she said in a gentle tone, "And Norbert... You may call me Tessia now that we are alone."

"Thank you... Tessia." I said, realizing this was a gesture of forgiveness for my huge blunder. I felt my shame lift slightly.

"Oh yes, we know Zamarrra quite well," Narrra said, her mouth full of fresh grass. "She was born in the tower.

93

The Blue Witch? Is that what she calls herself now? I remember her as a sweet baby girl who crawled in the pasture here."

Aware that sheep have relatively short lives, I asked, "How could you remember her, Narrra? Zamarrra is older than I am."

"Norbert, you are forgetting that we are enchanted sheep. We have been bred to give the sweetest milk and the softest wool and to live for a very long time unless…" She cast a glance at Tessia at the other end of the field. "Something eats us. You know there was another one of those who came here a fortnight ago."

"A dragon? There was another dragon here?"

"Not exactly a dragon. More of a transformed dragon like her," Narrra said, nodding at Tessia on the other side of the field.

"Did you talk with the dragon?"

"Oh, no," Narrra said. "We ran from her. She looked hungry."

She gave a slight shudder before continuing her story. "Zamarrra's mother was a beautiful young woman named Faba. Her father was the old witch Tatatungia who lived in the tower."

"Excuse me," I asked. "Zamarrra's father was a witch? How is that possible?"

"Therein lies a tale," Narrra said with a gleam in her eye.

"When Faba arrived here, it didn't take her long to realize Tatatungia was a powerful witch, so Faba used all her top and bottom charm to convince the older woman to reveal the twelve magics and the mutability of *mu*, and Tatatungia, completely swept away by the young woman, agreed. Of course, it took many years for Tatatungia to teach Faba the basics, and during this time, without meaning to, Tatatungia fell deeply in love with her student. However, the old witch knew Faba would never love her except in the way a child loves her grandmother.

"Thus, driven by desire and desperation, Tatatungia transformed herself into a handsome young man and knocked on the door of the tower. He introduced himself to Faba, saying his name was Tuguslar, the grandson of Tatatungia from whom he'd learned magic. Tatatungia, he said, had returned to her home far away and wouldn't be coming back, but before leaving she'd asked him to continue Faba's lessons in the many magics. In the following months, the two young people lived together in the tower and eventually gave themselves to each other in love.

"As you know, Mage, maintaining a lie night after night exhausts the spirit, especially for a great witch like Tatatungia who had devoted her life to serving the Goddess Nilene, whose name means Evening Star, but rather than surrendering the effort and confessing to Faba, Tatatungia sustained the lie until she fell ill. After Faba gave birth, her womb became infected and she developed a high fever, but Tatatungia was too weak to summon the power to cure her lover, for Tatatungia was dying as well. In their last moments, Tatatungia revealed her true identity to Faba and asked for forgiveness. Faba forgave her, and the two lovers died in each other's arms."

"What happened to the baby?"

"My sisters and I heard the baby crying, so we brought her down to the pasture and nursed her for two summers. We named her Zamarrra. Eventually, two silver-haired women came and took the child away."

"Were they witches?"

"I don't know. Perhaps. They had round ears and narrow feet, not pointed ears and broad feet like yours. Their skin was light blue like Faba's and Zamarrra's, not pink like yours or brown like Tatatungia's. The blue women went into the tower and came out carrying a large book."

"What kind of book?" I asked, feeling my curiosity rising with each thing Narrra said.

"'What kind of book?'" She laughed. "How would I know? Do you think a sheep would know how to read?"

"When they took Zamarrra, which direction did they go?"

"They flew that way," she said, nodding toward the cliff

on the other side of the river. "Then they rose high in the sky toward Sheonad."

"They flew?"

"Oh yes, they flew on brooms," she said offhandedly. "Does that mean they were witches?"

When Alaric got back, he reported that the trail up the cliff widened halfway up, and there was enough room for us to camp. He said he'd seen no people on the trail, so we should be safe and unobserved.

"Get on my back, Norbert," Tessia said, lowering her shoulders to the level of my waist.

I swung my leg over her folded wings and sat on the spot where I'd seen Tessia sit on Tyrmiss so many times. On dragons there's a natural saddle in the place where the shoulder joins the neck. There, the rider can hold onto the spines that run along a dragon's neck. It was actually easier than riding a horse, except of course you can't afford to fall off.

Tessia was about half the size of Tyrmiss, so carrying a human was much more difficult for her. She had to take a running start with outstretched wings before lifting into the air. I could hear her panting heavily as she beat her wings quickly to keep us afloat. I didn't know whether we could make the whole trip, and I thought she might have to give up and float back to the valley, but with a final burst of energy she landed in the clearing where Alaric was waiting.

"Remind me not to do that again," Tessia said, short of breath.

I looked up the steep trail that led to the top of the cliff. I didn't relish the idea of the long climb.

Alaric had caught a few trout in the river below, and I gathered some dandelion and monk's mallow from the cliffside clearing. Since we didn't want to call attention to our presence by starting a fire, we ate the food raw. Alaric and Tessia tore into the fish while I was content with eating only plants.

Afterwards, Tessia asked, "Norbert, based on what you know about Zamarrra, tell me who she is and why she attacked our kingdom."

"We still know little about her, Tessia. She's evidently the daughter of the powerful witch Tatatungia."

"Do you know of this witch?"

"I've seen the name in the chronicles in Windkeep's library, but I know little about her." I took a bite of dandelion and chewed it slowly, trying to put together what Narrra had told me. "Zamarrra's mother was a Blue Witch who died shortly after giving birth. Zamarrra's father was the witch Tatatungia who'd transformed herself into a male wizard. After the death of her parents, Zamarrra spent her early childhood in the enchanted meadow where Narrra and her sisters took care of her. Eventually, two women, probably Blue Witches, took Zamarrra to Sheonad where she grew to adulthood."

"Why has Zamarrra attacked our kingdom?"

"Perhaps because she was raised by women who have a tradition of resenting Dragonja for what was done to them a thousand years ago. The Blue Witches were the rulers of Dragonja until the people rose up, murdering many of them in horrible ways. A few witches escaped into the mountains and built their own city."

"Why have they waited until now to exact their revenge?"

"I don't know, your Majesty," I replied. "That's one of many questions we can ask the witches when we see them."

"I'm very tired now, Norbert," she said. "If I'm going to fly your fat rear end to the top of the cliff tomorrow, then I need to go to sleep."

She closed her leonine eyes, and soon she was breathing deeply. Alaric flew up into the branches of a nearby tree and tucked his head under a wing. An odd way to sleep, I thought, but never having seen a cat-hawk sleep before, I supposed it was natural for him.

I lay in my blankets looking at the stars and remembering all that had happened on our journey so far and wondering what lay in front of us. As I drifted off to sleep, I thought I could hear Tyrmiss saying, *not to worry, little Norbert. All that is, is good.*

Chapter Eight

The next morning, I woke to the sound of Tessia and Tyrmiss laughing. I wondered whether I was still dreaming because Tyrmiss had the head of an old woman. She still had her wings, her purple scales reflecting the morning light, her giant talons, twice the size of Tessia's, but instead of her great dragon head, there was the head of a normal-sized woman. She had long silver hair, blue skin, an aquiline nose, and a high forehead. She was really quite attractive.

She said, "I love what you've done with your head, Tessia. I've always thought of you as a lioness. Good job!"

"And you, Tyrmiss," Tessia answered. "Where did you get that beautiful head? Did you borrow it from someone?"

"Long story," Tyrmiss said waving her talons dismissively. "I'll tell you later."

Turning her gray eyes to me, she squinted in amusement at my surprise. "Good morning, Norbert." Her voice was no longer the deep rumbling thunder of a ten-thousand-year-old dragon, but the pleasant contralto of an experienced hostess greeting an uninvited guest.

Tessia looked at me with a huge smile, her lioness fangs showing, an expression that was intended, no doubt, to show happiness, but actually made her look frightening.

Alaric flew down from a branch above and stood beside our two friends. The cat-hawk, the dragon-lion, and the dragon-woman made a strange tableau.

"And whom do we have here?" Tyrmiss asked fondly. "Can this be Alaric? My, how you have changed!" She sounded like a maiden aunt talking to her favorite nephew. "And what has been going on with you, young man? Anything new?"

"Oh, nothing much," Alaric said, going along with the game. "I hope you will forgive me if I eat and fly, but there's lots to be done."

The three of them laughed at their little game of pretending everything was completely normal.

"Surprised to see me, Norbert?" Tyrmiss asked, changing her tone.

"Where have you been? We haven't seen you in over a month, Tyrmiss."

"Not even a 'good morning' for an old friend?" Tyrmiss asked feigning umbrage. "Very well then, I will tell you where I've been. But first, let's eat breakfast. I've brought a fat salmon from the river. Unfortunately, though, I've lost the ability to breathe fire, so we will have to eat it raw."

Not fancying raw fish for breakfast, I ate a handful of berries and nuts I'd gathered the day before. The three of them tore at the pink flesh of the salmon.

"I don't see how you humans can survive with such small mouths," Tyrmiss said, her mouth full of half-chewed fish. "Lately, I've had to eat all the time, just to get enough. Pardon me for eating while I talk. Let's see. Where should I start?"

"Start with you leaving us at your cave in the pass between the Two Thumbs of the Giant," Tessia said. "You were going to reconnoiter the valley and then fly up to Sheonad."

"Yes, and so I did," Tyrmiss answered, holding the head of the salmon in her talons while nibbling on it. "I flew down to the valley and followed the river south to the keep, but I got

100

tired, so I stopped in a clearing and took a nap. Dragons are usually nocturnal, you know, and all this flying around in the hot sun is exhausting.

"And when I woke, there was a mouse with the head of a rabbit right in front of my face. Without thinking about it, I whipped my tongue around the little thing and swallowed it. It was nothing more than a tasty morsel. Still hungry, I flew to the river, caught a few trout, then flew up the cliff where we are now and arrived in Sheonad by nightfall.

"It is, or at least it once was, a beautiful city built from the black igneous rock of the region. Evidently, what the witches did centuries ago was to quarry obsidian out of the side of the mountain to construct the walls and buildings, and then place their temple in the huge cavern they'd dug. A gargantuan undertaking. I doubt they could have done it without the help of magic. The black walls of the city are spectacular in the moonlight, reflecting the stars and mirroring the night sky."

Tyrmiss sighed. "Anyway, as I circled the city, two things struck me as odd. One was that the glacier from the mountain was crushing the west wall of the city. The walls had fallen on the buildings next to it."

"Have the witches lost their ability to control the weather?" I asked.

"Perhaps. Or perhaps they've abandoned parts of the city," Tyrmiss answered.

"Which brings me to the other thing that struck me," she continued. "As I flew around the city, I didn't see any lights. In my long life, I've flown around a number of cities at night, and normally in the evening, there are cookfires in the kitchens, lamps in the inns, and torches lighting the streets. But most of Sheonad was dark. And I smelled very little smoke. Only when I flew past the huge cave where the temple is located did I see fires of any kind, and then only a few."

"So, the witches are abandoning their city," I said. "And now the few that are left want to return to their ancestral homeland? Is this why one of them attacked our kingdom with violent weather? To weaken us before an invasion?"

"Perhaps, Norbert," Tyrmiss said, lifting her eyebrows at me, a very human gesture. "But you are getting ahead of yourself. We need to talk with the witches and let them tell us what they want from Dragonja."

"So, Tyrmiss," Tessia said, "I told you how we were transformed into these strange creatures. How was it for you? You ate a rabbit-mouse in the forest... and then what happened?"

"Yes, my dear, I ate a rabbit-mouse, then flew to Sheonad. As I circled the city, a strange feeling came over me. My neck and face started itching, and I grew tired. I stopped to rest on the roof of the temple. I heard a heavy door opening, and below me, I saw a tall majestic-looking woman with flowing silver hair and translucent blue skin walk across the courtyard. She stood in front of a large statue of a woman, perhaps the Goddess Nilene, her arms holding a sheaf of wheat grass and her eyes looking off into the distance."

"Was the woman Zamarrra?" I asked.

"No, Norbert, it was not Zamarrra, but another Blue Witch, an older one. Her name is Evanora. I learned her name later when I overheard one of her dreams." Tyrmiss looked at me with exasperation. I found it strange to see Tyrmiss expressing her feelings clearly in her face. "And please stop interrupting me.

"Anyway, my neck was itching horribly, and as I scratched, the scales fell off. This surprised me because I had molted last century, and dragons molt only every thousand years, so I gave out a small gasp. The woman, hearing me, looked up and our eyes met. She muttered a few words under her breath, perhaps some kind of protection spell, and she ran into the temple.

"Having been discovered, I flew away from the city of Sheonad, and up the mountain, I found a place where the glacier was thick, and there I melted enough ice to make a lair."

She turned to me and said, "As you know, the Goddess created dragons during the last Age of Ice and gave us our fiery breath so we could carve ice to make homes. I was born in the city of Ellulian which was carved from the ice by my ancestors. But all of that is gone now. The dragon world is no more."

After a few moments while we let Tyrmiss experience her grief, Tessia gently urged her friend, "And what happened next?"

"Ah well, I slept in the ice lair—they are quite comfortable you know—and when I woke, I felt something I'd never felt before. My skin was cold. I raised my talon to my face and realized that I'd been transformed. Needing to see myself, I walked out on the glacier, found a spot where the sun had melted the ice to form a small pool of water, and I looked at my reflection."

She sighed and lifted her talons in resignation. "And here I am."

"And this happened over a month ago?" Tessia asked, obviously concerned for the welfare of Tyrmiss. "What have you been doing since then?"

"First, I sheltered in my ice cave, thinking about what had happened. I wondered whether there was a residual spell in the rabbit-mouse that I ate, but I didn't know why I would have been transformed into a version of the witch in the courtyard. I waited a fortnight, hoping the spell would wear off, but it didn't. So, I flew down into the Iskar valley and went to the tower. I thought the mimic-sheep might know something, but I never had a chance to ask them because they ran away when I approached them.… Well," she added ruefully, "I can't say I blame them. I've certainly eaten my share of sheep through the years."

"Then I flew up the valley. I saw the six of you making your way along the river trail, but you seemed to be doing fine, so I went back to my rock cave where Rilla and I lived happily for so long. I felt safe there, avoiding people and coming out only at night."

"Did you see Hamlin, Zrul, and Bastian?" Tessia asked. "They were on their way to your rock cave. They've been transformed into a bear, a mastiff, and a badger."

"Oh, I did see them on the river trail, but they were in animal form, so I didn't know it was them," Tyrmiss replied. "I stayed in the rock cave for only a week or so. I couldn't stay any longer. The place reminds me too much of Rilla."

"Poor Tyrmiss," Tessia crooned, using her talon to stroke the white hair of the dragon-woman. "You must have been so lonely."

"Yes, I was, my dear. I often thought of you. I hope you will forgive me for saying that some part of me is glad that you've been transformed as well. I don't feel so much like a freak of nature being with you."

"Let's be freaks together," Tessia said, and reaching out to Alaric and Tyrmiss, she pulled them together in a group hug. They didn't seem to notice that they'd left me out of their gesture of solidarity, but I really didn't mind considering how high a price they'd paid for this sense of belonging.

Chapter Nine

"I don't see any reason why we don't just fly into Sheonad and take over the city," Tessia was saying, sharpening her claws on a rock.

"It certainly wouldn't be difficult," Tyrmiss said. "Even without breathing fire, I am sure I could easily kill any warrior, man or woman, who tried to stop us."

Alaric wasn't having any of it. "Shouldn't we at least try to talk to the weather witches before we kill them?"

"Why?" Tessia said, looking up puzzled. "I always saw the diplomatic mission as just a cover for our real goal of teaching them a lesson. Do you know how much damage Zamarrra did to our kingdom? It will take years for us to recover."

"I agree with Alaric, your Majesty," I added. "I would like to know why Zamarrra did what she did. Was this revenge for something that happened a thousand years ago? It hardly makes sense for the Blue Witches to be carrying out revenge now. There has to be more to their story."

"Love, I see Alaric's point," Tyrmiss said, pointedly leaving me out of the discussion. "If we kill the Blue witches, then we'll never know what was behind their attacks. I wonder whether they have allies. Also, do they have enemies besides us? It may be that the Blue witches are caught between powerful kingdoms, and they attacked us as a way to please an ally."

Tessia nodded, considering the issue. "Very well then, let us go to Sheonad to parley with the Blue Witches, and if we are not satisfied with their explanations for attacking our kingdom, then we can destroy them later."

Turning to Tyrmiss, Tessia said, "Bastian said that there's a pass leading into Sheonad which is heavily guarded. Did you see this pass?"

"I saw the pass, and it does form a natural barrier that is easily defended, but there were no soldiers there."

"So, we should be able to fly right into the temple where the witches are?"

"I believe so, Tessia," the dragon-woman said, with a hint of a smile.

Tyrmiss had said that Sheonad was high in the mountains where the wind was so cold it could cripple a man, so I spread arnica cream on her face to protect the skin, as well as on my own face and hands. Tessia and Alaric had fur to protect the skin of their faces, so they passed on my offer.

I also wrapped a heavy woolen cape with a hood around my body. Not only would it keep me warm, but the hood might be useful for theatrics. I had a reputation in Dragonja for being a mighty wizard because I'd killed the great Wizard Ludek, but the truth is that my defeating him was mostly a matter of luck and desperation. He'd attacked my wife and son, so I went to his lair and held him long enough for a great white she-bear, a friend of Idella's, to kill him. In truth, I was not a great wizard, but only a simple village mage. My strengths lay in helping people heal, and crops grow, and businesses prosper. My fights with my brother Ludek were the only times in my life I've ever used magic for violence. So, I was hoping that if I looked like a mighty wizard, wearing a hooded cloak and all, the Blue Witches would refrain from using their magic against Tessia. A thin hope, admittedly, but I did not want to fight them at all. Zamarrra had already proven she was much smarter and more powerful than I, so I hoped we could resolve the issues peacefully.

Tessia, on the other hand, had sharpened her claws, and Tyrmiss seemed to be excited by the prospect of battle as well. As far as I knew, the dragon had not killed any Drekavacs or humans since the war with Ludek ended seven years ago. Since we started talking about killing the witches, Tyrmiss' eyes had lost the gentle irony that was typical of the old woman she'd become, at least from the neck up, and her eyes were turning into the red slits I recognized from the days she killed Ludek's soldiers in revenge for the death of Rilla.

I climbed on Tyrmiss's shoulders. There were fewer spines running along her neck than there had been before her transformation, but I could still get a firm enough grip to keep my balance. She dove headfirst off the edge of the cliff, spreading her wings as she gathered speed, leveled off and made a wide bank and started rising. The contrast with my experience in riding Tessia was remarkable. Tessia had had to pump her wings hard in order to carry my weight, but Tyrmiss was sheer power, each smooth wingbeat lifting us higher toward the top of the cliff.

She landed on a wide snow field, bright with sunlight, to wait for Tessia and Alaric to catch up to us. Staying on the dragon's back, I looked down at the Iskar Valley far below us. The green valley stretched a long distance to the north from where we came and to the south which was still an undiscovered land.

"Well, it is certainly a lot easier to fly without Norbert on my back," Tessia said, skittering to a landing next to us. "How was it flying up here?"

"It was fine, very easy," I said.

Tyrmiss turned and looked at me with exasperation. "She was talking to me, Norbert. Of course, it was easy for you. All you had to do was hold on." Softening her expression, she said to Tessia, "There's a trick to carrying a load, dear. If you stay in this form, I'll give you flying lessons."

Tessia looked surprised. Evidently it hadn't occurred to her that she may be in her current form permanently. Changing the subject, she lifted her face to the sky and said, "It looks like Alaric has taken to flying. He doesn't seem to need to rest at all. He just floats up there, barely moving his wings."

"Yes, hawks have a different anatomy than dragons. Their wings are much larger in proportion to their bodies," Tyrmiss said looking at Alaric high above. She sighed, "I've often envied them."

"How far is Sheonad from here?" I asked.

"By foot, it would be a 30-day march, but by air, we can travel much faster. We should be there by nightfall."

"Love," she said to Tessia. "I noticed you're working far too hard, beating your wings constantly. You're not trusting your wings to hold you up. The art of flying is really all about the glide. Instead of trying to move your wings up and down, think of them moving front to back, pushing the air behind you. Also, if you tuck your head down and lift your feet against your body, you will allow the air to flow over your body, instead of resisting the air."

Tessia's feline mouth turned down at the corners, "That's lot to think about, the different parts of my body moving in different ways at the same time."

"I know, dear, but keep practicing and it will eventually seem like second nature. I'll fly slowly at first, so you get a chance to master your form. Once you get the hang of it, we can speed up."

Tyrmiss took a few quick steps and once again we were aloft. I turned my head to see Tessia fumbling her take-off a few times, then lifting off and climbing in our direction. I looked up but couldn't see Alaric. I wondered whether he'd flown ahead to scout the way.

Tyrmiss slowly rose with Tessia following. Up here, I could see a long way into the distance, but there was only white snow, broken up here and there by black patches of ground. I didn't see any animals and only a few birds who, no doubt, wanted nothing to do with two dragons and a hawk.

Tyrmiss slowed and Tessia was able to pass under us. It looked like she was taking to heart her friend's advice to depend more on the glide and to beat her wings less often, although still more often than Tyrmiss did. Tessia had always been naturally athletic, picking up new skills quickly, so I knew it wouldn't take her long to master the art of flying.

In midafternoon, Tyrmiss dropped down to fly beside Tessia and signaled with her head that it was time to land. Tessia was breathing very hard, and she shot a look of gratitude at us. She clearly needed a break.

We gyred down through the air and landed on a flat rock, free of snow. I guessed that Tyrmiss chose this spot carefully. Landing on the snow might be tricky, especially for Tessia; no telling how deep the snow was or what it disguised beneath the surface. Also, standing on this rock, we could see a long distance in every direction, so nothing could sneak up on us.

Tessia landed beside us, wheezing. "Thanks for stopping," she said between gasps. "I didn't know how much farther I could go."

She looked a little ashamed. All her life, she had been around men who admired her athletic abilities. She could run faster and longer than any other hunter or warrior and arrive at the destination ready to use her weapons. She didn't like being the laggard.

"It's okay, sweetie," Tyrmiss said patiently. "You're doing very well. Now if you could just trust your wings a little more and rest between wingbeats, then you won't tire yourself out as much." She looked up. "I wonder where Alaric is. I haven't seen him in hours."

I nodded. I was getting a little worried about my son as well.

Reaching into my kit, I brought out the arnica cream which I spread on my cheeks and lips. "May I?" I asked Tyrmiss. When she nodded, I spread some of the cream on her face as well.

"I never realized how thin and sensitive human skin is," she said between cracked lips. "What delicate creatures you are."

Tyrmiss and I lifted off again with Tessia not far behind. I noticed that Tessia was beating her wings less and gliding more. Also, she was keeping her head low and her feet tucked close to her body. She seemed to have less trouble keeping up with us, but I also noticed that Tyrmiss was flying more slowly than she usually did, a casual rhythm to her motion.

Late in the afternoon, when each small hill of snow was casting a shadow below us, I saw something black on the distant horizon. Tyrmiss was flying straight toward it. When I could just make out the walls of the city, we veered off toward the large mountain that loomed over it, Tessia close behind.

Tyrmiss flew next to the mountain until she saw a flat place where we could land. When we touched down, Tyrmiss gracefully stopping after a few steps, Tessia, coming in too fast, hit us from behind, knocking me free of my perch and throwing me over the side of the cliff. It happened so quickly that I didn't know I was in danger until Tyrmiss, diving off the cliff, caught me with her talons in midair and flew me back to the place where Tessia stood, her eyes bright with fear.

"I am so sorry, Norbert." Tessia said, shaking her head. "I didn't mean to…"

I held up my hand. As my breath slowly returned, I said, "It's okay, Tessia. I'm okay."

"Well, at least this time you didn't wet your pants," Tyrmiss said, referring to an unfortunate incident seven years before when I was in my first battle.

"Tyrmiss! You… I…" I sputtered. "You said you wouldn't mention that again."

Tyrmiss laughed. "Sorry, Norbert, but it's better to be angry than to be frozen with fear, so you should thank me for talking you out of your terror."

I checked myself and realized she was right. My shock at

falling off the cliff was gone. Now I was just feeling irritated at this insufferable dragon-woman.

W e stayed on the cliffside for a few hours until most of the lights had gone out in the temple. Without mentioning Alaric's name, all three of us were palpably aware that something was wrong. He should have rejoined us by now. It wasn't like him to lag behind or to disappear without letting us know when he'd be back.

"Have you heard any dreams that would give us a clue as to where Alaric is?" I asked.

"I heard something... a cage, a spell of some kind... I'm not sure," Tyrmiss said.

Finally, Tyrmiss said, "Norbert, climb up. We need to go search for your son." It was the first time she'd ever acknowledged my relationship with Alaric, and it showed a solidarity between us that I hadn't felt with her since the war had ended six years before. Tessia and I had flown into the siege of Dragonja on Tyrmiss' back, and I've never felt so alive in my life. Now, we were about to go into battle again, but this time, I suspected, it was going to be a battle of wits. I would need all my magical skills if we were going to find Alaric. And if he were already dead, may the Goddess forbid, I knew that Tessia and Tyrmiss would be out for revenge. Whether I, who'd always believed in peace, would join them in revenge... we would have to see.

Chapter Ten

We flew quickly down to the city and veered into the cavern where the temple lay. Tyrmiss let Tessia land on the roof first, in order to avoid a collision like the one that almost cost me my life earlier. Tyrmiss moved toward the edge of the roof and looked down.

"Norbert, drop down to the courtyard and look in the windows," she said.

I shimmied down a drainpipe and found myself next to a lit window. Inside was a woman with the exact same silver hair and radiant blue face that Tyrmiss now had. Obviously, this was the one she'd encountered during her last visit here. The woman was ladling water into a pot on a wood-burning stove. She was alone in the room, and I saw that her wand was on the table behind her.

Reaching over to the door, I tried to push it open, but it was locked. I took my wand from the sheathe at my belt, did a simple charm and opened the door, but she heard me and reached for her wand.

"I wouldn't do that if I were you," I said, pointing my wand at her and trying to look menacing. Pure bluff on my part. I didn't want to burn the place down by shooting fireballs at her, and besides I wasn't sure that I was a match for a Blue Witch of her powers whatever they may be. But she didn't know that

I was bluffing, so she hesitated while I walked over to the table, took her wand and put it in my belt.

"What is your name?" I asked.

"Evanora."

Still pointing my wand at her, I asked, "Where is Alaric?"

"Who?" she asked, genuinely puzzled.

"The cat-hawk you attacked this afternoon."

I saw a glimmer of acknowledgement in her eyes. *So, she does have him*, I thought, *or at least she had seen him*.

"Evanora, where is he?" I asked more forcefully.

"I don't know what you're talking about," she said, obviously lying.

"Let's go," I said, pushing her out the door and into the courtyard.

"Tyrmiss," I said, looking up. "Here she is."

When the witch saw Tyrmiss, she was startled. "You," she said. "Are you the dragon I saw a few nights ago on the roof? What are you doing wearing my face? What do you want?"

I looked from Evanora to Tyrmiss and back again. The two faces, the hair, even the eyes were identical. And yet one was a woman and the other a dragon with a woman's head.

When Tessia poked her lioness head over the edge of the roof, the witch almost screamed. I put my hand over her mouth and said, "No one will hurt you unless we have to, but you must be quiet. Do you understand?"

She nodded and I removed my hand from her mouth. Tyrmiss was now in the courtyard beside us.

"Now," I told Evanora, "I'll help you climb on the dragon's back. Once you're up there, hold onto the spine on her back. She's going to fly you to a place not far away where you and she can talk. You will have to answer the dragon's questions, and she will know if you are lying. Do you understand?"

She nodded and I helped her into the right position on Tyrmiss' back and then they were gone.

"Stand guard," I whispered to Tessia who was still on the roof. "I'm going to see whether I can find Alaric."

She nodded and I went back into the building. I quickly discovered that the temple which appeared to be a low building with a courtyard was actually just the top of a much larger underground complex with stairs that led in a wide spiral down the middle of the building and deep into the earth. As I descended, the air became warmer and I heard noises coming from below.

I found myself standing on the stairs looking down into a large chamber lit by torches in sconces on the walls. There were a number of cages containing strange creatures: a man with the head of a horse, a large snake with the head of a stag, a cow with six insect legs... In the middle of the room, three cauldrons were bubbling over low fires. Three women were stirring the cauldrons while talking among themselves.

I looked around the room and saw Alaric in a cage against the far wall. He was preening his wings and hadn't seen me. And then I saw her. I would have recognized the long silver hair, the mean eyes, the dishonest way she had of tilting her head: Zamarrra was sitting at a table behind the bubbling cauldrons. She was intently studying an ancient book, poring over it while slowly turning the pages. Something made her look in my direction, and our eyes met.

She let out a blood-boiling scream, pointing at me. The other witches looked at me and pulled out their wands. I pulled out both wands from my belt, mine and Evanora's, and pointed them at the witches in my now-customary bluff. After all, I was a Green Mage. What was I going to do, make bean sprouts grow from their ears?

But my bluff was enough to make them hesitate. I turned and ran up the stairs the way I'd come. I knew they expected me to run to the surface, so I opened the first door I came to. Inside was what appeared to be a library with books and scrolls lined up neatly on shelves. I hid behind one of the bookcases and waited to hear the footsteps of the witches running up the stairs outside the library door.

Once they'd passed, I stuck my head out to make sure the way was clear, then I ran down the stairs back to the chamber and used my wand to unlock each cage as I passed it. The last cage held Alaric whose beautiful furry face beamed at me as I freed him. We quickly embraced.

"They'll be back soon," I said to him. "Is there another way out?"

He shook his head, then looked at me and smiled. "But there is something we could try," he said.

He stood up on the table where Zamarrra had been working and shouted to the beasts in front of him. "Follow us if you want to be free!" Jumping off the table, he ran on his bird legs for the stairs with me and a dozen beasts stampeding behind him. The stairway was narrow, so I was squeezed between a charging goat-eagle and a lumbering bear-owl. Alaric was in the lead running up the stairs, so when the witches came down the stairs, realizing that they must have passed me in one of the rooms, Alaric crashed into Zamarrra. The two of them tumbled down the stairs, knocking the hybrid creatures down like dominoes. By the time the flailing arms, wings, legs and antlers reached me, it was an avalanche of freaks.

At the bottom of the stairs, we lay in a pile, holding our bruised heads and appendages, wondering what we should all do now.

I looked at Zamarrra, who also seemed completely baffled about what to do next. She looked at me sadly and sighed. I was surprised that she no longer seemed evil, just tired and desperate. I suddenly realized that the weather witches were not the enemies we'd thought they were, but rather they were caught up in something larger they couldn't control, just as Tessia and I were.

"How about we sit down and talk?" I suggested. "Let's try to work something out."

She nodded, and we moved over to the table and sat down.

"Zamarrra," I began. "I don't understand why you brought drought and floods to the Dragonja and Bekla Kingdom. You destroyed our crops, caused famine and disease, and brought hardship to our people. Why would you do such a thing?"

She looked down at the table and shook her head. I saw a few tears fall onto the table. "I'm so sorry for what I did, Norbert, but I had to. The Skarsland Drekavacs said that they'd destroy Sheonad unless we joined them in their war against your kingdom."

"I don't understand, Zamarrra. We're not at war with Skarsland."

"Oh, but you are, Norbert. It was my job to weaken you and to draw your Queen away. While you've been gone, the Skarslanders have attacked your kingdom and taken your Princess hostage. At this very moment as we speak, Drekavacs control your Queen's castle Windkeep, and now they're spreading their power through the Dragonja and Bekla Valleys."

My first thought was for the safety of my wife Idella, and Tessia's wife Princess Taja; I wanted to find Tessia and Tyrmiss and fly quickly over the mountains to save our kingdom and our loved ones. But then, I realized I needed to learn more from Zamarrra before I could leave.

"And what are you doing here?" I asked waving my hand around the chamber with its menagerie of creatures. "Are you creating abominations of nature as some kind of weapon?"

"Oh no," she said, shocked. "We're trying to learn how to reverse the spells that hold these poor creatures in thrall."

When I looked puzzled, she explained, "My father was a great wizard who lived in the tower in the Iskar Valley. I believe you must have been there. You probably talked to Narrra?"

I nodded. "Narrra was quite helpful to us."

"Yes, she was the closest thing I had to a mother until Evanora brought me here and adopted me."

116

I gestured toward the large book on the table which she'd been studying earlier. "Was that from the tower?"

"Yes, Evanora brought the book back here with me, thinking that when I was older, she'd give it to me. It's the only thing I have from my father. I've learned so much from it. Lately, I've been studying it to try to understand the spells he cast on the animals of the Iskar Valley."

I saw no point in explaining to Zamarrra the fact that the wizard she thought of as her father had once been a great witch. Perhaps someday Zamarrra would be re-united with Narrra who could tell her the tale of Tatatungia.

"Why would he distort the forms of animals? Has he no respect for the Goddess's creations?" I asked.

"My father meant no harm, I'm sure. According to the book, he started with trying to improve the productivity of the sheep, so they would have thicker wool and richer milk. And then he wanted to make the wild dogs of the valley more peaceful. But then he became ill. His spells became more erratic, and he couldn't undo them. Each spell caused more chaos in the natural order. And the spells became layered until they spilled over from one kind of animal to another. The result was..." She gestured toward the strange animals in the room.

"So, you are trying to undo the spells? How much progress have you made?" I asked, thinking of Alaric, Tessia, Tyrmiss and our three companions now sheltering in Tyrmiss' cave.

"Yes, I call it *un-spelling*, and I think I may have discovered how it works," she said, pushing the big book toward me and pointing her finger at one particular passage. It was a series of hieroglyphics unfamiliar to me.

"What does it mean?" I asked.

"These are very old symbols for certain rare earths and each one is paired with a constellation, but elsewhere in the book, my father notes that the constellations have changed through the ages."

"So, to make the spells work, we would need to know how far the stars have moved and which of the constellations we can see correspond to the ancient ones?"

"Exactly. But the mathematics of star measurements have never been one of my strengths," she said.

"Mine neither, but music is," I said, reaching out into my bag and pulling out my lyre.

Her eyes lit up, "So you could tune your instrument to reflect the shift of the spheres?"

"That's right, but we still need to know the degree of the shift that the stars have gone through over the ages since these spells were invented."

Zamarrra was delighted with this direction of thought. She turned the pages of the ancient book to a section of mathematical formulas: page after page of numbers and symbols, but every now and then there was a symbol that was different than the others. These unusual symbols were made of six vertical lines with a diagonal line slashing through them.

"I thought that the diagonal lines were excisions, indicating that something about the vertical lines was incorrect based on the mathematical calculations. But what if the vertical lines symbolize strings like the ones on your lyre?" she asked.

"And the slash marks indicate a shortening of the strings?" I was beginning to catch on to her line of inquiry.

She nodded. "Now that I look at them, the diagonal lines seem carefully measured, not just an excision, but rather an indication of a shift in key."

"Yes," I said, using my forefinger to measure the intervals. "It looks like this diagram indicates that I need to tune the lyre to a little less than half a note higher on the first string, three-quarters note higher on the second and so on in a spiral progression. Let me try it."

Using the tuning keys, I shifted my lyre to play a higher scale. I plucked a string.

"It sounds off-key to me," I said.

"Well of course it does," Zamarrra responded. "But doesn't music correspond to the world we know, and now we want to find the music of a world we don't know?"

This wasn't any kind of magic that I'd heard of, but on the other hand, a few months before, I'd never heard of Blue Magic either. Tatatungia had obviously been a brilliant witch, so perhaps it wasn't surprising she'd discovered a type of magic no one knew existed. I decided to follow Zamarrra's lead and see whether we could find a way to undo Tatatungia's spells.

"What was your father's name?" I asked.

"Tuguslar."

I slowly played the first four notes on the lyre while singing the syllables of the name. No result.

Didn't your father have another name?"

"I don't think so," she said, puzzled.

"Tatatungia, perhaps?"

"No, that's the name of a witch who invented most of the spells in the book, but she lived long ago, didn't she? My impression was that my father inherited the book of spells from her."

"Tatatungia's name may still be attached to the spells," I pointed out.

Again, I slowly played the first four notes on the lyre while singing the syllables of the witch's name. Still no result.

I re-tuned my lyre to a slightly higher scale and plucked it again while singing the syllables.

"Did you hear that?" Zamarrra asked, looking around.

"Hear what?"

"I thought I heard an echo in the room that wasn't there before. Try it again."

I played the four notes while singing the name Tatatungia as I did before, but louder.

There was definitely an echo in the room. The witch's name hung in the air around us.

"Let's move to the next scale," she said, turning the pages. After a long indecipherable series of mathematical symbols and formulas, there was another diagram made up of six vertical lines with a diagonal line through them, but the angle was different than the last one. I re-tuned my lyre to roughly correspond to the diagram and again I plucked the first four strings while singing the witch's name.

"OUCH!" Alaric yelled from behind me. I didn't realize he'd been listening to us.

There was a feather on the floor next to him.

"What happened?" I asked.

"I don't know," he said, licking a place on his wing. "It felt like something yanked one of my feathers out."

Zamarrra and I locked eyes. "It sounds like we're onto something," she said.

"Did your father have a lyre?" I asked.

"No, but he had a collection of small flutes that he often played."

"Were they tuned oddly?"

"I don't know. I was just a little girl and I had never heard anyone else play music."

"I remember in your father's workshop there were jars. Perhaps they contained herbs and rare earths that he used in combination with music to cast spells?"

"Yes, and I've worked out the formulas for the substances. There's a whole section of this book that explains them. It's written in clear language, so I've been able to gather the herbs and minerals from the woods around the tower and bring them back here. Do you want to see them?"

She led me up the stairs to the library where I had hidden before. At the back of the room, she opened a door. Inside was a closet which had jars lined on the shelves. On each jar was a symbol. It looked identical to the jars in her father's workshop.

"I've been experimenting with the ingredients, but not

getting any results. We should try using them with the music you discovered," she said, gathering samples from a few of the jars and putting them in small linen pouches.

We went back to the large chamber where the menagerie of animals was waiting. Evidently, many of them had been listening to us talk.

"I'd like to be the first to try your formula," a short creature with the head of a lizard and the body of a dog said. "I hate this form and I want to be a man again."

Zamarrra asked the creature his name, consulted the book, mixed a concoction of ingredients including a yellow tea from one of the cauldrons, and set down the bowl on the floor. As the dog-lizard lapped up the liquid, I strummed the six notes indicated by the book, sang his name which was Beslan. We waited, but nothing happened. I retuned my lyre by a half tone and tried again. Still nothing. I experimented with different scales, and just when I was ready to give up, the creature began to change. We watched for a few moments, and once we saw he was becoming human, we knew we were ready.

Alaric was next. I was overjoyed to see him start to lose the feathers from his wings and the fur from his face. The other creatures lined up behind him and we treated each one with the un-spell.

"Well," Tyrmiss said, after her head was restored to its dragon shape. "That was an interesting experiment, but I have to say I prefer being a dragon. You humans are so fragile."

"Each to her own, I guess," Tessia said, flexing her fingers, "I, for one, like having hands. Claws are a bit clumsy."

"I'm going to miss having wings," Alaric said, looking sadly up at the sky. "Too bad I couldn't have kept them a while longer." He looked at Tessia. "How are we going to get back home? From

121

what Zamarrra told us, the Skarslanders have invaded Dragonja. We are needed back home as quickly as possible."

"I'll have to fly you back to Dragonja in shifts, two at a time," Tyrmiss said. "But first, I think it's important for you to hear what Evanora has to say about the Skarslanders."

I'd been so busy working with Zamarrra to restore my companions to their true form, I hadn't even noticed Evanora standing with us in the courtyard. A surprising turn, considering how striking the older woman was. Her blue skin seemed lit from within, and her silver hair fell in cascades past her shoulders. She held herself like the Queen she was.

Evanora gestured that we should gather around her on the benches beneath the acacia tree. Tyrmiss made herself comfortable on the black flagstones.

"You're all aware, I believe, that the Blue Witches were slaughtered in Dragonja a thousand years ago," Evanora began.

Her tone was sad, but not angry. This was ancient history, and I was beginning to realize that a great deal had happened since then.

"The handful of survivors fled the Dragonja valley and wandered far up the Iskar River. We wanted to find a place where those who were hunting us would never come. We eventually came to this place which we called Sheonad, which in the ancient language means *The Wisdom of Women*. Since we had the skill of influencing the weather, we were not discouraged by the fact that this was an extremely cold, windy place. In fact, where we are now standing was a glacier at that time."

She gestured up at the black roof of the cavern. "One of the witches had the skill of cutting and moving large blocks of stone. She taught the lore to her sisters and together they melted the glacier, clearing a place for the city, then carved the cavern where we now stand, using the black stone to construct the walls and buildings of Sheonad.

"The Weather Witches, as your people knew us, created a

122

paradise here, a place where warmth and sunlight prevailed, and the snow was changed to warm rain as it fell. They grew abundant crops and tended orchards of many fruits. The problem of course was that without men, pregnancies didn't happen, and the witches had to search the wild places for girls who'd been lost or abandoned. The witches dared not go to cities such as Dragonja or Skarsland to find girls to take, and the witches had no wish to cause distress for families, so they looked for girls who were orphaned, abandoned, or abused. During times of war or famine, there were many children in need of a home, but as men became more civilized there were fewer, and our numbers dwindled.

"In recent generations, except for a brief time after the war in Dragonja, there were almost no children we could find." She looked at Zamarrra, sitting beside Tessia, "Before the war in Dragonja, we hadn't adopted a child in almost fifty years. You've seen that most of Sheonad is abandoned. There are not enough of us to maintain the weather to protect the city from the relentless creep of glaciers. The walls are crumbling, and our buildings are empty."

Evanora looked sadly at Tessia, "Our nation is dying."

"What happened with the Skarslanders?" Tessia asked.

"We'd always been on good terms with the people of the north," Evanora answered. "We traded with them a few times a year. They brought furs and metal goods, and we gave them fruits and vegetables from our gardens. But in recent years, they became more aggressive. Their king, a man named Kazko, is greedy. He came here, looked at our city and decided that there wasn't anything here that he wanted. However, he was aware of our reputation for being able to influence the weather. He threatened to destroy our city and enslave us unless we helped him conquer Dragonja."

Evanora looked sadly at Zamarrra, her adopted daughter. "We sent our most gifted witch to Dragonja with instructions to attack the city with drought and flood. She came up with an ingenious scheme to get you to invite her into the Windkeep in order to carry out her attack."

Zamarrra looked at me apologetically, and I looked at her and shrugged. I'd been played for a fool by someone whose magical skills far surpassed mine, but I was no longer angry at her. In her situation, I may have done the same thing. After all, unlike me, Zamarrra did not have Tessia and Tyrmiss to protect her and her loved ones. "You only did what you had to do to protect your people," I said.

"What?" Tessia cried. "You're going to forgive them just like that? After all they've done?"

"I agree, Father," Alaric wailed. "These witches put my mother and sister in terrible danger. They deserve some kind of punishment."

I turned to the two witches who were looking at the floor in shame. Tessia and Alaric were right. These two witches had committed crimes against Dragonja, but having worked the last few hours with Zamarrra, I was convinced she'd been coerced into doing evil things, and she deserved mercy. Besides, if they were right about the Skarslanders carrying out an attack against Dragonja, then we should consider allying ourselves with these weather witches.

"We are facing extreme danger now, and we need your help," I said. "Will you be willing to stand trial at a tribunal in Dragonja once we return? If you agree, then any help you now give us will be taken into consideration at your trial."

I glanced at Tessia and Alaric who didn't object. Tyrmiss also stayed silent. Later, when the two witches stood trial, I would learn about dragon-justice.

The two witches nodded. Evanora said, her voice turning more urgent, "As we speak, Kazko has invaded your city weakened by the violence of weather. I see now that what we did was wrong, and we'd like to help you."

Tessia, always practical in matters of war, said, "We welcome your help, Queen Evanora."

Alaric looked away, obviously unsatisfied with the compromise, but willing to go along with it for now.

Evanora, seeing that an ally is better than an enemy, replied, "All right then, there's something you need to know.

"What is that?" Tessia asked, raising an eyebrow.

"You need to be aware Kazko has three dragons with his army."

Chapter Eleven

Tyrmiss, who'd been nodding off as Evanora was telling the story of Sheonad which the dragon already knew, suddenly lifted her head. "*Three dragons?*" she shouted. "That is not possible. I'd have known if there were three dragons somewhere in the world. I'd have heard their dreams."

"Be that as it may, Mistress Dragon," Evanora said. "There are three dragons under the control of Kazko. I've seen them."

"Where did you see them?" Tessia asked, carefully.

"Kazko himself and two of his generals flew to Sheonad on them. It would have taken them weeks of marching across a glacier to get here otherwise."

"This changes everything," Tessia said.

"Three dragons?" Tyrmiss shook her huge head in disbelief. "I thought I was the last one."

Tessia patted the dragon's head. "This is good news, Tyrmiss."

"What worries me," Tyrmiss responded, "Is that I've never heard their dreams. It seems like at some point our paths would have crossed and they would have been close enough for me to hear them."

"Perhaps the dragons are from far away?" Tessia offered.

"They must have been from very far away for me to never know about them for these thousands of years."

Alaric and I sat silently and let Tessia and Tyrmiss adjust their thinking to the new situation.

After a while, Tessia asked Tyrmiss, "If the king of Skarsland is riding a dragon, then does that mean that he and the dragon have bonded in friendship in the way that you and I have bonded?"

"Not necessarily," Tyrmiss said, thinking about it. "Milon and the other so-called heroes of ancient times did not bond with the dragons they rode. Instead, they intimidated them, beat them into submission, or threatened their mates or off-spring in order to turn them into beasts of war. Remember the old tapestries? The dragons are always portrayed in chains with the hero controlling them. This was not friendship, Tessia. It was slavery."

"You think that King Kazko has some kind of hold over the dragons?" Tessia asked, musing.

"That would be my guess," Tyrmiss said. "What you and I have is very unusual. I've never heard of a dragon and a human becoming friends. Our relationship may be unique."

"So, we have a responsibility to free the dragons under Kazko's control, don't we?" Tessia looked at Tyrmiss with a gleam in her eye.

"And freeing the dragons would turn them into allies? " Tyrmiss asked, seeing the strategy to take back Tessia's kingdom forming as they spoke.

"While Kazko's army is occupying Dragonja, he has left his own city of Skarsland undefended," Alaric said. "What about the tribe of Renetu? Would they be willing to attack Skarsland now?"

"Bastian lived with the tribes for many years, and he's said the Renetu tribes hate the kings of Skarsland," I pointed out.

We continued discussing strategy and came up with a

two-pronged approach. Tessia, Tyrmiss and I would go to Dragonja, free the captive dragons and then take back the city from Kazko. Meanwhile, Alaric, Bastian, Zrul and Hamlin would go to the Renetu tribe and encourage them to attack the city of Skarsland. Even if they could not capture the city, they could at least disrupt Kazko's supply lines and communication. Once his troops learned that their homeland was being attacked, they would not want to remain in Dragonja.

Alaric shook his head, "There's a big problem with logistics. How are we going to get all the way to Renetu? It will take months of marching to go to the Iskar Valley and find Bastian and the others and then climb back into the mountains to meet and parley with the tribes."

"I think I can be of help," Evanora said, speaking for the first time in quite a while. "Please follow me."

We walked after her into the temple and down the circular stairs. She opened a door and inside the room, a row of brooms hung on the wall. Each one appeared to be different from the others. Some had short thick shafts, some had long thin ones. Some had straw brush tied with cord, others stiff twigs pushed into a wooden cap. A few had ribbons dangling from their handles. One had a red flag attached. Evanora swept her arm down the line in a graceful gesture showing her pride in the collection.

"With these, we fly," Evanora said simply, smiling.

It took several lessons from Zamarrra for me to master the basics of flying on a broom. On the other hand, Alaric, with his considerable experience flying as a hawk, took to it immediately. I can't say I liked it. Whereas flying on the back of a dragon was merely a matter of my holding on and not looking down, piloting a broom required a mastery of balance, an intuitive feel for wind and velocity, and deep concentration.

"After a while, the broom becomes part of your body,"

Zamarrra said repeatedly. "You will go up or down, fast or slow, right or left, simply by willing it. It's not something you do. It's something you feel."

For her, I'm sure that was true. For me, flying on a broom felt as unnatural as eating mud. I could do it, but only with great force of will overcoming my revulsion. Every time I got off my broom, I felt dizzy and nauseous.

It wasn't a problem with the broom. Zamarrra had chosen one of her best for my use. It had a thin shaft made of alder, and the brush was a handsomely sculpted gathering of elder sticks. It even had a short green ribbon that trailed behind me as I flew. The problem was my basic distrust of any magic not my own.

"Norbert, you're a mage. You should be able to master the magic of a broom easily. Look at your son," Zamarrra pointed at Alaric flying around the city as if he had been born to fly.

"It's not the same as Green Magic, Zamarrra." I heard myself whining, and I felt disgusted with myself. "Encouraging things to grow is completely natural. Making a middle-aged man fly is anything but natural."

Tessia rolled her eyes. "Would you please quit referring to yourself that way, Norbert? How old are you anyway? 36? 37?"

"You are only as old as you feel," I grumbled. I remembered my mother telling me I was born a grumpy old man.

Once again Zamarrra explained to me how important posture is. "Everything is in the gesture of the body. If you want to turn left, merely turn your head in that direction. Your body will slightly shift its balance, and the broom will bank left. The same is true for going up or down, or fast or slow. Merely think of the direction, and your body will signal the broom."

On the third day, Zamarrra told Tessia that I was competent enough to fly, but, she added, ruefully, "Don't expect him to do anything more than get to Dragonja without killing himself."

Shortly after noon, Tessia, Alaric, Zamarrra, and I packed our kits and mounted up. Tessia would ride Tyrmiss while the other three of us would ride our brooms. We would fly to Tatatungia's tower the first day, arriving there at sunset. After resting for the night, we would fly down the Iskar Valley, following the trail we'd taken before. We hoped to catch up to Bastian, Zrul and Hamlin. We needed to work our magic to transform them to their previous forms, assuming that they no longer wanted to be a badger, a dog, and a bear.

Once we were in the air, I realized we'd be flying east with the sun directly in our eyes. Fortunately, the wool hood I was wearing could be pulled down to shade my eyes. I left a small slit open so the others were visible in front of me. As Zamarrra had said, I was capable of getting where I needed to go, but I wouldn't be performing any tricks along the way.

I have to say that Alaric and Zamarrra were a sight to behold. They would fly next to each other, an arm's length away, shouting at each other in conversation. The one would veer off to inspect something on the ground, an old ruin or a band of Renetu hunters, then fly back up to join us. I envied their skill but was far too frightened to try anything more than just follow Tyrmiss's tail or creep up beside her to catch a signal from Tessia.

Very few people have seen a dragon close up in flight. At a distance, a dragon looks like a winged snake, wriggling through the sky, its purple scales reflecting light. This is the image we see on pottery and the old tapestries: the hero holds a spear as he rides the charging dragon who is breathing fire. But flying next to a dragon is a completely different experience. Up close, Tyrmiss did not look like a wriggling snake, but like a magnificent mare, stretched out in full gallop, her wings moving and gliding, the muscles of her chest taut as a drum, her legs tucked beneath her belly and her talons curled. With each drum beat of her body, her magnificent head stretched forward as if the energy began in her neck and spread through the rest of her body like ripples in a stream. She seemed to be not a beast but a great river pushing incessantly forward, her scales iridescent in the sunlight.

I knew that someday when I had my lyre and I had regained my peace of mind, I would write a song about this experience, but first we had to win the war. Then there would be time for music and poetry, the smell of baking bread, the taste of honey, and waking up in my own bed with my wife beside me. But not now. Now was a time of war, and there is a time when even a peaceful man must take up arms to defend his home.

We landed in the pasture next to the round tower at nightfall. The sheep kept their distance from Tyrmiss, but when Zamarrra approached them, they gathered around her, asking questions and rubbing their heads against her legs and arms. Zamarrra was smiling broadly. This, after all, was where she had spent her early childhood, and Narrra was the only mother she had known until she went to Sheonad to live with Evanora. She sat in the grass with the sheep and told them all about Sheonad and her life there. She apologized for not stopping to visit them when she flew between Dragonja and Sheonad, but the nations were at war, and she had her part to play.

The rest of us sat near the door to the tower, eating provisions that Evanora had supplied. We didn't talk about the plans for the next day or the overall strategy we'd put into play. We each knew what needed to be done, and we also knew that some or all of us would likely be killed. We were a small group, and we were taking on a large army. If the thought of facing thousands of trained soldiers didn't intimidate us, then the image of Kazko's three dragons certainly did.

As I lay in my bedroll that night, I looked up at the stars. There wasn't a campfire, lamp, or torch within a week's walk, so the stars were strewn like spilled milk across the sky. The moon looked down with her knowing eyes, and the shadow of the tower enveloped us. I could hear the sheep moving around as they found the most comfortable places and Tyrmiss was snoring with deep rumbles. I realized I hadn't thought of Idella in days, we'd been so busy with talking about strategy and getting ready for the journey home. I prayed to the Goddess for my wife's safety, turned over and tried to rest.

It turned out that Bastian, Hamlin, and Zrul had traveled much more quickly than we expected. They'd been following the river downhill, moving quickly since the trail had been made by animals like them. We found our friends halfway up the mountain and landed on a large flat stone just ahead of them. Bastian greeted us with a nod of his badger head and went immediately to Alaric and inspected the broom. He'd mentioned to me in the past that he'd heard of flying brooms, but had never seen one, so this one merited close attention. Zrul, like any dog, had to smell each of us carefully to make sure we were who he thought we were. Once the identification was certain, he licked our faces enthusiastically. Hamlin's behavior was odd, though. He lowered his bulk onto the warm stone and lay there, somewhat indifferent to us. He and Tessia had been friends since childhood, so his distance from her seemed out of character. She went over to him, spoke softly to him, then went back to sit beside me. I wondered if she was feeling a little hurt by Hamlin's indifference to her.

Once we all had had a chance to rest and drink water, Tessia caught up the others on what had happened in Sheonad. She said that Zamarrra and I would perform the un-spells necessary to change them back to human form, then we would develop a strategy for waging war against Kazko.

During Tessia's explanation, Bastian listened intently, his sharp black ears pointed at her and his furry face reacting with each new disclosure. I could see that once he had human form again, he would have lots of questions and ideas about strategy. Zrul was completely into his dogginess, panting and smiling happily as he sat beside Alaric, who slowly scratched behind Zrul's white floppy ears. Again, I noticed that Hamlin seemed disengaged from the group. We were talking about the liberation of the kingdom where he'd spent his entire life, but he seemed uninterested, staring off into the forest of aspens beside the trail. *Something is not right with him*, I thought.

Tessia nodded to Zamarrra and me, and we got started with the un-spelling of our three friends. Zamarrra unpacked her father's heavy book of computations, as well as her herbal and mineral concoctions, and I took my lyre out of my bag. We started with Bastian who seemed to be the one most interested in returning to human form, and after a short while he was standing in front of us, looking at his hands, feeling his nose and chin, and standing up straighter with each moment.

"By the Goddess," he said, stretching out his arms. "That was quite an experience! I'm glad to lose all that fur. It was hot, and my skin was starting to itch."

"How do you feel?" I asked.

He paused for a moment, thinking, then said, "I feel like a man."

Tessia laughed and gave him a hug. "Welcome back, my friend," she said. "We are going to need your help."

We all looked at Zrul, the big white dog happily sitting in our midst, obviously unaware that he was supposed to be a Drekavac.

Alaric patted Zrul's head, and the beast looked up at him affectionately, "It's almost a shame to change him back," Alaric said. "He's such a great dog."

"Yes," Bastian said, wistfully. "He's a much better dog than he was man."

"Drekavac," Alaric said. "He was a Drekavac, not a man."

"Drekavacs are men," Bastian said. "They just look different on the outside. On the inside..."

And this started a debate between the old man and the young one over whether Drekavacs and men are closely related, or completely different species. People in Dragonja have been arguing about this issue for centuries.

"We don't have time for this argument now," I interrupted. "We need to make a decision about Zrul."

Hearing his name, Zrul looked up expectantly. I had to agree with my son. Zrul was a great dog, and as a Drekavac he'd been surly and violent. It was tempting to leave well enough alone.

"We don't have to change him back to a Drekavac you know," Zamarrra said. "I never knew him as a Drekavac, so all I know is that I really like him as a dog." She looked at me, "It's your decision, Mage. I can return him to his Drekavac form or not."

"I say turn him into a chipmunk," Tyrmiss said wryly. "I never liked him."

At this point, Tessia, seeing that the conversation was not moving forward, exercised her prerogative as Queen and made a decision. "We have to change Zrul back to his true form. Not only is that the right and natural thing to do, but I need him. We are about to go to war with an entire army, and Zrul is my best warrior. Not only can he fight like a lion, but he can lead the attack on the castle if I should fall. We cannot afford to have a good dog when what we need is a great warrior."

All of us, even Tyrmiss, nodded silently at her decision, and for the thousandth time, I was proud to be led by this wise and fearsome Queen.

Zamarrra and I performed the un-spell on Zrul, and soon he was standing in front of us, scowling, furious we'd made a fool of him. It seems that he had indeed understood we were seriously considering letting him stay in canine form. He glared at Bastian and Alaric who sheepishly looked at the ground, embarrassed by the way they'd talked about him. He tried to glare at Tyrmiss, but the dragon merely ignored him, obviously indifferent to the feelings of men or Drekavacs.

Zrul bowed his head to Tessia, "Thank you, my Queen, for restoring me to my true form. I will serve you to my last breath." He seemed to have understood her praise of him. It seems what I'd long suspected was true: dogs understand more of what we say than we realize.

Next, it was Hamlin's turn. Zamarrra consulted her father's book, mixed some herbs in a cup with some water, and she and I moved toward the big blonde bear. Hamlin who had been sitting on his haunches, indifferent to the group, suddenly rose on all fours and looked at us with narrow eyes. A rough growl came from his throat. I signaled to Zamarrra and we halted about eight paces from Hamlin.

"Again, Mage," Zamarrra said, "I never knew Hamlin as a man, but I gather that you and the Queen knew him quite well. He doesn't seem to want us to approach. What should we do?"

I turned to Tessia, "Your Majesty, you've known Hamlin all your life. What is your wish?"

Tessia looked at the bear for a few moments, then signaled Zamarrra and me to move back. Slowly, the Queen moved toward Hamlin, not looking him in the eye and keeping her palms open in front of her in a gesture of peace. The bear relaxed his posture and allowed her to approach. Tessia took the great ursine head in her arms and hugged him and whispered in his ear. They went off together into the aspen forest away from the rest of us.

We sat in silence for what seemed a long time. Finally, Tessia returned. Ignoring the rest of us, she went to Tyrmiss and held the great dragon head in her arms the same way she had held Hamlin's and whispered in the wide ear. Tyrmiss listened, and silently nodded her head. Tessia walked back into the woods where she had come from.

Again, we sat in silence, and finally Tessia came back accompanied by the blonde bear.

"Hamlin chooses to remain as he is. He prefers being a bear to being a man. Tyrmiss has agreed to let him live in her cave. He is protected by the invisibility spell there. There are trout in the stream, deer and rabbits in the woods, and seeds and berries in the fields. He will not be joining us in our attempt to take back the city from Kazko."

I looked at Hamlin who sat on his haunches next to Tessia who had her hand on his shoulder. He seemed content with his decision, and I admired the Queen for having the wisdom to inquire what he wished, then putting her authority behind his decision.

Tyrmiss offered to make dinner, and she flew down toward the Iskar River. The rest of us, including Hamlin, followed Tessia up the steep trail to Tyrmiss's cave. By the time we got there, the sun was setting over the high cliff on the other side of the Iskar Valley, and Tyrmiss was already in the cave, two large salmon spread over the flat cooking stone. We put down our kits, sat down and watched the dragon breathe fire on the fish until they were crisp. Alaric and I shared the greens we'd gathered, and Tessia's heroes ate our last meal before the war for Dragonja began.

A Treatise on Dragon Anatomy
by Zakkik, Royal Sage to King Milon Redshield

~Fragments of a manuscript composed on vellum and stored in the Royal Library at Windkeep

*T*o many, dragons are horrifying creatures. To a few, they're impressive and miraculous [....] Like leeches, they have 32 brains, 2 hearts, 300 teeth grouped in 3 jaws, and five pairs of eyes although only the two frontal eyes are functional. Like snakes, they have a long body and scales. Like bats, they have leathery wings enabling some varieties to fly. Like men, they speak and consider their actions. However, one variety, the Iskar dragon, is the only creature known to breathe fire.

[...] unlike all other creatures which crawl or fly, dragons are capable of speech. It has been said they love poetry and song, have purpose and believe in a Higher Being. It is true dragons have been observed praying, but this activity may be merely a mimicry of human behavior. Moreover, dragons live many thousands of years, and in this way, it has been said, dragons develop wisdom. Tomacus of Itria goes so far as to say that in a comparison between dragons and men, dragons are the superior beings, but this of course is sacrilegious nonsense because dragons do not have souls [...] Hereon, I set aside theological debate and speak only of the anatomy of these remarkable creatures based on my dissection of 17 living specimens. I shall also recommend a policy for the king to consider as a final solution to the dragon problem which afflicts the kingdom.

[...]

Each of the two hearts of a dragon consist of two atria and a single ventricle divided into four chambers: the cave of echoes, the cave of green blood, the cave of crystal and the cave of hungers. As the blood shunts between these chambers, the creature becomes refreshed and thus more dangerous.

[...]

What are the parts of a dragon egg? Three membranes and a leathery shell with [...]

What are the colors of dragon blood? Red in the tail. Black in the belly. Green in the [...]

Do dragons have fatherless births as many believe? Virgin births have been observed in other reptiles but never in dragons [...] Dragons mate for life, and sires as well as mares teach and care for their young.

[...]

The elongate body and tail of dragons, as well as the way they reproduce, resembles that of snakes, but there are significant differences. In particular, dragons have four legs, and the front appendages are utilized in much the same way that men use their hands [....] The wings of a dragon are made of skin stretched tightly across a fan of thin bones, much like the wings of a bat. [....] likely the ISKAR dragons became fire-breathers only after the development of a third set of flat flint-hard molar teeth which when struck together create a spark that ignites stomach gases as they expel [...] an adaptation allowing dragons to create glacial caves for the purpose of shelter during the primordial Age of Ice.

Of the Different Species of Dragons

Arboreal dragons are the most elongated and slender of all, with the tail approaching half the length of the entire body. The body is often strongly compressed laterally, which permits greater rigidity of the body frame while crawling from branch to branch[....] Burrowing dragons are seldom large, and the true burrowers, the Tyfids and the Leptoe, living all their lives like earthworms, are the tiniest dragons of all. The burrowers have almost no tail, although some of them retain a spiny tail tip, which serves the animal as an anchoring point when crawling through the soil.... The tail of Sea Dragons is flattened to form an oar, used to scull through the water. Sea dragons are almost totally helpless on land, locomoting only with the utmost difficulty.

[...]

The spines of dragons are highly elongated and have more vertebrae than any other known animal—up to 600 in the Iskar Dragon, 405 in the body and 195 in the tail of one specimen [...] These structures permit lateral and vertical rotation while preventing almost entirely any twisting of the spine, thus achieving both flexibility and rigidity.

[...] The Iskar Dragon has a bone spur in the back of its mouth with a distinct coating of extremely hard enamel. These bone spurs click against the third set of molars and serve to ignite the stomach gas, so the Dragon's fiery breath is essentially a flaming burp.

The Skin of Dragons

Dragons are covered with scales, which upon close examination turn out to be folds of layered horn arranged in rows. In the

Iskar Dragon, the most magnificent of the species, scales are shield-shaped, and the number of rows can be as high as 180. A single scale is smooth, shiny, striated, and dark green although when a dragon is flying in sunlight the scales can take on the hues of the rainbow [...] The ventral scales of Sea Dragons, Worm Dragons, and Blind Dragons are used in locomotion.

The Eye of the Dragon

[...] lidless eyes that change shape and color [...] round and blue, but with provocation, the eyes become red vertical slits [....] The Iskar dragon has a bulging lateral eye which permits it to see activities directly below as well as above and to the side [....] The structure of the eye indicates their snake ancestor was a burrower and that all aboveground activity by dragons is a secondary invasion from an ancestral life underground. From this, we can conclude that dragons are not a natural part of our sunlit world but are denizens of the dark and thus agents of evil.

[...]

The reception of sound is entirely by bone conduction within the skull. The dragon has no external ear, but still retains an internal ear connected to other skull bones permitting transmission of sound waves of low frequency.

[...]

The dragon's skull is characterized by mobility. It is light, with a reduced number of bones, and there are hinge joints at several levels that permit slight rotation or movement of one segment upon another. The only compact unit is the central braincase [...] To swallow prey, the upper jaw is connected to the lower jaw by a joint that acts as a pivot point. The main bone of the upper jaw is elongated, with many fangs. [...] the rear-fanged dragons, such as the Iskar, usually (although not always) nonlethal to man. Dragon fangs are long, slightly recurved, and needle-sharp. [....] facilitates swallowing and prevents loss of food, because the only direction in which a food item, which may be alive when swallowed, can go to escape the teeth is down the throat. Modifications in food habits have often been accompanied by changes in tooth structure or the loss of teeth. The egg-eating dragons, for example, have only a few peg-like teeth left. The burrowing blind dragons have very reduced dentition and often have lost the teeth of one jaw entirely.

Iskar Dragon Skull

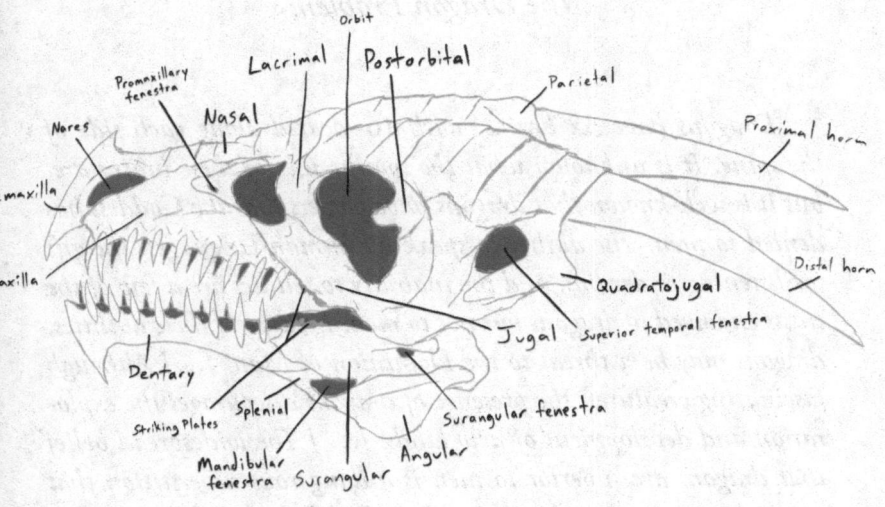

[...]

The reproductive system in dragons is completely different than that of men and women [....] Male dragons' testes are made up of two saclike structures that must be turned inside out to be inserted in the cloaca of the female and can be removed only by turning it back inside, because to draw it out directly would damage the female considerably.

[...]

Dragons, unlike many snakes and other reptiles, have no venom, and in fact their saliva, tears, urine and other bodily fluids are believed to have magical uses. Since magic has been outlawed in the kingdom, the gathering of dragon fluids should be outlawed as well. [...]

Dragons bury their clutch of eggs in warm sand, then stay nearby as the dragonlings hatch. Beware. Both male and female dragons guard their nests and are known to attack men or women who come near. [...] The six ovaries of dragons are elongate and located near the pancreas close to the kidneys.

The Dragon Problem

Dragons have 32 brains, with 16 located along each side of the spine. It is unknown what the specific uses of these brains are, but it is well-known that dragons have powers that the Goddess has denied to men. The ability to speak all human languages, the gift for listening to dreams, and the inability to tell lies are a few of the traits endowed to dragons but not to men. Because of these abilities, dragons may be a threat to the Dominion of Man. [...] Although fascinating creatures, the presence of dragons discourages the exploration and development of new lands. [....] The widespread belief that dragons are superior to men is a dangerous superstition that raises the creatures to the status of magical beings and prevents the King and his subjects from controlling the population of dragons. [...] Your Majesty, your humble Royal Sage, as well as many of your other subjects, believes that dragons pose a potent threat to men and must be eradicated from the kingdom.

Part Three: The Rescue

Chapter Twelve

After we ate, Tessia explained the strategy she'd developed. "Zamarrra, can you carry Bastian on your broom to Sheonad? There you can encourage Evanora and the Sisters to go with you and Bastian to the land of Renetu."

"Of course, my Queen," Zamarrra said, nodding. Alaric and I looked at each other, thinking the same thing. This was the first time any of the witches had recognized Tessia as their Queen, a good portent for the future of our two peoples.

"Thank you, Mistress Witch," Tessia said, recognizing the honor she'd been paid, as well as the future alliance it promised.

"Bastian is a former tribal chief of the Renetu people, so he will be invaluable in gaining the trust of the tribes. Since Kazko has led most of his army, including his three dragons, to our homeland of Dragonja, his own homeland must be largely undefended and will fall easily to the combined forces of the witches and the tribes." She turned to Bastian. "Do you agree?"

Bastian nodded his head. "A brilliant strategy, Your Majesty. The mountain tribes have hated the coastal flat landers for generations. The wealth of Osterbo City has been accumulated by robbing the inland people. If the tribal leaders can be convinced that it's possible to capture the city, they will join us enthusiastically."

"Very well, then," Tessia said. "The two of you can fly down the Iskar Valley now, spend the rest of the night with our friends at the tower, then you can be in Sheonad by tomorrow night."

Zamarrra and Bastian packed their kits, and at the cave mouth, Zamarrra turned to Tessia and asked, "If we are successful in capturing Osterbo City, how shall you know?"

Tessia nodded. "When the city is falling, there will be refugees sailing from the port of Skarsland and coming to our shores. They will carry the news."

As Bastian was about to follow Zamarrra, Tessia asked, "Can you limit the amount of looting and destruction the tribes do once they take the city?"

Bastian sighed and shrugged, "I will try, Your Majesty."

He hesitated. Tessia asked, "What is it, Bastian? We don't have time for doubts. What is your concern?"

"Pardon me, my Queen, but can the four of you take Dragonja City? Even with the help of a dragon, it seems impossible."

Tessia smiled and replied confidently. "Zrul is worth a regiment, as am I. Alaric is a genius at espionage and street fighting. And we have the legendary Green Mage with us," she said, nodding at me. "And Tyrmiss is made of fire and rage. Don't worry about us. We will be victorious."

Bastian gave a quick bow of his head to her and swung one leg over the broom.

After Zamarrra had flown off with Bastian balanced uneasily behind her, Tessia gathered Zrul, Alaric, and me in the cave and said she needed to explain our plan of attack on Dragonja City. In the dark before dawn, she said, Zrul would fly with Alaric on his broom, and she and I would fly on Tyrmiss.

"Here's what I need from each of you," she began. "While Zrul, Alaric and Norbert infiltrate the city, stir up rebellion and lead the citizens against Kazko's headquarters, Tyrmiss and I will strike at the heart of the occupying force."

Each of us had our assigned tasks. I would fly with Tessia and Tyrmiss to the city, and they would drop me off at the Silver Pony Inn to talk with Heikum and Femke. As leaders in the Citizens Council, they would know about the status of the government, and as proprietors of a popular inn, they would know the gossip from the soldiers and tradesmen. I would use that information to rally the citizens against Kazko's troops.

Zrul, never the diplomat, asked why I was flying behind Tessia on Tyrmiss when I had my own broom.

Alaric looked at the floor, and Tessia said, "With no offense meant to Norbert, his flying skills are not as strong as Alaric's, and he's too important to risk a mishap. We need each of us to arrive safely and unobtrusively inside the city."

She went on to say that Zrul would fly on the back of Alaric's broom, and once inside the city walls he would rally the Drekavac soldiers with whom he'd formerly served, and hopefully he would be able to recruit Kazko's Drekavac soldiers to our cause as well. Zrul had been successful in a similar mission during the war against Ludek, and he thought that Kazko's troops would be ripe for mutiny as well. And Alaric would infiltrate the underground which consisted of organized criminals in the marketplace and the gangs who dominated the back-alleys. Both groups could be easily encouraged to attack the soldiers who harassed them.

"What should we tell the soldiers and thieves to stir them to action?" Alaric asked.

Tessia met our gazes. Her green eyes were so intense that looking into them made a man feel taller. "Tell them," she said, "To grab their weapons and rise up against the oppressor. The Dragonqueen has returned and calls them to fight for their freedom."

Alaric nodded, and we all knew what the effect on the city's people would be once they heard that their Queen had returned.

Tessia went back to the business at hand, assigning Tyrmiss

the task of finding Kazko's three dragons and turning them against Kazko's army.

"Why would they turn against Kazko?" I asked.

"Norbert," Tyrmiss said to me slowly as if she were explaining arithmetic to a child, "Dragons do not naturally ally themselves with humans. We have a long history of being hunted and abused by your kind. We avoid humans and your wars and rivalries as much as possible. If Kazko is using dragons for warfare, then they have been forced into servitude."

"And why is it that you allow the Queen to fly on your back?" Zrul asked, impertinently.

"Because she is my friend," Tyrmiss answered, then answered, barely audibly, "My only friend."

"And how is a dragon forced?" I asked. "Dragons are so much more powerful than men."

"A dragon can be raised in captivity and never understand that it can break its chains and leave anytime it wants." Tyrmiss thought for a moment. "Also, it is possible that Kazko has some kind of hold over the dragons."

"A hold?" I asked.

"Yes, possibly Kazko is holding a loved one hostage."

I could see Tyrmiss's eyes turning into red slits. I knew she was becoming dangerous, so I stopped questioning her.

"And, My Queen," I asked, "What is your role in the siege?"

"I plan to find Kazko and kill him," she said, pulling out her Voprian sword and polishing the blue blade on a fist-sized stone she carried in her pocket. "Also, I want to find Taja and Caz. Kazko is probably holding them as prisoners until he has a firm grip on the citizenry, and he's planning to kill the Princess and First Minister later when he no longer needs them."

She looked up at all of us. "I suggest that you get some sleep. We'll be flying out of here before dawn."

A few hours later, I woke in the dark hearing Tessia's voice. She and Hamlin were in the far corner, merely shadows in the starlight coming through the cave mouth. Her arms were around his thick furry neck, and he was looking at her adoringly. She was whispering in his ear. I could make out a word here and there, and I gathered that she was telling him of her love for him. She reminded him how as children they'd run through the woods, learning to hunt, and how she still felt grateful for his bravery, how when they were still children, he'd killed a giant bear who was attacking her. He and his lover Anja were the only siblings she'd ever had, and poor Anja had loved Hamlin so much she gave up everything for him—her honor, her friends, her city—to bargain for Hamlin's release from Ludek's prison. Ludek had tortured Hamlin for an entire month but Hamlin had never given in. Tessia understood how Hamlin, having seen the worst that men are capable of, no longer wanted to be a man, instead to live as a bear among the mountain aspens, and he would shelter in this cave no man would ever find.

As Tyrmiss continued to snore in the back chamber, Tessia's voice eventually grew quiet. She and the blonde bear sat next to each other. She rose and packed her kit, and said to me, "My friend, today we take back our home."

Chapter Thirteen

"Weapons check, men," Tessia said, spreading out a leather sheet with various weapons tucked in pockets. The blades shimmered, reflecting the torchlight in the sconce on the wall. There were Voprian swords, copper knives, bows and crossbows lined up in front of us.

"Where did these weapons come from, your Majesty?" I asked.

"Oh, I stashed them here a while back in case of emergency," she answered as if it were obvious.

"How is your Voprian, Alaric. Is it sharp and ready for use?" Tessia asked Alaric.

"Yes, Your Majesty. It's ready," he replied.

"What about your sidearm?" she said, looking at his belt which had leather pouches, but no dagger.

"A short sword would just weigh me down," he answered. "I have a dagger in my boot for emergencies. That's all I need."

"And you, Sergeant?" she asked, looking at Zrul. "I know that you lost your weapons during the transformations." When he spluttered, at a loss for words, she lifted her hand. "No need to explain, Sergeant. We all saw what happened. The loss of your weapons was not your fault. Now what weapons do you need?"

"A Voprian, my Queen," he answered, his eyes running over

the deadly inventory that lay before him. "And that dagger with the hand guard. And that copper knife with a sheathe for my boot. And the knuckle-club…"

"What about a bow?"

"No thank you," he answered. "Never been much good with one, Your Majesty. And I expect I'll be doing mostly close-up work, hand-to-hand, you know."

Tessia turned to me, "Norbert, you are not wearing any weapons other than the copper knife at your belt. What do you need?"

"Nothing, Your Majesty," I answered. "My wand is all I need."

Alaric and Zrul looked at each other with their mouths open in surprise. "Mage," Tessia reminded me, "We are not going home, we are infiltrating a city controlled by the enemy. There will be hundreds of Drekavac soldiers there. And you will be unarmed?"

"Your Majesty," Alaric said. "I'd like your permission to accompany my father as his bodyguard."

"No," Tessia answered quickly and firmly. "I need you to act as a provocateur among the street gangs and criminals in the city. You are the only one they'll listen to."

"But— but…" Alaric started to protest.

"Your father is much tougher than you realize, Alaric," Tessia assured him. "In the last war, he and I attacked the Wizard Ludek's castle. When we invaded his throne room, I killed his two bodyguards, but the wizard used magic to knock me out cold. Your father saved me by bringing down the ceiling on the wizard's head, burying him."

Alaric looked at me with puzzlement and respect. I realized that I'd never told him about that incident because it had been mostly luck that allowed me to fight Ludek, who was a much more powerful wizard than I'd ever be.

"Show him what you can do, Mage," Tessia ordered me.

I thought *this is very unfair. Am I to perform tricks on command like a trained monkey?*

"Very well," I said, thinking that a Queen's order is not to be ignored, so let's do the demonstration and be done with it. "Follow me," I said, walking through the cave mouth and into the moonlit meadow outside.

Tessia, Zrul, and Alaric stood beside me as I dramatically whipped out my wand, pointed it at an oak tree and said, *"linte merge mai departe!"*

A steady spray of hard black pellets streamed from the tip of my wand and bounced off the tree.

Zrul guffawed, "And what were those, Laddie? Peas? Those are very dangerous. Be careful where you point that thing. You could put someone's eye out with those pebbles."

Tessia looked at me with pure disappointment in her eyes. "A pea shooter? That's your weapon of choice? Seriously?"

"They are actually, lentils, Your Majesty," I muttered. "I didn't want to injure the oak." Somehow, I'd thought my display of magic would be more impressive than it evidently was.

Alaric said, "Please let me accompany him, Tessia. He is going to get himself killed."

Tessia ignored Alaric's lapse in protocol in calling her "Tessia." Afterall, they'd known each other since he was a boy and she was a serving wench at The Silver Pony.

"Absolutely not, Alaric," Tessia said, looking at me with narrow eyes. I knew she was assessing whether I was up to the job of gathering intelligence through my friends at the Silver Pony. Making a decision I was fit for duty, or at least that she had to believe I was, she added, "I trust your father to do his part in this attack, Alaric, just as I trust you and Zrul to do yours. Don't underestimate your father. I've seen him do amazing things armed only with a willow stick picked up off the ground and used as a wand. Now, get your kits ready. We'll be flying very soon."

I was first to enter the cave, and before the others came in, Tyrmiss, who had not watched my inept display, but evidently having listened, said, "She's right, you know, Norbert. You're not much good at magic tricks, but when you're fighting for love, you're the best warrior here, even better than Tessia. Tessia is at her best in battle. She lives for the thrill of fighting, the way a dancer lives for the dance. You, on the other hand, hate to fight, and you will do so only when something huge is at stake. Tessia fights for victory. You fight for love."

When I looked at her in complete surprise, she added, "And if you tell her I said that I will light your pants on fire."

And I knew she meant it.

As Alaric waited for Zrul to join him outside the cave, I gave him a hug. He looked at me. "Are you going to the Silver Pony Inn to look for my mother and sister?"

"Yes," I said. In the past when things became difficult, the inn is where Idella sought safety. With a five-year-old in tow, she'd be even more vulnerable, and she knew that Heikum and Femke would take her in.

Zrul came out of the cave carrying his kit and looking over his shoulder at the massive pile of brush and rock that disguised the entrance. "I'll never get used to walking in and out of a rock wall," he grumbled. He uneasily straddled the broom behind Alaric, and they lifted off the ground slowly. Once above the trees, Alaric banked sharply in the direction of Dragonja City, pointed the broom downwards, and they dove down the mountain toward home. Entering the city from the sky without being spotted would not be difficult, especially at night. The Drekavac guards on the walls would not be looking upwards expecting infiltrators; instead, they would be looking down at the fields below them.

Unbidden, the chances of success came to me. There were only four of us, five if you count Tyrmiss, and we were facing an army of hundreds, perhaps thousands. No one needed to tell us it was unlikely any of us would survive this attack on Dragonja City.

We watched Alaric and Zrul as they turned in the direction of the city. Tyrmiss was crouched beside me, her red eyes looking up at the sky where Alaric and Zrul had passed. I turned my head expectantly to Tessia, ready for the command to climb onto Tyrmiss' back.

"We need to wait a little while, Norbert," she said. "We don't want to collide with them in midair, nor do we want to call too much attention to our entrance into the city."

"One thing I ask, Your Majesty," I said, remembering the last war when she and I flew into Dragonja to take back the city from an interloper.

"What do you ask, Sir Norbert?" she asked, using my official rank.

"When we flew into the city last time, you and Tyrmiss dropped me off on a rooftop we thought was the Silver Pony, but as it turned out, it was the roof of a neighboring building. I dropped through the thatched roof right into the bedroom of a lady who was... entertaining a male friend. It was rather embarrassing for them and for me."

She laughed, "Really? This the first time I've heard this, Norbert. What happened?"

"Well, she attacked me with the man's belt, and I had to flee."

She thought this was hilarious. "Very well, Norbert. This time we'll try to deliver you to the correct roof."

We waited in silence for a few moments which seemed like an eternity. I turned to look at Tessia who was looking up at the sky, and I realized I felt a great deal of gratitude to her.

"Thank you, my Queen, for assigning me to go to The Silver Pony."

"You're welcome, Norbert."

No more needed to be said because she knew, undoubtedly, that the inn was the most likely place for my wife and daughter to be hiding in this turbulent time, and the duty the Queen had assigned me was a light one, gathering intelligence from the locals and telling them to be ready for an uprising. Tessia knew that my first priority was not restoring her kingdom, but rather the protection of my family. I didn't have to tell her this. She simply knew, as my friend, who I was and what I needed to do. I looked at this amazing woman beside me, a fierce warrior, a brilliant general, a kind ruler, and a devoted friend, and I loved her now more than ever.

Finally, Tessia swung up onto Tyrmiss' back, settled herself into the natural saddle in front of the wings and offered her hand to me. "It's time," she said simply, and pulled me up onto the dragon's back.

We rose slowly above the treetops, Tyrmiss pushing her wings down and back methodically. She made a wide turn to the southeast, kept rising until we were past the ridge that ran like a spine between the two peaks that towered over the region. Then, she tucked her wings at her sides, and we shot like an arrow through the moonless night, the spilled milk of the stars lighting our way as we dropped toward the city. Enough time had passed, so Alaric and Zrul were inside the city walls by now, gathering their wits and searching out their friends who were sure to join the insurrection once they knew the Dragonqueen had returned.

Once we were close to the city, we dropped quickly, then leveled off, as we passed over the thatched roofs of the buildings next to the open market square. I got ready to jump, but we were traveling so fast, I lost my nerve and hesitated. Tessia pushed me off my perch and I fell onto the building below.

"Wait!" I managed to squeal before I dropped onto the thatched roof. Instantly, I knew where I was. I crashed through the thatch and fell into the bedroom below, landing on the same bed where I'd landed six years before.

"What the..." the woman shouted, uncoupling herself from the man who had been on top of her. "Wait, I know you..." She pointed a finger at me. "You are... *You!* You did this to me before."

The man, whom I noticed was a different man than she'd been with years ago when I dropped in, looked at her in puzzlement. "You know this man?"

"Well, I..." she looked at me in bafflement. "I... I... I..."

"Who are you?" the man asked me.

I blushed, brushed myself off, cleared my throat, and not knowing what else to say, I portentously announced, "The Dragonqueen has returned. Get dressed and prepare for the revolution." And with as much dignity as I could muster, I left the bedroom, ran down the stairs and into the alley behind the building.

The inn was dark, and everyone was asleep. I quietly went up the stairs and knocked softly on the door of Heikum and Femke's bedroom.

Heikum opened the door, rubbing his eyes, "What the...?" He peered closer at me in the dark hall. "Is that you, Mage?"

"Hello, Heikum," I said and waited while he adjusted to my surprise appearance.

"So, you're back," he said. "My friend, a lot of things have changed in the couple of months you've been gone."

"Yes, we'll talk about the situation in the city later, but first, where are my wife and daughter?"

He held up a hand to reassure me, "They are safe, sleeping in your old room down the hall."

I felt a surge of relief flooding over me. I realized I hadn't allowed myself to feel my fear for their safety. I hurried down the hall and lightly knocked on the door. I heard the voice of Idella, saying, "Who's there?"

"Your husband."

She opened the door immediately and went into my arms. We held each other for a long time.

"Idella, the Dragonqueen is back. We're taking the city tonight. Can we go downstairs and talk with Heikum and Femke about what is going on in the city?"

I looked at our daughter, Ena, who was sleeping sweetly in the bed. Her breath made a small high sound as she slept, and I thought of a baby bird in a nest. Thank the Goddess she was safe.

Idella and I went downstairs, and we sat with Heikum and Femke at a table in front of the bar. I looked around the room where I'd spent so much time drinking ale, singing the old songs, laughing with friends. Nothing had changed. And yet, everything had changed.

I quickly recounted what had happened with Tessia and our quest, ending with the fact that right now, Tessia was in the castle planning to kill Kazko while Tyrmiss was searching for the three dragons to free them. I added that Alaric and Zrul were in the streets instigating rebellion.

"Tell me what's happened in the city while I was gone," I prompted.

Heikum and Femke nodded toward Idella, indicating she should speak first.

"First, husband," Idella began. "Our daughter is safe. You needn't worry about her. Despite the great unrest in the city, she's had sufficient food and playmates while you've been gone. We left our house and sought safety behind the city walls when the first rumor of an invading army reached us. Heikum and Femke," she nodded to our friends. "Took us in as they've done in the past. I am so grateful to you." Her eyes filled with tears.

Heikum nodded and Femke said, "Of course, my dear. We would never turn away a friend."

Idella smiled at them and continued, "The invasion happened

157

very quickly. Kazko and two of his captains arrived on dragons. They landed in the market square and announced that the Dragonqueen was dead, and he was the new ruler of Dragonja. He said if we bowed to him as the ruler, then he would treat us with mercy. I was surprised that so many people bowed to him immediately. I stayed inside the inn so I wouldn't have to bow." She glanced at Heikum who was looking down at his hands. I picked up the signal that Heikum was one of the people who bowed to Kazko.

"If you thought the Queen was dead, and you were faced with a new ruler, what choice did you have?" he asked softly.

"The Dragonqueen is very much alive," I said firmly. "And right now, she's in the castle hunting the pretender. You are going to have to make a decision. Are you with your Queen or against her?"

Heikum and Femke quickly assured me that they loved Queen Tessia, and if they'd known she was still alive they never would have bowed to the pretender. Reassured, I signaled to Idella she should continue.

"Many of us were surprised at how easy it was for Kazko to take over the city," she said, shaking her head in disbelief. "Kazko took up residence in the castle. After a few days, his captains opened the city gates and let his soldiers enter the city. Kazko demanded that the Queen's soldiers swear allegiance to him—which they did."

Femke said, "And then Kazko's captains started issuing proclamations."

"What kind of proclamations?" I asked.

When Femke hesitated, Idella answered, "At first it was simple things we were already doing, such as honoring the Gods by not working every seventh day and taking disputes to the magistrates rather than fighting with each other, and having watchmen walk through the streets at night to keep the peace. But gradually, the proclamations became strange and onerous."

"Like what?" I asked.

"One proclamation ordered us to recognize Kazko's ancestors as gods," Femke said.

"Did the soldiers loot the city?" I asked.

"There was no outright looting," Idella said slowly and then looked at Heikum.

"Kazko's officials issued a proclamation that all innkeepers must provide food and drink to soldiers." Heikum blurted out angrily. "Soldiers were allowed to set the price for anything they consumed which of course gave them a license to loot." He clenched his fist. "The soldiers are drinking us into poverty. We cannot survive much longer."

"Soldiers are forcing families out of their homes. There are families with children sleeping outside the gates," Femke said, tears in her eyes.

"What else?" I asked.

Femke said quietly, "A few weeks ago, girls started disappearing."

"Disappearing?"

"Yes," she said. "Soldiers would see a pretty girl in the marketplace, follow her home, and arrest her, claiming that she was seen stealing. They would take her into the castle, and the girl would never come back."

"It wasn't just girls," Idella said. "Young matrons as well. I haven't been out of the inn in weeks, and when soldiers are drinking here, I stay upstairs. Out of sight." She dropped her eyes, and I knew she was remembering what happened to her in the last war.

"I've heard of the soldiers taking a few boys as well," Femke said. There was a rising anger coming from these two women. Heikum sat silent, no doubt still feeling the shame of having welcomed the pretender into the city, but I knew his anger would soon rise as well.

"Thank you," I said, "It sounds like it is the right time for a rebellion. We'll use the inn as a hospital to take care of our wounded."

I reached into the leather pouch on my belt and took out three small gold coins. Heikum's eyes lit up. Since he charged one copper coin for a tankard of ale, these gold coins represented half a year of income for him. I slid them across the table to him.

"Heikum, I want you to water down your ale and give free draughts to anyone who supports the Queen."

"I've never watered down my ale in my whole life," he harrumphed.

I ignored his lie and said, "Please water down your ale for the next couple of days, Heikum. We don't need drunken rebels running through the streets."

I turned to Femke and Idella, "We are going to need to feed the rebels over the next few days. How many soup cauldrons do you have?'

"Four, and I can borrow more from my friends," Femke answered. "I can have enough soup to feed an army ready by noontime."

"And how much bread can you make?" I asked Idella.

"I have two stoves behind the inn and plenty of charcoal. I can have fifty loaves ready by noon," she answered.

"Wonderful! Please give a bowl of soup and a slab of bread to anyone who says that the Dragonqueen has returned."

"Even Drekavac soldiers?" Femke asked.

"Especially Drekavac soldiers," I said. "Zrul is turning them to our side as we speak."

As I left the inn, the sun was showing itself over the East Gate of the city. The market square was in chaos. I hurried past a woman beating a Drekavac soldier with a chair as he held his hands up to protect his face. A farmer was threatening two other soldiers with a pitchfork. I heard a familiar rough shout and looking across the square, I saw Zrul leading a squad of

Drekavac soldiers. They aggressively engaged a group of confused soldiers who surrendered almost immediately. I walked up to Zrul and said quietly in his ear, "I used the Queen's gold to buy as much food and ale as your men need. Send your wounded to the Silver Pony Inn. They will be taken care of there." He nodded and went back to shouting orders at his soldiers.

On the other side of the square, I saw Alaric, a gang of rough-looking boys and girls right behind him, charging toward the inner gate that protected the castle. Two of the bigger boys gave a lift to a girl who scrambled to the top of the gate and dropped to the other side. A few moments later, the gate was open, and the gang of street kids charged into the castle courtyard, followed by Zrul and his soldiers.

I followed them into the castle, wondering where Tessia and Tyrmiss were. The contingent of Drekavac soldiers following Zrul had grown to several dozen and were skirmishing with Kazko's soldiers in front of the large wooden door of the keep. Since all the soldiers wore the same uniform, it was impossible for me to tell who was on our side and who was opposing the rebellion, but Zrul seemed to have no trouble sizing up the loyalties of each soldier, so I ran past him and opened the door of the keep. I was guessing that Kazko was holed up there because it was the most fortified of the buildings. I ran through the keep looking for Caz or Princess Taja, but all I saw were soldiers running around. Since I looked like a civilian, they didn't pay any heed to me. After a quick run through the keep, I was sure that this was not the place where Taja or Caz were being kept. I looked out the window and saw across the courtyard the old dungeon which hadn't been used in years. And closer on my right, the tall tower where Tessia had had her residence and on a floor below, the dragon lair she'd constructed for Tyrmiss.

Coming out of the keep, I saw my old friend Mina, the Red Witch I'd trained as a healer. She asked me where she was needed. I told her that the Silver Pony was being used as a hospital. There was plenty of food and drink there which the Queen had already paid for. She nodded, signaled a young man who was her assistant, and they ran through the castle gate on their way to the Silver Pony.

I made my way through the skirmishing soldiers to the door of the high tower. I took out my wand, waved it over the lock while saying a simple spell and the door opened.

Entering the first hall, I could hear a ringing noise coming from the upper stories, a cacophonous humming music I recognized as coming from the clashing of Voprian swords. This, I remembered, is why they call them *singing swords*. I ran up the winding stone stairs to the second level which was empty of people. The third, fourth and fifth levels were also empty. The soldiers and staff seem to have fled once the fighting started, I thought. On the seventh floor, I found out what had frightened everyone out of the tower.

Tessia, armed with her long Voprian blade in her right hand and a short sword in her left, was defending herself against a roomful of Drekavac soldiers. Kazko stood toward the back of his small regiment, his sword drawn as he shouted orders at his soldiers. This was the first time I'd seen Kazko, and I was surprised by how unimpressive he was. A short, thin man with a bald head and narrow features, he seemed more like a clerk than a king. Moreover, unlike Tessia, he was behind his soldiers, letting them do the fighting. Tessia was holding her own against the small army in front of her, moving so quickly that they didn't know where she would strike next. Feint, jab, lunge, slice, her Voprian was flying so fast it was just a purple blur of motion. At this rate, though, she would wear herself out, and if she slowed down, they would rush her, and the fight would be over.

Tessia saw me out of the corner of her eye and yelled, "Mage, use your wand!"

Following her order, I whipped out my wand and pointed it at the soldier directly in front of her, and…

A stream of wet lentil sprouts sprayed from the tip of my wand and splattered on the soldier's face. He was so surprised, he lifted his sword hand to his face to wipe the mess from his eyes, giving Tessia a chance to slice off his head which flew through the air and hit the soldier next to him. Meanwhile, the soldiers behind him who couldn't have seen Tessia's lightning move, looked at me in horror. They seemed to think that I had chopped off a man's head by spraying sprouts at him.

Several of the soldiers backed to the doorway behind them, turned and ran. The remaining soldiers in the room, seeing that Tessia was about to kill them, dropped their swords, fell on their knees and bowed their heads, hoping to be spared.

Tessia, out of breath, turned to me and smiled, "What was *that*, Norbert?"

"The lentils must have sprouted overnight," I said, and she laughed. I added, "I told you lentil sprouts are good for you." I looked around the room. "Where did Kazko go?"

"He must have run out the doorway with his men," she said. "Follow me."

She looked at the soldiers kneeling in front of her. "Do you swear allegiance to my crown?" She asked, her chest heaving from exertion. As each one nodded and murmured agreement, she said, "You are forgiven for your disobedience. You shall fight for your Queen now. Follow me."

As the soldiers stood up, confused to have gotten off so easily. Tessia turned and ran out the doorway followed by the soldiers and me, but instead of going down the stairs to follow Kazko, she climbed a flight up to the dragon lair.

Chapter Fourteen

As we entered the dragon lair, I saw something I will never forget. Tyrmiss sat on her haunches close to the wide opening, the landscape behind her sloping up to the mountains, the Dragonja River a blue and white ribbon stretching away to the south. Tyrmiss was weeping. In front of her lay three dead dragons, each one wrapped in chains and each one with a spear through one of its hearts.

As Tyrmiss looked up and saw Tessia, a low moan started in her throat, growing louder and louder until it was a rumble like thunder, so loud it shook the very stones of the castle. The sound grew louder until I had to cover my ears with my hands, but even then, the sound penetrated my bones, and I could feel her grief like a vise on my chest.

Tessia too started a loud wail that was the sound of an entire kingdom, an entire nation which was grieving for something so beautiful that the destruction of it was a high crime against the Goddess Nilene Herself.

As Tyrmiss's deep keening died down, Tessia went to her and put her arms around the great head of the dragon and their tears mixed and fell on the floor in a rivulet which ran to the opening and streamed down the sides of the stones. I remembered that dragon tears are full of magic and in ancient times were considered medicinal, and I wondered whether these tears would help our battered kingdom heal from these terrible times we were living through.

"Why would Kazko do such a thing? Why kill these dragons?" I asked Tessia.

"I'm not sure," Tessia said through her tears. "Perhaps the dragons refused to leave with him, and he didn't want us to have them."

"We would have set them free," Tyrmiss wailed, and she started sobbing again. Then, suddenly, she stopped and lifted her head, catching Tessia by surprise, "Wait," the dragon said. "What is that sound?"

Tessia looked around, wiping tears from her eyes, "I don't hear anything."

I listened hard, but all I heard were the scattered sounds of the battle winding down in the city below. Then, I remembered a dragon sometimes hears dreams.

Tyrmiss slowly moved between two of the dead dragons, leaning close to their bellies. "This one," she said, excitedly. "This female is pregnant. The pups are still alive!"

She turned to me, "Norbert, save the young ones!"

I walked over to the dead dragon and put my hand on her belly. I thought I could feel heartbeats, but it was hard to say, dragonhide being so thick.

"YOU HAVE TO SAVE THE BABIES!" Tyrmiss roared.

"Hand me your short Voprian sword," I said to the soldier closest to me.

The soldier looked at Tessia who nodded, and he passed his short sword to me handle first.

"I need to find Caz and Taja," Tessia said, moving toward the door.

"Go," I said. "I'll handle this situation."

Without being ordered to, the soldiers followed their Queen out the doorway. I was surprised by how quickly the soldiers had changed allegiance from Kazko to her, but I shouldn't have been surprised because I had seen many times that she had a natural ability to lead. Both men and women were drawn to her, sensing that she was serving something greater than her own glory. To follow Tessia was to serve the good and true, and deep down, this is what we all want, to make our lives mean something important.

Turning my attention to the dead dragon in front of me, I ran my hand over the area about two-thirds down the body where I knew the uterus lay. I'd never studied the anatomy of dragons, but I remembered the treatise on dragon anatomy I'd come across in the library.

"Where are you going?" Tyrmiss asked, panicked.

"To do some research!" I shouted over my shoulder. I ran down the stone stairs to the library, quickly found the oaken box and gently opened it to reveal the vellum manuscript. Although most of the pages were dust, as I skimmed the legible passages, I found a few things about dragon anatomy that were helpful, mainly though, I was surprised and disgusted by Zakkik's disdain for dragons. His arrogance toward these magnificent creatures and his recommendation to King Milon that the creatures be eradicated made me resolve to do everything I could to save the dragonlings and ensure that the species survived. I ran back up the stairs, and outside Tyrmiss's door, I stopped and composed myself. If I was going to help these babies, then I needed to trust that the Goddess had given me the skills I needed. I said a short prayer and walked into the dragon lair.

Tyrmiss had told me that dragons are closely related to snakes, and Zakkik's treatise confirmed that the anatomy had many similarities. Luckily, snakes had long fascinated me, and through the years, I'd dissected many types in order to learn more about them. As the treatise made clear, dragons give birth to eggs with a leathery shell, each containing a young one that is almost fully formed. Then the mother buries the eggs in warm sand until they're ready to hatch. Tyrmiss had told me that she came from a litter of six, so I was guessing that I would need to carefully slice open the mother's belly, remove the half-dozen eggs and put them in a warm dark place.

The shimmering purple blade easily sliced through the dead mother's tough belly-hide. I pulled back the layers of skin and saw what was probably the uterus, although the black and green fluids disguised the anatomy. I asked Tyrmiss to use her talons to hold open the incision, and I reached into the open belly and pulled out the end of the uterus, or at least what I hoped was the uterus. Using the tip of the Voprian, I made a small incision and very slowly took a look inside, then another incision, repeating until I could see the dark green eggs, each one the size of a man's head, clustered around what looked like a single branching fallopian tube. Using the Voprian, I gently detached each egg and set it aside on a blanket. After I put the last one down, I counted five eggs. I was heart-broken to see that three of them had been damaged by the surgery.

"Will they live?" Tyrmiss asked me, letting go of the mother dragon's belly-skin.

"I have no idea," I said. "It depends on how developed they are."

"I can hear them dreaming," she said, looking at the eggs with awe.

"We need a large barrel of warm sand," I said, looking around.

"I'll be right back," Tyrmiss said, leaping out the opening in the wall and flying down toward the river.

I put another blanket over the eggs to keep them warm. In a little while, Tyrmiss returned. She had a barrel in her talons and when she scooted it across the stone floor, I could tell it was heavy. She dumped out the sand on the floor. I laid the barrel on its side and cut it in half with the sword. I put a layer of sand in the bottom of the barrel and laid the two eggs a hand's breadth apart and covered them with sand.

"Will they be warm enough?" Tyrmiss asked.

"I think so," I said. "But I don't know how long it will take for them to hatch. All we can do now is wait."

Tyrmiss was leaning over the barrel, looking at the sand.

"How many of them are dreaming?" I asked.

"Two," she said. "We have two baby dragons."

Tessia found Caz and Princess Taja in their respective quarters in the high tower. The Princess said she'd not been harmed although Kazko had told her that Tessia was dead, so she'd been in mourning for weeks. Once she saw Tessia and heard the tale of her adventure, Taja quickly regained her good spirits.

Caz, on the other hand, had been treated roughly by Kazko and his men. Caz refused to help the usurpers in managing the kingdom. May the Goddess bless him, he stubbornly stayed silent in the face of their interrogations, not letting them know the location of the Queen's treasure or the sources of income, and they'd beat him mercilessly as a result. However, once they discovered Caz's meticulous records in the library, as well as his perfectly detailed accounting ledgers in his office, they didn't need him anymore, so they left him alone. Still, he would need time to recover from the wounds and trauma he'd suffered.

As for Kazko, he'd simply disappeared. Apparently, the last time anyone had seen him was in the high tower when he'd slipped out while Tessia and I were busy fighting the soldiers. No one we could find knew where the spry little king had gone. I shared my suspicion with the Queen that he'd used magic to fly out of the castle and back to his kingdom of Skarsland. I wondered if the weather witches had somehow helped him, but for the time being at least, his whereabouts were a mystery.

Also, the whereabouts of Bastian and Zamarrra were a mystery. The last Tessia and I knew, they were flying to parlay with the Renetu tribes in the hope that they would rise up against the throne of Osterbo in Skarsland. In the weeks since our return to Dragonja, we'd expected to see refugees showing up on our eastern shores, fleeing a civil war, but there'd been no news from the fishermen in the east, nor from the southern ports.

Meanwhile, the Kingdom of Dragonja and Bekla was in terrible shape.

"In less than a year, the nation has been ravaged by a drought, a flood, an occupation and a war," Heikum said to me as he drew an ale for a thirsty soldier. Although it was evening, the inn was almost empty.

"No one except the soldiers have any money," he said, eyeing the soldier in front of him. "And most of them are handing over their wages to their families."

"I'm a bachelor," the soldier said defensively and slunk with his ale to a corner.

"There's little food to be had," Femke said, coming in from the kitchen, wiping her hands on a dishcloth. "Every day, my helpers go out to the countryside to buy turnips and greens, but there's little the farmers will part with. We haven't seen any meat in months."

"I heard that farmers are doing the best they can to plant late season crops," I said, trying to interject some hope into the conversation. I took a long draught of my ale and looked at Femke. "The merchants and craftspeople are recovering, but it's going to take time for stability to return."

Femke tried to support my attempt at optimism. "I hear there's food coming in from the farms and pastures of the Iskar Valley," she said, nodding.

"Ya," Heikum said, his face flushing with anger. "That fellow Gaspar is getting rich by bringing food from there."

I remembered Gaspar, the trader we'd met in the mining camp. It seemed that despite my threatening him with Sergeant Zrul, Gaspar had been profiteering after all.

"Well, at least the brigands have been brought to heel," Heikum grumbled. "During the occupation, no one was safe within the city walls or without. Queen Tessia is not going to put up with any nonsense. She's assigned Zrul and your son Alaric to put together squads of trustworthy Drekavacs to patrol the streets and roads at night."

Indeed, Mina had told me that men and Drekavacs were being brought daily to the hospital with deep lacerations and head wounds. She'd actually lost one patient who died as she was trying to staunch the bleeding in his belly. There were specific patterns to the wounds which she recognized as the pitiless work of Zrul and his minions, and she worried that Queen Tessia had put too much trust in her former drill sergeant. I didn't mention to Mina or Heikum that I was worried Alaric might be part of these vigilante night squads as well.

O nce the countryside was safe, Idella and I moved back to our little house with Alaric and Ena and began cleaning and restoring. Idella rebuilt her ovens which had been damaged by the floods, and Alaric and I patched the roof and repaired the doors knocked in by looters. We had a lot of cleaning and repairing to do from damage done by squatters, but within weeks our home was humming, much as it had before the floods. Ena followed me around the house, helping with the chores and pretending to boss everyone around the way her mother did.

We were glad to resume our lives. Each evening, Idella and her helpers kneaded enough dough to make fifty loaves, and early in the morning, they went to the ovens and made the banked fires rise, and when the temperature was high enough, they slid the loaves into the ovens. When they were brown, they took the loaves out, put them in a wooden box, made a delivery to the Silver Pony, and then took the rest of the loaves to Idella's stall in the market. Idella's was a small but successful business, and she was thinking about building more ovens to meet the growing demand for her product. She was hoping that once honey and spices were again available, she could resume making pastries, which had a higher profit margin than bread. I was proud of her skill as a baker and her head for business, and like everyone else in the city, I loved eating her loaves and looked forward to the time she started making pastries again.

Working on the house with Alaric, my fears he'd become like Sergeant Zrul were allayed. Alaric had evolved into an effective officer in Tessia's guard. His squad had a reputation for being tough on criminals, but gentle with the populace, and walking through the city with my son was a joy. Everyone—shopkeepers, craftspeople, children, and farmers—smiled and greeted him as we passed. I envied his ease with people, and it reminded me of my youth as a shireman when people were glad to see me arrive in their village with my wares and my stories of their distant kin.

Nowadays, people were respectful of me, but kept their distance. I had the impression that some of my exploits in the two wars had been exaggerated in the telling and retelling, and people were afraid that I might drop a ceiling on them or decapitate them with a spray of lentil sprouts. However, the distance people kept from me had its benefits. As one of Queen Tessia's chief advisors, I didn't want to be in the position of having to fend off requests for favors or special treatment from the throne. If someone wanted a favor from the sovereign, then he or she needed to apply through Caz's office and not to approach one of her advisors on the street.

Over the months following the Queen's return, castle life gradually went back to normal as well. Mina, who was now both a Green Mage and a Red Witch, as well as the chief healer in the kingdom, personally saw that Caz's injuries were well cared for. His limp gradually lessened until it was barely perceptible. The right side of his face, which had been mangled by the beatings that Kazko's thugs had administered, had to be rebuilt, but no one was a better surgeon than Mina, and Caz gained back most of his former good looks. Occasionally, when he reached for a document on his desk, or stood up from his chair, I would see him wince, but he never complained, and the Queen, grateful for his resistance to the usurper, treated her First Minister as the brave hero that he was.

And Princess Taja seemed happy as well. She checked on Caz regularly and I noticed that there seemed to be a special closeness, even a tenderness, between them. Most of the time, though, the Princess busied herself with repairs to the castle. Lightning, flood, and war had damaged a number of the walls and rooms, and she oversaw the masons, carpenters, woodcarvers, and weavers with a zeal that inspired them to do their best work. Her love for Tessia was palpable, and the Queen thrived on the attention from her kind and beautiful wife. I was glad to see that the tension between them seemed to have been lessened by Tessia's absence. I convinced myself that theirs was a good marriage, as was mine. But looking back on it, I realize that I was lying to myself, and so was Tessia. In fact, our wives were coping with our neglect as best they could.

However, the one who changed the most after the war was Tyrmiss. She doted on the eggs until one night she heard a scratching coming from the barrel, and when she checked, she found two tiny dragons, each one double the size of a man's hand. Tyrmiss fell in love with them immediately and cared for them as if they'd come from her own body. I came by every few days to check on them.

One morning after a meeting with Caz and Tessia, I visited Tyrmiss's lair in the high tower.

"Hello, Norbert," the dragon said to me pleasantly. She was holding a large roasted fish in her talons and was tearing small chunks off and dropping them into the barrel in front of her. The two dragonlings were happily swallowing the chunks whole and looking up at their adoptive mother with adoration.

172

Although I'd grown used to seeing Tyrmiss pleasant and happy, I was still sometimes surprised that she was taking to her new role as mother so easily.

"How are they doing?" I asked, smiling at the beatific scene.

"Oh, they're doing fine," she answered, pausing between mouthfuls. "Banos had a little indigestion yesterday, and he threw up his dinner. But he seems fine today. And Rozae is right as fire today, as usual."

I wondered whether it was true with dragons, as it was with men and Drekavacs, that the females tend to be healthier and live longer than the males.

"May I check them?" I asked. One of the first rules every healer learns is to always check with the mother before reaching for her baby. A mother's love is both beautiful and dangerous, especially with dragons.

"Of course," Tyrmiss said pleasantly, but I saw her eyes narrow and turn red for just a moment before going back to blue. It seemed safe for me to proceed with the examination as long as I was careful.

I picked up Banos and held him in my arms as I would a human baby. He seemed to like it and gurgled up at me, his talons clenched next to his face. Tyrmiss had named him Banos Gentleheart, for her father. His eyes were blue like Tyrmiss's and I thought that when threatened they would certainly turn into red slits like hers. His wings were still clenched tight to his sides, unfurled, and the spikes that would run down the back of his neck were still only bumps. I was very aware that I knew little of the development of dragons. I stroked the purple scales under his chin, and he purred.

"He seems healthy to me," I said putting him back in the barrel of sand. "When do you expect his wings to unfurl?"

Tyrmiss shook her head, "Norbert, it's been ten thousand years since I've seen a baby dragon. As I remember, they grow in spurts, very quickly the first year, then slowly for a number of years, then a spurt at around twenty, then very slowly over the centuries. Dragons reach full maturity at the age of two thousand years. At that age we're considered adults and can get married and vote in councils…" Her voice trailed off, and a terrible sadness came over the room. I realized she was talking about the dragon civilization which had died out thousands of years ago, destroyed by men.

I picked up Rozae, The Gifted One. She seemed healthy as well, more alert than her brother, but with the same sweet personality. Of the two, Rozae seemed the braver, trying to scramble out of the crib; whereas Banos was content to sit and watch his sister with large blue eyes. I could see that Tyrmiss was taking excellent care of her two young charges. As a healer, I've seen many babies of various species, and I could tell when a baby was getting plenty of love. Reluctantly, I put Rozae back in the barrel next to her brother. I could have spent all day holding them.

"Do you have to teach them to fly, or do they develop that skill on their own?" I asked.

"I'm not sure," Tyrmiss said, sounding slightly disturbed that she hadn't thought of this aspect of mothering. "I suppose they'll learn it on their own, but they'll need gentle encouragement from their mother." She turned her head and looked at the wide opening of the lair. The drop from here was high enough to kill a dragon. "I suppose I'll need a fence of some kind in front of the opening."

I liked the fact that Tyrmiss was referring to herself as their mother. The adult and the babies were bonding nicely, I thought.

"I'll talk to Caz," I said. "He'll send over a carpenter to build a safety fence. Is there anything else you need?"

"Well, I have trouble going down to the river to catch fish. I don't like leaving the little ones alone."

"I'll talk to the cook about bringing up a large salmon or pike for you each day. Also, I'll see that four pails of fresh water

174

are brought here every day." I looked at her and realized there was something different about the dragon. Even though she was tired, she seemed to be positively glowing. "May I ask, Tyrmiss, how are you feeling?"

The dragon looked at me with puzzlement. "I feel..." She hesitated and cocked her head. "I feel happy for the first time since Rilla died."

At home, Idella and I were busy with our own little one. Ena had just turned six and was quickly becoming a child who knew her own mind. She accompanied her mother everywhere, helping to mix the pails of water and flour, kneading the dough and gathering charcoal for the ovens. She was fond of ordering her mother to add more flour to the mix or to make the oven hotter. Idella generally indulged her, treating the child as if she were in charge, but occasionally Idella had to put her foot down.

"Stop telling my helpers what to do, Ena," she would say. "It's rude for you to talk to adults in that manner."

"Well," little Ena would answer, her fists on her hips. "She was putting wood in the oven instead of charcoal! Can you imagine? Wood doesn't burn nearly hot enough to bake bread."

Her mother looked down at her. "You must be more courteous and respectful. No one likes to be ordered around."

"You order me around," Ena said, accusingly.

"That's different."

"Why's that different?"

"Because I'm your mother."

"Well, I'm your daughter which makes me the daughter of the boss. So, I get to order people around."

"It doesn't work that way..."

The two of them would bicker endlessly until I had to leave the house. I usually walked into the city and stopped at the Silver Pony. I would stand next to Heikum as he drew draughts of ale for customers. Ever since I paid him three gold coins to set up a hospital in the inn, he'd given me free ale, but today I had to be careful not to drink too much. Idella gave me the mean-eye when I stumbled home at night belching, slurring my words.

"How's your daughter?" he asked, making conversation as he worked.

"Bossy as ever."

He laughed. "Yes, girls are that way." He and Femke had raised two daughters who were now married and living in Kladd City on the coast. "I like grandchildren much more than children. With grandchildren, you can enjoy them as long as you like, and when they become a nuisance, you can hand them back to their mothers."

I laughed. "Your lessons in parenting are a constant inspiration, my friend." I lifted my tankard to him and took a long gulp.

A Drekavac soldier came in the front door, looked around the room and headed straight for me.

"Meister Mage," he began breathlessly. "Your wife said you'd be here. The Queen has sent me to find you."

As I ran for the inner gate, I heard a terrible roar and a ball of flame burst out of one of the windows of the high tower.

Tyrmiss, I thought. *Something must have happened to the dragonlings!*

I charged through the heavy doors of the royal chamber without waiting to be announced. Clearly, there was an emergency happening, and there was no time to waste. Tessia was standing in front of her throne. Taja was beside her with terror written on her face. Caz and Zrul stood with their backs to me, listening to their Queen give instructions.

Tessia, seeing me, said, "What do you know of this, Norbert?"

"Know of what, Your Majesty?"

176

"This… This kidnapping!" she answered.

And I thought, *By the Goddess, Tyrmiss will kill every human being in the kingdom if her babies have been taken.*

Tessia turned to Zrul. "Have your men search Windkeep from top to bottom. If you don't find the dragonlings here, widen your search to the city. Also, tighten the security at all the city gates. Don't let any package or bundle leave the city without being searched. Find those little ones!"

As Zrul hurried out the door with two soldiers behind him, Tessia turned next to Caz. "Where is Tyrmiss?"

"I… I… I don't…" Caz stammered.

Just then a soldier ran in, bowed his head quickly to the Queen and said, "Your Majesty, the dragon has taken the cook and carried him up to the top of the second tower. The man is screaming in terror."

We ran over to the window and saw Tyrmiss holding the man upside down from the roof of the next tower. She was holding one foot in her mouth while he screamed for help.

Tessia turned to me, "Norbert, get your broom and fly up there and try to talk reason to Tyrmiss. Tell her she is not helping things by terrorizing our cook."

I nodded, and as I ran to the storage room where the witch's brooms had been stored, I wondered *Why is Tyrmiss attacking the cook?* The broom carried me out the window and over the space between the two towers. Tyrmiss saw me coming. The slits of her eyes were the reddest I'd ever seen.

"Mistress Dragon," I said as I flew slowly toward her. "It is too early in the day to be killing cooks, don't you think?"

Tyrmiss swung the cook toward the spire and once he was clinging tightly to the haycock, she opened her mouth and released him. I hovered in the air in front of her, aware that if she decided to, she could easily light me on fire.

"They took my babies, Norbert," she said, eyeing the terrified cook.

"I know, Tyrmiss. As we speak, the Queen's soldiers are tearing apart the city looking for them."

The dragon scanned the city below her. People were in the marketplace looking up at her, pointing.

"How did it happen, Tyrmiss?"

The dragon looked at me through the red slits of her eyes, obviously trying to decide whether she should trust this particular human. "A salmon was brought to me by a soldier. He said it was gift from the Queen's cook. I ate it, shared some of it with Rozae and Banos, and then I fell asleep. The fish must have had a sleeping potion in it. When I woke up, my babies were gone."

"Did you know the soldier who brought the fish?"

She shook her head. "But when I find him, I will roast him slowly."

"You realize this cook you are terrorizing is almost certainly innocent."

She nodded, "Yes, if he knew anything at all, he would have told me by now."

"I'm going to take him down to safety and then Tessia and I will meet you in your lair, alright? If we're going to find your babies, we need to be clear-headed and move quickly."

Since she didn't object, I flew toward the poor cook who grabbed the shaft of my broom and hung there. After leaving him safely on one of the lower roofs, I flew to the entrance of Tyrmiss's lair. Tessia must have been watching from the window because she was already there with Caz, Princess Taja, and Zrul. As I joined them, Alaric flew through the outside entrance on his broom, followed by Tyrmiss, slightly calmer than she'd been, but still very dangerous.

Tessia was speaking to Zrul, "I need you to stay in Windkeep and guard the city. I made the mistake earlier this year of leaving our defenses weak, giving Kazko a chance to invade. Keep the defenses here strong. Let's not make the same mistake again."

Zrul saluted and Tessia turned to Caz and the Princess. "As

before, I'm leaving the two of you as my regents in the city. Zrul will report to both of you. I'm not sure how long I'll be gone, so you are empowered to make any decisions that are needed."

Tessia didn't seem to notice the slight smile on Caz's face as he glanced at the Princess. As had happened before, I had a bad feeling about leaving the two of them in charge, but Tessia was in no mood to have her decisions questioned, so I let go of the slight misgiving I had. I guessed it was based on nothing more than my growing uneasiness when I was around Caz. As for the Princess, I would have trusted her with my life, as I've done many times with Tessia.

"Alaric," the Queen said. "I need you to get on your broom and patrol the farmlands and pastures around the city. Try to find out from the locals which direction the kidnappers went. My guess is that they used magic to escape. Perhaps a broom. Someone must have seen something. If we know which direction they took, then we'll have a clue as to who took them and where they went."

"Could the little ones be dead already?" Tyrmiss asked in a flat voice.

Tessia shook her head. "If they were going to kill the dragonlings, they would have done it here. Why go through the trouble of kidnapping them unless they want them alive?"

"Why would they steal the little ones?" Princess Taja asked. "They're just babies. It will be centuries before they're big enough to have any value, right? Have the dragonlings been stolen just as collector items?"

"Not necessarily," Tessia answered her wife. "If someone has a long-term strategy for conquering another kingdom, then raising dragons from infancy would be a smart thing to do. The dragonlings would develop an attachment to their caretakers and they could possibly be used as offensive weapons, but as you say, it would take centuries. Whoever did this is building a future dynasty."

179

"So, my babies are going to be raised to be war-dogs?" Tyrmiss asked, smoke coming from her nostrils. "Or perhaps they will be put on display to entertain guests like trick ponies? Or perhaps," she asked, her rumbling voice breaking into sobs, "My babies will be killed and stuffed as trophies?"

"Tyrmiss," Tessia said evenly, "We are going to do everything we possibly can to bring back your babies, but I need for you to stay calm. Can you do this?"

After Tyrmiss nodded, Tessia turned to me. "Is it possible that Kazko is behind this?"

"Very possibly," I answered. "He could have hired someone from the city who could walk in and out of the gate without being noticed. A trader, for example."

Alaric and I looked at each other. "Gaspar!" We said at the same time.

Tessia asked who Gaspar was, and Alaric explained how we'd met the trader at the copper mines on the first leg of our quest.

"He always seemed a little too much in love with money," I said. "I had to threaten him with the wrath of Zrul in order to discourage the trader from price gouging during the famine."

"But who would he sell the dragonlings to?" Caz asked.

Tessia said, "It's been months since Bastian and Zamarrra left to parlay with the Renetu tribes. They planned to encourage the tribes to attack Osterbo, the capital of Skarsland."

"Could they have been successful?" Caz asked.

"There was certainly no major war in Skarsland." Tessia answered. "If there had been, then we would have had refugees showing up on our shores. So, it's possible that there was a bloodless coup, but…" Tessia's voice trailed off.

"But it's more likely that Bastian and Zamarrra were unsuccessful, and Kazko is back on his throne in Osterbo, causing this mischief," Caz said, finishing the Queen's thought.

"So, what is the plan?" I asked.

"Alaric," Tessia instructed. "As I said, make a tour of the

countryside. Try to find this Gaspar character. If he took the dragonlings, he's probably already handed them off by now. Find out who his buyer was."

"Caz and Taja," Tessia said, turning to her regents. "Announce to the castle staff that you will be ruling the kingdom while I'm away. Mention that Zrul will be in charge of defending the city and maintaining order. His name will discourage any ruffians or knaves from trying to take advantage of my absence."

After everyone had left but Tyrmiss and me, Tessia said, "Pack your kit, Mage. We have some dragonlings to find."

Chapter Fifteen

I flew by broom back to my house where Idella had just returned from delivering bread and pastries to the city. She was surprised to see me arrive on a broom.

"What is going on, Norbert?" she asked, suspiciously eyeing my means of transport.

I quickly filled her in on the kidnapping of the dragonlings and Tessia's request that I accompany her on a quest to find them.

"Another quest?" my wife asked, rolling her eyes. "You have been back from your last quest barely three months and you're leaving again?"

"I'm sorry, Idella," I said, trying to embrace her, but she stepped back, avoiding me. "The Queen needs…"

"The Queen, the Queen, always the Queen. What about me? I need you here."

"My love, Tyrmiss' babies have been stolen. Imagine if it had been us? Imagine if it had been Ena who was taken. We have to do whatever we can to bring them back. Don't you see?"

Idella allowed me to put my arms around her and kiss her on the cheek.

"Very well," she said. "I hadn't thought of it from Tyrmiss' point of view. Of course, you have to do what you can to help her." We kissed on the lips, long and deep. "You must be careful,

Norbert. Ena and I need you to live a long life with us, and there's something else I need to tell you."

"Can it wait? I need to pack my kit. And don't worry about me. After all, I'll be with the greatest warrior of our time and mounted on a dragon that will scorch anyone who dares to attack us." I was getting excited about going on another quest.

My beautiful wife nodded and smiled with her mouth, but her eyes were blazing at me. Oh well, I thought. When I get back, we'll have a long talk and she'll forgive me once she understands how important and necessary it is that I go with Tessia. I was too busy to think about Idella's moods right now.

I went into our bedroom and started packing my kit.

I was bringing my healer's bag, as well as a change of clothes and my harp. Although I'd be flying on Tyrmiss with Tessia, I also would be bringing my broom in case we needed to fly separately for any reason. I thought about bringing my book of spells, but it was large and heavy, and I needed to travel light. Although I never carried weapons, I did pack a small bag of yellow soil, a small bag of charcoal and a larger bag of saltpeter. I'd heard from a traveler that magicians in the east had developed an interesting concoction from these minerals. Also, I put the rune-stone in my pocket, knowing I could always use the black magic I'd picked up from the old books in Windkeep's library. I'd practiced the incantations in the Dry Hills and knew they worked. The power of these spells frightened me, but if I had to use them to protect my Queen, I would.

As I left the house, I blew a kiss at my wife. I couldn't help but notice that she was enraged at me, but I felt I didn't have time to argue with her right now, so I hurried out the door. Later, I came to understand that this decision was one of the worst of my life.

Tessia was in the dragon lair already, talking quietly with Tyrmiss and stroking the purple scales beneath her chin. When I walked in, the dragon turned her head to me; her eyes, which had been red slits, softened slightly as she looked at me, then she turned her head to look out the entrance at the mountain behind the castle.

Alaric flew in on his broom and made a graceful landing on the stone floor. "I found Gaspar," he said. "He was halfway up the trail on his way home to the Iskar Valley. It took a little persuading, but he confessed to stealing the dragonlings and delivering them to a witch outside the city walls."

"Did he say who the witch was?" I asked.

"He said he didn't know her name, but the description he gave sounded like Evanora."

Tessia and I looked at each other. We hadn't expected the most senior of the witches to be involved in this crime.

"Something odd, though," Alaric continued. "The witch didn't fly west toward the mountain pass to the Iskar Valley, which is the direction I would have expected Evanora to fly if she were going home to Sheonad. Instead, Gaspar said she flew east in the direction of the sea."

"If she were going to Osterbo City, she would have to fly east to the sea, then north to Osterbo," Tessia said slowly, working through the puzzle. "The mountains are too high for someone on a broom to cross."

We were all silent for a moment, thinking it through. Tessia looked at Alaric, "Where is Gaspar now?"

"I took the gold he was paid by the witch, and I told him that if I ever see him on this side of the mountain pass again, I will hand him over to Tyrmiss."

"You should have turned him over to me now," Tyrmiss said.

Tessia shook her head, "Gaspar might be useful to us in the future, and we can find him in the Iskar Valley if we need him. Alaric, give the gold to your father. We may need it to ransom the dragonlings when we find out where they are."

Alaric obediently handed me the small leather bag, heavier than it looked. I waved my wand over it, saying a simple cloaking spell, and put it in my kit. Tessia knew that in my youth when I was a shireman, I hid my money in this way.

Still speaking to Alaric, Tessia said, "I want you to fly down the Dragonja River and ask the farmers whether they've seen a witch on a broom fly past. Then meet us in two days at the place where the Nordtoppen Mountains meet the sea and tell us what you've learned."

I was tempted to tell Alaric to go home and say goodbye to his mother. He might be gone for a long time, depending on the strategy Tessia was inventing now, but I knew there was no time. We needed Alaric to move quickly and gather information as soon as possible. I hoped Idella would not worry too much, but Alaric had a tendency to disappear for days at a time, and he always returned without a scratch on him, so she wouldn't be surprised by his absence, and she'd probably guess he was working with Tessia and me. Thinking of Idella made me feel uncomfortable, but I wasn't sure why, so I put the nagging discomfort out of mind.

After Alaric had flown off, I asked the Queen, "What is your best guess on where the dragonlings are?"

"Nothing's sure at this point," she said. "Based on what we know so far, it seems that Evanora took the dragonlings to Kazko in Osterbo City, but I can't understand why she would do such a thing. Even though she sent Zamarrra to attack Dragonja with drought and flood, Evanora always seemed like an honorable woman to me. I'd think that kidnapping would violate her sense of decency."

I thought of Idella and the way she felt about Ena and Alaric. "Your Majesty," I said. "Do you know what the most powerful force in the world is?"

Tessia looked at me with curiosity. "I'm not sure, Mage. Dragon fire?" She was thinking, of course, in military terms.

"No, Your Majesty. The most powerful force in the universe is mother love. Think about it, the Mother Goddess Nilene Zeita has given us everything, the whole world. She has given us the forests, the streams, the pastures. She has given us life itself. So, what is more powerful than Evanora's sense of honor?"

"Her love for her adopted daughter Zamarrra?" Tessia hazarded.

"Exactly."

"We never heard anything from Zamarrra and Bastian after they left us a few months ago," Tessia said, musing. "I was hoping they were still in the mountains trying to build an alliance to attack Osterbo City. But what if their attempts went awry and they were captured and turned over to the leadership of Osterbo?"

"And when Kazko returned home after we defeated him here, he had a powerful bargaining chip in forcing Evanora to use her magic again."

"Do you think that Evanora's attempt to protect the people she loves in Sheonad was the leverage Kazko used to get her to send Zamarrra to attack us with violent weather last spring?"

"It sounds likely."

"Well then," Tyrmiss who had been silent during these deliberations, declared. "Let's fly to Osterbo, set everything on fire, find the babies and come home. It seems simple enough to me."

Tessia held up her hand. "No, no, Tyrmiss. We don't want to get the dragonlings killed. Remember what happened in this very room to the three dragons. Kazko would rather kill your kind, than let them ally themselves with a rival city. We need to have a more subtle strategy."

"And what might that subtle strategy be?" I asked.

"I'm not sure yet," she said. "Right now, we'll fly to the place where the mountains meet the sea and wait for Alaric to report to us. Hopefully, he'll be able to confirm our theory that the witch Evanora flew in the direction of the sea on her way to Osterbo."

I didn't want to ask what we would do if Alaric had no information.

Tessia swung up onto the dragon's neck and gave me a hand so I could settle in behind her. She carried her usual weapons— her Voprian sword in a sheath on the left side of her belt, a Voprian short sword on the right, a dagger in an ankle sheath, and a bow and quiver on her back. I carried my kit on my back which included my broom and my medical supplies, and my willow wand sheathe hung from my belt. I put my arms around Tessia's waist and held onto her belt. She held onto the last spine in the row that went down Tyrmiss's neck.

Tyrmiss turned her head to make sure we were secure and jumped out the lair entrance and into the air. As we dove, we picked up speed. Tyrmiss unfolded her wings, leveled off and pushed the air behind her as we followed the Dragonja River over the farms and pastures and toward the sea.

Chapter Sixteen

I'd never been to the place where the Nordtoppen mountains meet the sea, and I was struck by its majestic beauty. The high mountains form a natural boundary between the Skarsland to the north and the Dragonja valley to the south. The border area is largely uninhabited with salty soil unsuited for farming and a rocky coastline unfriendly to ships. The mountains march into the sea here with snow-covered peaks rising from the water and waves crashing around their base. I'd heard that trading ships traveling from our southern ports to Osterbo, the capital of Skarsland, had to go far out to sea before they could safely sail to the north to trade for gems, rare metals, and furs. Osterbo was also the source of the purple earth that Tessia's father, Kerttu, had smelted with copper to invent the Voprian alloy a generation before. Bastian and Caz were the only two people I'd ever known to visit that northern land, and both had brought back stories of a people who were toughened by the cold winds, but friendly to those visitors who'd managed to earn their trust.

We made camp on a high cliff overlooking the sea. I thought there probably wasn't a single person within two days walk of here. We hadn't brought any food with us because for Tessia and me it was a welcome chore to forage for food—even in such a sparse landscape as this one. Tessia scrambled easily down the cliff and gathered eggs from the birds' nests there while I gathered wild onion, orange seaberries, and small hat mushrooms. Then Tessia made a fire from her tinderbox, and I beat the eggs in a bowl. Once the pan was hot, I poured in the egg batter and when it was firm, sprinkled the ingredients. We ate the omelet straight from the pan using our knives. Afterward, we sat on a log beside the fire, resting. It had been a very long day.

"Where did Tyrmiss go?" I asked, having seen her fly off to the north shortly after leaving us here.

"I sent her north to look at Osterbo from the sea. I want to know the layout of the city before we get there. She needed something to do. She's so restless and agitated she couldn't possibly stay here, not knowing where her babies are."

"She won't be too tired to carry us tomorrow?"

Tessia shook her head, "Tyrmiss can go weeks without sleep. Her cycle of rest is different than ours."

We sat in silence for a while, comfortable in being silent together.

"Norbert," Tessia finally asked, looking into the fire, "What are you thinking about?"

"Oh, just the many adventures the three of us have had together."

She laughed, "It's been quite a ride, hasn't it?"

As she looked into the fire, her mood seemed to shift. "Norbert, Taja and I are thinking of having a baby."

"Really? I think that's a fabulous idea."

"Tell me honestly, do you think that two women should raise a child together?"

"I would guess that it depends on the two women and the situation in which the child is raised."

"Don't you think a child needs a father?" she asked. "My own father raised me, and I was always very close to him. Now he and I are so busy, I rarely see him. He has a thriving business

189

smithing Voprian weapons, and I'm busy being queen, which, as it turns out, is not much fun."

We both laughed. Then I turned serious again. "Yes, after my mother died when I was just a boy, my father raised me." Then I remembered who I was talking to. "But you know that."

"You must have missed your mother," Tessia said, looking at me with concern.

"Oh, yes," I said, feeling my eyes filling with tears. "I missed her terribly. And her death changed my father. He became cold and distant. I guess he was feeling a lot of grief as well, but we never talked about it."

"I never felt any grief for my mother because I never knew her. I was always jealous of the other children who had mothers, and I was curious about what I was missing."

"Perhaps this is the reason you and Tyrmiss have bonded? She's like a mother to you?"

Tessia thought about the question for a while. "No, Tyrmiss is not like a mother to me but more like a best friend. Or maybe like an older sister." She laughed. "A much much much older sister!"

Picking up the thread from earlier, I asked, "Would you and Taja choose a surrogate father?"

Hearing the panic in my voice, she smiled ruefully, "Don't worry, Norbert. You're not on the list."

"What would you be looking for in a surrogate?" I asked, trying to hide my relief. My being a surrogate would have complicated my friendship with Tessia, not to mention my marriage to Idella.

"Oh, a dashing young man, athletic, a warrior, perhaps with his own kingdom, and of course a dragon as his best friend."

"So," I said, laughing. "You want a male version of you."

She laughed, then grew serious. "Taja and I are looking for a man who is reasonably good looking, in excellent health, intelligent, hard-working, and preferably he has had children before."

"Somebody like your father?"

"Well, better my father than Taja's!"

We both laughed; neither of us liked the old wool merchant. Taja's father hadn't stood in the way of his daughter marrying the hero of Dragonja, but he hadn't been particularly warm toward Tessia either. Taja's mother, on the other hand, had always been very loving to Tessia, welcoming her into their home when Tessia was just a serving wench at the Silver Pony. It had been obvious to everyone from the beginning that the two girls were madly in love.

"I'm sure that you and Taja will make an excellent choice for a surrogate father of your child. And I wouldn't worry about the child needing a good man to help the child learn. There are lots of men around the castle who can act as the child's uncle. I, for one, will be glad to help teach your child."

"Thank you, my friend," Tessia said quietly. "I know I can count on you. I always have."

I blushed at her quiet faith in our friendship. "Any thoughts on naming the child?"

"If it's a girl, I think we should name her Jabir," Tessia said with a twinkle in her eye.

I laughed. "You're going to name your daughter after the legendary troll who used to eat men for breakfast with hot peppers on the side?"

"And if it's a boy we'll name him Snitch."

We both guffawed uproariously. "So, he can tell on his sister if she does anything wrong?" I said, breathlessly.

"Exactly," Tessia nodded, regaining her composure. "Caz has taught me that you can never have too many informers in the kingdom."

I laughed, thinking of Caz and how his years of living as a merchant in foreign kingdoms had taught him to be always suspicious of ambitious people, and to always pay attention to where the money was coming from and where it was going. "I wonder how he's doing. He and I have barely had a chance to talk in months."

"Caz is fine," Tessia said. "He does a very good job of managing the finances of the kingdom. Good thing he has that skill because money doesn't interest me in the slightest."

Tessia looked off into the distant gray line of the horizon. "I want the Dragonja Kingdom to be prosperous again, but first we have to deal with the threat that Kazko poses. It's clear that the kidnapping of the dragonlings is just a small part of a larger strategy he's employing against Dragonja."

The next day, there was no sign of Tyrmiss or Alaric, so Tessia and I spent the day taking care of the tools of our respective trades. Voprian blades held an edge so well that they rarely needed to be sharpened, but if you desired the purple shimmer the blades were famous for, then they needed a vigorous polishing on a regular basis. Since I hadn't used much more than basic magic since we'd been back to Dragonja, I thought it would be a good idea for me to get some practice. I walked along the edge of the cliff a good distance until Tessia was a tiny figure in a very large landscape. I needed privacy to concentrate, not to mention that if something went wrong with one of the spells, I didn't want Tessia to get hurt.

I started with the Green Magic my father had taught me when I was a child. Not only had he been a beloved shireman, but he was also a valued healer who could set a broken bone or assist the local midwife with a difficult birth. He knew the herbs and earths and what each of them did to help people in their simple lives. Blessing fields and streams to bring bounty was part of his daily activities, and at night, he'd sing an old song or tell an old story that almost everyone knew by heart. He was a good man, but the murder of my mother and the kidnapping of his favorite son Ludek had caused him to wall off any love or tenderness he might otherwise have felt for me. As I've grown older, I've learned to forgive him and to be grateful for what he did give to me.

In my pocket, I still carried the rune-stone from Windkeep's library. I'd been wanting to experiment with different spells, and the stone would help to amplify their power.

I waved my wand over a seaberry patch so that, almost imperceptibly, the leaves grew more vibrant and the fruit more juicy. Walking along the cliff, I saw a seagull with a broken wing, hobbling toward the cliff but afraid to fly. I picked it up, held it gently in my hand, waved my wand over the hurt wing, said a healing spell, then gently released the bird into the air, and it flew off toward the sea. Feeling a few raindrops carried by the wind, I lifted my face to the sky and thanked the Goddess for blessing us—let us not forget where all power comes from. One of the greatest of mistakes for a mage is to think that he or she is the source of magic when only the Goddess has that power. I am, at best, a mere vessel for Her will.

Feeling warmed up, I decided to practice some of the skills I'd recently learned from the old books. I've struggled for a long time over the proper uses of magic. If my power as a mage comes from the Goddess, and everything the Goddess creates is good, then is it permissible to use these powers to hurt people? My father taught me, and I've always believed, that magic should be used only to heal and to help, never to harm. But in my studies of the old books and scrolls, I discovered that there have been Green Mages in the past who were good men and women, and yet they developed spells that could protect their homeland from invaders. This contradiction was a shocking paradox for me. To use the Goddess's gifts as weapons was repugnant to me. But as I thought about the issue, it came to me that the Goddess has given the wolf fangs, the lion claws, and the dragon fiery breath. It is natural and good that these beasts defend their young with the weapons they've been given.

Muttering a few words under my breath, I pointed my wand at a stone the size of my fist, lifted it into the air high over my head, then flung it far out to sea. This is the Atlatl Spell, developed by the great wizard Uxius and recorded in the *Book of Transmutations*. I pointed my wand at a boulder and shot a ball of fire at it, repeating until it glowed red and I could feel the heat on my face. This was the Kharaba Spell carried from the far lands in the east by refugees from the Great War of the Wizards. And finally, I waved the wand in a circle over my head, spinning around and around while slowly lowering my wand and saying the Spell of Gayaba, making myself invisible, a dangerous maneuver that can cause the wizard to disappear altogether if he says it too loudly. These are the dark arts I learned from my brother Ludek when we fought and blended our spirits, but thus far I'd been afraid to use them.

When I got back to camp, Tessia was practicing with her sword. She paused in her movement and looked at the basket of orange seaberries I had in my hand, then nodded at the fire where there was a seagull roasting on a spit. I truly hoped it was not the seagull whose wing I'd healed. Well, such is the way of all things: we have to kill to eat, but I still believe it's best not to eat our friends.

Since Tessia was bored by philosophy, I didn't share with her my trepidations about the ethics of using magic as a weapon. Instead, I sat on the log next to the fire, ate the meat of the bird with a handful of berries and felt grateful for this life.

The next morning, Alaric caught up to us. He was exhausted from his search for clues about where Evanora had taken the dragonlings, so we let him rest. I offered him a leather water pouch as well as seaberries and bird bones left over from our dinner. He guzzled the water, gobbled down the berries, and broke open the bones to suck the marrow. I doubted that he had eaten in the two days since he'd flown from Windkeep, so I silently vowed to find him more food later.

Finally, he seemed strong enough to reveal what he'd found. "I talked to a lot of people in the valley. A few people thought they may've seen a witch flying by, but they weren't sure. Farmers and villagers have gotten so used to seeing dragons and witches they don't pay much attention anymore. However," Alaric said, looking at me excitedly. "There was a girl, a small child, who lives with her family in the Dry Hills close to the valley, who said that when she was playing outside her house a woman landed on a broomstick in the nearby pasture. The witch carried a wooden box to the well beside the house. She drew water and ladled it into the box while speaking softly. The child asked whether she had a baby in the box, and the witch said *yes*."

"I knew it!" Tessia could barely contain her glee. "I knew Evanora had to have come this way. She's on her way to Osterbo with the dragonlings!"

In the middle of the night, I woke feeling a familiar presence in my dream. *Tyrmiss is back*, I thought and went back to sleep.

The next time I woke, Tyrmiss and Tessia were arguing. A baby seal sat between them, turning its little black head back and forth as the conversation bounced between the queen and the dragon.

"But he's so cute," Tessia was saying.

"He's breakfast, Tessia," Tyrmiss said, shaking her huge head in dismay at her friend's sentimentality.

Alaric was sitting on the log next to the fire, clearly enjoying this contest between practicality and sentimentality.

"I'm not going to butcher this little thing," Tessia said firmly.

"Very well, then if no one else wants to eat him, I will," the dragon said, opening her mouth full of dagger-like teeth directly over the baby seal.

"No, no," Tessia said, rushing over to the little one, scooping him into her arms, and cooing to him as if he were her own baby.

"Tessia," the dragon said disgusted. "I have seen you disembowel men with a single swipe of your blade. I've seen you behead men, and women too if they were armed. So why are you choosing this one little beast to save?"

"That was different," Tessia said, continuing to murmur to the baby in her arms. "Those were soldiers who were trying to kill me. This little thing's never tried to hurt anything in its whole life."

"I beg to differ," Tyrmiss said. "When I scooped him up, he was on the shore at the bottom of this cliff devouring a seabass he'd caught. By eating this seal, think of how many fishes' lives we will save."

Tyrmiss looked at me. I shrugged, not wanting to get between these two.

"Very well, then," Tyrmiss said, rolling her large blue eyes. "I'll take him back to the shore where I found him and find a fish that is not cute enough for you to object to it being our breakfast."

Tyrmiss took the baby seal in her talons and leaped off the cliff. We watched her fly down the strand, gently deposit the baby seal, then fly out over the water. In a short while, she returned to us carrying a large mackerel.

"I almost brought you a baby shark, but I was afraid you might fall in love with it. So, here's the ugliest fish I could find. I saw a lovely tuna, but it had such a cute smile I knew you would object," she said sarcastically.

Alaric and I looked at each other, covering our mouths with our hands, so Tyrmiss wouldn't see us laughing.

"Perfect!" Tessia said, drawing her dagger and deftly gutting and cleaning the fish. Tyrmiss cooked it with her breath, and we ate with our knives.

After we'd eaten, Tyrmiss grew serious and reported on what she'd found at Osterbo City.

"It's highly fortified," she began. "Built next to the sea on the edge of a cliff like the one we're on now. The walls are very high, and in their turrets, there are large ballista crossbows that shoot arrows longer than a man is tall. In addition, there are archers in the battlements. It would be impossible to attack the castle from the sea. The ballistas would sink most ships long before they got close enough to shore to launch boarding vessels. And any men who stood on the strand below would be easy pickings for the archers."

"Did anyone see you?" Tessia asked.

"No, during the day I stayed up in the clouds observing the city from high above. At night I came down closer. Not only did I not want to be seen, but I am very afraid of those ballistas. They could send a shaft into both my hearts from quite a distance." She shuddered. "In the Great War between men and dragons, I saw many of my kin killed by ballistas."

"What about from the land side," Alaric asked. "Can we attack from that side?"

"Probably not," Tyrmiss answered. "The city wall is long and surrounds the whole area. There are only two gates, located at the northwest corner and the southwest corner. Both gates are protected by double turrets with ballistas. The wall is crenellated, so archers can shoot at anyone approaching the walls. Of course, the gates and walls are guarded day and night.

"And there's more bad news," Tyrmiss continued. "Inside the outer walls, there's a large area made up of houses, shops, and a market square. Then there are even higher curtain walls which surround the castle at the middle of the city."

We shook our heads. An assault seemed impossible.

Tessia, never one to admit defeat before she started, asked, "What about infiltrating the city with a spy? He could scope out the city, find out where the dragonlings are being kept, then report back to us. Once we know where your children are, Tyrmiss, we'll develop a plan to take them back."

Not for the first time, I noticed how Tessia inspired others by making it personal, in this case, reminding Tyrmiss, of why we were here—to save the dragon babies.

"A spy?" Tyrmiss asked, and we all turned to Alaric, the one who had the most experience in this kind of warfare.

Alaric looked up and noticed we were all looking at him. "I... I... uh, don't think it would work for me to go into the city. Most of the citizens are Drekavacs with white skin, thin white hair and pink eyes. I wouldn't be able to even get through the gates without being spotted as a foreigner." He gestured to his nearly black complexion, dark eyes, and dark curly hair.

"Could you disguise Alaric to look like a Drekavac, Mage?" Tessia asked, looking at me.

"Possibly, but I have a better idea," I said. "What we need is for one of us to be invisible."

It was a moonless night, so we decided to leave immediately. We packed our gear, and Alaric cleaned the campsite, so in the unlikely event that someone came through here, it would be difficult for them to see evidence of our stay.

I climbed up and sat in my usual perch holding onto Tessia's waist. Alaric had already left on his broomstick. We would catch up to him in a little while, then slow our pace so we could fly together up the coast. In order to avoid being spotted, we flew very high. Below us, the ocean reflected the starlight creating an expansive map of the heavens as we flew around the mountains which extended out to sea, then veered north and west toward Osterbo.

The plan was to drop me off outside the city under cover of darkness, and the next morning I'd use my invisibility charm to enter the gates with the farmers and merchants who normally entered. I'd search the city, especially the castle, find the drag-onlings and take them to the top of the highest tower. There, I'd set off a flare as a signal to Tyrmiss who would fly to the tower, collect the dragonlings and me, then carry us to safety.

Events didn't unfold exactly the way we planned.

Tyrmiss and Tessia landed next to a road which led to the city gate. Once I had my feet on the ground, and my kit and broom safely in hand, they flew off to meet Alaric in a clearing a short distance away. From that vantage point, they would be able to see my red flare at night, or my blue smoke by day.

Once they were gone, I checked to make sure I still had the rune-stone in my pocket. Then, I took out my wand, held it up in the air and making wide circles over my head said:

Božica me čini nevidljivim

I could feel a flush of heat come over me. I looked at my hand holding the wand, but it was still fully visible. I had no way to test my invisibility at present, so I decided to proceed cautiously. I sat on a rock, reached into my pack and drew out the bags of charcoal, yellow earth and potash. I mixed them thoroughly in a small clay pot, fastened the lid and put it back in my pack. Not knowing whether I was invisible, I couldn't risk being spotted flying on a broom, so I steadied my breathing and started walking toward the city of Osterbo.

I reached the city gate shortly after dawn. There was already a line of farmers with their carts of produce and merchants with donkeys loaded with trade goods waiting to get into the city. Two armed guards were inspecting each load and asking the people what their business in the city might be.

Just to make sure that the invisibility charm had been effec-tive, I walked up to an apple-wagon being driven by a farmer and lightly tickled his bulbous nose with my forefinger. He swatted the air in front of his face as if a fly had landed on it.

Satisfied that I was invisible, I climbed on the back of his wagon and made myself comfortable in the load of fruit.

Then, something strange happened. As the wagon got close to the gate, the guards seemed to recognize the farmer, and both guards bowed down to him, as one might to a king or a holy man. The farmer wasn't surprised by their supplication. He merely nodded to them and continued through the gate with me in the back of the wagon. Once inside the city, I jumped to the ground.

Tessia, who knew much more about defensive strategy than the rest of us, had guessed that Kazko would keep the dragonlings close to him, so his Drekavac soldiers could effectively guard both himself and the dragonlings simultaneously. Tyrmiss had said that the king's chambers were in the heart of the castle, which meant that I had to get through another gate.

Making my way through the crowded streets was difficult because I couldn't afford to bump into anyone accidentally. I suspected that people in Osterbo, like those in Dragonja, had grown used to spotting magical happenings. If I drew attention to myself, someone was liable to grab me or shout an alarm, so I moved through the crowd carefully, dodging this way and that, trying not to brush against anyone. Finally, I was able to get behind a large cart of hay and make my way in the direction of the inner gate that led to the castle.

Security was tighter at the inner gate. The guards were more alert, and they aggressively searched each pack and parcel before allowing it through. Fortunately, the cart I was following was heading toward the inner gate, so as we drew near, I ducked beneath the cart, held onto the undercarriage, and lifted myself off the ground. I wasn't sure how long my arms could bear my weight, so when the cart stopped in front of the gate and the guards started searching its contents, I let myself down onto the ground to rest. My heart was pounding so loudly, I was afraid the guards would hear it. But when a guard went down on all fours and peered under the cart, I stayed very still, barely breathing, and he looked right through me. Finally, the guards gave approval to the drover, and the mules pulled the cart into the courtyard of the castle with me hanging on below, catching a slow ride into what I discovered was the heart of evil.

It was easy to spot which building held the king's chambers. It had wide stone steps leading to a pair of heavy oaken doors. Two guards armed with Voprian swords and Voprian-tipped spears stood at attention at the entrance. As I climbed the steps, I was heartened by the way their gaze seemed to look through me. I stood to the side and waited. Eventually, the heavy doors swung open, and a high-ranking officer exited with a retinue of half a dozen soldiers behind him. I slipped through the entrance and found myself in a vestibule where courtiers stood in small groups, talking among themselves, no doubt trading influence based on their proximity to the king. At the far end of the room, there was another pair of doors, intricately carved and decorated with gold and precious gems. There was no doubt that on the other side was a person of great wealth and power. Again, I stood beside the entrance and waited. Soon, the door opened, courtiers were summoned, and I followed closely behind the bevy of sycophants to enter the Great Hall.

On the walls hung large tapestries with intricately woven images of castles with high turrets and cliffs that reached to the sky. Ships sailed through rough seas and warriors battled dragons. Here was the story that kings want to be told about their reigns. Of course, there was nothing portrayed that signified the terrible suffering brought about by warring kings. There were no burning cities, ruined crops or starving children. War is always portrayed heroically, and its constant companions Famine, Pestilence, and Plague are never shown. I'd seen war, and it's nothing like what the rulers want us to believe. The history books are written by scribes in the pay of murderers, and so the truth is forgotten, which is why each generation needs to re-discover the horrors of war, and the lessons it teaches are never passed down.

At the far end of the hall, Kazko sat on a tall gold throne encrusted with jewels. His short legs couldn't reach the floor and his feet dangled in the air. He looked like a small boy in his highchair, pretending to be emperor. On his ferret-like head was a large gaudy crown. It must have been very heavy because his head leaned forward with the weight. I thought of Tessia's slim diadem with a single gem which she wore for special state occasions, a symbol of her regal office and also a sign of her modesty. Tessia was a Queen, albeit an imperfect one, while this man was nothing more than a pretender, a toad in a small pond.

As each supplicant bowed before the throne, Kazko snarled.

"You again?" the diminutive king said to a young Drekavac who wore clothes that had once been elegant, but now showed wear.

"Your Majesty." The young man said, respectfully with only a small quaver in his voice.

"What do you want?"

"My sister, Your Majesty," the supplicant said, his eyes on the floor. "If the sovereign is finished with her, may I take her home?"

"Which one is your sister?" the king said, eyeing the young man. "The one with red hair?"

"Your Majesty, my sister has white hair. Her name is Celisile, known as The One who Rejoices. Our mother and father grieve at her absence."

"No," King Kazko said. "I've not yet finished with her. Now get out of my sight."

The young man was dragged away by guards, and another supplicant kneeled in front of the king.

Sitting on diminutive chairs behind the king were Evanora and Zamarrra, their translucent blue skin had lost its radiance and appeared slightly gray. They were cowering like beaten dogs. I wondered by what extortion the king had convinced these two women once again to perform an evil act.

Beside them was the half barrel which Tyrmiss had used as a crib for her dragonlings. An old woman, a Drekavac nurse, leaned over the crib, speaking softly to the babies. For the thousandth time, I felt grateful to Tessia for her strategic insight. She'd intuited that Kazko would keep the dragonlings close to him.

As I moved toward the front of the room, I heard a moaning sound behind me. I turned and saw in a dark alcove in the corner of the Great Hall, three women chained to the wall. Each woman's clothes were in shreds and all of them bore the marks of having been whipped. Great welts streaked across their bellies and breasts. One of them had white hair, one had black and one red. Rage rose in me as I imagined my lovely Idella held captive by this monster.

But rage, as it often does, made me stupid. I didn't see the guard walking toward me, and by the time I noticed him, he'd bumped into me and recoiled in surprise. His face turned from bafflement to understanding, and he reached out and touched me before I could jump back.

"WIZARD!" he yelled and pointed in my direction.

Chapter Seventeen

Suddenly everyone was alert and moving. The king stood up, pointed at the main entrance and shouted, "SEAL THE DOORS!"

The captain of the guard ordered his men to form a line and march toward the place where I'd been detected, but I was moving as well. I ran to the dais and stood beside the crib, thinking that Kazko's instinct may be to kill the dragonlings to keep them from being taken by his enemy, the same strategy that led him to kill the adult dragons in Windkeep. Evidently, the old nurse, although she was unaware of my presence, had the same impulse, so she and I stood in front of the crib, guarding the precious babies. When it was clear Kazko had decided his first priority was finding me, and he started giving his men orders different than those the captain of the guard had given, causing the soldiers to mill around uselessly, I decided to seize the moment and try to escape with the dragonlings.

I took the clay pot out of my pack and lit the fuse with a torch in a sconce on the wall, then set the pot down and used the Atlatl spell to sling it toward the double doors. At the same time, I pushed the nurse harder than I meant to, and as she fell behind the throne, I threw myself over the crib, protecting the babies.

The explosion was deafening. A few of the soldiers were

blown into the air, their helmets and shields hurtling across the room like missiles. I picked up the crib and started toward the entrance, hoping to take advantage of the confusion. But I suddenly realized that the crib hadn't been part of the original invisibility spell, so what Kazko and the others saw was the crib suddenly rising in the air and moving quickly across the room. There was absolutely no chance of my getting the crib out of the room undetected.

Meanwhile, the explosion had knocked one of the torches out of its sconce, lighting a tapestry on fire. As the fire spread across the walls, from one tapestry to the next, the room filled with smoke and people started to panic, trying to get out of the burning room. The women prisoners in the alcove were screaming in terror and begging to be released from their chains. The soldiers who'd started toward me carrying the very visible crib, stopped and realized that if they didn't leave immediately, they may be overtaken by smoke, so they turned and ran for the front entrance where the double doors had been blown open. Kazko, Evanora, Zamarrra and the nurse ran out of the room by an exit behind the throne, and I was close behind them with the crib. We found ourselves on a balcony overlooking the city.

Right in front of us, Tyrmiss sat on the stone battlement with Tessia on her back. Tyrmiss's eyes were red slits as she saw Kazko. He turned to go back into the Great Hall, but with a crowd of women and a crib floating in the air between him and the door, he was trapped. He looked at the crib and raised his sword to strike the box—one final act of cruelty before he died—but I stepped back with the crib, and he missed. Tessia quickly drew her Voprian blade and leaped forward crashing into the soldiers trying to get out of the smoke-filled room. Kazko shoved aside the people milling around the room, but Tessia pushed through the crowd and caught up to him beside the throne. Kazko looked back at the queen in time to see her singing sword whipping toward his neck.

Seeing the head, still wearing a crown, rolling toward the throne, Evanora cried out, "Kazko the Usurper is dead!" Suddenly, all the soldiers and courtiers stopped and looked around, confused about what to do next. It was clear that Kazko had had them under some kind of spell, but whether it was fear or magic that had held them, they no longer were in thrall to him.

Usurper? I thought. *If Kazko was a usurper, who was the rightful ruler?*

"I told you to send up a flare, Norbert," Tessia said strapping the crib onto Tyrmiss's back. "Not set the whole frigging city on fire."

And indeed, the fire was spreading through the castle, and there was no doubt that other buildings would catch fire as well. Below us, people were streaming out of the castle and out the gates into the city streets where crowds were looking up at the conflagration. Although the outer walls of the castle were constructed of stone, everything in the castle, the floors, the inner walls, the furnishings were made of cloth or wood.

"Don't leave us here to die!" the nurse cried in terror.

"We're not going to leave you here," Tessia said. "Mage, can you ferry this woman to the ground?"

"Of course, Your Majesty," I said, taking out my wand and waving it three times over my head while saying the spell. The nurse was very surprised to see a man suddenly appear in front of her, holding a wand.

"But your majesty, there are three women held in chains at the back of the throne room. They will surely die if not freed!" The nurse shouted.

I leaned over the edge of the battlement and looked at the outside wall of the throne room. "The women are chained next to the fourth window," I said, pointing.

Tessia swung her leg over the dragon's back, and they flew along the wall allowing Tessia to jump through the window. She reappeared in a few moments. "I cut them loose and they ran

206

out the hallway. I think that they'll make it to safety." I looked over the edge of the balcony and saw the three women emerging from the tower and running through the courtyard toward the inner gate. I hoped they'd find shelter with friends and family in the city.

As I showed the old nurse how to sit on the broomstick behind me, I heard Tessia say to Evanora and Zamarrra, "I will deal with you later," and she turned to tend to the business of getting people off the burning pile.

Alaric had chosen an excellent spot for our rendezvous with him—a meadow on the side of a mountain that looked down on the plain below. In the distance, we could see smoke rising from the city and beyond, the sea stretching to the horizon.

Tessia was standing in the meadow, her arms crossed, staring at Evanora and Zamarrra.

"This is the second time, the two of you have betrayed me. First, you attacked my kingdom with drought and flood enabling Kazko to take over the city. Then you helped Kazko kidnap the dragonlings. You have caused terrible damage to Dragonja and you have hurt my friend Tyrmiss. Why shouldn't I execute you right now?"

The two witches fell on their knees in front of the Queen.

"Please forgive us, Your Majesty," Evanora said, clasping her hands in front of her. "Kazko and his agent Bastian forced us to betray you."

When Tessia didn't respond, but just continued staring at the witch, Evanora continued. "Kazko held captive my daughter Zamarrra and threatened to kill her if I didn't do as he said. At his bidding, I went to Dragonja and hired the trader Gaspar to steal the dragonlings. Then I flew back to Osterbo with them. Please forgive me, Your Majesty."

Tessia turned to Zamarrra, "It is as my mother said, Your

Majesty," the younger witch said. "We did not wish to harm you or your kingdom. We were just trying to survive."

"Where is Bastian?" Tessia asked. "What was his role in all of this?"

"Bastian betrayed us," Zamarrra said. "When he and I left you at the dragon lair, we flew to the tribal lands of Renetu, as you asked us to do. But once we were there, Bastian told the chief and the council of elders that I was a witch, and they took me captive. They removed my wand and my herbal kit, and they tied a cloth around my mouth, so I could not practice spells."

"Bastian sent word to me," Evanora said, filling in the rest of the tale, "That if I didn't deliver the two dragonlings to Kazko, then my daughter would die."

"How long has Bastian been working for Kazko?" Tessia asked, her eyes narrowing as she began to see the whole pattern emerging.

"Oh, for many years," Evanora said. "He was the emissary between Osterbo and the Renetu tribes when Kazko sent him to spy on you. He told me that he thought you were a fool for trusting him."

"And you didn't know he was a spy?" Tessia asked Zamarrra.

"No, your majesty, I didn't know until he betrayed me to the Renetu leaders."

"Where is Bastian now?" Tessia asked.

"I believe he's still living with the Renetu," Zamarrra said.

"Well," Tessia said, looking at Alaric and me. "It looks like we're going to Renetu."

Tyrmiss, who had been silently listening to the interrogation of the witches, asked, "May I have these two?"

"What do you plan to do to them?" Tessia asked her friend.

Tyrmiss looked at the two witches who started trembling under her red-slitted gaze. "I thought I would roast them over a slow fire, then feed their hearts to the wolves."

Tessia looked at Evanora and Zamarrra for a few moments, considering her options.

"No, not yet, Tyrmiss," she said. "They may prove useful."

"You saw me cut off the head of Kazko?" she asked the witches.

They both nodded.

"And you understand that I can just as easily hand you over to this dragon to be roasted for her dinner?"

The two witches, still on their knees, nodded.

"Very well then," the Queen said to them. "If you come with us to Renetu and help us to capture Bastian, then I will show you mercy. But if I see the slightest hint of betrayal from you, then I will execute you. Do you understand?"

Evanora and Zamarrra nodded, "Thank you for your mercy, Your Majesty," the older witch said.

Tyrmiss looked disgusted, but soon she was leaning over the crib, talking to her babies, and she gradually recovered her composure. Later, as Tessia was strapping the crib on the dragon's back, Tyrmiss was bending her long neck around, so she could look at her babies and make soft noises to reassure them.

As we sat on rocks in the meadow, I asked Evanora, "When Tessia killed Kazko, you yelled that the usurper is dead."

Evanora nodded. "Yes, Kazko was not the true king."

"Who is the true king?"

"His name is Alin. He was known as the Gentle King."

"Where is he now?"

"He has a farm outside the city."

"Is he an apple grower with a large misshapen nose?" I asked thinking of the farmer that the guards bowed to at the city gate.

"Yes, do you know him?"

"I have seen him. Can you take me to his farm?"

Following Evanora, I flew up a river valley of many orchards. We landed in front of a small hut and knocked on the door. No one answered, so we walked through the apple grove and eventually came to an old man with a pruning saw on a long pole, cutting back dead branches from an ancient tree.

Noticing us, he said, "This old fellow still has a few more years of bearing fruit, but we have to be gentle with him."

The orchard-keeper made a pile of dead limbs, then turned, and I recognized the bulbous nose I'd tickled at the city gate. He stood in front of Evanora and me, patiently waiting for us to explain why we'd come.

"Are you Alin, known as the Gentle King?" I asked.

The old man looked off into the distance and answered, "I was once known by that name, but for many years I've gone by the name Eran."

"May I ask why you gave up your throne?"

He sighed. "It's a very unpleasant job being king. Everyone expects you to solve their problems, and usually there is very little you can do to help them. And besides," he said. "I hated meting out punishments. If a boy steals from the market, what good does it do to punish him? Tomorrow he's going to be hungry again. He may not learn how to avoid getting caught, but he's going to continue stealing as long as he keeps getting hungry."

"How did Kazko become king?" Evanora asked.

"He was my trusted advisor. He took care of things for me. After a while, it seemed pointless for me to be there, especially since all I really wanted to do was to take care of my apple trees." He smiled. "I grew up in a villa not far from here. We raised cattle and had orchards, and we had three dragons I played with as a child, but when my uncle who was king died, I inherited the throne and moved with my pet dragons to the castle in the city. When I left the castle, Kazko didn't allow me to take my dragons. I've always been surprised he didn't have me killed once he'd taken the throne, but I suppose he understood that I was glad not to be king anymore."

"You know that Kazko is dead now? The Dragonqueen killed him," Evanora said.

"Well, he was an evil man," Eran said, looking down at the ground and shrugging. "I heard that he used my three dragons as steeds of war and then killed them. What a shame."

"The throne is yours," Evanora said.

"I will not go back to the castle," Eran said emphatically. "Let the leaders of the city find a new king."

"You don't want to take the crown in order to find a successor?"

Eran shook his head. "I'm the one who let Kazko rule the nation. Why would anyone trust me to find a new king? Let the ones who want to be king fight among themselves. They can sort it out. I want no part of vying for power anymore." He picked up his pruning saw and walked away, looking carefully at each tree as he passed.

We followed him and waited. I felt he had more to say.

After a long while, Eran said, "You know a kingdom is like a mirror."

"I beg your pardon?" Evanora said.

"Whatever the king is, so are the people. If the king is just, the kingdom is just. If the king is cruel, the kingdom is cruel."

"And what kind of king were you, Eran?" I asked, beginning to see where he was going with this parable.

"I was a lazy king. I disliked the duties of office, so I did as little as I could, letting Kazko attend state dinners, welcome ambassadors, listen to disputes, see to the defenses of the kingdom…"

He looked up at the sky as if the movement of clouds could explain his failure.

"By the time I left to live in the countryside, Kazko had completely taken over the kingdom. Other than a few servants who tended my needs, I doubt that anyone even noticed I was gone." He continued picking up dead limbs and throwing them in piles.

Then he straightened up and looked at me with intense blue eyes. He seemed possessed, or perhaps inspired, and I saw the king he could have been. "Mage, I've heard of your Dragonqueen. Tell her to fly home and mind her kingdom because while she's gone, someone else is sitting on her throne."

Eran walked away, clearly having finished with us.

As we were mounting our brooms, Evanora shook her head, puzzled. "I don't understand. Rather than be involved in governing, he would rather his kingdom descend into chaos and civil war." She turned to me and said, "Those blue eyes of his were frightening. What do you think he meant about Tessia needing to go home?"

I didn't answer, remembering how Tessia had grown to hate the demands of governance. Would she eventually just walk away from her throne, as Alin had done? Or would she become despotic as Kazko and so many other rulers had?

Tessia had been shrewd to keep the two witches alive and use them as guides through the Nordtoppen Mountains. We never would have found Bastian without their help.

Having only two brooms, we gave Evanora mine, so she and her daughter could fly together while I rode behind Alaric on his. Tessia and the crib rode on Tyrmiss's back. We traveled through what seemed like an endless maze of deep valleys, occasionally crossing between peaks to find ourselves in yet another maze. Still, we traveled quickly with the two witches flying well ahead, but not so far away that Tyrmiss couldn't have caught them. Before we left, I'd heard Tessia tell Tyrmiss that if the witches tried to get away, she had permission to incinerate them in midair. Tyrmiss had nodded, a hint of a smile and a red twinkle in her eye. She was obviously hoping that she would have the chance to kill the ones who'd taken her babies.

After flying all morning, we finally came to a valley which

looked identical to a dozen other valleys we'd flown through except that this one was inhabited by humans. As we descended, I could see several groups of huts scattered along the riverbank. The witches led us to the largest hut in the central village, and we landed in the common area in front of the circle of habitations. Although there was still smoke coming from cookfires in the common area, there was no one here.

"They must have seen us coming," Tessia said.

"Are they in their huts?" Alaric asked, looking around.

"Perhaps," Tessia answered. "But more likely they went off to hide in the surrounding area."

I looked at the thick aspen forest sloping away from the river and climbing onto the shoulders of the peaks. In this rough country, it would be difficult to find anyone without knowing which direction they went.

Tessia and Alaric made a quick search of the huts and found no one.

"They must have just left," Alaric said. "There are half-eaten bowls of food in the huts."

Tessia, a tracker and hunter since childhood, was circling the perimeter of the clearing, studying the ground.

"Here we go," she said, pointing at the ground. "Half a dozen people took this trail into the forest just minutes ago. They have a dog and children with them, and they haven't even tried to cover their tracks. They'll be easy to follow. We'll catch up to them pretty quickly."

She looked at us, devising a plan. "Tyrmiss, you stay here with the witches. Do not harm them unless they try to escape." She looked at Tyrmiss who reluctantly nodded her head.

"Please don't leave us with the dragon," Evanora pleaded.

"Tyrmiss has agreed not to harm you. But don't give her any trouble, you understand?"

The two witches nodded.

Tessia signaled to Alaric and me that we should follow her,

and she turned and started up the trail at a fast pace, looking at the ground in front of her.

It didn't take long before we caught up to the fugitives, a band of three women, one old man and two small children who held onto their mothers' hands. The dog approached us barking ferociously.

"Call off your dog," Tessia said mildly, her hand on the pommel of her sword. "I don't want to hurt him, but I will if he doesn't back off."

The old man whistled, and the dog stopped barking and retreated to stand beside his master, both man and dog watching us carefully.

"My name is Tessia, Queen of the Dragonja and Bekla Valleys, and this is Captain Alaric of the Queen's Guard, and Norbert, the Green Mage."

Tessia paused, obviously expecting these people to be impressed by her title and to do what any civilized person would do, that is, bow before the Queen. But these wild mountain people, whose independence had never been compromised, knew nothing about the ways of civilization. Instead of bowing before the Queen, they simply stared at her, as if she were from the moon.

Tessia smiled, admiring the independence of these people whose freedom was not just an idea, but a daily fact. "We are looking for a man named Bastian. Do you know him?"

Although they didn't respond, I could see they recognized his name. Tessia leaned toward me, and I whispered, "They know him, but they're not going to tell us anything without rough questioning, and even then, what they tell us won't be reliable."

"What do you suggest we do?" she whispered while looking at them.

"I suggest that we make friends with them, give them gifts, provide a feast, and then, if they trust us, they will tell us what we want to know."

214

Tessia glanced at Alaric who nodded in agreement.

So, that is how we came to provide a feast for the Renetu tribe of the Wolfbron Rill Valley.

We told our new friends to invite everyone they knew to the feast. As it turned out, there were hundreds of people who lived in the valley and on the nearby slopes, so we would be needing a lot of food. Tyrmiss skimmed the river for trout. Alaric flew into the high peaks and killed a mountain goat. Tessia hunted an elk. I dug up water tubers and the two witches flew down the valley and found wild chokecherries and blueberries.

Our new friends were very impressed with the way Tyrmiss could light a bonfire with just a quick breath, and the women of the valley took over the cooking. As we waited for the feast to be ready, Tessia sat on a log in the middle of the village and talked with the people. The chief who, as it turned out, was the old man with the dog we'd tracked on the forested slope, sat next to Tessia with Alaric close by. His name was Juhu. The Renetu dialect was close enough to ours that we could converse with them, but Tessia asked Alaric, who had an excellent ear for languages, to occasionally translate a word or phrase. I couldn't follow everything, but I heard Bastian's name mentioned a few times.

According to Juhu, generations ago, the Renetu had lived on the plains, but the Drekavacs emigrated from the north and took their land. These mountains, which we call Nordtoppen, they call Scarsrich, which made me wonder whether the name 'Skarsland' which is the name of the whole region, came from the name 'Scarsrich.' The other tribespeople kept looking in Tyrmiss's direction. It seemed they didn't want to stare, but they were fascinated by the dragon. Tessia asked the chief whether he'd ever seen a dragon before. He answered that last year,

Bastian had arrived on a dragon. Then later, two more men arrived on dragons as well. They'd been very rude, demanding to be fed, and then they flew off to the west.

"So, Bastian did not live here?"

"No," Juhu answered through Alaric, "Bastian was from Osterbo City. Then, a few months ago, he returned with her," he said, nodding toward Zamarrra.

I was beginning to understand that everything Bastian had told us about having escaped from Osterbo to live with the Renetu, marrying the chief's daughter, and becoming their chief was an outright lie. In fact, Bastian had been a spy working for Kazko all along. I felt foolish for having been taken in by his story, but the fact that all of my friends had also been taken in made me feel a little better.

"Yes," Zamarrra interjected. "Bastian and I came here on my broom, as you instructed us, Your Majesty."

"Bastian told us she was a witch, and she planned to kill us in our sleep," Juhu continued. "So, we tied her up and covered her mouth to protect ourselves. Then, I went with Bastian to the river junction downstream from here where there is a small fort where the king's soldiers are stationed, and Bastian and the witch stayed with the soldiers, and I returned here."

"Bastian and a contingent of soldiers then took me to Osterbo," Zamarrra said, "And you know the rest."

Tessia explained to Juhu that Bastian was a traitor to his people, and he tricked Zamarrra into coming here. "We're hunting Bastian to make him pay for his crimes."

The old chief nodded, but he didn't reveal any more information, so Tessia let the subject drop.

After hours of smelling the roasting meat and the steaming pots, we were famished, and the feast was finally ready. We ate heartily, and once our first hunger was sated, the entertainment started. A fire-eater whom everyone called "the Dragon" performed his tricks and Tyrmiss eventually joined him for a fiery

216

duet. There was a juggler, a symphony of drums, and a chorus of girls who sang in beautiful harmony. Afterwards, Tyrmiss settled down with her babies, and allowed the children to pet the dragonlings. After our second round of eating, a storyteller sang one of the old sagas, and when he was finished, he handed Alaric his instrument, a large harp, and invited him to sing. Alaric shook his head and indicated that the harp should go to me. I improvised a song about the feats of the heroic Queen Tessia. I didn't have to exaggerate in the slightest since, as I said as part of the song, I had witnessed these feats with my own eyes. Tessia was modest enough to look down at the ground through the saga, and I could see her humility further impressed the Renetu.

After the feast and the songs, skins of fermented cider were passed around, each person took a long draught. When the skin of cider had gone around the circle a few times, the old man's eyes began to glaze over, and he began talking—with Alaric translating where needed.

Juhu revealed that according to legend there once had been many dragons in these mountains, but men had hunted them, killing them most cruelly although the dragons had never done anything to men. It had become great sport to capture a dragon and ride it. And if the dragon resisted or tried to escape, the man would run a spear through one of its hearts. In many of the great houses of the time, it is said, dragon skulls decorated walls, and dragon skins were used as tents, and talons were used as daggers.

The old man was saying these things with great sadness in his voice, and all the people were looking at the ground in shame for what their forebears had done to these magnificent beasts. I noticed Tyrmiss lying not far away, her mighty head resting on her front legs. The firelight caught a tear as it slid down the side of her snout. Tessia got up from her place at the fire and went to her friend. She put her hand on Tyrmiss's head and leaned down and kissed her scaly cheek.

Juhu said that when the dragons could no longer accept their treatment at the hands of men, they revolted, and there was a great war between men and dragons. For many generations, it's been believed all the dragons had been killed in this war. But now, Juhu was happy to discover there are still dragons in the world, and that there are two baby dragons who will carry their mighty race into the future. The chief swore that from now on the Renetu people would always be friends with the dragons, and if any man attacks them, the Renetu will always stand beside them as brothers and sisters in arms.

The old man had been speaking loudly and everyone at the dozen fires heard him, and the women started sobbing in sadness at what their ancestors had done, and the men stood as a group and raised their fists and swore to stand beside Sister Tyrmiss if she needed them. I looked at Tyrmiss and remembered how many times she'd saved me, my family, my Queen and my city, and I silently swore to protect this dragon and her dragonlings as long as I lived.

The Woodcarver

~A folktale told by the Bekla Valley people and here recorded on parchment by Mihai of Crota during the reign of Costica III

*T*here was once a young man with a talent for woodcarving who loved to walk through the forest. One day, in a part of the forest where he'd never been, he came to a house in a clearing. There were people working on the house, carving beautiful scenes into the doors and lintels. An old Mage with long white hair was standing nearby waving a willow wand, blessing the freshly turned dirt of a new garden. He greeted the young man and offered to introduce him to the people who worked here. The Mage showed the young woodcarver the nearby groves where people harvested food for the community kitchen, stables where the draft animals were cared for, and workshops where men split logs for shingles. Everywhere the young man looked, he saw people happily absorbed in their tasks. He was especially impressed by the quality of the carvings. When he showed the Mage a few of his own pieces, the old man called to two men working on a nearby lintel and asked them to take a look at the young man's work, and they too were impressed. The Mage invited the young woodcarver to join the community and help with the work on the house.

The young man enthusiastically agreed, but first, he said he had a few questions. How much of the house would be his? Which of the trees in the surrounding forest would be his? How much food from the groves and gardens would be his? Could he sell what he did not eat? If he found gold in the earth beneath their feet, would it be his? The old Mage sadly shook his head and asked him to leave. The young man became angry and said it was very unfair for the old man to invite him to join the community, and when he asked a few questions, the old man withdrew his invitation. The young man said he suspected the Mage had tricked all these people into working on his house for free. The Mage apologized and explained he had not intended to be unkind, but he could tell from the questions the young man would not be happy in the community.

The Mage explained that the house was not his; he was merely the caretaker. He was from the nearby village, and many years before, sick at heart after losing his wife and children, he'd come to the house in the forest quite by accident. It had been in disrepair with a roof that had collapsed and vines growing through the windows. Having nothing better to do and not wanting to return to his empty life in the village, he'd started rebuilding the ruined house. Soon, others joined him, and the community grew. It gave the Mage pleasure that the house had become so beautiful, and he was restored to happiness. He thought of himself only as a trusted servant of the community, not its leader. The house and the land around it were not owned by any individual, but rather by the community as a whole.

The Mage suggested that the young man go to the nearby village to seek work. The village was known for its many woodcarving shops, and a few master carvers had become wealthy and famous. In fact, the two woodcarvers who'd been impressed by the young man's pieces lived in the village and came to the house in the forest in their spare time.

The young man did as the Mage suggested, and after many years of work, the woodcarver, now an old man himself, famous throughout the world for his beautiful carvings, returned to the house in the forest. The community was in need of a caretaker, and there the woodcarver lived out his days.

Part Four: The Wisdom of Dragons

Chapter Eighteen

Tessia, Alaric and I spent all the next morning negotiating with Juhu and waiting for him to make a decision on whether to help us find Bastian. At first, we didn't realize that by asking him for help, we'd put the old chief in a difficult position, but listening to Juhu talk with the elders, we began to realize how complicated and demanding were the laws and customs of this isolated tribe.

"Revealing the whereabouts of Bastian represents a conundrum for me," Juhu explained. "My people have strict rules about the treatment of guests, and turning a guest over to the authorities is clearly a violation of these rules. However, after the council discussed the issue at length, one of the elder women pointed out that Bastian had never taken on the responsibilities of a guest. He'd never offered gifts, or been polite, or praised the tribal leaders, or offered mutual aid in the event of attack. He has lied to many people about being a chief of the Renetu, and of having a wife and children here. Moreover, Bastian behaved dishonorably by betraying Zamarrra, Tessia, and Tyrmiss. Worst of all, in light of their new vow to protect dragons, Bastian helped to kidnap Tyrmiss's young ones.

"Queen Tessia, on the other hand, has been a perfect guest, offering a feast and treating the tribe with respect and honesty.

She's made it clear we can rely on her and her warriors if we're ever attacked. Most important of all, Tessia has treated me, the chief of the Renetu, as well our laws and customs, with respect. The council concluded that Tessia is the honored guest whereas Bastian is merely a criminal interloper. Therefore, I am free to reveal Bastian's location to Tessia." Juhu looked around at us with pride, pleased that the council had found an ethical path that satisfied both the law and common decency.

Bastian's hideout, as it happened, was a cave straight up the mountain behind the village. Tessia and I looked up the mountain and could see the black speck of the cave entrance, and we exchanged a look. Obviously, Bastian could see the village from his cave and had, no doubt, seen us arrive yesterday. It was unlikely he was still in his hideout. Tyrmiss left her two babies with a couple of grandmothers who adored the little ones, and Tessia swung up onto Tyrmiss' back with me behind her.

It only took a few moments to fly up the mountain and dismount. Tessia drew her sword, entered the cave and said, "It looks like he's been living here for a few days, but he's gone now." She walked in a large spiral around the cave entrance until she picked up his trail. "This way," she said, gesturing to me.

Tyrmiss meanwhile flew into the air into the direction Tessia was walking. She flew over the high ridge and disappeared. Tessia and I were making slow progress across the loose gravel and stones on the slope. I was about to complain about the difficult climb when Tessia, reading my thoughts, said, "The rough path works to our advantage, Norbert. Bastian can't move any more quickly across this mountain than we can. Tyrmiss will catch up to him quickly."

She was right. In a couple of hours, Tyrmiss came flying slowly over the ridge with Bastian walking below her. When he slowed down, she blew a small ball of flame in his direction, scorching the seat of his pants.

"He ambushed me," Tyrmiss muttered angrily. "I was flying

low over a jumble of rocks, and he jumped out and tried to stab me with a spear. Luckily, his foot slipped, and he missed me. Good thing he's clumsy with a spear." She breathed fire in his direction one last time for good measure.

When Bastian was standing in front of us, Tessia looked at him with rage. "You've betrayed your friends, your country, and your Queen. You caused irreparable harm to many people," she growled.

"You and your Mage are such fools," Bastian blustered. "You were inviting a coup."

Tessia drew her sword and pointed it at the traitor's throat.

Realizing that his insolence was going to get him killed, Bastian fell on his knees in front of Tessia, and said, "I know what I did was wrong. Can Her Majesty find it in her heart to forgive me?"

Tessia turned to me, and I knew what she was thinking. It was not practical to take Bastian back to Dragonja for a trial. She could, of course, execute him now, but murdering an unarmed man was not something she'd ever done.

"Perhaps," Tyrmiss suggested, "We could feed him to the bears. The ones in these mountains are known to have a taste for human flesh."

"You have no right to detain me," Bastian blustered, forgetting his humility of a moment before. "I was just doing what I thought was right."

Tyrmiss's eyes narrowed to red slits, and I was worried she was going to light him up.

"Let's take him back to the village and ask Juhu what he suggests," Tessia said.

Back in the village, we left Bastian with his hands tied in front of the fire in the middle of the village. Tyrmiss made herself comfortable close by, the crib with her babies in front of her.

225

Meanwhile, Tessia, Alaric and I went into the large hut which served as a meeting place for the council of elders. Juhu had asked the council to decide on Bastian's fate, and they'd agreed.

While we were waiting for the meeting to begin, I could hear a boy outside singing to the music of a lyre. The melody unwound in a slow tempo, and the lyrics evoked a strange sadness, a sense of loss, a golden river, a blackberry field, rain falling. I repeated the lyrics to myself to remember them.

"What's the name of that boy?" I asked a woman passing by.

"Lorenc," she answered, pausing for a moment to listen. "It's a very old song. He has a gift, doesn't he?"

I nodded, and listening to the song fade away in the misty air, I sensed for the first time that these seemingly simple villagers had a great deal to teach us.

Tessia asked me to speak to the council, explaining Bastian's crimes. I told them about his ingratiating himself into Tessia's court, convincing us to trust him, and how he accompanied us as we traveled up the Iskar Valley where he was turned into a badger. I told them how Zamarrra and I developed an unspell that changed people back to their human forms.

Zamarrra then picked up the thread and told how she and Bastian had flown to this valley and how he'd betrayed her, handing her over to Kazko's forces. Evanora then completed the narrative by explaining her role in kidnapping the dragonlings and taking them to Osterbo to trade for her daughter's freedom.

Tessia then explained what laws Bastian had broken in her kingdom, but that it was too difficult to take him back to stand trial there, so she was requesting that the council, in its wisdom, would decide what to do with Bastian, and she in her role as Queen of Dragonja would accept their judgement.

Bastian was brought in and given a chance to tell his side, but he denied everything, claiming that he'd been an important advisor to Queen Tessia, and now she was trying to get back at him for having undercut her policies in her kingdom. He claimed he'd never stolen the dragonlings or betrayed his country. He was simply being made into a scapegoat for mistakes Queen Tessia had made.

By the time everyone had finished testifying, it was quite a long tale, and council members often interrupted to ask questions or clarify a point. It was late evening when we concluded, and Juhu suggested that we end the proceedings for the day and reconvene the next morning when council would make a decision. This delay had the advantage of giving council members a chance to sleep and dream about the case. In Renetu society, Evanora explained, dreaming was considered the most important part of any process involving the community.

Tessia, Alaric, and I were given a hut in which to sleep, and after a light supper of vegetables left over from the previous night's feast, we fell into bed.

The next morning, the boy Lorenc whom I'd heard singing came to our hut and said the council was ready to announce its decision. The elders had evidently woken early and gone straight to the meeting house to discuss Bastian's case. Once we were settled on the benches, we were very surprised to see the door open and Tyrmiss's head emerge through the opening.

"Since Tyrmiss is the most injured party, she has a right to address the council and hear our decision," Juhu explained.

"The council thanks Queen Tessia for apprehending the fugitive Bastian and for trusting the council with hearing the case," Juhu began. He went on to discuss the Renetu laws which pertain to the case and how the council had responded to each of the charges. He spoke eloquently and respectfully. It was clear to me that the Renetu tribe had a rich tradition of oratory, the council had taken its charge seriously, and the deliberations had been thorough.

"One important distinction," Juhu said, "Is whether a dragon should be considered a person or an animal. If Tyrmiss, and therefore her children, is an animal, then stealing a dragonling was basically a crime of property, like stealing a lamb, but if Tyrmiss is a person, then stealing her children constituted kidnapping, a much more serious crime."

I looked at the members of the council. Half of them were men and half were women. They were all paying respectful attention to Juhu. It was clear he was speaking the will of the council, not just his own opinion.

"Another question," Juhu continued. "Is whether Bastian lying about Zamarrra constitutes a crime. Generally speaking, lying about another person is considered a wrongful act, but not a crime, a wise rule since we don't want to waste the council's time with prosecuting gossips and braggarts. However, Bastian told a lie about Zamarrra which resulted in her being detained by the Renetu and turned over to the king's soldiers, so in the end, the council must treat his wrongful actions as a fraud which he perpetuated against the Renetu.

"On the more difficult issue of Tyrmiss's status, whether that of a person or animal, the council decided unanimously that the dragon is a sentient being and a valued friend of the tribe, and therefore, she is a person with full rights to be protected by the law as such.

"Is the council prepared to vote at this time?" Juhu asked, looking at each council member as he or she nodded.

"Then, let us vote first on the charge of kidnapping and then on the charge of fraud," Juhu said.

The council decided unanimously that Bastian was guilty on both charges.

Tessia, Alaric, and I smiled at each other and put our arms around each other's shoulders. I knew they felt as I did—a great sense of relief that Bastian was about to receive his just punishment. But then something happened which we didn't expect.

Under Renetu law, the punishment phase of the trial consists of the injured parties, in this case Tyrmiss and Zamarrra, making a suggestion of what should be done to the convicted defendant. So, it was up to Tyrmiss to suggest a punishment for kidnapping her children, and it was up to Zamarrra to suggest a punishment for perpetuating a fraud which led to her being taken captive by the king's soldiers.

Everyone in the room turned toward Tyrmiss. Most of her body was outside the meeting house. Only her huge head was in the room, the thick purple scales of her neck reflected the torchlight, giving her the appearance of an apparition from the underworld. I was fully expecting her to pronounce a death sentence on Bastian who sat on a low bench in front of the council.

"Let him go," Tyrmiss rumbled.

Members of the council looked at the dragon in disbelief. Juhu's jaw dropped. "Let him go?" Juhu asked, shaking his head slowly.

"Yes," Tyrmiss said. "Let him go." Noticing that the men and women in the room didn't understand the decision, she explained, "Dragon law is not vindictive the way that human law is. Under our laws, when an individual is found guilty, then they are required to make amends. Once the amends are completed, the guilty party is allowed to return to the community. It is assumed that the shame of having been found guilty is painful enough that the guilty party will not want to repeat his or her mistake. The amends are atonement, and once the process is complete, the crime is never mentioned again."

Alaric could not restrain himself any longer. He stood up and said to his friend Tyrmiss, "How can you let Bastian get away with having kidnapped your children? He needs to be punished. If the death penalty is more than you can bear to see happen, then he should be whipped or put in a stock. I want to see him suffer for his crime."

Tyrmiss shook her head and said gently, "And what would his suffering accomplish, my young friend? By killing him, we extinguish whatever good is in him and we eliminate the

229

possibility of the good he might do in the future. And by causing him pain, then we take the risk of twisting his soul in a way that would cause him to inflict harm in the world. No, it is better to let him go and let him learn from his mistakes."

At this point, Bastian stood up and asked, "May I address the council?" Juhu nodded, and Bastian said in a sonorous voice that sounded completely out of place, since everyone else had spoken in a plain way, "Honorable Council, the dragon is absolutely correct. I have learned my lesson. I made a terrible mistake in taking part in the kidnapping of the dragonlings and falsely accusing Zamarrra. Please let me make my amends. For example, I could become an advisor to this council, instructing them on the way of the larger world. I could bring wealth and power to the Renetu."

It could not have been a worse thing to say to the council. Juhu stared with undisguised contempt at Bastian. The idea that the council needed advice from this confidence artist who betrayed his friends and his country of birth for his own profit was a deeply offensive proposal to them.

Alaric sat down and tried not to laugh. Any chance of the council accepting Tyrmiss's proposal of leniency had disappeared.

Next, the separate charge of fraud was considered. Bastian had been found guilty of lying in order to cause harm to Zamarrra, so she was allowed to suggest a suitable punishment.

Zamarrra stood and addressed the council. Her blue skin had regained its radiance, but her eyes blazed in anger. She described the humiliation, fear, and dishonor she'd experienced at the hands of the soldiers and said that she suggested that Bastian be punished by magical transformation.

The council members looked confused. "Magical transformation?" Juhu asked, "We are not familiar with this act. What might it be?"

Zamarrra looked at me, and Juhu followed her gaze, "Mage, are you familiar with this act of magic?"

I rose to my feet and answered, "Yes, I am."

"Please explain it to the council," the chief instructed.

"The Great Witch Tatatungia of the Iskar Valley developed years ago a group of magical spells which can transform a person into an animal."

"And have you seen this spell performed, Mage?"

"Yes, I have. Queen Tessia herself was transformed into a dragon with the head of a woman."

"And you've seen other spells work in this way on men?" Juhu asked, methodically laying the groundwork for a decision. I was impressed by his courtroom skills, and I decided that when I got back to my courtroom duties in Dragonja, I would be much more conscientious about the proceedings. Juhu's diligent attitude and logical method had inspired me.

"Yes, I have," I answered. "My son Alaric was transformed into a hawk with the head of a cat. One of our party was transformed into a bear and another into a mastiff."

"And the defendant?" Juhu asked, following the thread I was spooling out. "Was he transformed into an animal?"

"Yes, he was," I answered. "He was changed into a badger."

"A badger?" Juhu looked at Bastian and couldn't help but smile. Bastian did indeed resemble a badger with his black and white hair, his short wide body and his large hands.

"And do you have the power to transform the defendant into a badger again?"

"No, I don't," I said. "I'm sorry. The spell requires the subject to eat the meat of a transformed animal."

"If I may," Zamarrra said. "I can be helpful here. It happens that my mother Evanora brought the dried meat of a transformed animal with her." Zamarrra turned to her mother who was sitting next to her and gave her a slight nudge with her elbow. "Tell them please, mother."

"Is this true, Mistress Witch?" Juhu asked, directing his attention to Evanora.

Evanora nodded.

"And what kind of animal do you have?" he asked.

"It is a small amount of dried flesh of a cat with the head of a sparrow," she answered, almost inaudibly.

"And why do you have it with you?" Juhu persisted.

Evanora mumbled something I couldn't catch.

"Repeat that, please," Juhu said. "Speak loudly enough so we can hear you."

"I brought the meat with the plan that I would slip it into the food of Queen Tessia and her retainers, so my daughter and I could escape."

"And why didn't you use it? Surely, you've had opportunities."

She nodded. "I… I was worried that the spell might not work on the dragon." She looked at Tessia and said, "I'm so sorry, my Queen. I only wanted to save my daughter."

Tessia was looking at Evanora with murder in her eyes. I thought, *the witch is lucky she will stand trial here, and not in Dragonja.*

"So," Juhu summarized, "Zamarrra, the aggrieved party, is suggesting to the council that Bastian who has been found guilty of causing harm to her and to others be punished by being transformed into a badger. Is that correct?"

Zamarrra nodded. Juhu turned to me and asked, "Mage, did you know Bastian when he was a badger?"

I nodded.

He asked, "Was he a good badger?" Juhu asked, a twinkle in his eye.

"Yes, he was," I answered. "In fact, I thought he was much better as a badger than as a man."

Juhu, turning serious, polled the council members, asking each one whether he or she agreed to the punishment of transforming Bastian into a badger. Everyone on the council agreed.

At this point, Bastian abruptly stood up, and said, "I object! This punishment is excessive! To change me into an animal is a ridiculous abuse of power!"

232

Juhu, only slightly amused, said, "Bastian, considering the many crimes you've committed through the years, you are getting off lightly, thanks to the extreme leniency of the dragon. Besides, in Renetu we call the badger the King of the Soil because he turns over the dirt, loosening it so seeds can grow. So, think of it this way, you are being elevated from the rank of despicable man to that of admired King. Be grateful."

As Bastian was led out, his hands still tied, Juhu gestured for me to join Evanora, Zamarrra and him. "How long will it take you to transform him?" he asked.

"Not long," Zamarrra answered. "We will prepare a soup for him and include the dried meat as one of the ingredients. He should be fully transformed by tomorrow."

"And if he refuses to eat?" Juhu asked.

"Then we will have to force him," Zamarrra answered.

Later, as we ate dinner beside the fire, I noticed Bastian resignedly eating his soup. Evidently, he'd decided that cooperating with his transformation was better than being force-fed. Besides, I actually did think he was better off as a badger. Badgers don't talk, and talking was the thing that had always gotten Bastian into trouble.

The next morning, I saw Bastian asleep beside the fire. His black and white fur gleamed in the sunlight. He woke, looked around at everyone staring at him. He examined first his right paw, then his left. He turned and looked at his right flank, then his left. He lifted his paw and felt his long snout and hairy throat. Then he wandered off into the woods to find his breakfast of grubs and beetles.

I never saw him again.

Chapter Nineteen

The next day was the trial of Zamarrra and Evanora.

I was asked to testify about the weather war that Zamarrra had conducted against the Kingdom of Dragonja and Bekla. I told the council about the terrible drought we'd experienced, how she'd tricked me into giving her a room in the high tower so she could cast her weather spells more effectively, and how she'd brought terrible flooding to the kingdom. Alaric and Tessia told their versions, confirming mine; then Tessia elaborated on the lasting effects of the drought and flooding on the kingdom and how it will take years for the nation to recover. When the testimony was over, the council asked Zamarrra to tell her side. She testified that King Kazko had forced her to do these terrible things by threatening her mother Evanora and their nation of Sheonad. She also said that she bears no ill will against Queen Tessia or her subjects, and she regrets the harm she caused them. She added that if she's given the chance to make amends, she would gladly do so.

Juhu announced that the council had decided early this morning that they would hear testimony today about both Zamarrra and Evanora, treating the two cases as one because they overlapped and were closely related to each other, and the council wanted to gain a sense of the whole picture before making a decision on the fate of the two women.

Tyrmiss was asked to testify about the kidnapping of her babies and the recovery of them in Osterbo. She sounded quite eloquent, I thought, explaining how each incident led to the next and how the involvement of Tessia and me was essential to the regaining of her babies. The council followed up with a few questions to Tessia. Evanora was asked to tell her side, and she verified what Tyrmiss and Tessia said. I was surprised that neither of the witches had offered any kind of defense. I wondered whether they felt so guilty that they were willing to accept whatever punishment the council meted out. Or perhaps, having seen that the dragon had asked for leniency for Bastian, they were counting on gentle punishments for themselves as well.

When the council members were satisfied that they understood the facts, Tyrmiss, Tessia, Alaric, and I were asked to step outside. Tyrmiss withdrew from the chamber. And guards escorted Zamarrra and Evanora out the door as well.

As we sat on a log next to the fire, a woman who seemed to be in charge of cooking brought us each a bowl of white porridge with sliced apples. I found myself admiring the simple nourishing diet of the Renetu. It seemed to me that they had discovered how to live a simple fulfilling life. Unlike the citizens of Dragonja, the people of Renetu were content.

As we ate, Alaric asked, "What do you think the council will decide?"

"The two of them are obviously guilty of the charges," Tessia said matter-of-factly.

I looked at Tyrmiss who had lain down on the other side of the camp with the crib next to her head. I wondered what she would advise the council about the punishment of the kidnappers of her babies.

When we were settled once more in the meeting house in front of the council, and Tyrmiss had nudged her head into the doorway, Juhu said, "Before the council renders its verdict, the members would like to thank Queen Tessia for trusting us with this important proceeding. She is the ruler of a mighty kingdom, and we are but a small group of villages. However, we've lived here a very long time and have developed laws that are just and fair. We deeply appreciate the Queen's recognition of the values of our traditions."

Juhu bowed before the Queen who nodded her head at him and then looked at each council member and nodded. It was exactly the right gesture the occasion called for, and it seemed to please the council members.

Juhu announced the verdict. "The council has found that Zamarrra the Witch did harm the Kingdom of Dragonja and Bekla, destroying crops, buildings and even causing death through her weather charms. Furthermore, the council has found that Evanora the Witch did kidnap the dragonlings which are the adopted children of Tyrmiss. In this way, she caused great distress to the dragon. Furthermore, by forcing the Queen and her retainers to rescue the dragonlings, Evanora did cause death and destruction in the city of Osterbo."

Juhu looked at the two witches. "Do you have anything to say to the council at this time?"

Zamarrra and Evanora shook their heads and looked down at their folded hands which rested on the table in front of them.

"Very well, then," Juhu said. "The council would like to hear from the injured parties. Who would like to speak first?" He looked around the room.

Alaric asked to be recognized and then stood up, "Considering how much harm these two witches have caused, I think that they both should suffer death."

Although I was taken aback by Alaric's suggestion of executing the two witches, the council members didn't seem surprised at the suggestion.

Juhu nodded solemnly. "Would the Queen like to address the issue?"

Tessia stayed silent for a few moments, then said, "I was very impressed yesterday by Tyrmiss' forgiving attitude toward Bastian. I've thought all night about what she said about the way we humans always want to punish lawbreakers, rather than to give them a chance to redeem themselves. These two witches have tremendous talents, and they have used them well in the last weeks to help others. I would like to see this council give them a chance to use their magical skills in a way that serves the people they harmed."

I raised my hand to be recognized, then said, "I hope the council will allow me to tell them a true story." When Juhu nodded, I said, "There was once a boy in the city of Dragonja," I glanced at Alaric. "This boy was strong and good, but when his mother was taken from him and he was alone without guidance, he became a ruffian of the streets, fighting and stealing every day. When his mother returned, she brought him to the city square and sat him down in front of their friends and neighbors. She told them what he had done, but she believed he was a good boy who'd lost his way. She praised him for his goodness and kindness, and she begged the community to help her save him. And then, as they'd planned to do, the friends and neighbors took turns praising the boy, talking about all the good things they remembered him doing. Even shopkeepers the boy had stolen from praised him for his basic decency. After a while, the boy was sobbing, and he went to his mother and embraced her. She took him home and served him his favorite foods and treated him with the loving-kindness that everyone wants and needs. This event happened five years ago, and that boy is now a man who serves his city with honor and distinction."

I glanced at Alaric who had tears in his eyes. Tessia reached over and took his hand.

"Thank you, Mage," Juhu said. "I would like to hear from the dragon Tyrmiss now. It was her babies who were stolen, and a mother's love is a true guide to wisdom."

"Be merciful to them," Tyrmiss rumbled. "One of the witches was trying to save her mother. The other witch was trying to save her daughter. Given no other choice, any of us would have done the same."

Tyrmiss looked at each of us, one after the other. Not for the first time, I wondered what a ten-thousand-year-old dragon thought about the frail, ignorant, selfish humans she lived with.

"However," Tyrmiss added. "Being merciful does not mean we've forgotten the harm they did. They must make amends to the ones they hurt."

"And what do you suggest, Mistress Dragon?" Juhu asked.

"I'm not sure," Tyrmiss said thoughtfully. "But their crimes are great. Zamarrra destroyed a kingdom with her weather spells, and Evanora stole two babies, endangering an entire species. Their amends must be proportional to their offenses."

There was a long silence as everyone pondered the issue. What amend could be so immense it could balance the weight of what these two witches had done?

Zamarrra tentatively raised her hand. When Juhu recognized her, she stood and said, "I would like to make a suggestion as to a way my mother and I could make amends to Queen Tessia, the people of her kingdom, and the dragon Tyrmiss.

"Last night when my mother and I were waiting for our trial, we talked about the events of the last few months, and we began to see how much harm we've done to innocent people, as well as to the dragon. We felt very sad we'd gotten carried away with our plots and devices and had no concern for those we hurt. We promised each other that if we were not executed…" Here she nodded to Alaric. "Then we would spend the rest of our lives using our magical skills to serve the people of Dragonja."

"And how do you propose to do that, Mistress Witch?" Juhu asked.

"In Queen Tessia's kingdom, there is an area called The Dry

Hills, located between the two great rivers of Dragonja and Bekla. It is a desert unfriendly to man and beast, inhabited only by bandits and the great white wolves people believe to be ghosts. But this area was not always so hostile to life. A thousand years ago, the hills were blanketed with a cedar forest. The trees were so tall they were prized as masts for ships, and the wood was so fragrant that small blocks were traded to foreign lands, so kings could sweeten the air of their palaces. And in these rolling hills covered with cedar trees, the ancestors of the witches who now live in Sheonad lived. They gently practiced their weather spells, so that the land of the two rivers was abundant, and the people were prosperous. However, some witches abused their magical powers. They hungered for riches and power. They dominated the rulers of the kingdom and set themselves up as priestesses, and eventually as gods. And the people rose up against the witches and slaughtered them and burned their cedar palace and set fire to the great forests. A handful of the witches escaped and made their way to the place they called Sheonad and established a kingdom there.

"Now the number of witches has declined and the city of Sheonad is in ruins. So, I suggest, wise council members, that you allow my mother and me to make amends to Queen Tessia's people by letting us go to our ancestral home in the Dry Hills. There we will plant cedar trees and *gently* encourage the weather, so we can help to restore abundance and prosperity to the kingdom. It will take the rest of our lives to reforest the desert, but we vow to devote all of our magical skills to the task."

"And what would you do to make amends to the dragon Tyrmiss for having stolen her babies?" Juhu asked.

At this point, Evanora stood and said, "My daughter and I will put all dragons under our protection. Let no man or Drekavac molest a dragon or a dragon's egg without suffering the wrath of the weather witches."

"And does the Queen accept this amend?" Juhu asked.

"She does," Tessia said.

"And does the dragon accept this amend?"

"I do," Tyrmiss said.

"And does the council accept these amends?" Juhu asked, turning to his colleagues.

Each council member nodded his or her head in agreement.

"Then let this be the decision of the council," Juhu proclaimed. "The witches Evanora and Zamarrra will go to the area between the two rivers known as the Dry Lands, which is their ancient home, and there establish a great cedar forest and a home for themselves and for those like them. And let them there gently encourage the weather in order to restore prosperity to the Kingdom of Queen Tessia."

And in this way, the wise elders of Renetu helped the Kingdom of Dragonja and Bekla make peace with its enemies and regain its prosperity.

Chapter Twenty

When I woke the next morning, I noticed that Tessia was not in the hut. I got dressed and went outside where I saw Tessia and Juhu talking. I ladled myself a bowl of porridge from the cauldron bubbling on the fire, sat down on a log and began eating. After a while, Tessia came over, helped herself to a bowl of porridge and sat down next to me.

"Juhu says we should stay another day and work out a plan for bringing the Dry Hills back to life. What do you think?"

I thought about it for a minute, pretending to be very interested in the lumps in my porridge.

"It would be helpful, I think, to know what we want and to develop a sense of what we need to do to get what we want," I said.

"Juhu has offered us the use of the meeting house for the day," Tessia says. "I'm going to accept his offer."

"Tessia," I said, and she stopped and turned to me. "Juhu has been very wise in overseeing this whole process. Please tell him that we appreciate his wisdom." I was thinking wisdom was what was most needed in Dragonja.

She nodded and walked over to Juhu who had been standing in front of the meeting house entrance with his arms crossed. When she walked over to him and started speaking, he dropped his arms and looked at me. Our eyes met and he nodded at me, indicating that Tessia had given my message to him.

Within the hour, Tessia, Alaric, Zamarrra, Evanora and I were sitting at the table in the meeting house. Tyrmiss was also in attendance, having pushed her head through the entrance. I thought how strange it must look to the Renetu villagers to see the huge body of the dragon sprawled across their village, the long neck extended into the meeting house. *These days will be recounted again and again by the Renetu for generations*, I thought, *the story of the dragon and the Queen and how Renetu saved their kingdom.*

Tessia began the meeting: "As you all know, we are here to develop a plan for transforming the Dry Hills into a cedar forest as it was in the times of old. Zamarrra," Tessia said, turning to the younger witch. "This was your proposal, a way that you and your mother could make amends for your crimes against Tyrmiss and the people of our kingdom. What would you like to see happen and how can we help?"

"The area known as the Dry Hills is a huge tract of land, comprising a large part of the Queen's nation," Zamarrra said, reviewing the facts. "These hills are located between the two river valleys, the Dragonja and the Bekla. Both valleys have prosperous farms, orchards and pastureland and produce wealth for the kingdom. The weather witches have known for a long time that the rain falls in the Dragonja Valley because the air rises as it approaches the mountains, and as the clouds rise, they cool and release their moisture. The rain falls in Bekla Valley because the wind blows from the sea and the clouds release their moisture as they move inland. These two weather patterns leave a gap where there is no rain. In the old times, the weather witches encouraged clouds to release some of their moisture over the hills as well. With wise management, spreading the rain more evenly over the kingdom should not cause hardship for the farmers in the valleys, but will bring a little more rain to the Dry Hills. The rainfall will not be enough to allow farming in the hills, but it should be enough to allow a cedar forest."

"And in the old days, the Dry Hills were covered by a cedar forest?" Alaric asked.

"Yes," Zamarrra said. "And with a little encouragement, they can be again."

"The Dry Hills are populated now by bandits and goat herders. What should we do with these people?" Tessia asked.

"Goats are very destructive," Zamarrra said emphatically. "They should not be allowed in the kingdom at all. And they cannot be allowed in the Dry Hills because they will eat all the cedar saplings, and they will eat the bark off the mature trees."

Tessia looked at me, "What does the Green Mage think?"

"She's right, Your Majesty. Goats can be destructive."

Tessia thought about it for a moment, then declared, "Very well, then, we will outlaw goats in the kingdom. We will offer to buy every goat for a fair price, slaughter it, and give the meat to the poor."

"What about sheep?" I asked.

"Sheep are also destructive, but they are easier to manage. I suggest that you encourage the sheep herders to take their flocks elsewhere," Evanora said.

"Seriously?" Alaric asked. "You want to outlaw goats? Goats have been raised in the Dry Hills for hundreds of years. How will you enforce the ban?"

"Perhaps we can trade each goat for two sheep?" I suggested.

"I think Alaric is right. We need to think about this problem before deciding," Tessia said. "We'll take the problem to the Queen's Council and let them decide on a policy."

"How many cedar trees will you be planting?" Alaric asked.

"Over the entire area of the Dry Hills, we'll be planting millions of saplings."

"There is a cedar forest in the hills to the west of the Iskar Valley," I pointed out. "We can harvest the cones there and then establish a nursery in the Dry Hills to sprout the seeds and care for the shoots until they are two or three years old. We can also transplant some of the saplings to the Dry Hills to start the forest."

"And where will you live while you are doing the work of planting a forest?" Tessia asked.

"Are you familiar with Mount Halibel which overlooks the Bekla Valley?" Evanora asked.

I nodded. It was not far from the village where I grew up. "Yes, when I was a boy, we used to call it Witches Castle."

"For good reason it was named that, Mage," Evanora responded. "It is the place where the weather witches lived for many generations. My daughter and I want to build a small hut there where we can live. We hope that other witches will join us, and we can re-establish our home in the hills above the Bekla Valley. Perhaps over time we can build more huts and eventually a castle."

"I would insist that a battalion of my guards be stationed near Witches Castle," Tessia said, obviously concerned by the possibility of the witches establishing an independent state inside the border of the kingdom.

"Of course, Your Majesty," Evanora said, bowing her head to Tessia. "As your loyal subjects, we recognize your right to station guards wherever you please."

And in this way, we spent the day talking about our plans for the Dry Hills, which had for a thousand years been a wasteland fit only for outlaws and goat herders and now would be transformed into a cedar forest where there would be birds and deer, meadows and wildflowers, and where the witches would have a home.

After we left the council house, I saw Tyrmiss at the edge of the village leaning over the crib. I walked over to her and looked at the dragonlings. They were larger than I remembered.

"Zounds!" I said, "Have they grown in the last week?"

Tyrmiss grinned at me, showing her rows of dagger-like teeth. Although I knew this was an expression of joy and kindness, I had never gotten used to the look of a dragon's smile. "Yes, dragons grow very quickly the first few years, and then their growth slows. As I believe I've mentioned before, we don't reach full maturity for about two thousand years."

"Tyrmiss," I asked, changing the subject. "You hardly spoke at the meeting today. What do you think of the plan for the witches to move to Mount Halibel and spend decades planting a cedar forest in the Dry Hills?"

"I think it's a marvelous idea, Norbert. As you may know, dragons are creatures much closer to nature and the Goddess than men or Drekavacs. I've never understood your kind's need to destroy living things."

"Do you remember the cedar forest between the two rivers?"

"Oh, yes," the dragon answered. "It was only a thousand years ago when the witches were wiped out, their castle toppled, and the cedar forest which they thought of as their soul, burned by men."

"Dragons are actually quite gentle, aren't you?"

"Yes, Norbert, we are," Tyrmiss said quietly, looking down at her babies. "It is only to defend ourselves against men that we've become fearsome and deadly."

"When Tessia and I first met you," I said. "You'd been on a killing spree for months, attacking Ludek's soldiers, both men and Drekavacs. You were hunting them, ambushing patrols, and picking off stragglers. In just a few months, you killed hundreds."

"Yes, I did," the dragon answered.

"You were acting out of revenge for the murder of your beloved Rilla?"

"Yes, I suppose I wanted revenge," she said, musing. "But really, I'd gone insane. Remember, men such as yourself had enslaved, tortured, and murdered all of the dragons in the world

245

except Rilla and me." She caught herself and looked down into the crib. "Well, at least I thought all of the dragons except Rilla and me were gone. Now, being with these two babies, I have hope there may be more dragons out there somewhere."

She looked up at the high mountains to the north. "You know that according to dragon mythology, we were created by the Goddess out of ice?"

When I shook my head, she continued. "The Goddess Nilene reached down and cleared the snow away, then using her gentlest hand, she scooped away the dirt and rock until she found the nest of the snake Scloglyg. The Goddess lifted two eggs from the nest and gently rubbed them in the snow until they hatched. Thus, the first dragons, the twins Zelby the Warm and Zipeidan the Firestarter were born. She gave them fiery breath so they could carve homes for themselves in the ice. She gave them dominion over all the rivers and forests, and she gave them wings so they could fly over their kingdom. Since the Goddess had entrusted us with all of nature and charged us with the protection of all living things, we thought the men who came onto the land were under our protection as well. But the men cut down trees, they polluted rivers, and they allowed their animals to eat everything they saw. At first, we tolerated men, thinking they were part of nature as well, and we trusted the Goddess to keep them in check, but it never happened. Finally, we realized men must be destroyed if creation was to survive. But in the great war that followed, men killed many dragons, leaving only Rilla and me who hid for thousands of years in the mountains until men no longer believed dragons were part of the world, but lived only in stories."

"And when the Drekavac soldier killed Rilla, you came down from the mountains to wreak your revenge."

"Yes, I did, but I'm not ashamed of what I did. Sometimes it is necessary to serve the Goddess through battle. Your brother Ludek had a twisted soul, and even more than most men, he was evil. So, I was glad when you killed him. I believe the Goddess wanted you to kill him."

It was a fact I didn't like to think about. I'd killed my own brother. I did it to protect my wife and son, but still I had used magic to drop a large timber on Ludek's head, and when I discovered he'd escaped and was still alive, I hunted him down, and with the help of Idella and a great white bear named Tayra, I killed him. I believed then and still believe now that it was the right thing to do, but I'm glad my mother and father were not alive to witness one of their sons murdering the other.

"You did what you had to do, Norbert," Tyrmiss said to me, kindly.

Sometimes forbearance from a friend is better than forgiveness from an enemy.

Chapter Twenty-one

The flight across the Skarsland plain was smooth and easy. We mounted Tyrmiss with Tessia in front, holding onto the last spine of the dragon's neck, the crib behind her strapped securely, and me behind, sitting between the wings. I liked this spot because it was the widest and most stable of the positions, and there was comfort in feeling the strong muscles beneath me as the wings moved up and down.

We went east, following the edge of the mountain range that separated Skarsland from Bekla, with Tyrmiss and her passengers in the lead and Alaric and the two witches on their brooms behind us. As we flew past Osterbo, I noticed that the ruined castle was no longer smoking. I wondered what the people would do now their king was dead. I hoped that when they chose a new leader, or a new leader chose them, he or she would be wise and forbearing, but it wasn't up to me to decide. I've come to believe that each nation gets the leaders it deserves.

We came to the sea and made a broad swing around the mountains which continued out into deep water. Once we were past the peaks, we turned south, then west and followed the line of mountains to the high cliffs where we'd camped before. Here, Tyrmiss landed, with Alaric and the two witches not far behind.

Sitting around the fire after a dinner of tuna steaks and

seaberries, I asked Evanora to elaborate on her strategy for re-foresting the Dry Hills.

"To start, we need a thousand cedar cones and a pair of shovels," she answered.

"There is that cedar forest in the hills beyond the Iskar Valley," I mentioned again.

"Yes," she said, "We'll go there to gather cones."

"I'd like to volunteer to help you plant the cones and tend the young trees," Alaric said.

Evanora laughed, "I thought you wanted to see us executed."

Alaric looked sheepish, "I'm sorry. I shouldn't have said that. Tyrmiss is my friend, and I was thinking only of how much Tyrmiss was hurt by the kidnapping of her children. But I see now that Tyrmiss's forgiveness of you was wise, and your willingness to make amends has changed my opinion. Will you accept the help of me and my friends in planting the cedars and restoring the land?"

"Of course, we will," Evanora said, smiling. "We're grateful for your help. For a thousand years, it's been a dream of the Blue Witches that we return to our homeland and restore the land to its beauty."

So it was decided that Alaric and his friends would join Evanora and Zamarrra in their quest to plant the cedar forest.

Later that night, I lay in my blankets looking at the boundless display of stars overhead. As I let my thoughts go quiet, I felt Tyrmiss as she entered my mind.

Norbert, she said. *You have now crossed into the twilight between waking and sleeping. Welcome. We can now speak to each other with complete honesty, for in this state nothing is hidden. Lies and evasions disappear. What you think is immediately clear to the other. You share your thoughts and I share mine and there is no division between the two.*

As she said this, I felt myself entering her mind, my large scaly body resting not far from the campsite, my head resting on my talons, my wings folded against my flanks, my long tail curled behind me. I now had the memories of ten thousand years: the comfort of sleeping with my littermates like puppies in a pile, our mother feeding us bits of fish, looking down at us with adoring blue eyes, covering us with her wing at night.

I remembered the great war with men when I flew into battle beside my brothers and sisters, a thousand dragons blackening the sky, the swarm of arrows and the great flaming bolts shot from the ballistas spearing the dragons and sending them crashing to earth. How we flew low over the men, our talons sweeping through their ranks, slaughtering many. But their numbers were too great, and finally I was the last dragon left in the sky and I flew off, arrows bristling from my body, my hide scorched, and I flew toward the mountains to die.

I remembered how Rilla, just a small dragon, not more than fifty years old, found me and helped me to the cave where her mother had hidden her, and she carried water from the stream to me in the only container she had, her mouth, and she pulled each of the arrows out of my hide, and she rubbed fish fat on my skin as a salve. As I healed, I came to love Rilla, and when she reached her two thousandth year, I took her as my mate, and we lived as sister-lovers for eight thousand years. By the light of the stars, we skimmed the river for salmon, and by day, we slept in the safety of our cave. For all those millennia, we could ignore the world of men and be happy. The joy of love was ours.

I remembered how the soldiers killed Rilla, destroying beauty for no reason other than because they could. And I found Rilla beside the stream where she'd found me after the great battle, but I was too late for her. She was dead, and the soldier who ran a spear through her right heart was dead beside her. And a great roar came from my throat, filling the valley below me. And when night came, I flew down into the valley and hunted the king's soldiers. Each time I found one, I engulfed him with flame. Each night I went out hunting and killing until Tessia came to me, and we merged. And now Tessia and I are one. We are dragon. We are woman. We are the Dragonqueen of the Dragonja and Bekla Valleys.

Because the dragon and the Queen had merged as I was merging with them, I remembered Tessia's life as well: hunting with her friends Hamlin and Anja in the forest; learning from her uncle Zygmunt how to fight with weapons and with hands and feet; and watching the Wise Queen Varvara gracefully administer a kingdom. I felt Tessia's shame of being a Queen who sometimes detests her own people, and her fear that she'd never discover the love that shapes a fit ruler. I knew the kingdom would continue to be in ruin as long as the Dragonqueen hated being Queen. I felt Tessia's grief, how she experienced the death of every soldier she'd ever killed, every animal she'd ever eaten, the heavy grief of mothers, sisters, wives and children of those she'd killed. I felt Tessia's certainty she would pay those debts in the next life.

This flood of memories coming from the dragon and the Queen was overwhelming, and I knew it would take many years to make sense of them, but one thing was clear: Tyrmiss, Tessia and I were now bound by something much deeper than blood ties.

When I woke the next day, the camp was already stirring. Alaric, Evanora and Zamarrra had packed their bedrolls and were preparing to depart. They planned to fly first to the pass between the Two Thumbs of the Giant where they would visit Hamlin the bear in Tyrmiss's old cave. Then they would fly down into the Iskar Valley to the cedar forest to gather bags of cedar cones and fly them to the Dry Hills where they planned to start their tree plantation. At some point, Alaric intended to

251

go to Dragonja City to visit his mother and recruit his friends to aid in the forestry project.

Shortly after my son and the two witches departed, Tessia and Tyrmiss returned to camp. Tyrmiss was holding a marlin in her claws which she laid on a flat rock, and with a single talon, she sliced the fish, taking a few pieces over to the crib to feed her babies. I followed her and peered into the crib. I was amazed to see that the dragonlings seemed to have grown since yesterday. Moreover, their yellow eyes—Tyrmiss told me that their eyes would change to blue as they matured—seemed alert, looking up at their adoptive mother with fascination and awe. I thought of my daughter Ena, now six years old, and how as an infant she looked at Idella with complete trust. I wondered whether dragonlings, as they grew, experienced the same phases as human children. Would they become difficult and emotional when they were two years old, wise and competent when they were ten, rebellious when they were sixteen? In a creature that lives for tens of thousands of years, how long do the phases of development last?

"Our phases are similar to yours, Norbert," Tyrmiss said, her eyes twinkling as she looked at me.

Tessia looked at me with a knowing smile. Evidently, Tyrmiss had told her about our merging of thoughts the previous night. Or did Tyrmiss not have to tell her? *Could Tessia read my thoughts now as well? Could I read hers?* I was unclear about how the merging worked…

"Don't worry, Norbert," Tyrmiss said. I looked at her to see whether she was actually speaking out loud or whether I was hearing her thoughts.

Tyrmiss and Tessia laughed. "You'll get it figured out," Tessia said. "It's not much different than speaking, except it's more honest. When someone is reading your thoughts, you can't lie to them."

"Unless you are lying to yourself," Tyrmiss added. "And

with humans, lying to themselves is extremely common." She shook her head in disbelief. "How did your species ever survive so many millennia with this muddle in your minds?"

"So, I'm looking forward to returning home," I said, changing the subject.

"Not so fast, big boy," Tyrmiss muttered.

"What? There's a problem?" I asked, surprised.

"Tyrmiss has picked up a few people's thoughts that indicate we should proceed cautiously," Tessia said.

"Are Idella and Ena in danger?"

"We don't have any details yet, Norbert," Tessia said. "We'll fly to Dragonja City, arriving after nightfall. Then Tyrmiss will hide in the mountains while you and I enter the city in disguise. After we know what the situation is, we'll know how to proceed."

We flew back the same way we had come, but this time much higher, so that we would not be alerting anyone to our return. As we flew over the Dragonja Valley, I looked down at the farms and villages that lined the river. To my left were the Dry Hills which Alaric and the witches were going to reforest, and to my right were the Nordtoppen Mountains with their steep cliffs and snowy peaks. I felt a strong love for this, my native land.

In the evening we came close to the city, and Tyrmiss veered off to the right and landed in a meadow on the side of a mountain. Here we looked down at the city where workers were heading home, and windows were lit by lanterns. I sensed that something seemed not quite right in the city. There were many soldiers in the streets, but not many civilians, and no children at all. I had a bad feeling about returning, and I was worried about Idella's safety.

We waited until the city quieted, and then Tyrmiss said, or rather thought, *Tessia is the best-known person in the city, and*

Norbert, you are well-known as well. Can you disguise the two of you?

"Of course," I said out loud. "Illusion is the simplest magic there is. The eyes can be easily fooled." The reluctance to use magic which I'd felt all my life had disappeared, replaced by a desire to serve my friends with the only skill I had.

I pulled my wand from the sheathe on my belt and waved it over Tessia's face. Instantly, her nose lengthened, her skin wrinkled, and her eyelids drooped. I waved the wand over her head and her hair turned gray. She looked fifty years older. "When you walk," I told her, "Stoop slightly."

"What have you done to me, Norbert?"

"I've made you appear to be eighty years old."

"What? You are going to change me back, aren't you?"

Tyrmiss laughed. "Well, if he doesn't, then you'll find out whether Taja loves you for your soul or for your face."

Then the mood changed, and Tyrmiss gave me an odd look. I tried to read her mind, but she was blocking her thoughts, a skill which she'd told me was not possible. I thought *something is going on with Taja that Tyrmiss is hiding.* Hearing my thought, Tyrmiss looked at me angrily and shook her head. *This mind merging business was turning out to be complicated.*

"Of course, I'm going to change you back, Tessia," I said, waving the wand over my own face and hair. "Now we appear to be an old married couple."

Tessia and I hiked down the mountain, crossed the Dragonja river at the shallows and headed up the road to the North Gate of the City. I knocked on the small door beside the gate, and a Drekavac guard appeared and held his lamp up to our faces.

"Don't I know you, old man?" he asked. In fact, he did. He'd grown up a few doors down from the Silver Pony Inn.

"Oh, yes, young man," I answered, my voice quavering. "My wife and I come here a few times a year to visit our grandchildren." Satisfied we were harmless, he allowed us entrance, and we headed across the market square to the Silver Pony where we went around to the back door and knocked.

"Who's there?" Heikum's voice bellowed.

"Someone who owes you money," I bellowed back.

His greed overcoming his suspicion, Heikum cracked the door open.

"Heikum, it's Queen Tessia and Norbert. Let us in," Tessia whispered.

He opened the door and I saw he had a club in his hand. Femke was behind him in her nightgown, wielding a frying pan. Evidently, things had become dangerous in Dragonja City.

Seeing us, both of them were taken aback, so I quickly explained. "We're in disguise because we heard there was trouble in the city. We came to you first in order to find out what has happened."

"Yes, well, you've come to the right place, Your Majesty," Heikum, said to Tessia. "I know just about everything that happens in the city." His wife rolled her eyes at this obvious inflation of his importance, but it was true that the reason we'd come here first is that between the two of them, they knew more than just about anyone in the entire city.

Tessia and I sat at the table and listened.

"Oh, Tessia..." Heikum caught himself. "I mean, Your Majesty..."

"It's alright, Heikum," Tessia said. "When no one else is around, you can call me by my first name. We're old friends after all."

Heikum nodded gratefully, acknowledging the honor she was bestowing on him. I thought about how far Tessia had come since we showed up in Dragonja City seven years earlier. She had been just seventeen years old, and the only job she could find was as a serving wench at the Silver Pony Inn.

"Tell me what is happening, Heikum," Tessia said gently.

"We're glad to see you've returned, Tessia," Heikum began.

"Things have turned for the worse since you've been away," Femke said.

"Why? Have Kazko's Drekavac troops returned?" Tessia prompted.

"No, no," Heikum said. "There have been no wars or incursions..."

"Then what is it?"

"It's the Drekavac you left in charge," Femke said reluctantly, not wanting to sound as if she were criticizing Tessia's decision.

"You mean Sergeant Zrul? Why, what has he done?"

"He's taken over the city," Heikum said, looking down.

"In what way has he taken over the city? He couldn't possibly have found the treasury," Tessia said, glancing at me. "It is very well hidden."

"His soldiers walk through the square, pushing people aside, grabbing fruit and bread as they wish. They come in here, demanding ale and food, and they leave without paying. Our regular customers don't even want to come here anymore," Heikum said, resentfully.

"Well, if it's just a matter of paying for the things they've taken, then we can solve that problem easily," Tessia said, sounding relieved.

"But it is worse, much worse," a voice I knew said from behind me. I turned and saw my wife Idella coming down the stairs. I jumped up, opening my arms and she glided into my embrace. I held her for a long moment, then held her at arm's length. She had gotten fat, but I knew better than to mention it.

"It is so good to see you, my love," I said.

"And you, my husband," she said. "Welcome home." Idella looked at my face, puzzled, and I realized that I still was disguised as an old man.

"It's just a disguise, love," I said. "Tessia and I thought it best

256

not to be recognized until we could see what was happening in the city."

Relieved, Idella curtsied to the Queen who threw her head back and laughed. The two embraced as the affectionate friends they were.

"You said things have gotten worse, Idella?" Tessia asked, growing serious.

"There are rumors that Zrul is holding Princess Taja and Minister Caz prisoner in the castle, so that the old soldier will be able to rule the city as he pleases," Idella said, looking at Tessia levelly. The look on Idella's face showed me she knew more than what she was saying.

Heikum and Femke looked down. It was clear they, too, were reluctant to say to Tessia what they knew about the situation.

"What are you not telling us?" I asked, looking from Idella's face to Femke's and Heikum's. They seemed very uncomfortable.

But before they could answer, Tessia interrupted, asking "Mage, will you follow me into battle?"

"Of course, my Queen." I said, thinking that the conversation with Idella, Femke and Heikum would have to wait.

Tessia walked to the front door of the inn and swung open the heavy door. Ten paces in front of us in the street was Tyrmiss, the red slits of her eyes burning. I noticed the crib was no longer strapped onto her back.

"Where are the babies?" I asked.

"Safe with a friend," Tyrmiss said.

I climbed on Tyrmiss's back behind Tessia, and we rose into the air, flew the short distance over Windkeep's wall and landed gently on the flat roof of the first building, the original keep, the oldest part of the castle.

As I climbed down onto the roof, I said to Tyrmiss, "You heard the conversation in the inn?"

"Of course," Tyrmiss said. "Tessia and I share all our thoughts. What she sees, I see. What she hears, I hear."

"So, what is the plan?" I asked.

"I will kick open the front door of the main tower, then release a fireball into the building. Tessia will charge through the door and engage any soldiers foolish enough to attack her. You and I, Mage, will fly to the open entrance of the dragon's lair where I will wait while you go up to the Queen's chamber where Princess Taja and Caz are being held. You will release them from their gilded cage and bring them down to the lair. I will fly them to a safe place out of the city. You, meanwhile, will make your way down the stairs of the castle and provide re-enforcement to Tessia."

She saw me swallow thickly, as I thought about how much was riding on my finding courage. I've never considered myself a warrior.

"Norbert Oldfoot, Green Mage," the dragon said to me softly, a hoarse whisper of her voice in my ear. "You are the greatest warrior in the kingdom. You are the only one who could beat your brother, the great Wizard Ludek, in battle. Even Tessia could not beat him."

Feeling fortified by her words, I quickly followed my Queen down the stone stairs on the outside of the building and stood in front of the double doors into the tall tower.

Chapter Twenty-two

Tyrmiss reared back like a huge horse and brought the full weight of her body against the oaken double doors. They burst open, flying off their hinges, and skittered across the stone floor. Then she let loose an enormous fireball into the foyer, and Tessia charged in with her two Voprian blades singing.

I climbed back onto Tyrmiss' shoulders, and we flew up the outside of the tower to the wide entrance of her lair.

"Go find Princess Taja and Caz, Norbert. Tessia is counting on you."

I ran through the dragon lair and up the stairs to the royal chamber with my wand ready in my hand. There were two Drekavac guards in front of the door. I pointed my wand at them, cocked my head at the stairs and said, "Scoot!"

The two guards exited down the stairway, looking at me over their shoulders. Sometimes, it's good to have a reputation for being able to make horrible things happen.

In the room, Taja and Caz were standing beside the door. Caz had a heavy candle stick in his hand and almost hit me on the head with it before stopping himself.

"Norbert, old boy," he said, as if we were running into each other at the market. "How nice to see you."

Taja ran over to me and embraced me. "Thank you for

coming for us, Norbert." She looked over my shoulder. "Where's Tessia?"

"Downstairs fighting a regiment of Drekavacs, I believe. Tyrmiss is in her lair. Let's get you out of this castle."

We ran down the stairs where Tyrmiss was waiting. I helped Caz and Taja onto the dragon's back and quickly explained how to hold on and maintain balance while in flight.

"Tessia and I will meet you at the Silver Pony," I said to Caz and Taja and stepped back.

Tyrmiss leaped into the open air, extended her wings and glided down to the market square, bringing the Princess and the First Minister to safety.

I turned to go downstairs to help Tessia fight the soldiers, knowing that Tyrmiss would guard the front door, keeping reinforcements from coming into the tower.

Running down the stairs, I could hear the singing of the Voprian swords and could tell that Tessia was keeping the soldiers busy.

The first thing I saw was Tessia halfway up the first flight, fighting off the onslaught of soldiers who were coming at her from below. She'd shrewdly chosen a position where they could come at her only two at a time. Her position allowed her to keep them from going up the stairs, protecting me as I rescued Taja and Caz. As I came down the stairs, I shouted at her so she wouldn't think I was a soldier attacking her from behind. I stationed myself half a flight above her, pointed my wand at a soldier at the bottom of the stairs and let loose a fireball at one of the Drekavac soldiers. It hit him on the arm, and the fire spread quickly over his torso. He screamed and beat his clothes with his mailed fist. Another fireball hit a soldier who was on the other side of the hall. Two of his friends knocked him down and put out the fire. At this point, the soldiers panicked and ran through the front door where Tyrmiss waited. She lit a few of them on fire and the rest scattered, running in all directions.

Tessia dispatched the last soldier standing in front of her on the stairs, and the battle was over.

"Where is Zrul?" Tessia asked, looking around.

"I don't know," I said. "I didn't see him upstairs."

"It's not like him not to be at the front of the battle."

Tessia and I looked at each other and said at the same time, "The Silver Pony!"

"You think he guessed we would hide Taja and Caz at the Silver Pony while we fought his soldiers?" I asked. "Idella is there too!"

Tessia and I ran out the door, jumped on the back of Tyrmiss who flew us over the battling soldiers. It looked like the ones who were loyal to Tessia were fighting against Zrul's Drekavacs, but I didn't care right now. I just knew we had to get to the Silver Pony quickly.

While Tessia burst through the front door of the inn, I went around to the back.

Zrul was backing out of the door into the alley. He had his forearm under Idella's chin who was struggling to free herself. He was trying to pull her into the alley while someone in the kitchen was swinging a frying pan at his head. He was fending off the attack with his other hand which held a dagger. As I walked up to them, I could see it was Femke who was wielding the pan. I was tempted to let the two women beat him, but I was afraid he might stab one of them and make his escape.

"Let her go, Zrul," I said, pointing my wand at him.

Zrul turned, saw it was me, and laughed. "What are you going to do, Mage? Shoot a sprout at me?" He swung his dagger at Femke, missing her face by inches. Then he roughly turned Idella around and punched her hard in the stomach. She doubled up in pain and he let her fall to the ground.

I shot him once. A hard, dry lentil, traveling fast, hit him in the eye. With a surprised look on his face, he dropped his dagger and lifted his hand to his eye. Blood ran between his fingers.

I ran over to Idella and turned her over. She seemed to have a broken rib and her breathing was ragged. I was worried she had internal injuries.

Tessia appeared in the back door, looked at Zrul standing in front of her in shock and asked, "Healer, how is she?"

"I'm not sure," I answered. We need to get her to the hospital, so Mina can look at her." I looked at Tessia.

"The hospital is still functional, and Mina is treating patients there," Tessia said, answering my question before I could ask it.

Tessia ran into the market and returned with two loyalist soldiers who improvised stretchers out of spears and capes. We laid Idella carefully in the stretcher, and I accompanied them double-time to Mina's practice in the castle. I assumed that the soldiers would go back for Zrul and carry him to the hospital as well, but I didn't really care what happened to him right now.

I volunteered to help treat the wounded, but Mina, my good friend and former assistant, sent me away, saying I was too distraught to help in the hospital.

"Go lie down, Norbert. You've done plenty for one day. You need to rest. I'll take good care of Idella."

On the way out, I saw Heikum coming into the hospital with a large bandage covering his right eye. Beside him was Femke holding him up.

"Zrul was in the market square when Tyrmiss flew you and Tessia into Windkeep." Femke explained. "He ran to the Silver Pony to hide. Later, he saw Tessia coming through the front door, so he grabbed Idella and started dragging her out the back door, using her as a hostage. Heikum tried to protect Idella, but Zrul punched him with his mailed fist. I picked up a frying pan and swung at him but missed."

"Where's Ena?" I asked, feeling a terrible burden of guilt that I'd forgotten about my daughter.

"She's fine," Heikum said. "She's with Tessia and her soldiers. The fighting is over, so they took her to the castle."

"Thank you for your bravery, my friends," I said to Heikum and Femke. "Are the Princess and the Minister safe?"

"Who?" Femke asked, puzzled.

"Taja and Caz…"

When they both looked at me with baffled looks on their faces, I felt a panic rising in me.

"Tyrmiss dropped off Taja and Caz at the Silver Pony where they could hide until the battle was over," I said.

They both shook their heads. "We never saw either of them, Norbert," Femke said, leading her husband into the hospital.

Chapter Twenty-three

Queen Tessia was in a rage. The city was in chaos. The Princess and the First Minister were missing. Everything in the kingdom felt out of balance. Many of the soldiers we fought against, especially Zrul, had been among the most loyal to the Queen. How could they have turned against her in the few weeks we'd been gone?

Although Idella had been seriously injured, she was recovering. Our daughter Ena, who'd been upstairs at the Silver Pony during the battle, felt confused and afraid because her mother was hurt, but under the vigilant care of Femke, she was gradually becoming calmer. Today, she was helping Femke in the kitchen and charming everyone who came into the inn.

A few days after the battle, I was visiting the hospital when Mina pulled me aside and said she had to discuss something important with me. She took my hand in hers, looked me in the eyes, and said, "You know that Idella was seriously injured, don't you?"

I nodded and said, "But she's recovering, isn't she?"

"Yes, she is recovering. However, the blow to her belly caused her to miscarry."

"Miscarry?" I asked, shaking my head.

"You didn't know she was pregnant?"

"No, I didn't." I sat down and put my head in my hands.

"Did she know she was pregnant a few weeks ago before I left?"

Mina nodded her head.

"Why didn't she tell me?"

"Perhaps because she knew you had to go with Tessia to find the dragonlings, and she didn't want you to feel obliged to stay."

I remembered Idella had said she had to tell me something, but I was too busy with preparing for another quest with Tessia to listen to her. I felt a flood of guilt and regret over my own willful blindness. If I hadn't gone to Osterbo and Nordtoppen, then I'd have been with Idella to protect her. I sat down in a chair and leaned my head into Mina who stood over me, and I cried. I grieved for the lost child. I grieved for my wife who was suffering. I grieved for my nation which suffers one catastrophe after another. I grieved for my friend Zrul whom I blinded and for my brother Ludek whom I killed. The sadness I hadn't allowed myself to feel for years came flooding over me, and I sobbed, leaning against Mina, my friend, who stroked my brow and let me cry.

And finally, when I was through with my sadness, my self-pity, my shame at being less than I should be, I went to my wife and sat beside her as she slept. And I looked at this brave beautiful woman whom I loved.

Queen Tessia had sent runners and spies to comb through the kingdom for news of her wife and her minister. Finally, a few weeks after our return to Windkeep, a messenger came with news that the two had been seen.

"Well, where are they?" Tessia asked, rising from her throne, ready to rush off to save her wife.

The messenger seemed reluctant to speak. He was very young, and I wondered whether the more senior messengers had given him this task because it might be... unpleasant. I could see what was coming.

"Tell me!" Tessia shouted at him.

"They were seen getting on a ship together at the southern harbor," the boy said, sinking to his knees and bowing his head. He was starting to tremble.

"Together?" Tessia said. "They were being forced to board a ship?"

"No, Your Majesty." The boy said, his voice quavering. "They were not being forced."

"Son," I said, taking pity on the boy. "Is there anything more to the message?"

"No, sir," he said, quietly.

"Then you are dismissed," I said. "Go down to the kitchen to refresh yourself."

After the boy left, Tessia said, "This cannot be true."

"This was only one report. We'll check with other sources, Your Majesty."

"Taja would not do this to me," Tessia muttered, shaking her head in disbelief.

I sent word to Femke to come to Windkeep right away. Femke had always been Tessia's stalwart friend and defender. Together they'd stood atop a table at the Silver Pony and fought off all the men to protect Tessia's honor when she'd been nothing more than a serving wench. Now, Tessia needed her friends beside her more than ever. As the old songs tell us, a hero can be brought down by a broken heart more easily than by a charging bull.

After Femke had put the Queen to bed and I'd prescribed a sleeping potion for her, I went down into the depths of Windkeep to the library. There behind the wall of scrolls was a secret passage which I'd disguised with an invisibility charm. If you knew the opening was there, you could easily crawl through it. There, where there should have been a pile of dragon gold, there was nothing but dust. Caz, the trusted First Minister, had absconded with the Queen's treasury. Fortunately, this was only one of several caches I'd hidden for Tessia. It was the smallest one and the only one that Caz knew about. So, most of her wealth was intact. Still, the missing gold confirmed that Caz and Taja had run off together, a treachery that would wound Tessia more deeply than any Voprian blade.

Idella was recovering at the hospital under the expert care of Mina, whom I'd trained years before, but who'd far surpassed me in her ability to help people recover from injury and illness. The hospital was well-run, but there were a lot of people suffering from illnesses having to do with starvation and bad water. And now, the staff also had to deal with battle-wounds. I'd offered to help in the hospital, but Mina told me I was needed in the castle. She wisely said that the problems in the kingdom had come largely from the leaders' neglect and abuse of citizens, and if I wanted to help people recover from their wounds and illnesses, then I should work on healing the kingdom.

Having lost the baby, Idella was suffering. I sat beside her bed and held her hand. She didn't want to talk, or even to look at me.

"I'm sorry I wasn't here when you needed me, Idella."

She said nothing.

After a while, I left and walked down the hall. In a large room, a dozen cots were lined up, each one holding a wounded soldier. Sergeant Zrul was lying on a cot with a bandage covering his right eye.

"I told you to be careful with that peashooter of yours, Mage, or you'd put out someone's eye," he said with a straight face.

"Lentil-shooter."

"What?" He asked.

"I put your eye out with a lentil, not a pea."

"And you're here to finish me off?" He didn't seem worried, just defeated.

"No, I dropped by to find out how you're feeling."

"My head feels like a boulder fell on it."

"Well, my friend, you've gotten yourself into a pickle."

"I told the Queen not to promote me to the rank of officer. Every officer I've ever known was an ass except her and her uncle. What was she thinking, putting me in charge of the city?" His one good eye squinted at me. "She's going to execute me, right?"

"Maybe not," I said, shrugging. "I have an idea."

Windkeep was all abuzz with activity. From what I could gather, Tessia was walking the halls, yelling at people, issuing orders, then contradictory orders.

"Where is she?" I asked one of the soldiers.

"Her Majesty is in the dragon lair," he answered. My impression was that everyone in the castle was staying aware of where she was, so they could avoid her.

Coming up the stairs, I could hear Tessia yelling at Tyrmiss. "WHY WON'T YOU HELP ME? WE HAVE TO LEAVE NOW! THEY ARE GETTING AWAY!"

Tyrmiss was ignoring her. The dragon's attention was on Rozae and Banos who were happily wrestling on the floor.

Tyrmiss looked up at me and said gently, "Hello, Norbert. How are you?"

Tessia turned to me, fire in her eyes, and said, "Norbert, fetch your broom. We need to fly to the coast."

When I didn't respond, Tessia looked with rage at Tyrmiss and me, and growled, "Why won't you two help me? I thought you were my friends."

"We are your friends, Tessia," Tyrmiss said gently.

"Then help me catch up to Taja and Caz."

"And what will you do if you find them?" Tyrmiss said, still watching the little ones on the floor.

"I will gut them and feed them to the sharks," Tessia said, burning with anger.

"Yes, and that is exactly why Norbert and I are not going to help you find them. If you kill Taja, you will regret it for the rest of your life," Tyrmiss said.

"I am your Queen, and I order you to help me catch them," Tessia said, her eyes narrowing.

"You are not *my* Queen, Tessia," the dragon said, matter-of-factly.

Tessia turned to me, "I order you to fetch your broom, Mage."

"Tessia," I said. "My friendship with you is more important than my duty to my Queen. As your friend, I cannot help you do something that will harm you."

Tessia sat down on the floor and covered her face with her hands. "I loved her, and she ran off with that little weasel, that lying cheating excuse for a man," she sobbed.

I sat beside her and put my hand on her shoulder, but she shrugged it off.

"I know, dear," Tyrmiss said. "But we can't let you kill them." I noticed a tear rolling down Tyrmiss's purple-scaled cheek. I reached up and caught the tear on my fingertip and carried it Tessia's cheek where it joined her tears. Dragon tears are believed to heal sentient beings, and if anyone needed healing, it was Tessia.

Chapter Twenty-four

It was a slow afternoon at the Silver Pony. Heikum was behind the bar, washing tankards and getting ready for the evening trade. Femke sat beside me, her soup simmering in the kitchen.

I couldn't restrain myself any longer, I had to ask. "Did you know that Taja and Caz were lovers?"

Heikum pretended not to hear me and continued wiping tankards. Femke looked down and stayed silent for what seemed an eternity before murmuring softly, "Everyone knew."

"Everyone didn't know," I responded. "I didn't know." Then, something occurred to me, "Did Idella know?"

Femke nodded.

"Why didn't she tell me?"

"She wanted to, Norbert," Femke said. "But we convinced her not to tell you."

"Why?" I was completely baffled that everyone in the city, it seemed, knew about Taja's betrayal except Tessia and me.

"If you knew about the affair, it would have put you in a terrible position," Femke said.

"We were trying to protect you, lad," Heikum said, looking at me in a gruff but affectionate way.

"Protect me from what?"

"If you'd known about the affair, you would have felt it was your duty to tell the Queen." Femke explained. "And what do you think that Tessia would have done if she found out that her wife and her First Minister were carrying on while she was running around fighting witches and Drekavacs?"

I realized that they were right. Tessia would have murdered both Taja and Caz within moments of hearing about it.

"I don't understand what has happened to this city," I said dejectedly. "Treason, betrayal, sickness, death…"

"'Tis true," Heikum said resignedly. "While the Queen's been gone, everything has fallen apart. People do not respect each other anymore. Laws are broken. People think nothing of stealing or lying. I don't know what's happened to us."

"How could the city fall apart so quickly?" I asked, not expecting an answer. "Six months ago, the people here were prosperous, happy and law-abiding, but now, we return to find that the Princess and the First Minister have embezzled gold from the treasury and run off together to another kingdom. And Zrul, the Queen's military mentor, her most trusted soldier, has been preying on the people he'd sworn to protect. How could these things happen?"

Heikum shook his head and sighed. Femke looked like she wanted to say something but was reluctant. "What is it, Femke?" I asked.

"It's the Queen, Norbert," she said in a soft voice.

"What do you mean?" I felt a sense of panic rising in me.

"When the Wise Queen Varvara was the ruler, we could feel her love for us," Femke burst out. "Queen Tessia doesn't seem to care about the people. She cares only about flying around on her dragon and fighting in foreign lands. Zrul was a brutal mercenary, but Tessia brought out his best qualities—his loyalty and his idealism—when she was gone, he reverted back to his true character. Of course, the drought was difficult, and the floods damaged or destroyed almost everything we had, and the war was terrifying. But we could have come out of the time of

271

troubles if Queen Tessia had been here to lead us, to show us what we're made of, appeal to our better natures. We needed to be inspired, and she let us down."

Femke put her head down on her arms and sobbed. She'd been neglected and betrayed by her Queen who was also her best friend. I realized she was right, and it was partly my fault. Tessia and I had accomplished what King Kazko and the weather witches never could. Our pride and neglect had broken the spirit of the people.

A few weeks later, Alaric returned to Dragonja City. He'd heard that his mother was injured, and as soon as he'd heard, he came flying home.

Idella was in our bedroom on the second floor of the Silver Pony. She'd said she wanted to stay there, close to Femke and Heikum whom she'd come to see as her family. I saw this as another sign of my failure to be the husband she needed me to be.

Seeing her son cheered up Idella. They laughed and talked about his work with the witches in the Dry Hills. He said they'd planted over a hundred cedar trees in a dozen different places, and they had a nursery with a thousand seedlings. They were now thinking of bringing in other trees, but they needed to plant ones that could withstand dry summers and harsh winters. They'd hired locals, who for generations had been only scavengers, goat herders and bandits but now were learning trades such as wood working and stonemasonry, and construction on the huts where they would be living with their families was coming along. Eventually, Alaric and the witches hoped to reconstruct the ancient castle, but it would take generations to finish a project so large.

Alaric seemed happy with his work, and the witches treated him well. I looked at the two of them together, mother and son so much alike. When they threw back their heads and laughed at the same time, I was struck by how the pitches and rhythms of their voices were identical. I loved him as my adopted son, but he was clearly the great love of his mother's life.

I was beginning to understand something about the last six months. I'd been a fool pursuing adventure, wanting to be a hero, trying to save the kingdom, all the while risking the loss of the most important thing in my life.

The Queen got word to me that I was to come to Windkeep, so I hurried across the market square through the castle gate and into the great hall. A soldier told me that the Queen was in the dragon lair, so I walked up the stairs and entered Tyrmiss's realm. I was relieved to see the Queen sitting calmly in a chair talking with the dragon while the dragonlings played with a toy bear in the corner.

Panting, Zrul sat on the floor beside Tessia, his tongue hanging out. With his one good eye, he looked up at Tessia adoringly. She scratched him behind the ear, praised him and promised him steak for dinner. Zrul had been given a choice. He could be executed for treason, or he could live out his days as a mastiff. Everyone agreed that in his new form he was a very good boy.

I sat in a chair beside Tessia and waited. I had the impression we were going to be instructed in dragon-wisdom by our ten-thousand-year-old friend.

"Tessia and Norbert," the old dragon began. "I have held back from giving you advice because it is generally best, in my experience, for people to learn things on their own, rather than to have things explained to them. I've always viewed this reluctance to learn from instruction a strange failing in men and women. What, after all, is the point of this complicated thing we call *language* if it is not to learn from one another?"

She sighed, lifting her large chest and letting it fall. "Nevertheless, it seems to me that it is time for the two of you

273

to pay attention to a few key principles you both keep ignoring. So, let me start with an observation. Both of you have failed marriages—"

I lifted my hand to object, but then realized Tyrmiss was right. My marriage was not just going through a rough patch, but was falling down like a neglected house. I despised myself for allowing my family to suffer.

Nodding to me, the dragon continued, "Both of you have spent the last six months fighting kings and witches. You've been successful. You've vanquished your enemies and saved the Kingdom of Dragonja and Bekla. Congratulations. You have also explored areas that were largely unknown to your people, and you've established important alliances with the witches of Sheonad and the tribes of Renetu. Again, congratulations. You are heroes."

"But..." Tessia prompted, realizing as I did, that Tyrmiss had not brought us here to shower praise on our heads.

"But," Tyrmiss continued, "You have been a complete failure as a Queen, Tessia."

Tessia's jaw dropped. Obviously, she had not seen this criticism coming.

"And you, Mage," Tyrmiss said. "You have made the situation worse by encouraging her in her failures."

Tyrmiss let the heavy silence remain between us. I was offended. But deep in my bones, I knew she was right.

"The kingdom is a mess," Tyrmiss pointed out. "The people are starving. The craftsmen can't sell their goods. The farmers have been wiped out by drought and flood. The water is polluted and making everyone sick. The army hasn't been paid and is on the verge of mutiny. Your chief military leader, who was also your close friend and mentor, betrayed you and was blinded and then transformed into a mastiff by Norbert, your advisor. Your Princess has run off with your First Minister who embezzled a pile of gold from the castle. Let's see... am I leaving anything out?"

"My friends have been lying to me," Tessia said, resentfully. "Did you know that Taja was being unfaithful to me?" she burst out.

Tyrmiss nodded sadly, "Yes, I did, Tessia. Everyone knew except poor dumb Norbert here. No one told you because you would have killed your wife and her lover. And also, given your penchant for killing people, you may have killed the messenger as well. People have become terrified of you."

"Taja and Caz stole my gold," Tessia blurted, her anger still showing.

"It was not *your* gold, my dear," Tyrmiss said patiently. "It was a small portion of the gold that I gave to your predecessor, the Wise Queen Varvara, in trust for the people of the kingdom. You are angry at Taja and Caz, not because they took the kingdom's gold, but because they took your pride. Pride is an expensive luxury you are better off without."

Tyrmiss looked out the entrance of the lair into the empty air and beyond to the brown fields that had yielded no crops this year. "Tessia, you are a magnificent warrior, and you are my dear friend, and I will always be grateful to you for bringing me out of my dark despair after Rilla was killed. And, Norbert, I am grateful for your help in bringing my babies home to me. If we hadn't saved them from the clutches of Kazko, my babies may have been turned into sconces by now. Or worse. But, Tessia, despite my great love for you and my gratitude for your skills as a warrior, I need you to know that for a queen, not everything is about battle. Your predecessor the Wise Queen Varvara was not a warrior, nor was she a proud woman, nor did she enjoy wielding power. Instead, she was a shrewd judge of character and a woman of admirable moral fiber who understood she'd been handed a huge responsibility. Being a Queen is not about wearing the crown and everybody flattering you and doing your bidding. Being a Queen is about serving the people, and herein lies your failure."

Tessia said, looking at the floor, "Yes, Queen Varvara always put the needs of the people first, even when they didn't know what they needed."

"Exactly. And is this what you have done?"

"No," Tessia admitted.

"What is it that you have done?"

"I love battle, so I saw every problem as a fight I had to win."

"Exactly. Now we are getting somewhere. You need to think about what your people need, and then find ways to make those things happen."

Then Tyrmiss turned to me, and I thought *uh oh*.

"Norbert, your wonderful wife has not left you yet, but she will very soon unless you change your attitude and your behavior. Marriage is not about finding the most beautiful woman and making her yours. It's about working together to build a life. You've been so busy being a hero you've forgotten how to be a human being. For the life of me, I don't understand how you, a healer who's trained many midwives, could not have noticed Idella was pregnant when you left a few weeks ago."

"She wasn't showing yet," I said, lamely trying to defend myself.

"She *was* showing, you fool. It's not just through a large belly that a woman shows she's pregnant, but also through her behavior, her skin, her eyes, her smell... I'm a different species than she is, and even I could tell she was pregnant."

I fell silent. I knew Tyrmiss was right. I was a fool. I was married to the best person I'd ever known, but I'd rather go flying around on a broomstick than to spend time with her when she needed me. I hoped it wasn't too late to save my marriage.

Tyrmiss looked at the two of us, not even trying to hide her disgust with the mess we'd made of our lives and of the kingdom. I was beginning to realize the problems in our respective lives were caused by the same neglect as the problems in the nation.

"What shall we do?" Tessia asked, sounding as desperate and forlorn as I felt.

"First, you are going to let Taja go. There were good reasons why she left you. Your friends are not going to let you make the problem worse by killing her or by killing Caz. And second, you are going to start acting like a Queen. Your people are desperate for leadership. There are huge problems that need to be solved, and like it or not, they are your responsibility."

"Norbert," Tyrmiss said, "You are going to go back to the Silver Pony and explain to Idella what an utter fool you've been and beg that good woman to forgive you. And then, starting immediately, you are going to pay attention to her needs. Understand?"

I nodded.

"Very well. Leave. Go to your wife now. Tomorrow, come back here, and the three of us will start working on a plan to save this kingdom from famine, disease, and anarchy."

Following the dragon's instruction, I ran down the stairs, through the front hall and into the street. I rushed into the Silver Pony and looked at Femke who took one look at me and said, "She's upstairs."

I burst into our room and saw my wife sitting on the edge of the bed looking down at the floor. She looked up at me, her beautiful dark face drawn tight with sadness. I fell to my knees in front of her and told her everything that was in my heart: what a fool I'd been, how sorry I was to have neglected her, how seeing her in pain was destroying me, and how I would do anything to save our marriage if only she would forgive me.

Idella reached out and placed her hand on my bowed head and said, "Of course, I forgive you, Norbert. I love you."

That was easy, I thought. *Too easy*. I waited for the rest.

"Norbert," Idella said quietly. "Ena and I are going to move back home."

"Wonderful!" I said. "We can move back to our lovely little house, and I can work in the orchard, and we can be happy again."

"Norbert," Idella said, her brown eyes meeting mine. "You won't be coming with me. Alaric has agreed to move in and take care of me until I'm healed, and Mina will be dropping by every few days to check on me."

"But I love you and I want us to be a family again," I said, not wanting to believe what was happening.

"Norbert," Idella said softly. "We haven't been a family for quite a while. Even before you left, you were spending most of your time at the Silver Pony or at the Queen's court. Family life bores you. You'd much rather be drinking with your friends or flying around having adventures. Femke says you can stay here in this room as long as you like. You've always loved singing in the tavern in the evenings, haven't you?"

"But I love Ena. I want to help raise her."

"And you will help raise her, Norbert. We'll invite you to dinner every week, and you can come over to the house and play with her in the orchard. You're still her father. She loves you, and nothing can change that."

I looked around the room and noticed burlap bags stuffed with clothes sitting beside the door.

"Alaric and Heikum have offered to help me move my things back to the house, so you don't have to bother with them."

"Does this mean you'll be taking lovers?" I asked, thinking of Taja and Caz and not caring how foolish and selfish I sounded.

She looked at me the way a mother looks at a child who's asked for a third piece of pie. "No, Norbert," she said, emphatically. "I've had quite enough of men to last me the rest of my life." Then taking pity on me, she said, "I need to heal, Norbert. My body and soul are injured. I need time alone. I hope you understand."

I nodded. Alaric who must have overheard our conversation,

knocked lightly on the half-open door and came into the room without looking at me. He picked up the two burlap bags and took them downstairs.

Idella leaned toward me, kissed me lightly on the cheek. "Take care of yourself, Norbert. Queen Tessia needs you. Dragonja needs you."

"But I love you," I said, desperately.

"I know you do," Idella said, and she left.

The next morning, I returned to the dragon lair where Tessia and Tyrmiss were already in discussion about the problems of the kingdom. They both looked at me sympathetically, but tactfully didn't mention my collapsed marriage. Close by, a scribe sat at a small desk, taking notes.

Tyrmiss was pointing out that the gold she'd given to Queen Varvara years ago had been hoarded for just such an occasion as this. Caz had absconded with only a small portion of the wealth of the kingdom. Tessia should spend as much as she needed to repair the damages caused by drought, flood, war and lawlessness. If Tessia ran out of gold, then Tyrmiss would ask the Renetu to give them more.

"The Renetu have reserves of gold?" I asked, remembering their simple huts and primitive tools.

"Yes, Mage," Tyrmiss answered patiently. "The Renetu are among the richest people of the world, but they're wise enough to know that simple things provide a good life. A warm hut, good food, music, sound laws and the presence of family and friends. These are what people need, not castles and foreign luxuries. You were wise to make friends with the Renetu. They will be very helpful to you in these dark times.

"We must first pay attention to the urgent needs of your people," Tyrmiss said, turning back to the Queen. "You must decree that all water must be boiled before drinking. Second,

279

you must send expeditions to the farms of the Iskar Valley, the fishing villages on the coast, the hunting tribes in the mountains and the ship captains in the harbor. Buy as much food as these communities can spare and bring it back to the city. You needn't worry about the people in the countryside. Our farmers have their stores and resources to feed themselves and their own families, but they have nothing left to send to the city.

"Once the emergency is taken care of, then we need to look at long-term solutions for supplying safe water and abundant food for the kingdom. Mage, you will need to oversee the restoring of plant life to the streams and marshes. Water plants will help to clean the water. Also, aqueducts need to be built in the mountains, bringing fresh spring water to the city. As for food, you will need to train groups of mages who will spread out through the kingdom blessing fields and pastures. Fecundity must be restored to the land."

After Tessia and the scribe left, I said to Tyrmiss, "I thought you didn't care about the affairs of men?"

"I've been thinking about that very issue, Norbert," she said, looking at Rozae and Banos. "And I've come to realize that the only way that my children will be safe is if people learn to act wisely. The way that people treat each other is also the way they treat Creation. If people are selfish, destructive and wasteful, then all Creation suffers, but if people can learn to live in peace and generosity with each other, then Creation will also be healthy."

"So, you're saying we should learn to live the way the Renetu do?"

"Well, you could certainly do worse than imitating the Renetu... I have things to do, Norbert. The little ones need their flying practice and I could use the exercise as well. So why don't you go back to your beautiful wife and have lunch with her. Love requires spending time together."

When I got back to the Silver Pony, Femke had laid out a lovely meal for us: a rich beet and carrot soup, with slabs of barley bread Idella had made. As we ate, we discussed renovations to our little house outside the city. Although I wouldn't be living there, Idella still wanted me to be part of the family because Ena needed a father.

As for me, I was hoping Idella would let me move back home someday. I was looking forward to building a stone wall around the orchard. Soon it would be summer, and the apricot trees would be heavy with fruit. And in the fall, we could walk beneath the arbor and gather grapes for wine.

"Oh, I've been meaning to tell you," Idella said, excitedly. "Ottolo has come back and is living with us now."

"Ottolo has returned?" I asked, excited. The old donkey had been my companion when I was a shireman traveling from one village to the other. He was the wisest being I'd ever known. "I thought he was gone forever."

"He was stolen," Idella said, nodding. "The thieves sold him to a mean farmer in the upper Bekla Valley. Poor Ottolo was pulling a plow every day and being beaten if he refused. Then, one evening when the farmer walked behind him, Ottolo gave the farmer a swift kick and ran away. And now he's home."

"And you know this story how?"

"Ottolo told me, of course," Idella said.

"Of course," I said. My wife did have a way with animals. Her mother, after all, was a Brown Witch.

Chapter Twenty-Five

Twenty-seven mornings in a row, Tessia and I listened to Tyrmiss dictate and explain the laws that would govern the Kingdom of Dragonja, Bekla, and Iskar. She outlined the ways that the courts would hear cases and how judges would be chosen in order to ensure they could decide cases independently of any pressure from the monarch or the merchants. She explained the functioning of the Citizens Council and how they had to approve any new laws proposed by the monarch.

Tyrmiss argued emphatically for the advantages of a limited monarchy. The Queen, for example, could charge a citizen with a crime, but a court would decide guilt or innocence. The budget for the kingdom, including the Queen's household expenditures, had to be approved by the Citizens Council. In order to diminish the recent resentment against the Queen for having spent the nation's wealth on luxuries for her wife, it was declared that the Queen's personal property would be held separately from the property of the kingdom which, in turn, would be held in trust for the people. It was clear under the proposed constitution that the Queen was a trusted servant of the kingdom, not its ruler. Most significantly in terms of limiting the Queen's power, the monarch held her post for only ten years, and at that time, the citizens had the power to give her another term or to elect a new monarch.

The Queen did not vote on the council except to break a tie which, as it turned out, was a much more important provision than I'd foreseen.

Some of the proposed sections of the constitution were surprising. The status of the Iskar Valley would be decided by a popular vote of its residents. Under the new constitution, it would become either a part of the kingdom with its citizens having full rights, or the Valley would become a separate kingdom, subject to its own laws.

Some of the laws intended to clarify property rights were very specific. For example, if a farmer's cow goes into his neighbor's field, the cow still belongs to the farmer, but the neighbor may charge a reasonable amount for the grass the cow eats. A deer belongs to the farmer on whose land the deer is located at a particular time; if the deer wanders onto another farmer's land, the deer becomes that farmer's property as long as it remains on his land. Since most of the citizens of the kingdom made their living either as farmers or as tradesmen who dealt with farmers, the specificity of these laws was important. Having served as a magistrate, I knew how many disputes over livestock and pastures resulted in protracted lawsuits, and the decisions of one magistrate often hadn't been consistent with the decisions of another. These new laws would solve a lot of problems between neighbors.

Other laws applied to the realm of magic and magical beings. All mages, witches and wizards must identify themselves at the Queen's court; no one is allowed to practice magic in secret. No mage, witch or wizard may cast a spell on a person without that person's permission. If a spell is to be cast on more than one person, then the mage, witch or wizard must get permission from the Queen or her agent to cast it. The punishments for the use of dark magic were severe.

Dragons were given special recognition under the law. All dragons were under the protection of the Queen. No dragon could ever be tortured or killed for any reason whatsoever. Dragons could not be tormented, contradicted, pestered, or questioned without the express permission of the monarch. (As Tyrmiss dictated this law, Tessia looked at me and rolled her eyes. I too had reservations about enshrining Tyrmiss's crankiness in the law of the land, but I thought we could discuss the issue later.)

All magical beasts, including, but not limited to giants, unicorns, trolls, two headed mice, people with three tongues, ghouls in their second lives, those funny little lizards that change color when you touch them, and the transformed beasts of the upper Iskar Valley fell under the special protection of the Queen. Certain "noble beasts," including but not limited to bears, eagles, hawks, lions, whales, dolphins and wild horses, cannot be trapped or killed without special permission from the monarch.

Some of the laws gave protection to the realm of the Goddess. For example, rivers, forests and marshes were recognized as "nature citizens with equal rights to humans." Each nature citizen was assigned a human or Drekavac trustee responsible for protecting the nature citizen. Nature citizens held their special status in perpetuity.

All Drekavacs were declared citizens, the equal of "men and women," and have full rights thereof.

Women are hereby declared to be superior to men, and in marriage, men are under the dominion of women.

When I objected to this law, Tyrmiss and Tessia shouted me down, pointing out the many obvious ways that women are superior, but I pointed out that this law would never get a majority in the Council which is made up of exactly half men and half women. After much argument, the three of us agreed to propose this law because as, Tessia put it, "At least one man on the council may come to his senses and agree to vote for it."

At the end of the month, Tyrmiss stopped dictating laws

and instructed the scribe to make copies. Then Tyrmiss instructed Tessia to call a meeting of the Citizens Council.

The Citizens Council had been appointed by Queen Varvara. She established it as an advisory board that discussed the issues of the day and made non-binding proclamations. Queen Varvara attended the Council meeting, but stayed silent and listened, depending on the Council to give her a sense of the will and concerns of the people and to draw her attention to the problems that the monarch should address.

Tessia, on the other hand, had found the Council meetings boring and stopped attending shortly after she was crowned. After a while, the council members stopped attending as well since their whole purpose was to advise the Queen and if the Queen was not listening, what was the point? As a result, no council meeting had not been held in over a year.

In the new constitution, however, the Citizens Council had real power. The Queen could not pass laws, declare war or spend money, even for her own household, without the Council's consent. In addition, all important appointments, such as ministers, judges and generals, had to be approved by the Council.

The Citizens Council was comprised of 100 people, half men and half women, who represented all the important groups of the kingdom. Heikum, for example, represented the merchants of Dragonja City while Femke represented the cooks and serving wenches. Idella represented the bakers and potters. Horak represented the farmers of the Bekla Valley. Mina represented the healers and midwives. There were also non-voting members of the council such as Evanora and Zamarrra who represented the witches of the Dry Hills, a growing contingent which was going to be important to the future of the kingdom. Also present was Juhu, a non-voting member representing the independent tribes of the Nordtoppen. I proudly represented the interests of the green, red, and purple mages.

Once the Council was seated, with Tessia and me at the front of the room, the Queen ordered the scribe to read the new constitution. It took most of the morning to read the whole document. The council was completely silent through the whole process, the scribe's voice droning on, as the members realized they were being given the kingdom. The Queen would no longer be their ruler, but rather she would be the first of equals. After the scribe read the last words of the constitution, his words hung in the air for a long moment, and then the council members broke into uproarious applause. They stood and cheered Tessia the Dragonqueen who hereafter would be known as *Tessia the Wise* as her predecessor had been known. (As it turned out, though, the citizens preferred the name *Tessia Dragonqueen*, so it remained in popular usage.)

After the excitement died down, Council was given recess for the midday meal. When we returned, the difficult work began. Each section of the Constitution was read aloud and then voted on by the council. Some of the provisions passed quickly and unanimously, including the ones limiting the power of the Queen. It had become clear to everyone that a lot of the problems the city now faced had their origins in the fact that all power resided in one person, subject to her whims and misjudgments. The citizenry as a whole, as represented in the council, was far wiser than any one person, no matter how admirable she may be.

The law protecting dragons was passed unanimously as well. It was clear this was a sign of respect and gratitude for Tyrmiss and all she'd done for the kingdom. However, protecting other noble beasts was difficult for many members to agree to.

"What about whales?" the captain of a sailing ship asked. "Are whales actually noble beasts? What about giant squids, fish that glow in the dark, and the jellyfish that use sails to travel the

286

oceans? Are they noble? If a sea-beast attacks my ship, we need to be able to defend ourselves."

"The white wolves of the Dry Hills may be noble, or they may not be," Evanora said. "It depends on how you define 'noble.'"

In the end, it was decided that dragons were protected by law, but other species would be discussed in the future and decided on individually. Thinking of Hamlin in his cave in the mountains, I proposed that bears be protected, a resolution that was passed without debate.

There were endless discussions about the laws concerning individual trades. Fishermen wanted to know where they could throw their nets because they were tired of fighting among themselves over the most productive coral reefs. The farmers quibbled over the laws determining ownership of wandering livestock. For example, Horak asked hypothetically, "If a cow wanders into my field and needs milking, do I get to keep the milk?"

Smiths wanted licenses to forge Voprian swords to be spread among them because currently only Kerttu, Tessia's father who discovered the Voprian alloy, had a license. Kerttu stood and vigorously defended his monopoly, saying it was necessary to ensure quality. The other smiths grew angry and accused him of exploiting his relationship with the Queen for his own gain. The dispute was boiling over, with burly men facing off and other council members starting to take sides.

Tessia stood on the table and shouted, "I ORDER YOU TO CEASE!"

The room grew quiet, and she said, "Kerttu the Smith is hereby ordered to take in apprentices and teach them how to make the Voprian alloy."

When the other smiths grumbled that Kerttu already had apprentices and this new decree would not help the other smiths, Tessia pointed out that their own sons and daughters would make excellent apprentices to Kerttu, and once they learned the skill, they could return to their fathers' smithies and apply for a license. I looked at Kerttu who was silent and pensive. He was being asked to give up a very lucrative monopoly in order to cooperate with his daughter's desire to make the kingdom less autocratic. Tessia's reign had made a few people rich at the expense of the prosperity of the kingdom as a whole, and now the wealth would be spread more equitably. It was inevitable that the people giving up their lucre would resent the new laws. Finally, Kerttu, understanding that he'd be setting an example for other tradesmen, agreed to take in apprentices who'd transfer what they learned to other smiths.

After much argument, various other strategies for distributing wealth, although they'd take years to implement, seemed to satisfy almost everyone, and the council was able to move on to other issues.

Shopkeepers said there should be a standard coinage, rather than the assortment of copper and silver coins of different sizes and purities. Tessia agreed to appoint a special committee to look at the possibility of establishing a royal mint to standardize coinage. She didn't mention that Caz had been advocating for a royal mint for years.

The issue that raised the most vociferous debate was the proposed law declaring that women were superior and therefore should rule over their husbands. I wasn't sure why Tyrmiss would have put that provision in the constitution since it was bound to raise the ire of the men and make women want to defend it. Since the council was made up of fifty men and fifty women, a vote was almost certain to be evenly split. The provision seemed like an unnecessary provocation to me.

The passage stated: *Women are hereby declared to be superior to men, and in marriage, men are under the dominion of women.*

When the passage was read out loud by the scribe, the room was silent. You could have heard a feather drop. Then a few women laughed and applauded, and they were joined by all the other women, except Tessia who was watching the men carefully. Then a man shouted angrily, "YOU BARNYARD BEVY OF HENS! I WILL DIE BEFORE I LET YOU RULE OVER ME!"

Then, other men stood up and started shouting as well. Then, women stood and pointed at the men and shouted back. Long-married couples such as Heikum and Femke were shoving their faces close to each other, shouting at the top of their lungs, neither one listening to the other.

Tessia let the loud melee continue for quite a while, but when the first violence occurred, she reacted immediately. A woman slapped her husband in the face, and before the man could hit her back, Tessia jumped into the crowd, pulled the woman away to the corner and spoke fiercely to her. No one could hear what was said, but the woman seemed chastened as she returned to stand in front of her husband. She spoke softly to him, and they embraced and sat down together. Seeing this, other men and women stopped shouting and sat down. Finally, the room was quiet.

Tessia called for a vote. As expected, it was evenly split, all the women, including Idella and Femke, were in favor of the law, all the men, including Heikum and me, against it. Tessia then reminded the council that as Queen, she had the power to vote in order to break a tie. A few men grew red in the face. It was clear they felt they'd been tricked into voting to approve the power of the Queen to cast a deciding vote.

"THE QUEEN VOTES AGAINST THE RESOLUTION," Tessia shouted. All the men sighed in relief.

A few young women expressed outrage at having been betrayed by their Queen. But the older women smiled and nodded their heads, laughing softly to themselves.

Evanora, the senior witch who'd gained respect in the kingdom for the work she and her daughter were doing to restore the Dry Hills, rose, "Our wise Queen has taught us a valuable lesson. Men and women are equally matched. Let not one have dominion over the other."

There was a gasp from many in the council, then scattered applause, then more applause until the whole room resounded with the approval of the men and women in the chamber. Heikum and Femke hugged each other, and men and women who'd been friends for years smiled at each other. At last, women felt they'd been recognized as equal to men, and men realized they need not fear domination by women; in fact, when given the chance to rule over men, women refused it, wanting nothing more than equality. The fact that equality was achieved by a slim margin of one tie-breaking vote was not lost on the men or the women. Indeed, a valuable lesson about equality was taught that day, engineered by Tyrmiss and executed by Tessia.

On and on, the discussions simmered, boiled and sometimes exploded, but each time tempers flared, Tessia was able to propose a fair compromise. No one got everything they wanted, but everyone got what they needed. The wording of laws was refined, objections were noted, and scribes kept careful notes. And finally, after weeks of discussion and debate, a body of laws for the kingdom was passed unanimously.

On the evening of the last day of council, I walked out of the city's South Gate and crossed the bridge to Idella's house where she was preparing a dinner of mashed tubers, quail eggs and the first of the spring greens. As Ena and I set the table, my daughter recounted the latest gossip from the playground, who was now friends with whom, and which boys weren't playing nice.

I thought about our good fortune.

The long hungry winter was ending, and farmers were planting their fields. Soon strawberries would be ripe in the gardens, and in a few months fishermen would have trout and bass for sale at the docks. By the fall, water would be flowing through new channels from the springs in the mountains. People were glad to have peace in the kingdom. We knew it would take years for prosperity to return to the kingdom and for tradesmen, farmers and soldiers to understand the new laws, but we were at last on the right path.

Idella, Ena and I were perhaps the happiest subjects in the kingdom. Idella had told me the miscarriage was her last pregnancy; she was getting too old to go through another birth, and knowing this made my love for Ena all the greater. Watching her play with her dolls in front of the fire on a cold spring night, my wife at last in my arms as we lay on the wool blanket on the floor, I silently thanked the Goddess for all She'd given us. A wise Queen, a flourishing land, a nation at peace with our neighbors.

Epilogue: The Way of Dragons

I didn't see Tyrmiss for months except at a distance. She was teaching Rozae and Banos how to fly, and as they left the lair in Windkeep's tower, they were quite a sight. In the city, people would often stop and point at the three dragons being carried by updrafts into the mountains.

One morning in early fall, the Queen summoned me, and I found Tyrmiss and Tessia waiting in the dragon lair. Rozae and Banos were within sight, playing chase in the air over the city. Their flying skills had become sophisticated, and they were doing acrobatic turns and twists as they tagged each other.

"Good morning, Norbert," Tessia said to me, smiling brightly. "Would you like to come with us to visit Hamlin at his cave?"

"Certainly," I said, equally cheery, although I sensed that something bigger than a picnic was happening. "I'd enjoy a little trip into the mountains."

I climbed onto Tyrmiss's back and settled into my usual place behind Tessia. It had been quite a while since I'd flown with them, and I'd forgotten how comfortable this perch is. Tyrmiss took a few steps toward the open mouth of the lair and leapt into the air, falling into a quick dive to pick up speed, then leveled off to fly toward the pass between the Two Thumbs. The dragonlings fell in line behind their mother, excited to go on an outing with humans. I looked down at the bustling city, my city, the place I'd made my home for the last seven years, the place where I'd met Idella, the place where my daughter Ena would grow up. To my right, I could see the long green snake of the Dragonja River with the fields and pastures and small houses of the farmers climbing into the hills. And beyond were the Dry Hills, now speckled with green where Alaric and the witches were planting cedar trees. As we climbed through the air, the silver birches gave way to golden aspens and Tyrmiss landed in the meadow next to the cave still hidden behind the illusion of brush and rock.

Once Tessia and I were on solid ground, Tyrmiss flew off again.

"She's going down to the river to bring back a fish for lunch," Tessia said, watching her fly off with the two dragonlings following behind.

Out of the forest came Hamlin, his large furry blonde head inclined in surprise. He approached us on all fours and put his head next to Tessia's. She stroked his face and scratched under his chin. Hamlin came to me next and brushed his cheek against mine. I hugged him around the neck and said, "Hello, my friend. It's wonderful to see you again."

Remembering that Hamlin couldn't speak, but understood our words, Tessia and I sat on a log and he sat upright in front of us, and the Queen began to speak to him, telling the big bear all that had happened since we last saw him a year before. She spoke of the trip to Sheonad and the taking of the Osterbo castle and the time we spent with the Renetu. She told him about her realization that she had to lead the kingdom and not just wear a crown. Then she let me tell him about the new constitution and how wise Tessia had been when she willingly surrendered most of her power to the Citizens Council. I told him how he was now protected under the law as a "noble beast," and no one was allowed to hunt him. About the time I was going over the new laws about fishing and Tessia was starting to yawn, Tyrmiss showed up with a large pike-fish in her claws. Her two children were close behind her, eyeing the fish hungrily.

After asking Hamlin for permission to enter his home, we passed through the illusion of the brush and boulders, a trick the two youngsters thought was fun, so they went back and forth through the entrance again and again until their mother told them to stop their nonsense and come in for lunch.

Being inside the cave reminded me of old times when Tessia and I had first met Tyrmiss, and while it had taken much longer for Tyrmiss to warm to me than to Tessia, I'd developed enormous respect for the dragon's wisdom and her strong sense of honor. I'd been terrified of her for a long time, but now felt confident of our friendship, based in part on our shared love of Tessia and in part on our experiences together in war and in peace.

After cleaning the large fish, Tyrmiss plopped it on the flat stone in the center of the cave and cooked it with a sustained blast of her fiery breath. When the fins and gills were crisp and brown, we knew lunch was ready. Tyrmiss sliced the fish with a talon and gave a large piece to each of her children, who swallowed the meat in one gulp. She then placed smaller pieces on flat leaves for Tessia and me, and a larger piece for Hamlin. The remainder of the pike, almost half of it, she flipped into the air and caught in her open mouth. Dragons don't take small bites.

After the fish, Hamlin led Tessia and me into the meadow where a blackberry patch grew at the edge of the woods. It held the last berries of the season, so we had to search for them on the canes covered in thorns. After we'd eaten our fill, a light rain began to fall, so we returned to the cave. The dragonlings played in the misty air outside, and Hamlin made himself comfortable on the dry-stone floor while Tessia and I sat on large rocks. All three of us looked at Tyrmiss expectantly, waiting for her to speak.

"Norbert," Tyrmiss said. "Would you sing us a song, please?"

I took up my lyre and felt a sadness in the air that may have been the lingering presence of Tatatungia and her lover Faba who once lived beside the Iskar river not far from here. I pushed away my self-pity at having lost my mother at a young age and instead thought of Ena and how happy I was when I was with her. Songs, even sad songs, made me happy as well. I remembered the days Tessia, Alaric, Tyrmiss and I spent among the Renetu and the song I'd learned from the boy Lorenc. The poets say that if we love someone truly and completely, then we become immortal by singing of them.

> *How much of the golden river*
> *will we remember?*
> *How many times*
> *Has the meadowlark fallen*
> *Before coming to the field*
> *Of blackberry cane?*
> *Where have you been?*
> *Where will you go?*
> *Share a song with us*
> *As we sit and listen*
> *To the music of rain*

We sat for a while in silence, thinking of the ones we love and how soon we lose them. Then Tyrmiss said, "Friends, it is time for Rozae, Banos, and me to leave you."

I was caught entirely by surprise. I looked at Tessia and noticed that her eyes were filling with tears, but she didn't seem surprised. Evidently, Tyrmiss had already told the Queen.

"What do you mean by *leave*?" I asked. "Where are you going?"

"My children and I are going away to live in the Nordtoppen, far from humans."

"May I ask why?"

"I don't know whether you will understand, Norbert," the dragon said, sighing. "But it is not good for dragonlings to grow up around humans."

"Please help me to understand, Tyrmiss."

"I have no wish to offend you, Norbert, but since you seem sincere in your desire to understand, I will tell you…. Compared to dragons, humans are cruel, callous, and corrupt."

For a moment, I regretted having asked, then catching myself, I said, "Go on."

"Take, for example, the murder of Rilla," Tyrmiss said, her eyes starting to turn into red slits.

"A soldier found her lying in a meadow near here and ran a spear through her right heart," the dragon said, "Ever since it happened a number of years ago, I've wondered why. Can you answer that riddle for me, Norbert?"

"It was not a man who killed Rilla. It was a Drekavac."

"Norbert, as a healer you know that the bodies of men and Drekavacs are identical. It is only in their outward appearance—skin, hair, eyes—they are different, so let's don't pretend that men and Drekavacs have different ways of being in the world. They don't. So, tell me why this human killed a beautiful harmless sentient being."

I fumbled for an answer, "Well, it's impossible to know why anyone does anything…"

"Nonsense, Norbert. You are evading the question. So, tell me why the soldier committed this abominable act. What did he hope to gain from killing Rilla?"

"Honor, perhaps? He thought that killing a dragon would prove that he's a brave warrior?"

"Perhaps so, Norbert. But he killed her while she was sleeping. What honor could there be in such an act?"

"He was planning to tell the other men that he'd fought her in battle?"

"Whether it was for honor, sport, or simple joy in destruction, a human killed a dragon for reasons that make no sense to a moral rational being."

"I suppose that's true…"

"You know that's true, Norbert."

A fly landed on the head of the fish in front of me and walked across the sightless eye. Without thinking about it, I swatted the fly with my hand, barely missing it.

"Norbert, that's exactly what I mean. That fly has done nothing to you. It was simply trying to eat and to survive, and yet you tried to kill it. Why? A dragon would have ignored the fly, but a man must kill everything he can't control. It is the way you are. Your kind has no capacity for either morality or rationality. Look at the way you treat each other. From my lair in the high tower, I have looked down at the streets of the city. I see mothers hitting their children for small infractions—is this any way to teach their young? I see rich merchants pass legless beggars in the street without even looking at them, much less giving them a copper so they can eat for a day. I see Drekavacs stumbling out of the Silver Pony so drunk they can barely walk, looking for trouble, yet they're allowed to amble around the city armed with Voprian swords and daggers. A prostitute, a girl no more than fourteen, was stabbed the other night in an alley, and no one seems to care."

"Do you know who did it?" Tessia asked, hoping to salvage the situation by arresting the murderer.

"You *all* did it," Tyrmiss said emphatically. "Every man who paid for the girl's services did it. Every woman who turned her back on her. Every person who judged her or shamed her without knowing how it was she found herself in such a life. Her mother who sold her virginity when she was eight killed her. Her pimp who beat her for not bringing in enough money killed her. You killed her, Mage, by walking past her every day outside the inn and not seeing her. You, Queen, killed her by being bored with serving the people. And your attitude is that if everyone is to blame, then no one is to blame, except of course, for the poor girl herself who wanted nothing but a decent life."

Tyrmiss's voice was starting to rise in anger, but she caught herself and softened her tone. "You look at an individual crime and you want to blame someone for it. But nothing happens by itself. Every action has a thousand causes. Every situation is connected to every other situation. Nothing in the Goddess's universe is isolated."

Tyrmiss looked at her dear friend, "I know, Tessia, you grow impatient with philosophy. You are a person of action. But I am trying to explain that I want my children to grow up wise. It takes two thousand years for a dragonling to reach maturity. What do you think two thousand years of living with humans will do to them?"

We sat in silence for a moment and then a question nagging me for years, ever since I first met Tyrmiss, burst out of me. "Are there are more dragons? I mean, besides Rozae, Banos, and you?"

"I'm not sure, Norbert," Tyrmiss answered shaking her head. "When Rilla died, I thought I was the last dragon left in the world, and I'm ashamed to say I went insane out of anger and grief and loneliness. I killed a lot of men and Drekavacs, hoping that one of them would eventually kill me. But after finding out about the three dragons of Osterbo, and now having Rozae and Banos, I'm beginning to have hope that somewhere, perhaps in a distant land, there may be more of my kind."

Tessia put her arms around Tyrmiss's neck and leaned her forehead against the dragon's scaly cheek. Tyrmiss was crying too, and their tears mixed and fell onto the stone floor of the cave. I felt my eyes misting as well.

"Thank you, my friend," I said, extending my hand to her. She lifted a talon and we touched briefly. I could see now, for the first time, that this dragon was the living embodiment of the Goddess. I would never be closer to the life force than now.

Outside the cave, Tessia, Hamlin and I stood and watched Tyrmiss, the dragon to whom we owed so much, spread her wide wings and fly off to the west, the evening light catching her purple wings and her two dragonlings following close behind.

FINIS

About the Author

Born and raised in Texas, Michael Simms has worked as a squire and armorer to a Hungarian fencing master, stable hand, gardener, forager, estate agent, college teacher, editor, publisher, technical writer, lexicographer, political organizer, and literary impresario. He is the author of eight collections of poetry and a textbook about poetry. In 2011 Simms was recognized by the Pennsylvania State Legislature for his contribution to the arts. Simms and his wife Eva live in the Pittsburgh neighborhood of Mount Washington overlooking the confluence of the Allegheny and Monongahela rivers. *Windkeep* is Simms' third novel.

The author would like to thank Kim Davis, Jacqui Davis, Liz Evans, Cat Smith, and Andrew Dunn for their tireless and brilliant attention to the publication of this novel.

www.ingramcontent.com/pod-product-compliance
Lightning Source LLC
Chambersburg PA
CBHW011346010726
47493CB00011B/2970